ROTTER WORLD

ROTTER WORLD

by Scott M. Baker

Scott M Baker

Also by Scott M. Baker

Novels
Operation Majestic
Nurse Alissa vs. the Zombies
Nurse Alissa vs. the Zombies: Escape
Nurse Alissa vs. the Zombies III: Firestorm
Nurse Alissa vs. the Zombies IV: Hunters
Nurse Alissa vs. the Zombies V: Desperate Mission
Nurse Alissa vs. the Zombies VI: Rescue
Nurse Alissa vs. the Zombies VII: On the Road
Nurse Alissa vs. the Zombies VIII: New Beginnings
The Chronicles of Paul: A Nurse Alissa Spin-Off
The Chronicles of Paul II: Errand of Mercy
The Ghosts of Eden Hollow
The Ghosts of Salem Village
The Ghosts of the Maria Doria
Frozen World
Shattered World I: Paris
Shattered World II: Russia
Shattered World III: China
Shattered World IV: Japan
Shattered World V: Hell
The Vampire Hunters
Vampyrnomicon
Dominion
Yeitso
Rotter World
Rotter Nation
Rotter Apocalypse

Novellas
Nazi Ghouls From Space
Twilight of the Living Dead
This Is Why We Can't Have Nice Things During the Zombie Apocalypse
Dead Water

Anthologies
Cruise of the Living Dead and other Stories
Incident on Ironstone Lane and Other Horror Stories
Crossroads in the Dark V: Beyond the Borders
Rejected for Content
Roots of a Beating Heart
The Zombie Road Fan Fiction Collection
The Collector

A Schattenseite Book
ISBN-13: 978-1-7365915-8-1

Rotter World
by Scott M. Baker.

Cover Art © Mat Yan

BOOK ONE

BOOK ONE

CHAPTER ONE

THE MOAN OF the living dead shattered the stillness of the night. Over fifty rotters congregated around the warehouse's front façade, stumbling along with slow, awkward movements. A handful lumbered around the abandoned military-green shuttle bus parked to the left of the building. Those in front of the warehouse clawed and banged at the sliding metal door built into the wall, each swipe leaving a smear of rotten flesh and blood. Undeterred by the futility of their attempts, they kept up their assault, desperate to get at the food inside. A quiet but steady droning underscored the scene, coming from the thousands of flies feeding off the living dead.

The small rescue party carefully studied the rotter horde from their position on a hillock a quarter of a mile distant.

Tibor snarled between clenched fangs. "There are many."

"Too many," said Mike Robson. The living dead resembled bees swarming over their hive in the green glow of the night vision goggles. Robson removed his goggles and placed them on the ground. As the group leader, he was responsible for the lives of his team, and right now, they were about to go into harm's way. He looked across the narrow sound toward the naval shipyard. He did not need night vision goggles to know it had been overrun. "This whole fucking place is swarming with rotters."

"I don't like this." Dravko stared at the warehouse, the irises of his eyes fully dilated to see in the dim light. "We haven't come this far into rotter territory in months. And for what? To save half a dozen survivors? It's not worth the risk."

"The boss thinks otherwise," Robson protested half-heartedly.

"Then let the fucking boss get his ass out here and save them." Lee O'Bannon spat out the words from underneath his night vision goggles.

"Knock it off," Robson ordered. Though he would never admit it to the others, he did not like this mission one damn bit. It violated every rule of engagement they operated by, rules that had kept them alive until now. It was dumb ass shit like this that would get them killed one day.

But orders were orders.

"Come on." Robson crawled back down the reverse side of the hillock, followed by the others. Even with the rotters out of their line of sight, the ungodly moaning still echoed through the dark.

The remainder of the rescue party stood a quarter of a mile away, milling around their vehicles and scanning the area for approaching rotters. Robson had brought the usual contingent for a rescue party: nine humans and three vampires; the two Mack trucks equipped with snowplow blades and twin gun mounts in the dump bed; the school bus reinforced with mesh steel gratings attached to the window frames and a cow catcher from an old steam engine welded to the front; and his command car, a Subaru Outback. It should have been more than enough to handle the situation. At least, he thought so until he found a swarm of the living dead between him and the survivors. He suddenly felt obscenely outnumbered.

Daytona, seated in the driver's seat of one of the dump trucks, saw them approach. He reached out between the foot-long steel spikes welded around the bottoms and sides of the windows and quietly slapped his hand against the door to get the others' attention. Everyone turned to Robson.

Daytona nodded toward the hillock. "What's it look like?"

Robson waved over the others so he would not have to

shout. "We got about fifty rotters hanging around the warehouse, mostly by the front doors. A few are wandering around the parking lot."

"What about the survivors?" asked Jordan, who crouched in the open doorway at the rear of the school bus, nervously rolling the tip of a toothpick between his lips. "Did you see them?"

Robson shook his head.

"Maybe we're too late," Jordan said hopefully.

"Those things wouldn't be trying to claw their way into that place if it were empty. Someone's still alive in there."

"So, what do we do now?" asked Clark, the second truck driver.

"We get them out." Eleven sets of eyes focused on Robson, waiting for orders. "Daytona, Clark, you go in first and plow the area, then set up a barricade on either side of the doors. Dravko, Tibor, and Sultanic are with me on the bus. Lee, you and Rashid take the Outback and hang back. Keep an eye out for swarmers."

Jordan sighed. "I wish Mad Dog was with us. He could take out a dozen of those things without breaking a sweat."

"Screw that," said O'Bannon. "The smell of blood would only incite 'em into a frenzy with that open cut on his arm."

"Knock it off." Robson said it louder than he wanted and then lowered his voice. "We don't have Mad Dog with us. If we do this right, we should be in and out in a few minutes. Any questions?"

None.

"All right. Let's rock."

Daytona pulled the brim of the black baseball cap emblazoned with the NASCAR logo down over his brow and started the truck's engine. Clark did the same. In the bed of each truck, the gunners took up position in one of the mounts welded onto the front corners of each dump bed, strapped themselves in, and switched off the safety locks on their AK-47 assault rifles.

Caylee, the petite brunette who manned the forward gun position on Daytona's truck, looked down at Jordan and blew him a kiss. He removed the toothpick, responded with a flirtatious smile, and then placed it between his lips.

The hiss of airbrakes and the grinding of gears accompanied the sound of revved-up MP8 diesel engines as the two Macks set off, pulling away from the rest of the party and slowly gaining speed as they disappeared around the hillock.

As Whitehouse turned over the ignition on the school bus, Jordan, Dravko, Tibor, and Sultanic stepped inside and took up seats near the rear. Robson climbed in last, closing and securing the rear door behind him. The bus lurched forward and set off after the trucks. O'Bannon followed close behind with the Outback.

The noise of the approaching vehicles attracted the rotters' attention. The horde turned to watch the twin Macks cross in front of the hillock and race around the outer rim of the parking lot. The trucks swung left in front of the warehouse and increased speed, Daytona hugging the front wall with Clark directly behind and to his left. Oblivious to everything but the approaching food, the living dead lumbered en masse toward the vehicles.

Daytona slammed into them, the truck shuddering with the impact. Clark hit the outer edge of the horde a second later. Bones shattered and bodies ruptured. Some of the older, more decayed rotters exploded, venting noxious fumes from pent-up bodily gases and decay that filtered into the cabs. A gore-laden mist of human blood and dislodged flies formed around the plows, splattering the windshield of each vehicle. Others not smashed outright were dragged along the building's façade and torn apart or knocked down and crushed under the wheels. Within seconds, the two trucks had cleared the doorway, leaving behind a small lake of blood and body parts, as well as a few rotters that struggled to get back on their feet.

The trucks circled and made another sweep in front of the

warehouse door, taking out the few that had escaped the first pass. This time the vehicles veered left into the parking lot and stopped a few yards from the warehouse. Several living dead lumbered toward the Macks, instinctively knowing food was inside. High-pitched beeping echoed across the lot as Daytona and Clark shifted into reverse. Clark's truck slammed into one rotter as it climbed to its feet, knocking it back onto the pavement. The rear wheels backed over it, bursting its torso and spraying its organs across the asphalt, leaving only its head and arms thrashing about. The trucks pulled up on either side of the doorway, leaving just enough room between them for the bus to back into. A pair of rotters roamed between them, staring aimlessly at the vehicles.

No one noticed the single rotter in a naval officer's uniform, its legs crushed to pulp, crawling on the ground along the wall as it disappeared under the rear of Daytona's truck.

Whitehouse drove the school bus into the parking lot, swung it perpendicular to the warehouse, shifted into reverse, and backed the bus between the trucks, placing the rear quarter between the two vehicles. He looked over his shoulder at the men in the back.

"Go!"

Robson opened the rear door. He paused, fighting back the urge to retch as the stench of rotting bodies wafted through the door, along with hundreds of flies. The sound of automatic rifle fire snapped him back to his senses. They needed to haul ass before the remaining rotters closed in on them.

Sensing food, the two caught between the trucks shambled toward the school bus.

"We've got this," growled Dravko.

Dravko morphed into his vampiric form. The facial features transformed, his ears elongating, his forehead furrowing, his nose flaring, his teeth becoming a mouthful of fangs, until he looked more bat-like than human. His fingers lengthened, and the fingernails extended into three-inch-long talons. He jumped to the ground in front of the closest rotter, which stood only a few feet away. It jerked toward Dravko and moaned, its arms outstretched to grab its prey. Dravko slapped the rotter's arms away and grabbed its head by the jaw and skull, careful not to get his hand close to its teeth. It bit frantically at thin air. Turning his hands in a circular motion, Dravko spun its head around. The rotter went limp. Dravko let it go, and the body dropped to the pavement.

Tibor lunged off the back of the bus, morphing into his vampiric form in mid-flight. He landed on the second rotter's chest, clutching its head and knocking it backward. As they toppled to the ground, Tibor used his strength and speed to slam the rotter's head against the pavement with such force that the back of its skull collapsed beneath his hands, covering them in gore. Tibor wiped his hands on the thing's soiled clothes and kicked the corpse under Clark's truck.

Dravko morphed back into his human form and turned toward the school bus. "It's clear!"

Robson jumped out and ran the twenty feet to the warehouse. Jordan followed, taking up a guard position by the left of the sliding door. Dravko and Tibor fell back and joined Sultanic by the open door to the bus.

Robson banged on the door with a closed fist. The clanging metal reverberated over the moaning of the living dead. "Open up!"

The rate of gunfire from the Macks' dump beds increased, accompanied by an increase in moaning. A dozen rotters converged on the vehicles, those from the parking lot and some that stumbled around from the sides of the warehouse, each desperate to feed. Most crowded around the cabs, clawing at the metal and frantic to get at the drivers but unable to reach through the rows of foot-long spikes surrounding each window. A few attempted to push between the school bus and the trucks, only to be taken down by the gunners. Out in the parking lot, O'Bannon and Rashid stood by the open doors of the Outback, shooting through the head the few rotters that approached.

Robson banged much harder. "Damn it! Open up!"

He heard the door being unlatched from the inside and watched as it lifted off the ground and above his head. Two men faced him. One was about fifty, with a graying beard and disheveled hair. The other wore an Air Force camouflage field dress with the nametag Thompson embroidered on his left chest. Thompson pointed a shotgun at Robson.

"Relax, man." Robson tried not to focus on the steel gray barrel aimed at his face. "We're your rescue party."

Thompson lowered the shotgun. "Can't be too careful."

"How many of you are there?"

"Six," responded the man with the gray hair, "including myself."

"Well, haul ass if you want to get out of here."

The gray-haired man turned back into the warehouse. "It's safe. Come on."

Four people emerged, one man in Air Force cammies, two in blue overalls, and a woman in her mid-twenties in a blood-stained lab coat. Robson ushered them toward Dravko and Tibor, who helped them into the school bus. He turned to the gray-haired man.

"Is that everyone?"

"Yes."

"Then let's go."

Robson led the two men toward the bus when Jordan suddenly screamed with an intensity that made his blood run cold. Robson turned around to see a rotter in a naval uniform that had emerged from under the rear of the truck and snuck up on Jordan without being seen. It had wrapped its arms around Jordan's ankle and buried its teeth into his calf. Jordan pummeled his fist into its face, trying to push its head away, but the rotter had broken skin. Blood gushed from around its mouth. Yanking its head back, the rotter tore off a chunk of

Jordan's flesh and chewed it. Jordan withdrew his .44 Magnum, placed the barrel against the rotter's skull, and pulled the trigger. Its head disintegrated, showering Jordan and the wall with gore. Jordan fell back against the wall and slumped, his face contorted in pain.

Robson ran up to his friend and examined the leg, already knowing the prognosis. The wound measured four inches in diameter and sunk through the skin deep into the muscle. Blood flowed around the jagged edges and formed a puddle on the asphalt.

From above him in the truck's dump bed, Caylee cried out. She unhooked herself from the gun mount and started to climb down. Robson yelled up to her. "Stay there!"

"But Jordan's—"

"I've got this! Just keep the rotters off my back!" When he saw Caylee crawl back into her mount, Robson turned to his friend. "Are you okay?"

"Damn." Jordan averted his gaze from the wound and winced. "I'm infected."

"Come on. Doc can fix you up."

"It's no use, and you know it," Jordan grunted through clenched teeth.

"At least he can give you some morphine for the pain."

"I'll turn before you get me back." Jordan spat out the toothpick and placed the barrel of the Magnum against the base of his jaw. "I just hope it was worth it."

Before Robson could stop him, Jordan pulled the trigger. His youthful features distorted grotesquely as the bullet ripped through his skull, fracturing the bones in a dozen places and splattering his brain across the wall.

From above him, Robson heard Caylee scream. She abandoned her gun mount and started crawling up the rear of the dump bed, tears streaming down her face. Robson knew if she made it to Jordan, he would never get her back onto the truck. He refused to lose two people on this rescue. Picking up the

Magnum, he aimed it at Caylee. "Get back to your position."

"I want to be with Jordan."

"He's dead. Get back to your position."

"No!"

In a single move, Sultanic jumped onto the side of the Mack and vaulted over the rim of the rear bed. He scooped up Caylee in his right arm and dragged her to the front of the truck, holding her in place. She pounded her fists against his face, screaming to be released until her yelling became a pitiful sobbing. Sultanic hugged Caylee tight, as much as to comfort her as restrain her.

"Hurry up!" yelled Dravko.

Robson sprang up and raced back to the bus. Dravko offered his hand, but Robson shoved it aside as he climbed in. Dravko closed and secured the door and then yelled up to Whitehouse. "Let's get out of here!"

Whitehouse shifted into gear and pulled away from the building, pushing aside the rotters gathered around his cowcatcher. Daytona and Clark fell in behind him. O'Bannon and Rashid climbed into the Outback and brought up the rear.

Once the vehicles were clear of the immediate threat, Dravko sat down in the seat across from Robson. "There was nothing you could do for him."

"Easy for you to say. It wasn't one of yours that we lost."

Dravko glared furiously at Robson for a moment before storming toward the front of the bus. Robson knew Dravko was only trying to be consoling but, at this moment, he did not care.

As the rescue party pulled away, Robson took one last look at Jordan. Several rotters had already descended on the corpse in anticipation of a warm meal.

CHAPTER TWO

THE WAREHOUSE DISAPPEARED behind the hillock as the convoy raced out of the parking lot. The four vehicles rushed along the single road leading off the island. They entered downtown Portsmouth near the on-ramp to the Piscataqua River Bridge, an old drawbridge dating back to the early twentieth century. Rather than cross the bridge back into Maine, which would have brought them dangerously close to the shipyard, the convoy turned left and entered the city center. Thankfully, rotter activity had long since drifted away from the downtown area. The convoy made its way south without incident to the rotary that connected the region's main roads, swung north onto Route One, and crossed back into Maine via the 1950s-era bridge.

As the convoy raced down Route One, Robson noticed that rotter presence remained heavy around Kittery's outlet malls, the result of the raiding party's frequent visits during the early months of the apocalypse to the various stores to gather supplies. The rotters continued to hang around, hoping the food would return. It had been quite a while since they had last fed, so they were unusually slow and in an advanced state of decay. A few close to the road wandered out onto the asphalt, attracted by the sound of the approaching engines. Most of these were quickly dispatched by the plow blades.

A few miles beyond the outlet malls, the convoy turned onto Harley Road and navigated the circuitous country road that led to camp.

No one spoke on the ride home. The survivors from the warehouse still suffered from the shock of their ordeal. Each member of the rescue party dealt privately with their grief over losing a friend. Nor did it help that tensions were strained between humans and vampires over the exchange of words between their respective commanders.

Eventually, the gray-haired man stood, made his way to the back of the bus, and took a seat opposite Robson.

"I'm sorry about your friend. We didn't mean to get anyone killed."

"It's not your fault." Robson tried to sound convincing. Deep down, he blamed everyone, especially himself, for Jordan's death. "We all take the same risks every time we leave camp."

"Still, he'd be alive if you hadn't come for us." The gray-haired man extended his hand and forced a smile. "By the way, I'm Dr. Robert Compton."

"Mike Robson." He gave the hand a weak pump, too physically and emotionally drained to offer a proper handshake.

"Thank you all for saving us," Compton said loudly enough for everyone on the bus to hear. "We wouldn't have been able to hold out much longer."

"What were you doing in that warehouse?" asked Robson.

Compton lowered his voice. "We were ordered there."

"By whom?"

"The government-in-exile in Omaha. They told us a military contingent had been set up at the Navy yard, and we'd be safe from the revenants until the government could figure a way to get us out."

"They were partly right," said Robson. "A couple of thousand people were holed up in the Navy yard.

What they did not realize is that rotters can walk underwater. The ones from Portsmouth crossed under the sound one night and attacked the Navy yard on its exposed flank. Everyone was wiped out in a matter of hours. We heard it all on the short wave."

"We didn't know. Communications have been spotty since the East Coast fell." Compton sighed and shook his head. "It cost us a lot of people."

"How many?"

"When we started out, we had close to seventy. We lost seventeen to revenants and gangs along the way. A dozen of my people deserted outside of Manchester. They tried to make their way to Canada. The rest died at the Navy yard."

"What happened?"

"We made it into the Navy yard without seeing any revenants. Only after we had gotten off the buses did...." Compton's voice trailed off into a croak. He swallowed hard and continued. "The revenants were scattered among the buildings. By the time they emerged, we had wandered away from the buses. They caught us in the open. We lost twenty-one people in the first few minutes. The rest of us fought our way back to the bus and tried to escape. We got as far as downtown Portsmouth when we ran into a mass of revenants blocking the road. We turned to avoid them and became trapped on the island. A few of our party abandoned the bus and set off on foot. I don't know if they made it. The rest of us wound up in the warehouse surrounded by revenants until you rescued us."

Robson saw the doctor struggling to process everything that had happened to him. Pulling a lighter from his pocket, the doctor flipped the cover open and shut repeatedly, seemingly oblivious to his actions. He had a shell-shocked aura about him, typical of someone who had experienced unspeakable horrors and still tried to come to grips with it. Robson had been there himself. Too many times. Thankfully, Compton did not have the thousand-yard stare, that vacant look people developed when they could no longer take the pressure and mentally shut down. Robson got the impression, however, that one or two more incidents like tonight and Compton could easily go over the edge.

"It's okay," said Robson. "You're safe now."

"Not yet." Compton sat back in his seat. He slipped the lighter back into his pocket. The aura of despair changed into one of grim determination. "But soon we will be."

The convoy made a brief stop just before dawn for Sultanic to dismount the Mack and join the others on the bus, where the vampires covered themselves with large wool blankets for protection from the approaching daylight. The sun already had crested the horizon, evaporating the terrible uncertainty of night, when the convoy finally arrived back at camp.

"Camp" was Fort McClary, an early-eighteenth-century fort that occupied twenty-five acres along the Maine coast where the Piscataqua River navigated around a series of small islands before emptying into the Atlantic. Originally one of a series of colonial forts built to defend the harbor, the structure now offered a safe haven from which to sit out the downfall of mankind.

A ten-foot-high granite wall surrounded the compound. The southern exposure, which faced the ocean, overlooked a steep cliff that dropped almost one hundred feet to the water, making it impossible for rotters to approach from that direction. Trees surrounded the fort on the land-bound sides, blocking it from the view of Route 103 that ran past the compound a hundred yards to the west and north. The camp used the security gate that blocked off the parking lot from the main road to prevent rotters from getting in, reinforcing the support posts and strengthening the gate with sheet metal. Rows of barbed wire were strung ten yards from the outer edge of the woods, far enough from the fort to prevent any stray rotters from wandering too close and far enough from the road to prevent human passersby from noticing the defenses and becoming nosy. Every morning and late afternoon, a security detail walked the perimeter to dispose of the living dead tangled up, using a crossbow to prevent the noise from attracting unwanted visitors.

Not that the camp had seen any these last few months. The area was relatively isolated, halfway between Portsmouth to the west and the beaches at York to the east. Fortunately for those living here, the outbreak had reached the coast in March when few tourists populated the area, so rotter activity was minimal. Even though Portsmouth and its suburbs succumbed to the outbreak in a matter of days, the living dead never ventured away from the city in search of food, being drawn instead to the military enclave held up at the Navy yard. Thankfully, it kept the rotters out of their hair. However, now that the Navy yard had fallen, it became anyone's guess where they would wander next.

As the convoy approached camp along Route 103, the guards manning the entrance unlocked the security gate and swung it open. The four vehicles turned off the road, entered the compound, and rolled to a stop in the parking area along the north wall. Robson noticed Natalie Bazargan standing on top of the abutment wall, scanning the entrance for rotters or human raiders that might try to swarm the open gate. Her black leather pants and jacket glistened in the sunlight. Their eyes met as the bus drove past. Robson gave her a single wave. Natalie returned the gesture with a friendly salute and then used her hand to push several brunette strands away from her face and back behind her ear.

The gate was already closed and secured when everyone dismounted their vehicles. Hodges and his mechanics met the drivers as they climbed out of their cabs, asking them about any repairs that had to be made. Dravko and the other vampires, still covered by the wool blankets, darted off the bus and into the steel container adjacent to the tunnel entrance that provided an emergency dark room where the vampires could sleep until nightfall. The humans trickled into camp through the rebar-reinforced wooden doors mounted on either end of a tunnel cut through the fort's granite wall. Thompson and the other rescued survivors followed, the camp regulars promising the newcomers they would be set up with hot coffee and living quarters. Robson and Compton exited the bus last.

Paul Martin, the human commander of the camp, stood by the tunnel entrance. Of average height and build, he would have easily blended into the crowd were it not for the thick red beard. No one spoke to him as they passed. Robson harbored mixed feelings about Paul. Part of him liked and respected their commander because he cared about his people. As the principal of York High School back when the niceties of civilization mattered, he had more than enough qualifications to lead the group, and his knowledge of the region had proven invaluable. Not only had he kept them alive this long, but the group lived in relative comfort thanks to his ingenuity. Without Paul, they would all be dead, if not from rotters, then from starvation. Yet he took the loneliness of command shit a bit too far, always seeming aloof and out of touch. Robson found that persona unsettling.

Paul took a step forward to greet Robson as he approached. "How did it go?"

"Jordan didn't make it."

"Shit." Paul closed his eyes and said a silent prayer for their fallen comrade. "What happened?"

"A rotter crawled under one of the trucks. No one saw it until after it had taken a chunk out of Jordan's leg."

"I'm sorry."

"He'd been with us almost from the beginning. Closest person I had to a friend here."

"What happened after...? I mean, did you...?"

Robson shook his head. "Jordan took his own life."

Paul let a moment pass before asking the next question. "What about the survivors from the warehouse?"

"There were six of them. We got them all out safely." Robson looked over his shoulder to see the doctor standing behind him. "This is Dr. Compton."

"You can call me Robert." Compton stepped up alongside Robson and extended his hand.

Paul clasped it and gave it a firm pump. "I'm Paul Martin, one of the group's leaders."

"Are you the one I spoke to on the short wave?"

"The same."

"I can't begin to tell you how thankful I am that you saved us."

"It's our pleasure. We can always use a few extra hands around here." Paul gestured toward the fort. "Come up to my office. We have a lot to talk about."

Robson watched Paul and Compton disappear into the tunnel before following. As the two men headed for the nineteenth-century blockhouse in the center of the compound that served as the command post, Robson veered left toward the south wall where rows of steel containers served as living quarters.

Mad Dog approached from the opposite direction. A bandage spotted with soaked-through blood covered his right forearm. The man presented a macabre image, towering over everyone at camp at six-foot-three with a bald head, dark blonde goatee, and emotionless brown eyes that had witnessed things no human should have. Robson had no clue what Mad Dog had endured for he never spoke about what had happened to him before arriving here four months ago.

Mad Dog slowed as he drew closer. "How'd it go out there?"

"We rescued all six survivors but lost Jordan to rotters."

"Fuck that, man. Jordan was a good kid."

"Tell me about it. I can still see—"

"Son of a fuckin' bitch!"

The outburst took Robson aback, but not nearly as much as when Mad Dog reached for his Glock 23 and withdrew it from its holster. For a moment, Robson thought the anger was directed at him. Then he noticed that Mad Dog aimed past him and toward the stairs of the blockhouse where Paul and Compton were about to enter the building. Acting on instinct, Robson reached out with his left hand, grabbed Mad Dog by the wrist, and pushed his arm down and to the left, spoiling the shot. With his right hand, he grabbed the Glock by the barrel and twisted it, yanking the weapon out of Mad Dog's grip. Robson stepped back several feet, ejected the magazine, and slipped it into his pocket. He cocked back the slide, ejecting the chambered .40 caliber round into the dirt.

Mad Dog massaged his bruised wrist. "What the fuck was that about?"

"You tell me." Robson handed back the empty Glock. "You were going to kill Paul."

"Fuck that, man." Mad Dog took the weapon and slid it back into his holster. "I was aiming for Compton."

"You know Compton?"

"Fuck yeah." Mad Dog looked at Robson like an aggravated father looked at a ten-year-old who could not grasp the obvious. "Compton is the fucker who created the Revenant Virus."

CHAPTER THREE

ROBSON ENTERED THE door to the eight-by-twenty-foot steel container that served as his quarters and trudged over to the cot. He stripped out of his boots, jacket, and military gear, leaving them in a pile in the center of the floor. Taking the pack of Camels off his nightstand, he flipped open the lid. Damn, only four left. He hated using them up, but he sure needed one now. Pulling out one between his lips, he closed the pack, tossed it back on the nightstand, grabbed the nearby box of matches, and lit up. Robson opened the window above his cot to let the smoke filter out and flopped down to rest, staring up at the stark steel ceiling.

Usually, after a raid, the adrenaline rush shut off once they got back to camp, and he would be fast asleep within thirty minutes. Not today, however. What Mad Dog had said to him about Compton being responsible for the Revenant Virus weighed too heavily. Robson wanted to ask more, but Mad Dog had stormed off, angrier than he had ever been in the past. Robson did not want to press him about it, so he returned to his container to sleep, but that turned out to be futile. The minute his head touched the pillow, the repressed memories flooded his consciousness like the waters of Katrina.

Despite everything that had happened, Robson still found it difficult to believe that only eight months ago society had teetered on the brink of extinction without even knowing it. At the time, he had been a deputy in Kennebunkport, with an excellent service record and on the fast track to becoming sheriff. His life had been so normal, with a house on the beach and a fiancée, Susan, who, while high maintenance, loved him dearly and made him feel like a man. Like everyone else throughout the world, he had remained blissfully ignorant that in a research lab in Fort Detrick, Maryland, the U.S. Army had created a virus that killed off living tissue and reanimated it, with the horrific side effect that the reanimated tissue required living flesh to obtain the necessary nutrients to sustain reanimation. At least, that's how the government and the media had described the process once the outbreak began. Officially the government referred to it as the Revenant Virus, or R Virus. For those caught up in the months-long feeding frenzy that followed, they had called it by the more appropriate name of Revenant Virus.

Unfortunately for mankind, the R Virus had come to the attention of the vampires, another nightmare most humans had been completely unaware of. Vampires had lived among men for thousands of years, farther back than they could remember. By the twenty-first century, more than eight thousand had intermingled with humans, being careful how they fed so as not to draw attention to themselves, hoping their victims would be counted among the mass of missing persons. Small bands of humans had known about their existence and hunted them with surprising success, mainly because the undead had to regenerate during the day and avoid sunlight, their immobility making them vulnerable to attack. The Vampire Council, the decision-making body comprised of the masters of the ten most influential covens, had developed a plan to steal the R Virus and release it on mankind to keep the humans so occupied battling the living dead they would stop hunting vampires.

It was the biggest miscalculation since Hitler had invaded the Soviet Union. The vampires had failed to consider the rotter's constant need to sustain their reanimation through the nutrients found in flesh, even if it came from the undead. Rather than dealing with a small number of hunters who could only take down a few of their number at a time, the vampires now faced millions of rotters that tracked them down with a ferocity unmatched by man, sniffing them out in the dark recesses where they hid. If the vampires' inability to move about by day had been a detriment when dealing with human hunters, it became their demise when confronted by rotters. Vampires had practically become extinct within four weeks of the outbreak.

Not that Robson or anyone else gave a fuck considering the holocaust the rotters had brought to humankind.

No one knew how the vampires had gotten hold of the virus since those who masterminded this insanity fittingly had been among its first victims. Nor did it matter. Once the vampires had stolen it, they created a small army of rotters across the world, confining captured humans in isolated buildings and injecting them with the virus, waiting until it killed the host and reanimated the body. The virus was highly contagious with an unusually rapid gestation period. A single bite from one of the infected could turn a human in a few hours. Multiple bites could turn a person in minutes. Once bitten, there was no cure.

That's how it had begun. One morning mankind had gone about its business, oblivious to the fate that awaited it. That night, the vampires had released the virus-infected humans. Twenty-four hours later, society had begun to sound its death knell.

The first rotters had been a fucking nightmare. Recently reanimated, the bodies had only started to decay, which meant they were still relatively limber. As a result, the initial attacks on humans by these living dead, or swarmers, had been fast and vicious. They had descended on humans like packs of rabid dogs. As weeks and months passed and decay set in, the rotters slowed, their attacks becoming more rambling and less deadly. By that time, though, the damage had already been done and the living dead overwhelmed humanity.

Air travel had been banned on the third day when an outbreak occurred on a trans-Atlantic flight from London to New York. A passenger had snuck past security, concealing that he had been bitten on the thigh, and turned halfway across the Atlantic. Every terrifying moment had been captured on video cell phones and transmitted to the BBC until the amateur camera operators became food. The following day, most countries closed their borders to international travel. Mass evacuations had jammed the roadways out of most cities, making travel around urban centers virtually impossible. The situation had grown so bad that FOX Business News had dedicated its entire coverage to reporting on traffic and road conditions around the country.

The virus had spread most rapidly in dense urban populations. Within a week, the world's largest cities had succumbed to the rotter holocaust, carried live by around-the-clock cable news. The images would remain scarred in Robson's memory forever. Tokyo in flames. Military units in Beijing's Tiananmen Square gunning down the living and living dead. Moscow's Red Square filled with tens of thousands of swarmers. Rotters crowding the base of the Eiffel Tower, trying to get to the handful of survivors left on the structure. New Yorkers trapped and slaughtered along the Hudson River by hordes of swarmers, the river turning crimson with blood and body parts. Marine One lifting off the White House lawn, carrying the First Family to safety as Washington crumbled around them.

Then cable news began going off the air. Most of the correspondents had fallen victim to the swarmers or the gangs and thugs that took advantage of the downfall. A few had died on camera while filming, which would have been fantastic for ratings if anyone cared about such shit anymore. Slowly, one by one, as the world's cities fell to the living dead, the cable news shows went silent, followed shortly after that by the local channels. An involuntary news blackout had descended across the world. By the third week, the primary source of information came from short-wave radio, which the survivors used to stay connected.

The ones who had survived had been those smart enough to choose the right location to hold out in and who had the courage to cull the infected from their ranks. For the most part, these had consisted of secure military facilities, although some civilian enclaves made it through the initial holocaust. The walled, medieval island city of Mont St. Michel off the coast of France. The underground bunker complex built beneath Moscow to withstand a nuclear war. The Crimea, until the rotters had learned how to walk underwater and had waded ashore near Sebastopol.

Less populated areas had come through relatively un-scathed, at least in the beginning. Thousands who had made it to mountain regions found themselves safe from the living dead but died en masse from exposure during that first winter. Other areas had fared much better. Most of the smaller Pacific islands. Siberia. The Australian outback. Africa, although by last accounts, the continent faced an imminent invasion from millions of rotters wandering south from the Arabian Peninsula.

And the American Midwest. After abandoning Washington, the President had set up a government-in-exile at Northern Command Headquarters in Omaha, Nebraska. Needing to face the reality that the living dead had overrun most of the nation, the President had made the necessary but unpopular decision to write off the two coasts and the urban centers along the borders and had established a defensive perimeter in the untouched center of the country. The Rocky Mountains and the Mississippi River formed natural barriers, although the latter had to be fortified with hundreds of miles of fence and barbed wire to deter any rotters that crossed the river. With the east and west flanks secure, the President had sent every physically able man and woman north and south to stop the living dead. Most had never even held a firearm before, let alone possessed military training. This makeshift army had set up defensive positions on whatever terrain they could find – interstates, rivers, high ground – and fought until overwhelmed or forced to fall back. As of a month ago, the northern boundary of the uninfected United States ran through northern Wyoming and South Dakota to just south of Cedar Rapids. The southern border followed a meandering line north of Flagstaff, Albuquerque, Oklahoma City, and Little Rock.

Robson found all this out much later. In those first few weeks, he had been preoccupied with maintaining order in Kennebunkport. That had been tough enough with television's round-the-clock coverage of the fall of civilization. Most town folks preferred to stay put, reasoning that the Revenant Virus would burn itself out before it reached this far north. This had suited Robson fine since that meant he only had to contend with the steady stream of traffic on I-95 racing north to the supposed safety of Canada and Nova Scotia. Everything seemed under control until a military helicopter flew in one night to transport the former President and his family to safety. The tenuous order collapsed in hours.

With that collapse had come the unraveling of the bonds of humanity that used to hold society together. The sheriff and two of his deputies had abandoned the town before dawn, taking most of the firearms and ammo with them and leaving the people to fend for themselves. One of the deputies had stopped by the local gas station to gas up his SUV and stockpile supplies, demanded not to pay for any of it since he was law enforcement, and shot the store owner in the head three times when he refused. That act of cowardice had set off a firestorm of violence. Town folk Robson had known for his entire life turned on each other. As everyone tried to escape, dozens of vehicle accidents and fistfights had erupted on the roads out of Kennebunkport. Anyone who had a means of transportation out of the area, or food and water, had become targets for those who failed to adequately prepare for the evacuation. The number of assaults in town had quadrupled overnight and, as the rotters drew closer, the murder rates spiked. The once quiet coastal community had devolved out of control, overwhelming what little law enforcement stayed behind. Robson and the last few deputies had lingered long enough to warn the remaining citizens that they should seek the safety of a less populated area. Then they gathered whatever supplies they could muster, wished each other luck, and got out of town.

He and Susan had headed west for either Vermont or up-state New York. In retrospect, he should have paid more attention to the news. If he had, he might have chosen a better escape route. They made it as far as Newington, just outside Portsmouth, where bogged-down traffic blocked their path. Before he could figure a way around the jam, the cars had been set upon by swarmers. Their only choice had been to set out on foot.

Sweat poured down Robson's face and soaked his shirt. The rapid, shallow breathing and racing heartbeat constricted his diaphragm, making him feel as if his chest would cave in. He jerked upright on his cot, planting his feet on the steel floor and breathing deeply, trying to calm the anxiety attack. Slowly his breathing and heart rate returned to normal. It happened every time he recalled that afternoon, which was why he tried to block out that memory. He had replayed the events a thousand times in his mind. Other drivers and passengers being overrun by swarmers, dragged to the ground, ripped open, and eaten alive. The screams of the living and the moans of the living dead. Susan, frozen in terror, refusing to open the car door, wasting valuable seconds as the swarmers approached. Himself yanking her out with one hand while shooting swarmers with the other. Susan plodding along, whining that he was running too fast. Running too fast? Jesus Christ, they had been running for their fucking lives.

Robson chastised himself for constantly revisiting that day. Each time he did, he told himself that what had happened had not been his fault, and each time his conscience would not allow him to accept that. Closing his eyes, he concentrated on the sound of the surf through his tiny window as it crashed on the rocks below the fort wall. Robson lifted the cigarette to his lips for a much-needed nicotine fit, pissed to discover that the tobacco had burned itself out during his attack. He tossed it aside and massaged his sweaty forehead.

The days following the swarmer attack in Newington remained a blur to him. Somehow, he had survived and returned to Kennebunkport, staying on the back roads where rotter activity was minimal. Eventually, he stumbled upon Fort McClary, where Paul had already established the camp and gathered survivors. Robson joined them and, because he was a sheriff's deputy, Paul placed him in charge of the raiding party sent out to gather supplies. It had taken a couple of months and more trips into rotter territory than he cared to remember before they had transformed the fort from a tourist attraction into a semi-modern and viable camp to sit out the apocalypse.

Despite their safe situation, an underlying uneasiness had filtered through the camp. Distrust would be a better word. Having faith in other people proved difficult enough after watching civilization come crashing down around them and witnessing mankind default to its basest instincts. That distrust had been most pronounced among the women who arrived at camp, especially those who had experienced their own sexual hells while on the road. Everyone who had stepped foot into camp had no idea what to expect and had been relieved when Paul demanded that those who stay provide their fair share of the work. After those few first months of the Revenant Virus, trust had been the toughest emotion to rebuild.

What little trust Paul had been able to restore had been severely tested when he allowed the vampires to join their ranks, especially since they had been the ones to release the virus on mankind. Paul had argued that the humans needed to put the past behind them and unite forces against the more significant threat. He had explained that the vampires significantly increased their fighting capability and would be a minimal strain on resources given that they had agreed to feed off livestock. No one had believed the bullshit. In those rare candid moments shared between one another, most people at camp had thought that, at best, Paul was being naïve and probably would get them all killed. But Paul ran the camp, so everyone had reluctantly agreed to admit the vampires, although Robson felt certain most of the others carried a wooden stake and kept it under their pillow at night.

In time, the vampires had proven they were not a threat to the camp. At least not an immediate threat. They had accompanied Robson's raiding party on every nighttime run and, as Paul predicted, had significantly increased the party's strength. He knew of half a dozen people who owed their lives to a vampire. In time, much of the camp accepted their presence, and he increasingly found wooden stakes discarded with the rest of the camp's garbage. As the months passed, the mutual distrust between the vampires and humans slowly eroded, and both sides settled into a routine that gave them some semblance of a normal life.

Until today. Something did not settle right with Robson when Paul ordered them to rescue Compton's party from Portsmouth. He could not put his finger on it, but that did not matter. As a sheriff's deputy, you learn to trust your instincts. In this case, they were spot on. By rescuing Compton, they had brought into camp the man responsible for creating the virus that had caused the apocalypse in the first place.

Robson's instincts told him nothing good could come of this.

CHAPTER FOUR

N ATALIE CROUCHED ON the top of the fort wall for several
minutes after the rescue party and those they saved
climbed out of their vehicles and entered the compound. She
ignored the commotion their arrival created, though she took a
few quick glances at Robson. Slowly the others filtered through
the gated tunnel into camp, heading back to their containers or
the blockhouse for breakfast. This was the only safe environment they now knew. Natalie, however, did not have the
luxury of feeling secure. She scanned the tree line and the main
entrance off Route 103 for signs of rotter activity. Or for
humans watching them from a distance. She knew all too well
that not all the dangers they faced came from the living dead.

Several minutes passed, and Natalie saw nothing that
threatened the camp. She glanced over her shoulder, hoping to
catch another glimpse of Robson, but he had left the area.
Below her, Hodges and his motor pool staff checked out the
returned vehicles, ensuring they were filled with gasoline and
ready to roll in case the camp needed to be evacuated quickly.

Natalie stood, groaning as her muscles strained against the
stiffness caused by crouching for so long. She massaged her legs
through the leather pants and worked out the kinks. Breakfast
would be served for another forty-five minutes, so she decided
to walk the perimeter and check for anything that required
attention.

As Natalie made her way along the wall, she secretly hoped
to find something out of the ordinary. A breach in the outer

perimeter fence or a structural defect in the fort wall. A stray rotter that had made its way through the barbed wire. Anything that would keep her distracted. Distraction was good because it occupied her mind and repressed the memories that were as clear and disturbing as if they had happened yesterday.

Natalie owed her life to an impulsive act. She used to be a reader for a large literary agency in New York City. The day before the outbreak began, she had decided to drive to Maine to surprise her lover, Dave, who owned a real estate agency in Portland. They had spent the first night together making love and sleeping in each other's arms, blissfully unaware of the unfolding apocalypse. The next morning, after some more lovemaking, they switched on the television during breakfast and sat transfixed as the news carried live coverage of the end of the world. For close to forty-eight hours, she and Dave had sat glued to the set, hoping the infection would burn itself out or be contained, and life would return to some semblance of normalcy. That hope had died with video images of rotters filing across the bridges out of Manhattan and the military blowing up the pedestrian-choked spans in a futile attempt to stem the virus' spread.

When Boston fell on the fourth day, Dave had decided they were no longer safe in Maine and had opted to head north to Nova Scotia where the combination of cold weather and isolation should keep rotter activity at a minimum. However, gathering supplies for the trip had proven as dangerous as being exposed to the infection. By then, most grocery and convenience stores had been stripped of bottled water, canned goods, and medical supplies. When a tractor-trailer showed up at one nearby Stop-and-Shop with water and food stocks, the employees confiscated it all for themselves and abandoned the store to looters. Even more mercenary, most of the gas stations had taken advantage of the crisis to price gouge, one station charging fifty dollars a gallon, with cars lined up for a mile to get fuel. Only at the gun store had a dozen heavily armed clerks maintained order despite hundreds of people waiting to arm themselves against the rotters, including the head of the local chapter of the Brady Center.

Getting out of Portland had been next to impossible. Route 95 north had been gridlocked with traffic, so David had made his way for the coast road. They had joined a slow-moving line of traffic heading north, traveling less than ten miles in three hours, when everything suddenly ground to a halt. Swarmers had overrun the road ahead, stopping traffic and trapping the cars behind it. They had made their way down the line of vehicles, feeding on those not quick enough to escape, David among them. She had watched him hold off three of the living dead long enough for her to stumble down the embankment of an underpass and escape along a county road. She was still haunted by his screams as the swarmers ripped him apart.

Not familiar with the area, Natalie had headed south toward the only place she thought might offer safety – Portsmouth Navy Yard. She had walked for a full day before finding an abandoned SUV with a quarter of a tank of gas, then wound her way along back roads until eventually running dry north of York Beach. Natalie had abandoned the SUV and continued on foot until she reached the center of town, fortunately long since deserted. She had raided the local convenience store and stocked up, mostly on soda and junk food, which were the only things left, and then broke into one summer rental condo. She had held up there for five days planning her next move when Robson's raiding party came through town looking for supplies. Her fear of being left alone overrode her uncertainty about what would happen if she joined this group. Thankfully, she had ventured out and flagged them down.

Natalie stopped where the wall veered south and paralleled the ocean. Crouching down, she dropped her legs over the side and sat on the edge, looking out over the water. She always thought it ironic that in a world gone completely to shit, anyone could call themselves lucky, but she fell into that category. She still could not think of David without tearing up and experiencing an emptiness that tore a void in her heart. What made Natalie one of the lucky ones was making it here without having been brutalized.

A breakdown in humanity accompanied the collapse of society. Much of it could be attributed to people doing whatever they had to survive, which was understandable given the situation. More than half of the camp members had been robbed of food, weapons, or a vehicle. Several had been turned away from another sanctuary because they would have been a drain on already-strained resources. Daytona had narrowly avoided being executed by a New Hampshire sheriff who mistook a cut on his forearm for a bite mark. Survivalist instincts had replaced compassion.

A small but significant segment of the population had taken advantage of the collapse to prey on the weak. In the first few weeks after the outbreak, hunting parties had roamed the countryside shooting everything in sight, living or living dead. Several camp members had related harrowing stories about their own encounters with these groups or what they had seen done to others. They told stories of families who had survived the outbreak only to be robbed by gangs, then murdered or shot and left for dead. Of one gang that had captured outsiders and tied them to posts surrounding their perimeter to serve as a human early warning system for approaching rotters. Of other gangs that had commandeered the women and let the men go on their way. Three girls in her unit had joined such parties, trading sex for safety until they could escape and set out on their own. One of her girls, Josephine, had been the plaything of a roving rape gang from upstate New York, having been debased nightly by each gang member until deaders eventually overran it outside of Manchester. Josephine had survived the attack and wandered the countryside until picked up by one of

Paul's raiding parties near Newington, nearly catatonic and unable to remember how she had gotten there. With a little time and much kindness, Josephine came out of shock and became one of Natalie's girls.

Her girls, Natalie thought derisively. It sounded so fucking sexist, but the term aptly applied. Out of all those who had found refuge at camp, slightly less than half were women. Very few, either male or female, had brought along skills that would benefit the group's survival. For better or worse, Paul had erred on the side of survival over egalitarianism. Anyone with military or law enforcement experience had been drafted into raiding parties. Those without such experience had been confined to camp and assigned more mundane chores such as farming, the motor pool, the mess hall, planting, and the like.

Natalie had been among the latter until she grew tired of sitting around on her ass contributing nothing. After one raid to Kittery, Robson had returned with a cache of World War II-era Mauser rifles. None of the men in the raiding party had wanted them since they were already equipped with more powerful semi-automatic rifles and shotguns. Natalie had convinced Paul to let her have the weapons and train those who stayed behind so they could defend the compound in an emergency. She had set up a training schedule of an hour a day. Everyone had attended at first but, after a week, attendance had declined as most people felt confident in their ability to handle a rifle. By the end of the second week, the only ones who had continued to show up were the fourteen women in the camp.

Natalie never knew for certain why these women stayed with the training. She had always assumed it was because it had given them a sense of empowerment after being at the mercy of a collapsed society for so long, or maybe because of the camaraderie. Or maybe they had been bored and were looking for something to keep them preoccupied. For whatever reason, the fifteen trained every afternoon for almost two hours. Emily, who had hunted before the outbreak, led the training. Only a few of the girls had ever shot a weapon before. Over time, their skill levels had become more than just proficient with the Mausers, with most of the girls being able to hit their mark at fifty yards at least two-thirds of the time. Along with the newfound skills had come an increased confidence in their abilities and themselves. All of which had paid off two months ago.

It had happened shortly after the raiding party had returned from a morning run to Wells. Someone had forgotten to secure the main gate, and a pack of sixteen rotters had stumbled onto the entrance and easily pushed their way into the outer compound. Thankfully, Natalie and the girls had been training at the time. They rushed into the outer compound, formed a line abreast in front of the gated tunnel, and systematically took down each one. It had taken only a minute to eliminate the threat, and not a single rotter got closer than twenty yards to the tunnel, but that single incident had solidified the girls' place in the camp hierarchy.

After that incident, Paul made Natalie head of camp security. Because she and the girls were now responsible for protecting the compound, they were excused from all other duties, a sweet deal considering they now did little more than take care of stray rotters that wandered too close to the compound or occasionally accompany the raiding party on supply runs. All the girls still helped around the camp to prevent themselves from going stir-crazy. It gave them a newfound sense of self-worth and importance, making them feel in control of their lives again. For many, it gave them a reason to go on living.

At first, they had a few detractors who had made fun of the girls, calling them Nat's Brats behind their backs. That teasing ended when Robson finally chose the name everyone now referred to them. During a pre-brief for one of his raids, he had used it when asking Natalie if the girls could provide armed backup. The girls loved it because they knew he had meant the name as a sign of respect.

The Angels of Death.

Swinging her legs back onto the wall, Natalie continued her rounds along the perimeter. The more their prestige grew, the greater the uneasiness that nagged at her. She tried to ignore it, writing off the feeling as her natural pessimism bubbling to the surface but, deep down, she knew there was more to it than that. Natalie would never downplay the Angels' success. Her Angels had kept the camp safe from the few rotters that wandered too close for comfort. Even when they accompanied the raiding party, they never encountered more than thirty or forty at a time. Not the kind of odds from which legends are made.

That was the problem. In her opinion, the Angels had become legendary at camp for no good reason. Fighting off the living dead at three-to-one odds was not extraordinary. It created false expectations among the others. Worse still, some of the Angels had begun to believe the hype, which threatened to make them overconfident and sloppy. Natalie trained them relentlessly, but she would occasionally overhear some of her girls talk about how they were invincible.

This feeling of impending doom had gotten much stronger since Paul announced that the raiding party would head into Portsmouth to pick up an important group of survivors. Although the rational part of her brain tried to convince her these feelings were merely paranoia, her woman's intuition warned her to listen. Something told her these survivors were bad news for the camp, her, and her girls. If only she knew why.

Arriving at the gated tunnel, Natalie used the inside ladder to climb off the wall. Wiping her hands together to brush off the dirt, she made her way to the blockhouse for breakfast.

CHAPTER FIVE

T HE KNOCK ON the container door echoed through the room's confines, jarring Elena awake. She stirred and sat up on her cot, wondering if she had only imagined it. A moment later, a second knock confirmed that someone was outside.

"Miss Elena, are you in there?" A third knock, slightly louder, accompanied the question.

"I can't open the door. It's daylight."

"I understand, Miss Elena. Paul sent me to tell you that Dr. Compton and the others have arrived."

"Thank you. Please tell Paul I'll join them after sunset."

"Of course, Miss Elena."

Elena settled back onto the cot and stared up at the ceiling. She wished she could have been there to greet Compton, but the raiding party's late return had prevented that. Now Compton would have an entire day with Paul to tell his version of how the vampires had stolen the R Virus and used it to destroy civilization, a version that in all probability would undermine, if not completely shatter, the fragile accommodation between her and Paul. She feared how the coven would be treated once night arrived. A part of her expected the humans to burst into the containers sometime during the day and drag every coven member into the sunlight.

Elena sighed. She would not blame the humans if they did.

Elena found it ironic how events had played out. She had never supported stealing the R Virus and releasing it against mankind, even when some of the more extreme covens were bantering about the idea. Her objections had not been based on any emotional bond to the species she once belonged to, nor were they derived from any sentimentality to what a living dead outbreak might do to the humans. Her objections had been entirely cynical and selfish. She had considered humans a source of nourishment and worried that a living dead outbreak might wipe out the covens' food supply, much like Mad Cow Disease culled out entire herds of cattle. Back then, Elena had viewed humans with the same emotional detachment as a rancher had for his livestock.

If she had the courage and the strength of her convictions, she could have prevented this apocalypse when the Vampire Council, the supreme decision-making body, had met sixteen months ago in Prague to debate stealing and releasing the R Virus. As master of the New York City coven, the largest in the United States and the fifth largest in the world, her opinion usually carried considerable weight. However, that day the dissenters had been outnumbered eight to two. The only other voice protesting such insanity had come from Hu Yi, the master of the Beijing coven, who fully understood what such an outbreak could do to a country with a billion and a half people. Unfortunately, the older covens from Rumania, Moscow, and London had carried the day, their centuries-long struggle to stave off human hunters swaying the masters from Tokyo, Manila, Mexico City, Cairo, and Abidjan. Had they known what the results would have listened to her and Hu Yi.

What no one on the Council had foreseen was that the rotters needed to sustain their reanimation through the nutrients found in flesh and, to the living dead, the flesh and organs of vampires were as nourishing as humans. Because the covens had to find refuge from the sunlight, they had found themselves in imminent danger as outbreaks erupted in the world's major cities. A few covens had been smart enough to move by night, staying ahead of the rotters, but that merely delayed the inevitable. Most of the covens had been trapped indoors when rotters swarmed them. Within weeks of the initial outbreak, vampires had nearly become extinct.

Because of New York City's massive population, the infection spread rapidly. Only one of the three scouts she had sent out that first night to survey the carnage returned, the single terrified vampire describing how he watched the city being overrun. Elena had prepared the coven to evacuate at nightfall and seek refuge in the country. She had planned various escape routes and safe havens to hole up in during daylight, ran through her mind all the contingencies they might encounter, and felt confident she had counted for every possibility. Except for the possibility that the living dead would find them first. On the morning before their departure, a dozen rotters had stumbled across the coven and attacked, excited by the prospects of food. Half the coven had been wiped out within minutes. The survivors had escaped to the sewers, only to find their underground world also infested with the living dead. Even worse, the coven now faced their recently butchered comrades reanimated as super rotters with all the speed and agility of a swarmer and the strength and voracious appetite of a vampire. The sewers had turned into a charnel house.

Only sixteen vampires had escaped New York City. Once outside the city limits, five members of her coven had disappeared into the night, no longer trusting her judgment or respecting her authority. Elena hoped they had found safe refuge somewhere but doubted they still existed. The remaining members were slowly whittled away during the next few months. Once the largest in the States, her coven now numbered only four vampires besides herself. As far as she knew, all the other covens had been wiped out and every vampire destroyed, including the members of the Council who had initiated the holocaust.

Elena would have laughed at the irony, except she no longer found humor in anything.

Of all the members, she trusted Dravko the most. After herself, he was the second oldest, having been turned in the 14th century when vampires took advantage of the Black Death to ravage their way across Europe, hiding their feeding under the guise of the pandemic. Whereas most vampires do not survive more than a few hundred years before hunters tracked them down, Dravko possessed a natural survival instinct and lived long enough to hone his skills for hunting, fighting, and evasion until he became a powerful and fearful vampire in his own right. Elena had discovered him in 1689 as a rogue prowling the countryside on the outskirts of Budapest, living off the local gypsy tribes, and had welcomed him into the fold. Dravko rewarded her generosity with unfettered loyalty and soon became the coven keeper and her right-hand man.

Tibor's loyalty was also secure, albeit to Dravko, who sired him back in 1812. When Napoleon had marched on Moscow, Elena's coven followed close behind, assured that the most violent war to date would allow the best opportunities for feeding. Dravko had stumbled across Tibor hidden in a grove of trees, bleeding out from a gunshot wound to the stomach and left for dead by the retreating Russian army. Dravko had offered him a chance for salvation and immortality, and the opportunity for revenge, which Tibor readily accepted. Tibor came into his own right as a vampire during Napoleon's winter retreat from Moscow when scores of French soldiers succumbed to his bloodlust. By the time they reached Poland, he had become the fiercest fighter in Elena's coven.

Less reliable was Sultanic. Elena had found him in London in 1888 after he had butchered five prostitutes in the East End, giving rise to the Jack the Ripper legend. She spent weeks tracking him down before his slaughtering brought the weight of the city's police down on the coven. She and Dravko had captured Sultanic shortly after the mutilation of Mary Kelly and moved him to the country. Common sense had dictated that Elena should have disposed of Sultanic to prevent any future killing sprees, but something stayed her hand. Maybe she connected with Sultanic's Polish heritage. Maybe she understood that he directed his rage at prostitutes because he had been sired by a vampire posing as a street whore. Or maybe she empathized with the confusion of a newly-turned vampire trying to find his way in a strange world. In any case, she had taken Sultanic under her guidance and tutored him in the ways of the vampire. In return for giving him a second chance, Sultanic devoted himself to Elena, loyally sticking with her through good times and bad. It did not get much worse than this.

Elena had a similar situation with Tatyana, the youngest member of the coven, both in physical and vampiric age. A nineteen-year-old student from St. Petersburg, Russia, Tatyana had emigrated to America to start a better life for herself. Instead, like so many other naïve and vulnerable girls before her, she got sucked into a culture of physical and psychological abuse, first being forcibly addicted to meth and then sent out to turn tricks to pay for her habit. One of those tricks happened to be Sultanic. Taken with her beauty, he had sired Tatyana rather than feed off her, bringing her into the coven.

Tatyana had encountered extraordinary difficulties adjusting to her siring. Most vampires underwent incredible hardship transitioning to their new lives, often taking decades to become comfortable with their vampiric form, enhanced strength, sense of immortality, and loss of inhibitions. For Tatyana, this displacement had been intensified by the abuse she had endured after coming to the States. Her adjustment from human to vampire, strained enough to begin with, had been crippled by her hatred and distrust of others as well as her sense of self-loathing. Tatyana drew inward. She rarely explored her vampiric side. She preferred the company of humans over her own kind, and one human in particular. Typically, such regression could be compensated for over time. However, these were far from normal times.

Elena knew that fact better than anyone. She wondered what the Vampire Council would say about her alliance with the humans if any of them were still alive. Even the surviving members of her coven had opposed the idea when she first proposed it. They had acquiesced only when Dravko spoke out in support of the alliance. She knew Dravko considered the idea insane and had agreed to it only out of loyalty to her. Truth be known, Elena had not liked the idea of trusting their lives to the humans, but she had been left with few choices. She had been amazed that the coven had survived as long as it had, living off stray animals and wildlife, and holding up by day in any building where they could find refuge. Too many times, they had to clear a building of rotters to occupy it for the night and, in the process, lost Christophe, her lover, as well as Svetlana and Toshii. Elena knew their luck would soon run out, which left an approach to the humans as the only viable option to ensure their survival.

Elena never knew why Paul accepted the offer. She had spent those first few days lying awake all day, waiting for the humans to break into their containers and drag the coven out into the sunlight, exacting revenge for what vampires had brought onto mankind. Thankfully, that never happened. The threat of death, however, always hung beneath the surface. She chalked up their continued existence to the humans having the same loyalty to Paul as the coven did to her. Just as she knew her coven's loyalty was growing tenuous and could be shattered by the slightest incident, she assumed the humans' loyalty to the alliance to be as shaky. Elena feared Compton's arrival could be the catalyst that broke the bond.

Elena stared intently at the ceiling, guessing where the sun would be in the morning sky. It would be another seven hours before the sun set again, and she dared not imagine how much discord Compton could sow in that time.

Not since the first weeks of the outbreak had Elena felt so uncertain about the coven's future.

CHAPTER SIX

D RAVKO SPREAD OUT on the bottom bunk, desperately trying to fall asleep. He could not doze off, partly because of the adrenalin rush of the raid, and partly because he always felt uncomfortable in the steel container the vampires used as their emergency quarters when they returned to camp after sunrise. It had nothing to do with their safety, for the container was the ideal haven. The outer layers were covered with steel plates welded onto the outer frame to ensure sunlight could not filter in, and the only door was secured from the inside with four heavy-duty slide bolts. He felt uneasy having to rely on their hosts to ensure their survival.

In the bunk above him, Tibor stared up into the pitch dark at the ceiling. "I don't trust the humans."

Dravko mentally sighed. Having to listen to Tibor's complaints did not help him relax. He pretended to be asleep, hoping Tibor would do the same.

Unfortunately, Sultanic was less astute. "Shut up and get some rest."

"I can't. What if the humans are waiting for us to doze off so they can kill us?" Tibor nearly spat the word "humans."

"You're paranoid," said Sultanic.

"And you're naïve," Tibor shot back.

Dravko reasoned it was time to end the conversation. "The humans have done nothing to threaten us. Why distrust them now?"

"I've *always* distrusted them."

"So why complain about them now?"

"Because of last night's raid." Tibor leaned over the edge of the top bunk and leered at Dravko. A large scar ran down his face, the result of being sliced centuries ago by a hunter who dipped the blade of his knife in holy water. The scar stretched from the right forehead, across his eye and cheek, and over his lips before ending on his chin. "Didn't it bother you?"

Dravko hesitated before answering. "I admit it was unusual."

"Unusual?" Tibor snorted. "Get your head out of your ass. We haven't gone near Portsmouth since the Navy yard fell to the rotters. We didn't even send a scouting party to look for survivors. Yet last night, Paul and Elena risked the entire raiding party to rescue six humans."

"Quit exaggerating. It wasn't that bad."

"They didn't know that. Do you remember the last time they sent a raiding party deep into rotter territory?"

Of course, Dravko remembered. It had happened five months ago when the Seabrook Nuclear Power Plant on the New Hampshire-Massachusetts border threatened to go critical and melt down, which would have contaminated most of the coastal region, including their camp. Elena and Paul had dispatched a raiding party of four humans and two vampires to shut down the plant. It turned out to be a suicide mission. The party had succeeded in shutting down the reactor. However, no one ever heard from them again. Both commanders promised they would never send out their people on such a mission again, a promise they had kept until last night.

Dravko wanted to avoid any further discussion. He rolled onto his stomach, breaking eye contact with Tibor. "I'm sure they had reasons for ordering last night's raid."

"Really?" Tibor rolled out of his bunk and dropped to the floor. Crouching by Dravko, he sneered at the back of his commander's head. "Did you even bother to ask Elena why she approved it?"

Dravko did not want to discuss this any further.

"Well?"

Dravko rolled over to face Tibor. "Yes, I did."

"And?"

"She told me to stop asking questions and do as I was told."

"I thought so." Tibor's words dripped with self-righteousness. He sprang back up to his bunk and settled down, content that he had won the argument.

As infuriating as he found Tibor's attitude, Dravko could not fault him. Even he was bothered by the cavalier way they had been ordered into rotter territory and Elena's curt response to his question. As far as he knew, Paul was as mysterious with the humans.

It had not always been this way. As mistress of the New York City coven, Elena used to be forthcoming with Dravko and the others, especially after her vampires began to fall victim to the R Virus. As the living dead overran the city, Elena had evacuated her coven and headed north, holing up in the basements of abandoned buildings during the day and traveling through the countryside by night. Realizing they could not survive on their own, Elena sought out a human colony to join forces with. Not just any colony, however. She had wanted one whose members she felt had the intelligence and the ability to survive, yet which was small enough that if the humans turned on the vampires, the coven would have a fighting chance. After weeks of searching, they stumbled upon Paul's group. One night, Elena approached the camp under a white flag to propose an alliance. Fortunately for her, Paul had seen the advantages of bolstering the camp's strength by including the vampires, so he accepted the offer and made Elena his co-commander.

At first, neither the humans nor the vampires accepted the arrangement. The entire situation would have fallen apart if Paul and Elena had not struggled to make it succeed. Still, words and insults had been exchanged, followed by threats.

The mutual hatred had boiled over one night when one of her vampires, Vladimir, and two humans went after each other. Elena had banished Vladimir from the camp, condemning him to almost certain death out among the rotters. Paul had sentenced his two humans to serve as blood cows for the rest of the coven for a month, giving up a pint a week to feed the vampires. After that, even though distrust existed between each group, everyone had internalized their feelings and refused to act on them.

The downside was that Elena had violated the openness and trust she once shared with the coven. From what Dravko could surmise from Robson and the others, Paul had not kept them informed either. The secretive mission had severely strained the goodwill Elena and Paul had built up these past few months.

Although Dravko would not publicly admit it, he felt that, for once, Tibor was justified in his paranoia.

Dravko leaned out from his bunk and looked up at Tibor. "I agree that Elena shouldn't have kept us in the dark. But she's done well by us so far, so she must have her reasons."

Tibor responded with a frustrated huff.

"Don't lose faith in her." Dravko rolled over. "As for the humans, we still have to work with them, but that doesn't mean we have to like them."

Under his breath, Tibor muttered, "Some of us like the humans way too much."

At last, thought Dravko. Something we can agree on.

CHAPTER SEVEN

L EE O'BANNON TRUDGED across the compound toward his steel container, avoiding those who came to greet the returning raiding party. The well-wishers meant no harm and only wanted to express their appreciation that they made it back safely. Yet these homecomings irked the living fuck out of him. None of these assholes who came to greet the raiding parties had ever left the confines of the camp. For them, it was a way of living vicariously, of pretending that they exposed themselves to danger. Maybe if they put their lives on the line once and came along on a run into rotter hell, O'Bannon might tolerate the hollow gesture. Until then, these well-wishers were nothing more than pains in the ass.

God, how he hated these raids. Not because he was a coward. Hell, the last person at camp to accuse him of that lost a tooth and suffered a fractured jaw. O'Bannon had been on every raid since arriving at camp five months ago and had volunteered to lead the ill-fated mission to Seabrook before Paul told him to stand down because they needed him here. Going one-on-one with the rotters did not bother him, either. Unlike some of the do-gooders around here who still harbored pre-apocalypse sensitivities about how to treat the dead, he saw the living dead for what they were: lifeless, soulless predators. He had about as many qualms about putting a bullet through a rotter's skull as he did about squashing a bug.

No, he hated taking the bloodsuckers along on the raids with them. The damn vampires had brought this whole rotter hell down upon themselves and mankind, so as far as he was concerned, the rest of the camp should drag them into the sunlight and watch them burn. As always, Paul thought otherwise. We need to cooperate to survive, Paul would preach, spouting tired old phrases about working together and strength in numbers. The others bought into it, but not O'Bannon. If the bloodsuckers' superior senses and strength were so beneficial to the raiding party, why had five humans died over the past five months but not a single bloodsucker? Too fucking coincidental for him. Good luck getting that asshole Paul to see the truth, however. If Robson and the others kept listening to Paul, the human contingent of the raiding party would be dead by the end of the year.

Not if O'Bannon had his way. Before the toughest and strongest humans were all wasted in these useless raids, he would kill the bloodsuckers.

Arriving at the door to his quarters, which sat at the far end of a row of containers situated along the interior side of the barricade closest to the farmyard, O'Bannon removed the keys from his pocket and unlocked the door. As he stepped inside and closed the door, he noticed the heavy blackout curtain had been pulled tight over the window and taped to the wall. His eyes scanned the confines of the container, unable to distinguish a thing until they adjusted to the dark. Slowly, he slid his gear off his shoulder and gently placed it on the floor. A faint rustling sounded from the far corner.

"Who's there?"

The movement stopped. O'Bannon took a few tentative steps into the container. He reached out with his left hand, blindly feeling around.

"I know you're there."

Something moved behind him. O'Bannon spun around, only to have a strong hand grasp his outstretched arm by the elbow. A leg swung out and clipped him behind the knees, bending him over backward. He tumbled to the floor, his fall broken only by the hand clutching his left arm. As he lay sprawled out, his attacker dropped onto his waist while a pair of strong hands pinned his shoulders to the floor.

"Damn it. Can't you say hello like everyone else?" asked O'Bannon.

"It's more fun this way."

One of the hands lifted off his shoulder and reached to the left, flicking on a kerosene lamp by the foot of the cot. As its soft yellow glow lit the interior, O'Bannon looked up into the opal-colored eyes of Tatyana. Her raven-black hair cascaded over her shoulders, chest, and back, with several loose strands hanging in front of her face. The dim light only accentuated her natural beauty, from her stunningly gorgeous eyes to her seductive smile. She wore nothing but a sheer white nightgown that nicely complemented her pert breasts and cleavage. Robson had once said Tatyana's elegance reminded him of one of the Sirens from Homer. O'Bannon understood why. He surmised that Tatyana had used her beauty to seduce many a man to his death in the days before the outbreak.

"Not tonight." O'Bannon tried to sit up, but Tatyana pressed his shoulders back against the metal floor. She slid her pelvis onto his crotch and began slowly gyrating.

"What's the matter?" she cooed. "Not up to it?"

Despite his best efforts, O'Bannon felt himself becoming aroused. "We had a rough night."

"Just the way I like it."

When in one of these moods, Tatyana was insatiable. Rolling to one side, O'Bannon tossed Tatyana onto the floor beside him and quickly jumped to his feet. "Damn it. I said not tonight."

Tatyana crawled over and knelt before him. She reached up with her right hand, her fingernails stretching into two-inch-long talons, and gently ran the talon of her forefinger along the bulge in his trousers. "You're saying no, but *this* is saying yes."

Before O'Bannon could protest any further, Tatyana

plunged her lips around his erection, taking all seven inches into her mouth and down her throat. She held him there for several seconds, her tongue massaging the shaft. Slowly she pulled back, sucking while gently running her fangs along the shaft. O'Bannon groaned, his inhibitions instantly melting away into wild, violent lust. Grabbing Tatyana by the hair, he held her head in place and began to fuck her mouth, plunging his cock down her throat as hard and fast as possible. Tatyana moaned lustfully with each thrust.

As his balls began to tighten and churn, Tatyana pushed herself away.

"What's your problem?" he demanded.

"No problem." Tatyana smiled and licked her lips. Rolling over, she got onto her hands and knees, her ass raised toward him. She glanced over her shoulder, admiring him through matted strands of hair. "You know how I like it."

O'Bannon stepped over, dropped his trousers around his knees, and yanked the nightgown over her thighs. Kneeling behind Tatyana, he plunged his cock into her ass, shoving it in until his groin slammed against her butt cheeks. Tatyana moaned from deep in her throat. Her anus closed around him. Unlike a human, her ass felt cold and lifeless. But it was inviting and willing, and that's all he cared. He fucked her with wild abandon, slamming his erection into her, practically raping her. Tatyana dropped her cheek to the floor, her face contorted in ecstasy, grunting like an animal with each thrust.

O'Bannon clutched Tatyana around the waist, holding her in place as he ass fucked her harder and more violently. A year ago, he might have been turned on by watching a woman react to him like this. Now he looked down on Tatyana with contempt. She mistook their fucking for passion or lust. For him, she was merely a convenient way of venting his anger and hatred for how his world had gone to shit. For the bloodsuckers who had brought this on them. For that asshole Paul, who wanted to make nice with them. For having to go out and face the rotters night after night while more than half the camp sat around on their fat asses. For losing what few friends he had left. For being impotent to do anything in a world overrun with the living dead.

With each thrust, O'Bannon vented a little more anger and hatred, but far from enough to purge his soul. As he felt his erection throb, he plunged his cock as far into Tatyana's ass as he could, blowing his load deep inside her. Tatyana pushed back against him and howled as she came. Her body went limp. She slid off his dwindling erection, lying exhausted on the floor.

He stripped out of the rest of his clothes, flinging them into the corner. Tatyana rested on the floor at his feet, exhausted after whoring herself for the last fifteen minutes. As he walked over to his cot, Tatyana rolled over and looked adoringly at him. "You want me to join you?"

"I'm exhausted." He did not care how unfeeling he sounded.

"I understand." Tatyana did not do a good job of hiding her disappointment. "You had a rough night. I hope I helped a little."

"You were just what I needed." O'Bannon grinned at his inside joke.

Tatyana smiled. O'Bannon wondered what she would think if she knew a part of him wanted to open the door and throw her out into the sunlight.

CHAPTER EIGHT

ROBSON ENJOYED THE communal dining facility, and not only because of the food, which was much better than could be expected in the midst of an apocalypse. The cooks could supplement the mundane supplies of canned goods and dry rations with fresh fruit and vegetables from the gardens Paul had planted in the common area and smoked pork or beef jerky from the camp's livestock. They could even count on the occasional egg from one of the chickens though, at the moment, there were only enough chickens for every person to get a single egg once a week. Considering almost everyone here had known days or weeks of starvation out in the rotter world before finding sanctuary within the camp, even the skimpiest of meals seemed a feast.

Robson enjoyed the fellowship. In the dining hall, everyone was equal. Raiders, Angels, mechanics, farmers, maintenance crews. It did not matter how dangerous or mundane your job, or whether it was mentally or physically draining. Breakfast and dinner were the two times people could get together with old friends. They sat at the benches that ran in rows down the length of the dining hall, talking, joking, laughing, and flirting.

Especially the flirting. Robson had noticed a lot more of that in the past few months. As life slowly took on a semblance of normality and people began to realize they might survive and have a future, human desires worked their way back into the psyche. Several couples already had openly declared themselves in a relationship, with as many keeping their trysts secret. Paul encouraged it, constantly stressing that if society was ever going to survive, people had to procreate. Robson smiled to himself. Although he agreed with Paul, he prioritized things differently. People needed to feel comfortable about loving someone without fearing they would be devoured alive before they would start having children.

Thinking of relationships made him suddenly think of Caylee. He scanned the tables, eventually spotting her sitting alone at the farthest end of the last table in the hall. The red, bloodshot eyes and the dark circles beneath testified that she had been crying all night. She sat at a slight angle that kept her back to most of the dining hall, sullenly staring at her plate and pushing the food around with her fork. Caylee had taken a chance on falling in love with Jordan and trying to live a normal life, only to have another loved one ripped away from her. Robson admired her strength, unsure he could have mentally survived another loss.

He started gathering up his tray to sit with Caylee when he heard an unfamiliar male voice from behind him. "Mind if we join you?"

Robson looked over his shoulder to see two people standing there. Thompson stood holding a tray of food, looking clean-shaven and refreshed, but still wearing the same camouflage uniform from last night. He had a bearing about him that would have defined him as an officer even without the cammies, from the crew-cut blonde hair to the ramrod-straight posture. Robson guessed him to be about fifty, mostly because he wore the rank of colonel, though it would be difficult to guess his age from his appearance. His body had the lean, hard look of someone who worked out regularly, though the bagginess of his uniform around the waist indicated he had been living off reduced rations for a while now.

Beside Thompson stood the young woman they had saved along with the others. Last night she was dirty and scared, and looked like the hell she had lived through. Since then, some of the girls at camp had made her feel at home, obviously getting her a hot shower and a change of clothes. Auburn hair fell to her shoulders in gentle curls, and she had abandoned the soiled clothes and lab coat for a white blouse and tan slacks. A broad smile lit up when Robson motioned to the empty seats opposite him.

"Please, be my guest. This must be your first hot meal in a while."

"Tell me about it." Thompson sat directly across from Robson, with the young woman sitting to his right. "We've been eating MREs for months. And we ran out of those when the group that set out on its own in New York took all our supplies with them. By the way, I'm Colonel Glenn Thompson."

"Mike Robson." Robson shook the colonel's outstretched hand, trying not to grin at the officer's strong Alpha male grip.

"Sorry about pointing my weapon at you last night."

"Don't worry about it. I've had worse things greet me when I've opened strange doors."

"I'm Jennifer," the young woman said, holding out her hand, "Jennifer Wilson."

Robson shook her hand, preferring the gentler grip. "No rank?"

"Nope. I'm a civilian detailee to the Department of Defense, at least when there was a DOD."

"Well, welcome to paradise."

"Is that what you call this place?" asked Thompson as he shoveled a fork full of green beans into his mouth.

"Depends on who you talk to. Some around here think of it as paradise compared to what's outside. Others call it Martin's Madhouse or the Tenth Circle of Hell."

"What do you call it?"

Robson forced a smile. "Home."

"Whatever you call it, you've got a nice setup here. I took a walk around the compound this afternoon." Thompson bit off a piece of beef jerky and munched it as he talked. "Your own garden and livestock, a secure perimeter. Pretty nice accommodations, even if they are a bit Spartan."

"You've probably seen worse."

Thompson nodded. "Desert Storm. Mogadishu. Bosnia. Iraq. This place is a five-star hotel compared to them."

"What about you?" Robson asked Jennifer.

"It's not my townhouse back in Maryland, but it's much better than being out there."

"Amen to that." Robson took a drink of coffee. "Paul's done well by us. He made sure that we not only survived but thrived. It took a while to bring in the steel containers, generators, and livestock, but we're at a point now where the camp is self-sustained and can easily ride out the rotters."

"It's impressive," said Jennifer.

"It seems your commander's only problem is identifying the enemy," added Thompson.

"You mean the vampires."

"Roger that."

"It does seem strange," Jennifer said, carefully choosing her words so as not to start an argument with her hosts. "We wouldn't be in this mess if it wasn't for them."

Robson nodded. "It took us a while to get used to the idea, too, but it works. And you should see them in a melee. They can take out ten times the number of rotters we can without even breaking a sweat."

Thompson stopped eating and swallowed what he had in his mouth. "Which means the five bloodsuckers could take out this whole camp if they had half a mind to."

Robson did not respond. He could not. All these months he spent convincing himself the vampires were a benefit to the camp because of their strength and fighting skills, and never once had he considered the vampires could just as easily turn on them. What other dangers had he been so fucking naïve about?

Jennifer realized the conversation had reached an awkward point. "What do you do here?"

"I head up the raiding party," said Robson, grateful for the change of subject.

"That's all?"

Robson took a drink of coffee. "Paul has a rule that if you go out into rotter territory and put your life on the line to keep the camp supplied, then you don't have to do any menial work on the compound."

"Sweet deal," said Thompson through a mouthful of food.

"It is. But most of us still help around here. Otherwise, the boredom would drive us nuts." Robson put down the empty coffee mug and pushed it aside. "What about you two?"

Thompson picked up the last piece of jerky and popped it into his mouth. "I'm chief of security for the eggheads."

"And I suppose you're one of the eggheads?" Robson asked Jennifer.

"More like an assistant egghead. I run lab tests for Doctor Compton and take notes for him."

"What's so important that you'd still be working on it during the outbreak?"

Thompson raised his left hand and held it up between Robson and Jennifer. "Sorry, but we're not at liberty to discuss that."

You can kill off most of mankind, but bureaucracy survives, thought Robson. Even though he knew the answer to the next question, he asked it anyway. "Is it true that Compton is the one who created the Revenant Virus?"

Jennifer became uneasy and looked down at her plate.

Thompson stopped eating and fixed his eyes on Robson. "Where did you hear that?"

"From Mad Dog. He mentioned it this morning when you arrived."

"Who's Mad Dog?"

"He's over there. Two tables over, facing us."

Only then did Robson realize that Mad Dog was staring at them intently, the same look of disgust on his face as he'd had that morning when he first saw Compton. His gaze locked onto Thompson, and the two glared at each other for several seconds. A cold hatred flared in Mad Dog's eyes. He stood up, dropped his tray off in the plastic barrel to be washed, and headed their way, never once breaking eye contact with the colonel. For a moment, Robson thought Mad Dog would start something, but he continued past the table. Thompson kept an eye on him until he left the dining hall.

"Do you know him?" asked Robson.

Thompson pretended he did not hear the question. "What's his name?"

"He never told us."

"Where's he from?"

"He never told us that either. We ran across him about five months ago held up in a gas station outside Newington. A pack of rotters had jumped him while he was fueling his Hummer. He had taken down over a dozen with nothing more than a baseball bat. We call him Mad Dog because of the way he tears into them."

"I wonder what his story is," said Jennifer. Robson could not be sure if her curiosity stemmed from genuine concern.

"You'll find many stories around here," said Robson. "Most of us lived within sixty miles of this place before the outbreak. Some tried to escape but were overtaken by rotters and eventually made their way here. Others tried to hold out in their homes, which was where we picked them up during our supply runs."

"Which one are you?" asked Thompson.

"I was a deputy up in Kennebunkport. My fiancé and I tried to head west when the outbreak got bad. Rotters overran us not far from here. Susan didn't make it. I did." Robson felt that familiar self-loathing blackening his soul. He reached for the cup of coffee as a distraction, annoyed to find it empty.

"I'm sorry." Jennifer noticed his discomfort, mistaking it for anguish. "I shouldn't have brought it up."

"Don't worry about it. There's not a single person here who hasn't lost family or loved ones. The guy in the NASCAR cap is Daytona, one of our drivers. He made his way up here from Florida. Witnessed the whole east coast go to hell. The guy sitting with him is Whitehouse. He used to be an ambulance driver in Boston. He was at Mass General when the first bite victims turned and attacked the other patients and hospital staff. He barely made it out alive. And see those girls over there?" Robson pointed to the table where Natalie's Angels sat, each wearing leather pants and a white shirt. "One of them spent weeks in a rape gang until rotters overran their camp. She's probably the only person here thankful for the living dead."

"What's with the leather?" asked Thompson. "Some type of fetish?"

"No. They're the camp security detail. The leather outfits make it impossible for the rotters to bite anything but exposed flesh."

Thompson shrugged.

"What about you two?" asked Robson. "Did you lose someone during the outbreak?"

Thompson shook his head. "I've been a widower for ten years. I have only one son who was with the Army in Baghdad when the shit hit the fan. Last I heard, his unit had fallen back to a defensive position somewhere in Saudi Arabia."

"I lost my parents in a car accident when I was eight," said Jennifer. "Ever since I started working with the military at Fort Detrick, I've been too busy to even date. Right after the outbreak, I was assigned to Doctor Compton's staff. Shortly after that, we flew out to Site R. I hadn't even seen a rotter until we tried to make it to Portsmouth."

"You gotta understand," added Thompson, "the military did it that way on purpose. Everyone assigned to Compton's staff had no family, so there were no families to worry about. They thought we would all concentrate on our work and not be distracted by wondering where our loved ones were."

Robson opened his mouth to ask where Site R was located when Paul entered the dining hall. He stopped in front of the middle table, picked up a spoon, and clanged it against the side of a water glass until everyone had quieted down. Paul placed the spoon back onto the table.

"Ladies and gentlemen, listen up. We're going to have an all-hands tonight at seven o'clock. Everyone needs to be here, so pass the word around. Thank you."

Paul turned around and left the dining hall as quickly as he had entered. Robson did not know what to make of it since Paul was never that abrupt. "What the hell was that all about?" he said to no one in particular.

Thompson stood, picked up his tray, and headed out. "I guess you'll find out tonight."

Robson noted that the colonel did not say "we."

CHAPTER NINE

R OBSON ENTERED THE dining hall a few minutes before the all-hands began. The din of dozens of people idly talking could be heard on the way up the stairs to the blockhouse. The dining tables had been folded and stored against the rear wall, replaced by rows of metal folding chairs. Almost all of them were filled. Robson scanned the crowd. The four vampires, except for Elena, sat in the rear corner seats, Tibor's scarred face looking exceptionally disgruntled at having to spend any more time than necessary with humans. The Angels sat next to them in the back two rows, talking amongst themselves in small groups. In fact, nearly everyone sat in their cliques: Daytona, Clark, and Whitehouse huddled in the middle with Hodges' motor pool crew; the cooks, farm hands, medical staff, and various work crews all hung out together. Even the newcomers seemed to have been accepted, for he noticed the two engineers joking with the maintenance crew and the Air Force non-com chatting with Hodges.

Robson looked around for Mad Dog, surprised to find him sitting in the front row near the podium Paul spoke from. Mad Dog always sat at the rear of the hall, pulling a chair over to one of the blockhouse windows to be as far removed from the group as possible, and that was on those rare occasions when he even showed up for such meetings. Robson knew that Mad Dog's presence tonight was because of Compton, which did not bode well. Thankfully, O'Bannon sat between Mad Dog and the podium to intervene if trouble erupted.

Natalie sat directly in front of the podium, looking extremely attractive in her leather pants and white blouse that she filled out quite nicely, her long brown hair cascading over her shoulders. Robson suddenly remembered what Thompson had said about the Angels having a fetish appearance and smiled, knowing he would never get that image of her out of his mind. When Natalie spotted him, her eyes beamed. She greeted him with a smile and waved him over to the empty seat to her right. Jennifer, who sat in the next chair, turned to him and nodded.

"Any idea what this is about?" asked Natalie.

"None," said Robson as he slid into the seat. He glanced over at Jennifer. "I hoped you'd know since this deals with Compton."

Jennifer responded with a shrug. "The doctor kept me out of the loop on everything. I was little more than his office girl."

Robson wondered what other services she provided for the good doctor but chastised himself for thinking so crassly. Suddenly realizing that someone was missing, he scanned the room. "Where's the colonel?"

"After supper, he met up with the doctor and your bosses. I haven't seen him since."

"That figures," grunted O'Bannon from a few chairs down. "This place has become too damn secretive ever since Compton showed up. No offense, miss."

"None taken," said Jennifer. "It's been like this since the Pentagon assigned me to work with him. He and Thompson would go off somewhere and talk for hours, sometimes by themselves, other times on a VTC with Omaha. They never told me a thing. Half the notes I'd type up for him were so cryptic—"

A bustle at the door announced the arrival of Paul and the others. Paul entered first alongside Compton, the two chatting quietly. Elena followed next. Usually, Paul took special care to show that he and Elena were equal, a deliberate effort to display the unity between humans and vampires. This time he and Compton took center stage, with Elena merely along for show. Robson did not like the hold Compton seemed to have over him. Thompson followed several feet behind, the dutiful officer bringing up the rear and protecting his boss. The four gathered around the podium, with Paul in the middle and Elena and Compton on either side. Thompson hovered in the background. Paul stepped up to the podium and called out over the noise for everyone to quiet down. The talking died off as the room focused on the group standing before them.

"I know you've all been curious about last night's raid into Portsmouth and whether it was important enough to risk so many lives and to lose a good friend, to rescue a handful of people. I apologize for all the secrecy. Trust me. It was worth it." Paul gestured toward the doctor. "This is Dr. Robert Compton, chief biologist out of Fort Detrick."

"He's a fucking murderer."

Everyone turned. Mad Dog had stood up, pointing at Compton, his face scarlet with fury. O'Bannon sat forward in his chair, ready to tackle Mad Dog if he tried anything violent. Robson noticed that Thompson took a few steps forward, prepared to do the same.

As usual, Paul attempted to be conciliatory. "Mad Dog, please. You'll have your chance to spe—"

"Did Compton tell you he's the creator of the Revenant Virus?"

A murmur erupted throughout the hall.

"Is that true?" asked O'Bannon.

Paul started to respond, but Compton held up his hand and cut him off. He stepped up to the podium and looked O'Bannon straight in the eyes. "Yes."

Rage erupted through the hall, interrupted only by Mad Dog yelling, "Then you admit to genocide."

"Nothing of the kind," said Compton. His voice was firm, with no guilt or defensiveness.

"Bullshit!"

The colonel placed himself between Mad Dog and Compton. "You better watch your language, son."

The entire hall was in turmoil by now. Compton quickly took control of the situation.

"Both of you stand down and let me explain." Compton glared at the colonel. Thompson stepped back and took up his position by the wall. Then Compton faced off with Mad Dog. The two men stared each other down, neither one giving in. O'Bannon finally sat forward in his chair and whispered for Mad Dog to take his seat. Mumbling under his breath, Mad Dog dropped back into his chair, his arms tightly folded across his chest.

Compton took a deep breath and exhaled slowly. "Yes, it's true I created the R Virus, or what you call the Revenant Virus, but I never intended it to be a bioweapon. My unit was trying to find a way to rejuvenate the scar tissue on vets wounded by IEDs in Iraq. We finally had some success with one strain, albeit minimal, and concentrated on that one. Unfortunately, the final variation not only succeeded in reanimating dead scar tissue, it also killed off all the living tissue and reanimated it. Once reanimated, the revenants possessed an uncontrollable urge to feed off the living. As best as I can tell, the original virus must consume live tissue to replicate itself. Of course, we didn't realize this until almost a dozen researchers and guards were bitten and reanimated as revenants."

"Why didn't you destroy the virus?" asked O'Bannon.

"We didn't weaponize it, if that's what you're referring to," answered Compton. "But you can't destroy something like this and hope it'll go away. It's like nuclear weapons. If one country knows how to make it, others do, too. The Pentagon classified all information about the virus as compartmented Top Secret and restricted access to the data to myself and a few trusted members of my staff. We were working on countermeasures to the R Virus in case some other country developed it. Unfortunately, our enemies used the R Virus against us before we had developed a defense against it."

Elena lowered her eyes at the comment. Robson heard Tibor in the rear corner mutter, "Fuck you."

If Compton heard the vampires' mumblings, he did not notice it. "Once the outbreak occurred and Fort Detrick was threatened, the government moved us to a secret underground facility where we continued our research. Working under such conditions and with limited resources wasn't easy but, after three months, we completed our work. The government told us to bring it to the Portsmouth Navy Yard and they would extract us. They had no idea the Navy yard had fallen. We lost everything when the revenants attacked us. That's why we must return to the facility and get more."

"Wait a minute," Robson stood up, waving his hand to catch Compton's attention. "You keep on referring to 'it.' What are you talking about?"

Compton stared at him, a confused look on his face. "I'm talking about the vaccine for the R Virus, of course."

CHAPTER TEN

A STUNNED SILENCE filled the hall as everyone registered what Compton had said.

Robson spoke first. "You discovered a vaccine for the Revenant Virus?"

"Yes," Compton said in a matter-of-fact tone.

"Then you can reverse the outbreak?" asked Natalie.

Compton shook his head. "Nothing can cure the virus. Once infected, death and reanimation are imminent. The vaccine will only prevent its further spread."

"That's more than enough," said Robson.

"More than enough for what?" asked Ari, one of the Angels.

"To take the fight to the rotters."

"But we face them all the time."

"We avoid them and defend ourselves when necessary." Robson shifted in his chair so he could face Ari. "Up to now, we've always been cautious when dealing with rotters because even the smallest bite is a death sentence. Think about it. How many other camps fell when someone snuck in without revealing they'd been bitten, turned, and spread the virus? We don't have to fear the rotters anymore. They can't turn us. We can face them down and kill them."

"We can start taking back the planet," added O'Bannon with a more optimistic tone than anyone had heard from him in months.

"Exactly," said Robson. "With this vaccine, we're the dominant species again."

Mad Dog snorted. "If the fucking thing works."

A somber mood returned to the hall.

"Trust me," said Compton. "It works."

The doctor stepped in front of the podium. He unbuttoned his right sleeve, pulled up the cloth, and held his arm above his head. Two sets of teeth marks six inches apart disfigured his forearm. The wounds were deep and left permanent scars, but were old wounds, long since having scabbed over and healed.

"I tried out the vaccine on myself six weeks ago." Compton lowered his arm and pulled down his shirt sleeve. "I didn't even run a fever."

A stunned awe greeted Compton's remarks. Even Mad Dog seemed impressed, though that did not prevent him from being argumentative.

"I don't buy it. You gotta be naturally immune."

"Really?" Thompson approached Mad Dog, unbuttoning his right sleeve to reveal a pair of scarred-over teeth bites on his arm. "I suppose I'm naturally immune, too?"

"My God," mumbled Natalie.

"God had nothing to do with this," Compton replied pleasantly. "This was all science."

"What good will it do us?" asked Dravko. "You said the vaccine was destroyed when you were attacked at the Navy yard."

"It was. But before we left, I made extra vaccine and stored it. I also stored away a portion of the virus sample from which I derived the vaccine and several copies of my notes. The vaccine is not permanently lost. We only have to go back there and get it."

That uneasy feeling began to creep down Robson's spine. "And where's 'there'?"

"Site R in Pennsylvania." Thompson stepped forward, taking over his part of the briefing. "It's an underground military facility outside Gettysburg. Washington originally built it for continuity of government in the event of nuclear war but gave up on the idea when the Soviets designed nuclear weapons large enough to bust it open. But it's more than strong enough to keep out the revenants."

"Unless one of them has a ten-megaton bomb," quipped O'Bannon. No one laughed.

"Logistically, it's gonna be a nightmare, boss." Hodges directed his remarks to Paul. "We'd have to carry enough supplies to get us there and back, which means taking along the tractor-trailer."

"We only need enough supplies to get there," said Thompson. "Site R is well stocked with fuel, MREs, ammunition, and anything else we'll need. When we left, we locked down the facility and secured the compound so nothing could get in. We can open it up and walk right in."

Paul stepped forward and forced his way back into the briefing. "Elena and I have discussed the situation with Dr. Compton and Colonel Thompson. We're sending a group to Site R to retrieve the vaccine and bring it back here. The group will consist of the doctor, Colonel Thompson, the raiding party, and the Angels."

"Are we included?" asked Dravko.

Elena quickly moved forward. "Of course. We're all in this together."

Dravko shook his head. "Unless you plan on driving like hell and getting there in one night, what happens to us after the sun rises?"

"We've got that covered," Paul responded. Elena slinked back a few steps, clearly having lost much of her authority with the arrival of the newcomers. "Hodges' team is preparing the Ryder for the trip. They're covering the trailer with sheet metal and installing two blackout curtains behind the rear door. You'll have a mobile dark room for the journey."

Natalie shifted in her chair, looking between Paul and the rest of her girls. "Is it a good idea to send the Angels on this mission?"

"Afraid?" asked Thompson, the derision evident in his tone.

"No." Natalie bristled but maintained her composure. "But is it a good idea to send both the raiding party and us at the same time? You'll be stripping the camp of all its defenses."

"It's a risk I'm willing to take," said Paul. "We've never had any significant rotter activity around here, so the camp should be able to defend itself while you're gone. And it'll only be for a week, ten days at most. Just long enough for the doctor to produce enough vaccine for the camp and to prepare copies of his notes and the core sample."

"How accessible is this facility from the outside?" asked Robson.

"You're referring to revenants?"

Robson nodded. "You're bringing a lot of firepower with you. I want to know what we can expect."

Thompson smirked. "There are more revenants around Site R than you and your girls can handle."

Natalie bristled again and started to say something, but Robson reached out and gently squeezed her hand. She bit her tongue. He noticed, though, that she did not pull her hand away.

Thompson continued. "Most of the revenants are effectively contained, so you don't have to worry. Besides, we have a special way of getting in."

Compton moved in front of Thompson, preventing a further clash of personalities. "The biggest threat doesn't exist at Site R, but on the way. I don't think you realize how dangerous it is out there. I requested that Paul send all his best-trained personnel to make sure we get to the site and back. He concurred."

Paul took over the briefing again. "Everything's settled. Robson and Natalie, prepare your people. Hodges' team will finish getting the vehicles ready. Besides the Ryder, you'll be taking the school bus, one of the gun trucks, and the armored car. Any questions?"

The tone of Paul's voice indicated none were to be asked. Robson asked anyway. "When do we leave?"

"Tomorrow at midnight."

CHAPTER ELEVEN

EVERYONE WORKED AROUND the clock during the next twenty-four hours. Hodges' motor pool crew put in a double shift, preparing the vehicles to ensure they were road worthy and loading them with supplies. Robson, Daytona, Whitehouse, Mad Dog, and Thompson studied the maps and satellite photos of their proposed route until they practically memorized every mile of the journey. Natalie's Angels spent most of the day filling ten-round magazines with 8mm ammunition for their Mausers.

Even though Paul had ordered those going on the mission to get some sleep, no one did. Everyone was apprehensive about what they would find out there. The few who tried lay on their cots staring at the ceilings, unable to doze off, until frustration got the better of them, and they went back to prepping for the trip.

After dinner, Paul held the final briefing around an easel in the now-empty dining hall. All of those who would go on the mission were in attendance. Robson counted everyone as they wandered in and took a seat. Twenty-nine people were assembled between his raiding party, the Angels, Compton's team, and the drivers and gunners. Over half the camp and everyone who could expertly handle a weapon. He frowned as the full extent of the foolishness of Paul's plan began to sink in. It was one thing to send out the raiding party and the Angels on a quick supply run to Kittery. Paul's plan would leave the camp defenseless for over a week while placing most of its key personnel in harm's way. The more he thought about it, the more dangerous this entire scheme sounded.

Paul waited impatiently for the last stragglers to show up, looking at his watch every few seconds as if that would speed them along. Mad Dog arrived last, entering the dining hall without an apology for being late and taking his usual seat by the window away from the others. Paul stood and cleared his throat to get their attention.

"Ladies and gentlemen, I'll only take a few minutes of your time because I know you have to prepare for departure. I want to go over the final arrangements for the convoy and see if there are any last-minute questions.

"We have four vehicles heading out to Site R. Daytona will drive the gun truck with Caylee riding shotgun in back. Whitehouse will drive the school bus, which will carry the Angels and most of the raiding party. Robson will drive the armored car and take Compton and Thompson as passengers."

"Wouldn't it give us better protection if we left the armored car behind and took along the second gun truck?" asked O'Bannon.

"It would. But I chose the armored car to protect the vaccine so we don't have a repeat of what happened at the Navy yard." Paul spoke louder so Mad Dog could hear. "Mad Dog will drive the Ryder. Elena's people will rest in the back during the day. They'll take over the driving at night so the rest of you can get some sleep. Food and ammo will be divided among the four vehicles. Daytona will carry all the fuel in the dumpster bed, enough to keep all four vehicles fueled for seven hundred miles. Sorry about that, Caylee."

The young woman shrugged.

Natalie lifted her hand and caught Paul's attention. "What do you mean seven hundred miles? I looked at a map this morning, and Site R is only five hundred miles from here."

"It is, as the crow flies. I'll let Windows explain."

Paul motioned to a young girl in the front row in her early

twenties with a short-cut blonde bob and librarian-style glasses. She stood up and crossed over to the easel, unfolding an old road map of the eastern seaboard. Flattening it against the easel's surface, she anchored it with pushpins. Robson noted a yellow highlighted line running from the coast of Maine west through New England and New York, then turning south into Pennsylvania. Windows placed a folder filled with paper in the chalk tray. When she turned to face the group, a huge smile brightened her face.

"I spent the day checking out satellite images and talking to the survivors of Dr. Compton's party." Windows glanced over at Compton. "You chose one of the most infected routes to get here. It's a wonder any of you made it as far as you did. I compared the satellite photos of the Internet against the maps, and I've come up with a route that should get you down to Pennsylvania while avoiding most major highways and population centers."

"You still have Internet access?" asked Thompson.

Windows shook her head enough for the blonde strands to slap across her cheeks. "The 'Net crashed months ago. Before it did, we set up a bank of computers and downloaded everything that could be of use: medical journals, how-to books, road maps, and commercial satellite photos. We kept updating these photos until the 'Net finally went offline. By that time, the world had fallen apart, so these are up to date."

Windows handed the colonel a manila folder with dozens of printed satellite photos showing various scenes of the proposed route to Site R. He thumbed through them as Windows returned to the map and referred to the highlighted route.

"A straight run to Site R like your convoy took will go through or near every major population center. I've picked a route that bypasses most of that, but it adds another two hundred miles to your trip. I briefed all the drivers on the routes earlier tonight so they know what to expect."

When Windows finished, she looked over at Paul. He nodded his approval and motioned for her to sit down, then continued the briefing.

"Once you leave here, Robson is in command until the convoy reaches Site R. Dravko and Natalie will be his backups, in that order. Upon arrival at the facility, Compton will be in charge of all decisions related to the vaccine, and Thompson will be in charge of security. Once you leave Site R to return here, command reverts to Robson. Anything else?"

Robson suppressed a wry smile. He had a thousand questions about this mission. They all did. Most of them knew they would never get an answer or would be fed some bullshit about being for the good of what little mankind remained, so the questions went unasked.

"Yeah," said Thompson pointing to Mad Dog. "I want him removed from the raiding party."

Mad Dog started to rise from his seat, his glare fixed on Thompson. Paul motioned for Mad Dog to sit. He hesitated, uncertain whether to obey Paul or his instincts. Only when Robson turned to him and mouthed the word "sit" did Mad Dog comply.

Paul turned his attention back to Thompson. "Why do you want to leave Mad Dog behind?"

"He's a coward and a deserter."

"Fuck you, asshole," screamed Mad Dog as he jumped out of his chair again.

Thompson stood up and faced him from across the dining hall. "When we went into lockdown, you abandoned the facility."

"Is that true?" Robson asked.

Mad Dog stared at Robson, his mouth slightly agape. "Come on, man. You know me fuckin' better than that. I left to get... something. When I got back, they'd already sealed up the facility, and I couldn't get back in. I had no choice but to set out on my own."

Thompson refused to back down. "You were warned along

with the others that maintaining the integrity of the facility was the primary concern. You left the facility and got locked out. That's not my problem. But bringing you along is. I won't risk the success of this mission on someone unreliable."

Mad Dog looked over at Robson, an uncharacteristic tone of desperation in his voice. "You know this is fuckin' bullshit, man. I've never let you or the others down. You can't leave me behind."

Robson had never seen Mad Dog like this, nor did he know why Mad Dog was so adamant about going. Not that it mattered because it would not alter his decision. He looked alternately between Paul and Thompson. "Mad Dog is one of the best rotter fighters I have. He's going."

Mad Dog responded with a barely perceptible nod and mouthed the word "Thanks."

Thompson shook his head. "I'm responsible for security at Site R, and I refuse to allow him on this mission."

Robson did not need this machismo bullshit and decided to put an end to it. "If I don't have control over my team, then I'll sit out this raid."

"Fine with me," said Thompson. "Who's second in command?"

Dravko raised his hand. His voice dripped with contempt. "I am. Or do you have a problem with that?"

Tibor leaned closer to Thompson and offered the colonel an exaggerated smile, enough to expose his fangs.

"Enough!" bellowed Paul. "All of you. These arrangements were already worked out and are not open for discussion. Colonel, if you have a problem with Robson or the people under his command, I suggest you take this up with Dr. Compton."

Thompson bristled at the dressing down but said nothing.

"All right. If there's nothing else, you're all dismissed."

Everyone stood and filtered out of the dining hall, most trying to escape the tension-filled room as quickly as possible.

Thompson stuck around long enough to flash withering glances at Robson, Mad Dog, and Paul before leaving, pushing through the others as he made his way to the exit. Only Robson and Paul stayed behind, watching the others until the last one departed.

Well," said Paul with a heavy sigh. "That didn't go as I had planned."

"Do you trust these guys?"

"Actually, I do." Paul stepped over to the easel and pulled down the map. "I spent several hours talking with Compton. He's created a vaccine for the Revenant Virus and it's sitting at Site R waiting for us. Compton's convinced that once we get the vaccine to the government-in-exile, we'll be able to turn this whole situation around, and I believe him."

"What about Thompson?"

Paul folded the map and placed it into the folder with the satellite photos. "I've dealt with his kind before. He's opinionated as hell, but he'll do whatever Dr. Compton tells him to. The doctor assured me he'll keep Thompson on a short leash."

"I hope you're right."

"Of course, I'm right. That's why I'm in charge." Paul smiled and headed for the exit, with Robson close behind. "Is everything ready to roll?"

"Hodges is finishing checking out the vehicles. Once he's done, we'll be good to go."

"Great." Paul looked at his watch. "You still have a few hours. Get yourself some sleep. You have several long days ahead of you."

CHAPTER TWELVE

A S THE COVEN exited the blockhouse and made their way down the stairs, Elena raced after them.

"Tatyana, wait up."

The young vampire stopped. The others each quickly glanced over their shoulder before continuing, all except Dravko, who stood ten feet away.

Elena slowed as she approached Tatyana. Placing her arm around the young vampire's shoulder, Elena gently directed her down the stairs and away from the stream of people. Dravko followed at a discreet distance.

"I need to talk to you for a minute," said Elena.

"About what?"

"I don't want you going with the others."

Tatyana became defensive. "Why?"

"I don't think you're up to it."

"I feel fine."

"You're not ready psychologically."

"I don't understand."

"It takes decades for a newly-sired vampire to become accustomed to their abilities. You've not had enough time to grow familiar with them yet, and I can't send you into battle like that. It's too dangerous."

"How can you say that?" Tatyana shrugged off Elena's arm. She took a step away and turned to face the master. "I fought alongside you and the rest of the coven all the way from New York. No one had to hold my hand or look out for me, and no one has ever questioned my fighting skills. So why the sudden concern?"

"I'm not questioning your fighting skills. I'm questioning your judgment."

Tatyana clenched her hands together. "This isn't about me. It's about O'Bannon."

"Your relationship with O'Bannon is one of the things that calls your judgment into question." Elena feared she was losing control of the discussion. "He's not right for you."

"Because he's human?"

"Because he mistreats you."

"Well, that's none of your business." Tatyana started to walk away.

Elena raced after Tatyana, grabbed her by the arm, and spun the young vampire around to face her. "As the mistress of the coven, it is my business."

"Really? And did you have this same conversation with Sultanic after he sired me?"

Elena could not respond because Tatyana was right. She never took the others to task for their sexual transgressions as long as their actions did not endanger the coven. Maybe it was her natural prejudice against humans or some long-dormant maternal instinct that caused her to react so differently with Tatyana.

Tatyana sensed Elena's faltering. "I know you're only concerned about my well-being, but I'll be fine. What type of vampire would I be if I let the others go off and fight without me?"

"I'm sorry. My mind is made up."

Tatyana looked to Dravko. "Do you agree with Elena?"

Dravko moved forward to join the women. Elena could tell by the hesitation in his response that he disagreed with her. "It's ultimately the Mistress' decision, but given what we're likely to face out there, I want as many of us as possible on the team."

With Dravko having turned against her, Elena gave in to the inevitable. She bowed her head, avoiding the stares from both Tatyana and Dravko. "You can go."

Tatyana responded like a teenager being told she could go on her first date. Rushing forward, she hugged Elena. "Thank you. I promise I won't let you down."

As Tatyana ran off to prepare for the mission, Elena turned to Dravko. Her voice contained no anger or recrimination, only resignation. "Now it's official. I've lost all control over the coven."

"No, you haven't."

"There was a time when no vampire would dare challenge my authority, especially you." Elena headed back to her container.

Dravko followed. "I'm not challenging your authority. I'm merely offering my guidance and counsel."

"Apparently, I need it."

"You're being too hard on yourself, just as you were being too hard on Tatyana." Dravko chuckled. "You and Tatyana have a lot in common."

"How so?"

"You're both trying to grow accustomed to your new circumstances. Tatyana with her vampirism, and you with leading the last coven while living amongst humans."

Elena lowered her head and smiled so Dravko could not see her. She was fortunate to have him as her deputy and knew they would never have gotten this far without him. "Promise me you'll bring the coven back safely."

"No need to worry. There's nothing we'll run into out there that we can't handle."

THOMPSON EXITED THE blockhouse a minute after the vampires. He watched Elena race after the young female vampire and lead her away from the structure. Stepping to the corner of the landing, he observed the exchange between them. Although he could not hear what they were saying, their actions were visible even in the dark. Thompson assumed they were arguing about something, though he could not hear about what. Eventually, the exchange ended, and the young vampire hugged the leader before running off. Like she was happy about something. Like she was a fucking human.

Thompson averted his gaze. This place disgusted him. It seemed as if everyone here had lost their sanity. They had one of the few ideal locations to sit out the rotter apocalypse, and then fucked it up with their asinine security procedures. He had checked their outer perimeter earlier in the day and could not believe how weak it was. Except for the reinforced gate blocking the driveway, the perimeter defense consisted of only a few strands of barbed wire strung through the woods. If a rotter horde converged on the camp, the barbed wire fence would not last more than a few hours at most. And while the fort wall would keep out the living dead indefinitely, it would also trap everyone inside with no way to escape. No one had even thought to tie up boats at the base of the cliff in case rotters overran the camp and they had to evacuate in a hurry.

Then there were their amateurish attempts at security, with cops pretending to be soldiers and girls playing at war. And if all that was not enough, he had to contend with the camp's ungodly alliance with the bloodsuckers. Shit, a first-year ROTC student knew enough not to bring the enemy into your camp if you wanted to live. These people did not have a fucking clue about what it was like to be in the military, to be professionally trained, to face real combat. How any of them had survived this long was a miracle, one that Thompson felt certain had more to do with sheer luck rather than skill. During his career, he had been in enough units with poor leadership to know that eventually luck runs out and, when it did, the result was disastrous.

Thompson's thoughts wandered to his son, Michael, some-where in the Middle East. He had been stationed in Iraq when the outbreak occurred. His unit had been cut off when rotters overran Iran, Turkey, and the densely populated Mediterrane-an coast. Those coalition and Iraqi forces not already turned had retreated south through the deserts of Saudi Arabia, crossed the Red Sea into Egypt, and joined the defensive perimeter trying to contain the rotters from spilling out of the Levant into Africa. At least that was where Michael had been the last time they had talked five months ago. Worldwide communications had fallen apart shortly after that. For all Thompson knew, his son still fought a retreating action to protect Africa or was now one of the rotters spreading into the Dark Continent.

The entire situation infuriated Thompson. His son was highly trained and well equipped yet, by now, he was either already one of the rotters or living on borrowed time. Mean-while, the idiots here managed to survive despite themselves. Even worse, they coddled the creatures that had brought this onto mankind and would eventually get his son killed. He wanted to get as far away from these people as possible and would have already set out on his own if he did not have an obligation to keep Compton alive. He had reached the end of his patience. Once the colonel ensured the vaccine got to the government-in-exile in Omaha, he would request a transfer to a combat unit to get some payback on the rotters for what they did to Michael. If he lived that long.

"Is everything all right, Colonel?"

Thompson glanced over to see Compton standing beside him. His thoughts consumed him so much that he did not even hear the doctor approach. *Shit*, he chastised himself. Screw up like that in the field, and you'll become dinner for the living dead.

"We're all ready to go, doctor."

"Good to hear. But that's not what I asked."

At first, Thompson wanted to keep quiet, but that would not work since Compton knew he was upset. "To tell you the truth, I've got bad vibes about returning to Site R."

"Because Mad Dog's part of the team?"

"I can handle that little coward. I don't like bringing the bloodsuckers with us."

Compton rested his forearms on the railing. "They're the least of my worries right now."

"You're not afraid they'll turn on us while on the road?"

"They need us to get to Site R alive as much as we need them."

For a moment, Thompson was taken aback. "It sounds like you want the bloodsuckers along."

"Actually, I don't mind. Paul may be an idiot about a lot of things, but he's right about the bloodsuckers increasing the fighting strength of his group. Having them along increases our chances of success." Compton pushed himself off the railing, turned around, and leaned against it. He glanced around to make certain no one was in earshot, then spoke softly so only the colonel could hear. "And I like the idea of knowing where they are at all times."

Thompson grinned. "You mean keep your friends close and your enemies closer."

"Something like that. Besides, bringing the bloodsuckers with us makes it much easier to finally deal with them once we reach Site R."

CHAPTER THIRTEEN

"**I** WONDER WHAT it's like out there." Ari stated it not as a question but as a way to fill the gap in the conversation as she loaded 8mm rounds into the ten-cartridge Mauser magazine.

"Same as before," responded Leila, "only much more hellish."

"How so?" asked Doreen, brushing a long strand of red hair out of her face and back behind her ear.

"There are no people out there now." Leila looked up from loading ammunition into a magazine. She had a pretty face, with emerald eyes and dark hair that cascaded over her shoulders, but her expression had hardened, the result of her experiences before arriving at camp. "Right after the outbreak, you could find survivors all over the place. It didn't matter if they were friendly or not. They were human. When we were out there, we didn't feel alone. Most of them didn't survive the last eight months so, when we go out tonight, we're entering a dead land. Literally. There's nothing out there but rotters."

"You're a cheery bitch." The comment came from Stephanie, the oldest member of the Angels.

"It's true," said Leila.

Stephanie cleaned her rifle, never once looking at Leila. "Stop trying to undermine morale."

"You have a problem with the truth?"

"The truth is you have no clue what it's like out there."

Leila threw the half-filled magazine into the box of 8mm

rounds. "Considering what I went through out there—"

"We've all heard it before. 'I had to fuck ten guys a night every night to survive'." Stephanie slid the Mauser's bolt back into its stock and locked it. She laid the rifle across her lap and glared at Leila. "We all have a story to tell, you just don't hear the rest of us dwelling on them."

"That's not fair."

"Yes, it is. I watched my husband turn into a rotter and attack my son, and then I had to kill them both. Sandy lost her entire family on the Brooklyn Bridge when the Army blew it up. Tiara made it from Boston on a broken leg. We're all carrying emotional baggage."

Leila refused to let go. "You don't have any idea what I went through."

"We do." Josephine, a petite young woman of Asian descent, pushed the last round into a magazine. She motioned to Amy, who sat beside her. "Both of us also traded sex for security. We decided, for whatever reason, that it was better to be a whore than a rotter. We made our own hells, but we made those decisions ourselves. Some of us made terrible decisions, and others didn't have a choice."

Most of the Angels cast a sympathetic glance at Sarah, who had spent five weeks with a rape gang before the living dead attacked the group, giving her a chance to escape. She still bore a deep, three-inch scar across her left cheek where one of her attackers slit her with a knife for not cooperating. Sarah pretended to concentrate on filling her magazine, though she slightly lowered her head so the sandy hair fell across the scar.

"And it doesn't bother you?" asked Leila.

"Every fucking day." There was no anger in Josephine's voice, only sorrow. "I think of my husband and whether he survived the outbreak, and what he would say if he ever found out what I did to survive. And then I hope he doesn't find me, even if he is alive, so he'll never know what I've become."

Stephanie stifled back a tear. "I never knew that."

"Because I don't talk about it. None of us talk about our experiences. They're too painful." Josephine sounded almost pleading when she turned to Leila. "You shouldn't dwell on it either."

Leila opened her mouth to speak. Instead, she bent her head and sobbed. Emily, who sat to her left, wrapped an arm around Leila and pulled her close. Her southern accent added a soothing quality to her voice. "It's okay, honey. We all have demons haunting us. It's the bond that keeps us so close to each other. Right?"

Emily glanced over at Stephanie, hoping for support.

"Right," said Stephanie, relieved at finally bringing the awkward moment to a close. She patted the Mauser in her lap. "That, and our kick-ass fighting skills."

"Yeah, but we still have a long way to go before we're as good as One Shot over here." Josephine leaned over and nudged Amy.

"That's true," said Ari, pushing her eyeglasses back up her nose. "Ever since we stood up the Angels, you've been able to take down a rotter with a single shot. How did you get so good? Were you a hunter before this?"

"Never fired a gun before in my life," Amy responded as she pinned her long blonde hair into a ponytail with a rubber band. Raising her Mauser, she aimed it at a point on the opposite wall and sighted down the barrel. "Whenever I line up a rotter, I pretend it's one of the guys I used to fuck in the biker gang. Works every time."

"Hell," said Bethany, who, at nineteen, was the youngest member of the Angels. "If it's that easy, I'll picture my first boyfriend who dumped me when I wouldn't put out."

"My ex-husband," chimed in Virginia.

"Both my ex-husbands," added Katie with a chuckle.

Leila still sobbed against Emily. Emily squeezed her arm gently. "Who are you going to picture?"

"Probably me," said Stephanie with a good-natured grin.

"No." Leila snorted back her tears and ran a hand across her eyes. The stern expression had softened, making her look vulnerable. "It'll be my mother-in-law."

Doreen chuckled. "She can't be that bad."

"You never met my mother-in-law." Leila looked up, a forced smile on her face. "That woman was so mean she could scare off rotters."

The fourteen women around the room laughed. Not that they found the joke especially humorous. They all realized they needed to bond and reaffirm their camaraderie for what lay ahead.

Natalie crouched outside the blockhouse, far enough away from the open window so none of the Angels could see her, but close enough so she could listen in on their conversation.

Leila's outburst bothered her, and not because of the tension it caused within the group. Fourteen people couldn't live in constant proximity to each other, especially under these conditions, without tempers flaring. No, Leila's outburst was merely a symptom of something more troubling. As Josephine said, every one of them carried demons because of the outbreak. And everyone dealt with those demons in their own way. No one had exorcised them yet, and those inner tensions threatened the camp more than a hundred rotters. Even after pinpointing the problem, she could not come to terms with her guilt over losing David and act on her feelings for Robson. She was not sure that she could.

"If I got caught spying on your girls like this, they'd call me a stalker."

The voice startled Natalie. She whipped her head around to see Robson standing behind her. "Jesus, you startled me."

"Sorry." Robson crouched beside her. "Is everything

okay?"

"Yeah. I'm just worried about them, that's all."

"Because of the fight?"

"No. There's a lot of pent-up emotion among my girls."

"I wouldn't worry about it. They're the best fighting force in camp, thanks to you." Robson placed his hand on Natalie's shoulder. It felt pleasant, even through the leather jacket. For a moment, she wondered what his touch would feel like against her naked skin.

"What about you?" she asked, trying to draw him out. "What demons are you fighting?"

Robson withdrew his hand and became sullen. "I'd rather not talk about it."

"Are you afraid of digging up bad memories?"

"I'm afraid you'll think less of me."

"I doubt that. If it wasn't for you leading the raiding parties, none of us would have survived this long."

"Thanks."

Robson did not pursue the matter, so Natalie dropped it. Laughing from inside the blockhouse caught her attention. She checked on the girls, relieved to see the argument had ended and them joking amongst themselves.

"I'm concerned about how they'll handle this trip." Natalie stood up and brushed dirt off her knee. She strolled toward the sea wall overlooking the ocean, with Robson walking beside her. "This will be the first time they've traveled this far from camp."

"It's the first time any of us have. But your girls came from out there, some as far away as New York and Pennsylvania. They have more experience with what we'll encounter than us locals do. I wouldn't worry about them."

"I hope you're right."

"I usually am."

Natalie flashed him a flirtatious smile, though she doubted he saw it. They stopped at the sea wall and looked out. Without a moon, darkness enveloped everything. She could barely see the whitecaps as the waves crashed against the base of the wall a hundred feet beneath them. A year ago, prior to the outbreak, you could trace the outline of the shore off in the distance by the lights of the numerous coastal communities. Now water and land merged into a single black void. All the lights had long since gone dark, and not even a fire burned to indicate where humans once lived.

In a few hours, they would be entering that unknown void.

CHAPTER FOURTEEN

P EOPLE BEGAN GATHERING in the motor pool twenty
minutes before midnight, both those going on this mission
and those bidding them farewell. Paul and Elena were among
the first to arrive. Paul refrained from giving a speech or
offering a last-minute pep talk. Instead, he wandered among
the vehicles, shaking hands and wishing everyone luck, working
the crowd like a politician outside a polling station pimping for
votes. Much less comfortable with such public displays, Elena
hung back, quietly offering best wishes to her coven.

Oblivious to the commotion around him, Hodges walked
the drivers around their vehicles and showed them the latest
innovations. His team had welded extra foot-long spikes along
the bottom and sides of each window in the truck's cab to
prevent rotters from getting at the drivers. They also reinforced
the mountings for the truck's plow and the school bus cowcatcher, giving them extra support if they had to push out of
the path something more substantial than rotters, and checked
the welding on the grates that covered the school bus windows.
In addition, four floodlights had been set up on the front of
each vehicle.

The Ryder truck was only recognizable by its yellow cab.
Working like banshees, Hodges' team had completely transformed it, welding metal plates onto three of the cargo bay's
sides and the roof, turning it into a mobile safe haven for the
vampires. Two rows of blackout curtains covered the rear of
the bay to prevent sunlight from entering when they opened

the sliding door. Inside, four hammocks strung across the width of the bay provided shelter for the vampires during the day.

By ten till midnight, most of those going on the mission waited at the motor pool, already having stored their gear and weapons in their respective vehicles. Compton arrived last, with Colonel Thompson and Jennifer in tow. As Paul and the doctor exchanged a few last words, Robson moved among the group, telling them it was time to go. One by one, they said their farewells and boarded their vehicles.

Daytona climbed into the cab of the dump truck, closing the door behind him. O'Bannon joined him in the front seat. Caylee crawled up the side of the bed, took her position in the forward gun mount, and strapped herself in. She flipped off the safety on her AK-47 and made sure she had easy access to her ammo bag.

Whitehouse pulled open the front door to the school bus to allow entry to Natalie and the Angels, Tibor, Sultanic, Tatyana, and Jennifer. The Angels each took a window seat at the rear of the bus, leaving the aisle seat available to place their Mausers in case they had to reach them quickly. Each Angel wore a melee weapon attached to their utility belt for use against any rotters that got in too close for them to use their rifles. Most of them preferred either the bayonet that came with their rifles or an eighteen-inch crowbar. Sarah and Emily bucked tradition, opting for a machete and a hunting knife, respectively.

Whitehouse walked around the exterior of the bus, checking all the emergency exits to make sure they were secured from the inside, and then climbed into the driver's seat.

Robson drove the armored car that served as the convoy's command vehicle, with Compton joining him up front to help lead the way, and Dravko and Thompson taking the smaller travel seats in back. Mad Dog drove the Ryder, with Rashid riding shotgun.

One by one, the engines thundered to life before settling

into an idling rumble. As the vehicles warmed up, Hodges led his motor pool crew to the main gate. As two of the men stood on either side of the entrance, M-16 semiautomatic rifles raised and at the ready, a third man unlocked the gate and swung it out of the way. Hodges cautiously stepped outside the compound onto the main road, scanned the area, and visibly relaxed when he saw no rotters nearby. Raising his right arm, he pumped it up and down several times.

Hodges closed his eyes against the glare as sixteen floodlights and four sets of headlights switched on, bathing him in white light. He stepped aside until he bumped into the gate post and stopped.

With a hiss of air brakes and the revving of its diesel engine, the Mack lurched forward. It passed slowly through the gate. Hodges gave a thumbs up to his friend Daytona, who returned the gesture by tipping his NASCAR hat. The truck climbed the slight incline and swung right onto the road, slowly moving off into the night.

Whitehouse followed two hundred feet behind Daytona. Several Angels waved to Hodges as they passed by, a nervous gesture to cover their trepidation over traveling into the unknown. Natalie turned to check on Robson, who followed a hundred feet to the rear in the armored car. He returned Hodges' salute as he passed through the gate.

Mad Dog shifted into first gear and stalled the Ryder, not properly compensating for the additional weight of the metal plates. He turned over the engine and tried again, giving the truck more gas. The Ryder lurched forward and threatened to stall, but Mad Dog pushed harder on the gas pedal. Gaining momentum, the truck moved forward. He shifted into second gear as he passed through the gate, nodding at Hodges.

Barely had the Ryder turned onto the main road when Hodges closed the gate behind the convoy and secured the locks. Everyone else filtered back into the fort, a feeling of anticipation for their comrades hanging heavy in the air.

Only Paul stayed behind. He walked over to the gate and watched as the Ryder's taillights disappeared around a bend in the road, silently praying that this would not be the last image he had of his raiding party.

BOOK TWO

BOOK TWO

CHAPTER FIFTEEN

T HE CONVOY WOUND its way along the tree-lined road without spotting any signs of life save for the wildlife that had rapidly repopulated the area. Each time the vehicles rounded a bend, a deer or small animal would scurry into the woods, dissolving into the darkness on either side of the road. A feral cat, at one time someone's pet, hunched down in the overgrown grass along the shoulder and carefully studied each vehicle as it raced by. Its eyes flared crimson from the headlights, giving the creature an ominous stare.

Robson lifted his foot off the accelerator five seconds before the brake lights on the school bus flashed. He knew instinctively that the convoy was about to turn onto the main road north of the Kittery. He could drive this route with his eyes closed. Each of them knew every inch of it by heart, even at night. They had driven this way God knows how many times previous because it was the only road out of camp that took them around the rotter-infested Navy yard.

Up ahead, Daytona slowed the Mack to make the turn onto Route 1A South. The other vehicles followed, keeping a safe distance from one another. As usual, they encountered no rotter activity until they reached the half-mile stretch of road that held the city's outlet malls. Hundreds of rotters milled around the surrounding parking lots and stores, having been drawn here by the numerous raids they had staged to gather supplies. Scores of corpses with bullet holes gouged out of their foreheads lay in small clusters throughout the area, marking previous battle sites. Upon hearing the approaching vehicles, hundreds of lifeless eyes turned in their direction. Robson could imagine the collective moan as the living dead lumbered toward the road in a vain effort to reach the food. Daytona quickly dispatched the few rotters in their path, their smashed bodies thrown aside by the plow. Robson glanced in his side mirror, watching as a few of the more determined living dead stumbled after them in pursuit.

A minute later, the convoy crossed the overpass that put them onto Route 1 South. The twin towers of the 1950s-era lift bridge loomed in the dark sky ahead of them, the red aviation warning lights on each structure still blinking. Before the convoy reached the bridge, the vehicles veered right onto Route 103 and began their run alongside the Piscataqua River.

Robson looked across the river onto the New Hampshire side. Though he could not see it through the trees lining the banks, he knew that Newington sat only a few miles away. The images of his and Susan's failed escape attempt eight months ago invaded his thoughts no matter how much he tried to forget. For a moment, he wondered what had happened to her. Was she fortunate enough to have been stripped clean by the rotters, leaving nothing left to reanimate? Or did she become one of them, now aimlessly wandering amongst the abandoned cars in search of food? The all-too-familiar pangs of guilt wracked his conscience, this time accompanied by nausea over picturing Susan as one of the living dead.

Thankfully, Daytona's voice came through his radio, providing a welcome distraction.

"Hey, boss? Are you there?"

Robson lifted the handheld push-to-talk radio from the dashboard and keyed the microphone. "What's up?"

"Do you realize this is the first time we've gone this far west?"

"So?"

"Just mentioning it," Daytona replied sheepishly. "Welcome to the brave new world."

"A rotter world," sneered Dravko from the back.

Robson placed the radio back on the dashboard. He doubted this brave new world would be any better than the one they were leaving behind.

CHAPTER SIXTEEN

THE CONVOY HAD been driving for less than an hour when the brake lights on the Mack lit up. Robson slowed, coming to a stop fifty feet behind the school bus. He watched as Daytona climbed out of the truck and walked down the road until he disappeared around a bend. Robson picked up the radio and pressed the microphone button.

"Daytona, what's going on?"

No answer.

"Daytona, are you there?"

Still no answer. Robson shifted the armored car into park and removed his shotgun from its vertical lodging mount. "Dravko, you're with me. Colonel, stay here and keep an eye on the doctor."

"Roger that."

Robson and Dravko climbed out of the armored car and headed for the Mack. As they passed the school bus, Natalie and a few of her girls disembarked. Josephine, Leila, Stephanie, and Tiara each stood by one corner of the bus, scanning their respective quadrants for rotter activity and holding their Mausers ready for quick-fire. Natalie waited by the open door. Ari stood on the stairs behind her, her rifle pointed at the ground.

"What's up?" asked Natalie.

"Damned if I know. Daytona's not answering his radio."

The two women fell in behind. Robson heard Ari pull back the bolt on her Mauser, loading a round into the chamber.

Daytona knelt by the front bumper of the dump truck, unwinding lengths of chain off the winch.

"Everything okay?" asked Robson. "You didn't answer your radio."

"Sorry. I left it in the truck."

"Why'd you stop?"

Daytona pointed over his shoulder while he continued to work. "Because of that."

The others turned to look up the road. A few yards ahead sat Eliol Bridge. Two vehicles blocked the entry ramp. The first, a red Toyota Camry, sat in the eastbound lane. A Dodge Ram heading west had swerved and crashed into the Camry's left front fender and now sat at a seventy-five-degree angle across its lane. Flies swarmed around the point of impact.

"Can't you push your way through?" asked Dravko.

Daytona stood up, holding the coiled chain in his hand. "Not at the angle that pick-up is in. I'm gonna have to pull it out of the way."

"Let me check it out first," said Robson.

"Better you than me." Daytona leaned back against the Mack's bumper and pushed the NASCAR cap back on his head.

"Watch yourself," said Natalie.

Dravko approached the Ram from the left as Robson circled around the accident to the right, carefully watching the vehicles for movement. Dravko checked the Ram's bed, then stepped forward and peered into the cab. Not seeing anything suspicious, he opened the driver's door and scanned the interior.

"Nothing here. Looks like whoever drove it walked away and took everything of value with him."

As he neared the Camry, Robson switched on the flashlight mounted under the barrel of his shotgun and shined the light onto the driver's side. The window had been shattered, with shards of glass littering the ground. A figure sat in the driver's seat, motionless. As he approached, Robson raised the shotgun, keeping it trained on the figure. Only when he got to within a few feet did he realize that the driver had been lucky, having been devoured so badly the body could not reanimate. The back of its head had been pried open and the brain eaten. Flies swarmed around the corpse, feeding off what remains had not already decayed. The chest under its shirt pulsated, probably from maggots. He placed the shotgun's barrel against the corpse's temple and pushed. The head broke away from its neck with a loud snap and dropped onto the passenger's seat.

Robson stepped back and turned to the others. "All clear."

As Daytona came forward to wrap the chain around the Ram's trailer hitch, Robson opened the back door of the Camry and peered inside. The flashlight fell on a duffel bag lying on the floor. Robson pulled it out and slung the strap over his left shoulder. He would rummage through it later to see if he could find anything of value.

Two minutes later, Daytona went back by the dump truck and turned on the winch. The electronic whir of the engine mixed with the clinking of the links as the chain grew taught, soon accompanied by the creaking of metal as Daytona dragged the Ram away from the wreck. Robson heard the moan of a rotter.

Jumping back from the Camry, he swept the accident scene with his flashlight. A rotter lay stretched on the ground where the Ram had sat, wedged under the pick-up during the accident. It tried to stand up, but its legs had been crushed, and instead thrashed its arms futilely. Robson stepped forward and aimed the shotgun at its head. The rotter turned to stare at him, its mouth snapping violently. He approached to within five feet and squeezed the trigger. The sharp retort of the shotgun cut off the moaning as the shell blasted its head from its body, spraying brains and skull fragments across the asphalt.

Natalie raced forward. "Are you all right?"

"Nothing to worry about. A rotter was trapped under the

pick-up."

More moaning from farther down the bridge caught their attention. Robson swung the flashlight in that direction. The light illuminated only a hundred feet. In the darkness beyond, several shadows shambled toward them. Robson and Natalie backed up and joined the others. Ari moved up alongside them and trained her Mauser down the bridge.

"Where did they come from?" asked Natalie, a nervous edge to her voice.

"The noise must have attracted them."

"How many?" asked Dravko.

"Don't know. According to the map, Dover is a few miles across the river."

Natalie moved close to Robson until they practically touched. "Which probably means hordes of rotters."

Ari leaned her cheek against the stock of the Mauser and kept the weapon sighted. "Should I call the others?"

"Hold on." Robson turned to the dump truck. "Daytona, can we get across now?"

"Sure. Just give me a minute." Daytona detached the tow chain from the Ram's hitch and began frantically rewinding it onto the winch. After seconds that dragged on like hours, he respindled the chain and secured it. Daytona stood, wiping his palms against his trousers. "All set."

Robson spun around to face the others. "Let's roll."

Moving around to the driver's side of the Mack, Daytona opened the door and climbed into the cab. Natalie headed back to the school bus. Ari retreated a few steps back, her Mauser still aimed down the bridge, then lowered her rifle and followed. Natalie had already ushered the other girls on board and stood by the door waiting. Ari ran up the stairs and to her seat. Natalie jumped on last, closing the door behind her.

The first rotter slowly emerged from the shadows. From this distance, it looked like it might once have been a young woman, long scraggly hair falling across what remained of its leathery face. Its clothes had long since been stripped away, revealing naked, desiccated skin. It reached out for Robson, flailing away desperately with the stump of its right arm. Two more rotters emerged from the shadows a few yards to its rear. One wore light blue hospital fatigues stained dark brown with dried blood. The other, a man in the tattered remains of a business suit, limped toward them, dragging a nearly severed left leg behind him.

Dravko stepped up beside Robson. "We need to get going."

Robson snapped back to reality. The two men jogged back to the armored car. Thompson stood by the open rear door. "Is everything all right?"

Robson circled around to the driver's side. "Rotters are crossing the bridge. Nothing to be concerned about."

They crawled in and secured the doors, and Robson shifted into drive. Daytona was already heading across the bridge, maneuvering between the wrecked vehicles, with the school bus close behind. Robson surged forward and kept a safe distance to the rear.

A dozen rotters moved across the bridge, the ones in Daytona's way easily being pushed aside by the plow. The rotter in the business suit became lodged on the right corner of the blade and was dragged along, its shattered leg tearing free and sliding across the asphalt. Daytona snapped the steering wheel to the right, throwing the rotter free. It fell into a heap by the side of one of the bridge abutments and immediately began crawling toward the convoy.

Once across the bridge and on the road leading to Dover, Robson saw another dozen of the living dead spread out across the area, a couple on the road itself and the rest struggling up the embankments. The convoy easily brushed aside the few that got in its way and slowly increased speed. Robson glanced in the side mirror as the armored car raced past, watching as the rotters along the embankment turned en masse and stumbled after them.

In the back of the armored car, Dravko looked out the rear window with a growing sense of concern. Not about the rotters, which were rapidly falling behind, but about the sliver of light blue sky spreading across the eastern horizon.

CHAPTER SEVENTEEN

DRAVKO MADE HIS way to the front of the armored car. He leaned in between Robson and Compton and motioned with his head in the direction they had just come from. "Have you looked east lately?"

Robson glanced in his side mirror, not realizing what Dravko meant. His eyes widened when he noticed the first tints of the rising sun. He glanced at his watch. It was a few minutes before dawn. He had lost track of time back at the bridge. All he could think to say was, "Shit."

"That's the same as what I was thinking," responded Dravko.

The first two vehicles of the convoy were already half a mile ahead of him. Robson grabbed the radio from the dashboard and keyed the microphone. "Daytona, the sun's coming up. We need to pull over now and get Dravko's people into the Ryder."

"That ain't gonna happen, boss."

"What do you mean?"

"You'll find out in about thirty seconds."

Robson began to argue when he saw movement to the right and left. As he drew closer, the floodlights fell onto a sign off to the right announcing they were entering Dover. Close to twenty rotters milled around on either side of the road, living dead sentinels for the town. Their numbers increased the closer the convoy got to the center.

Robson keyed the microphone again. "Daytona, we need

to find a safe place to stop, and fast. So, haul ass."

"I'll do my best, boss. But this town is heavily infested."

Robson took another glance toward the east. The horizon glowed reddish orange. Robson looked around for a secure location to stop, but rotters jammed the road and sidewalks.

The road suddenly ended at an intersection where it connected with a cross street. Daytona decelerated to a near crawl and pulled the Mack into a sharp left turn. As each vehicle slowed to make the turn, rotters closed in, most of them descending on the bus. The living dead slammed decayed hands against its flanks, trying to claw their way inside. Flashes erupted from the windows as the Angels fired back, dropping several. Robson could see the streaks of gore left on the side panels. As he entered the turn, he had to maneuver around the rotters, those lumbering toward the armored car and those littering the ground.

By now, they were well into town. Rotter activity was thicker than anything they had ever encountered at Kittery. Between the moaning, revving engines, and gunfire, the racket they made attracted every living dead in town. There were not enough to pose a threat to the convoy so long as they kept moving. But it also meant they could not stop to get the vampires safely into the Ryder. They would have to—

Daytona's truck came to a sudden stop. Robson watched the brake lights on the rear of the school bus light up. He slammed his foot on the brake pedal. Because of the added weight of the armored plate, it did not stop right away. The tires squealed in protest and the rear jackknifed slightly. The armored car came to rest a few feet short of the bus.

Robson keyed his microphone. "Daytona, what the hell's going on up there?"

"Hang on, boss." Daytona left the mike open. Robson could hear him arguing with O'Bannon. "Which way?"

"I don't know," O'Bannon yelled back, his voice accompanied by the rustling of papers.

"Well, figure it out before we're swarmed and can't move."

"I can't. Windows' maps are fuckin' useless."

Something slapped against the window by Robson's head. A hand with all its fingers missing swatted at the window, trying to break the glass, but only smeared the surface with blood and chunks of decayed flesh. The hand belonged to a rotter dressed in a police uniform, its lower mandible ripped off. Another dozen began to swarm around the front bumper and flanks, with more closing in. The Angels shot through the open windows. Caylee hung over the side of Mack's dump bed, firing down on those crowding the truck.

Dravko leaned forward, the tremor in his voice belying his outward calm. "We don't have much time."

Robson looked in his side mirror. Half the eastern horizon was lit up, with the undersides of the clouds glowing red from the approaching sun. He keyed the microphone. "Uh, guys? Anytime now would be helpful."

"There, there, there!" O'Bannon's excited voice came over the speaker. "Off to the left. A sign for Route 9."

The Mack lurched forward and turned left, shoving aside a swarm of the living dead that frantically clutched at its sides. A rotter grabbed one of the support beams and attempted to pull itself onto the bed until a well-placed shot from Caylee exploded its head. The decapitated body tumbled to the ground.

Whitehouse accelerated, moving into the path cleared by Daytona. Robson followed, constantly switching his attention from the road ahead to the rapidly lightening sky to his left. Rotter activity remained too heavy to attempt a switch here, but at least Daytona was booking it to find a safe place. They were already doing over sixty, which was risky on a city street clogged with the living dead and abandoned vehicles.

Daytona swerved right, smashing through two cars blocking the road. One of the vehicles, a Saturn, spun off to the left where it smashed through a glass-enclosed bus stop. The second vehicle, a Subaru Outback, got caught on the plow blade. Daytona pushed it along for a hundred feet, chunks of metal breaking off and falling by the wayside. Finally, the Subaru broke free and slid off to the right, forcing Whitehouse to swerve around it.

Natalie's voice came across the radio. "I have three vampires on this bus who are freaking out."

"Maybe you haven't noticed," responded Daytona, "but we have a rotter problem."

"In case *you* haven't noticed, the vampires are going to have even bigger problems unless you pull over in the next few seconds."

A glance to the east confirmed that. The sun had already crested the horizon, a few rays of light shining through the spaces between the buildings. They had a few minutes at most. A quick scan of the area showed about twenty rotters. Not ideal, but enough for them to handle.

Robson lifted the radio to his mouth. "Okay, guys. We need to stop now."

"Too dangerous, man," responded O'Bannon. "We have to wait till we clear town."

"We don't have time."

"I won't risk anyone's life needlessly."

"That's not your decision to make," Robson practically yelled into the radio.

Daytona cut into the argument. "Boss, there's an overpass about a hundred yards ahead of us. There's only a few rotters on it, and our flanks will be protected. We could easily do the switch there."

"Go for it," said Robson. "Natalie, did you hear that?"

"I copy. Already have our friends ready to make a run for the Ryder."

"Good. Mad Dog, do you read me?"

No response. Robson looked in his side mirror. To his horror, he did not see the Ryder. He keyed the radio again.

"Mad Dog, where the fuck are you?"

"Look in your right mirror, asshole," Mad Dog responded.

Robson glanced to his right and saw the Ryder passing him. "When we hit the overpass, stop alongside the front door of the school bus."

"Way ahead of you."

Daytona reached the overpass and raced across, sweeping away the few rotters on the span before screeching to a halt on the far end. Whitehouse pulled into the left lane directly behind the Mack. Tibor, Sultanic, and Tatyana rushed off the bus even before it came to a complete stop. Natalie joined them, and the group raced to meet Mad Dog. Robson pulled up behind the Ryder and climbed out as the first rays of sunlight broached the top of the buildings. A line of sunlight moved across the asphalt toward the convoy.

Natalie reached the Ryder first. Jumping onto the loading dock, she swung the latch into its unlocked position and flung open the sliding door. Tibor leapt up and rolled inside. Sultanic paused to help Tatyana onto the landing, then climbed up himself. Natalie helped them through the blackout curtains and turned to Dravko and Robson.

"Move it!"

The two were a few feet from the Ryder when the sunlight washed over them. Dravko cried out but kept running. As Natalie reached out a hand, grasping Dravko by the arm and helping him onto the loading dock, Robson tried shielding the vampire with his own body. Dravko rolled into the back of the truck and out of the sunlight. When he stood up, Robson saw that he only had been lightly burned on his right cheek and hand. Painful as hell, but nothing that would not regenerate.

"Thanks," said Dravko, rubbing the burnt spot on his hand.

"Don't mention it." Robson reached up and grabbed the handle of the sliding door. "You should be safe until sundown."

Robson began to slide shut the door when Dravko shot out

a hand, holding it in place. When he gazed into Dravko's eyes, he saw an emotion he had never seen in the vampire before. Fear.

"What's wrong?"

Dravko took a deep breath. "Promise me you won't leave us stranded in rotter territory."

"Are you serious?"

"You know there's a lot of people at camp who would see this as the perfect chance to get rid of us."

"I'm not one of them," said Robson.

"Neither am I," added Natalie.

Dravko nodded and offered the two a slight smile. As he moved through the blackout curtains into the rear of the Ryder, Robson lowered the door and secured the latch into the closed position.

CHAPTER EIGHTEEN

A PLEASANT MID-MORNING sun heated the cool air and shimmered off the placid surface of the Suncock River. A flock of ducks floated by, occasionally quacking at the intrusion of humans into their solitude. The peaceful silence was broken when the fifty-five-gallon drum of gasoline Daytona and Whitehouse were lowering from the rear of the Mack landed on the grass with a muffled bang, sending the ducks scattering frantically toward the opposite bank. The frenzied flapping of wings drowned out the metallic echo, and then silence descended across the area again. The serenity of the autumn day presented a sharp contrast to their encounter from the night before.

Robson sat on the trunk of an uprooted tree a few yards from the river, a granola bar and a tin cup of lukewarm coffee resting on the grass in front of him. The others sat nearby in groups having breakfast while Daytona, Whitehouse, and Mad Dog refueled the vehicles. The Angels gathered a few yards off to his right in a circle near the school bus. Compton and Thompson sat on the rear bumper of the armored car, which was parked in front of the school bus, being served coffee by Jennifer. To his left, Rashid rested up against the front bumper of the Mack with Caylee, munching away on his granola and talking up a storm while she stared absentmindedly into her cup. O'Bannon remained off by himself, standing on the road and staring in the direction they would soon be heading, a cup of coffee in his hand. The Ryder sat in the grass on the opposite side of Parade Road, directly across from them. In their own way, everyone enjoyed a few moments of relaxation. Hell, after last night, they had earned it.

After getting the vampires aboard the Ryder, the convoy had headed out of the Dover area without incident, traveling northwest for under an hour before coming to the town of Barnston. Thankfully, they had encountered no rotters there. The convoy picked up this country road north of town, which paralleled Route 28 and the Suncock River. Since the road seemed isolated, Robson had decided to pull over for a rest stop.

As the others went about their meal, Robson opened the duffel bag he had removed from the Camry on the Eliol Bridge and searched through the contents, hoping to find something useful. He found the type of stuff anyone would expect. Mostly clothes. A few paperbacks, ironically horror novels from Stephen King and Brian Keene. Two plastic bottles of spring water, which he put aside for later. And a travel photo album.

Robson opened the album. Attached to the inside front cover was a pink Post-It note written in an elegant, feminine hand. It read:

Jude,

Now you can look at me every night before you go to bed. See you in a few weeks.

Love always,
Tess

He smiled as the memory of those days when he had been in love filtered back into his conscious even though those days seemed centuries ago. Turning to the first page, he thumbed through the album.

Each 3 x 5 photo stared back at him. Most were of a young woman in her mid- to late twenties, slightly pudgy but still quite attractive, and with a well-proportioned body. She smiled in all the photos. A few contained a young man about the same age, though he looked too serious in most of the pictures, as if too macho to express his feelings for the camera. Robson assumed by the range of photos that each marked a special occasion – Tess in a long black evening gown and Jude in a tux. Tess in jeans and a sweater kneeling by open gifts under a Christmas tree. Tess in a red bikini on a beach. Tess in the bikini and Jude in a tacky Hawaiian shirt sitting at a bamboo bar drinking cocktails. Robson could not help but wonder what had happened to her. Was she still alive? Had Jude been trying to get to her when the accident occurred? Or had he already found her, either dead or among the living dead, and had been running away from his nightmare? Robson felt his eyes water as his mental rambling brought him to images of Susan's last moments.

The last few pages were of Tess in a full-length see-through negligee that left nothing to the imagination. Robson quickly closed the album. The photos made him uncomfortable. Not because he was a prude. These pictures were intended for two people in love, not for some voyeur. Stumbling across them made him feel like he had invaded their personal lives. He placed the album beside the bottled water, deciding to burn it later to ensure their privacy stayed that way.

Rummaging through the duffel bag some more, he found some underwear and socks which were too small for him. His eyes widened in excitement when he reached the bottom of the bag and found buried treasure, to him anyway. Sitting there underneath all the clothes sat an unopened carton of Camel cigarettes. It would be a sin to let those go to waste.

As Robson repacked the duffel bag, placing the items he intended to keep on top, Natalie came over and sat beside him.

"Find anything useful?" she asked.

"Just a carton of smokes."

"You know they're bad for your health," Natalie teased. Her smile faded and she looked down into her coffee cup. "I'm sorry I snapped at you back there in town."

"When did you snap at me?"

"Back in Dover when I yelled at you to pull over so we could get Dravko and the others into the truck."

"That? Forget about it."

Natalie looked up and met his eyes. "I don't want you to think I don't trust you. To protect them, I mean."

"That thought never even crossed my mind."

"There's a lot of people who would have been just as happy if you didn't stop and let Dravko and the others burn."

"I'm not one of them."

"I know that." Natalie grinned. "I don't want you to think I'm an ass."

"I happen to like your ass." Robson regretted the words the moment he spoke them. "Sorry, I shouldn't have said that."

"Don't be." Natalie reached out and gently placed her hand on his. "I'm glad you're looking."

THOMPSON GLARED AT the others as he wolfed down his granola, trying to wash away the stale taste with a tin cup of weak, lukewarm coffee. He could barely swallow the shit. Once the colonel got it down, he took another sip to clean out his mouth and tossed the rest of the bar onto the grass. The meal left an acidic aftertaste in his throat.

It matched his mood.

Beside him on the fender, Compton popped the last bite of his granola bar into his mouth. As the doctor chewed, he crumpled the empty wrapper into a ball and stuffed it into his jacket pocket. "What's on your mind?"

"Nothing."

"I know you too well, Colonel." Compton swigged down the last of his coffee. "You're pissed off about something, and I can only assume it's because of this morning."

"Do you blame me?" Thompson glared over at Robson

seated on the log rifling through the corpse's duffel bag. The colonel did not bother hiding his look of disgust. "We could've gotten rid of the last of the bloodsuckers last night if Golden Boy hadn't decided those things were worth saving. Even worse, he endangered all of us in the process."

"Don't be too hard on him."

Thompson turned to the doctor. "You agree with his saving the bloodsuckers?"

"Paul and I both agreed that this mission's best chance of success was to include them because they gave us added strength. Mr. Robson only did what we asked, like a good soldier. Which you should appreciate." Compton flipped the remaining drops from his tin cup onto the grass, and then used a paper napkin to wipe the inside dry. "As much as I hate to admit it, we need the bloodsuckers. At least until we get to Site R. Once we've secured the vaccine, we won't have any use for them."

"But do you think Robson will see it that way? If you ask me, he's drinking the same Kool-Aid Paul does."

Compton thought for a few moments. "You do have a point. He seems to have developed a level of trust with them, especially the one called Dravko. It makes it difficult to predict how he'll respond."

"There's at least one person who hates the bloodsuckers as much as we do." Thompson focused on O'Bannon, who stood in the center of the road looking west. The colonel handed his tin cup to Compton. "I think it's time he and I had a chat."

Thompson strolled over to O'Bannon and stood alongside him. "Morning."

O'Bannon cocked his head slightly toward Thompson and nodded.

Thompson ignored the sullenness. "You and I haven't had a chance to talk since I arrived at camp."

"I didn't think we needed to."

"We probably should."

"Why?"

"Because we have something in common."

"What's that?" The distrust was evident in O'Bannon's tone.

"It seems like you, me, and Doctor Compton are the only ones who find it appalling how much trust the others have placed in the bloodsuckers."

For a moment, O'Bannon did not respond. He eventually glanced over at the colonel, a scant hint of friendliness on his face. "You're right. We do have something in common."

"I thought so. You hate the bloodsuckers as much as I do."

"I do. But for different reasons."

"How so?"

All hints of friendliness rapidly faded, replaced by an intensity that scared Thompson. "You and the doctor hate them because the bloodsuckers stole the Revenant Virus and released it on mankind. It was one evil using another evil. And you're as responsible for that as they are."

Thompson started to defend himself but paused, partly because he did not want to alienate O'Bannon, and partly because he feared the reaction. All he managed to say was, "So why do you hate them?"

"Because those fuckers ruined my life before everyone else's." O'Bannon turned his gaze to meet Thompson. A fury burned in his eyes that bordered on insanity. "They killed my Maria three years ago."

Thompson considered dropping the topic, but he had to know. "Who's Maria?"

"Maria is my wife. *Was* my wife. She had spent the night with some of her friends. A vampire attacked her in the parking garage and drained her of blood. A security guard found her lying beside her car and called an ambulance, but it was too late. She was already dead. The police labeled it a homicide. A nurse at the hospital told me that Maria had died from blood loss, but no blood was found at the crime scene. When I asked the police about it, they told me the case was closed and threatened to make me the prime suspect if I didn't drop it.

"The worst part was she was eight months pregnant at the time. The police said the baby didn't survive the attack. The same nurse told me the baby had survived but had been infected with something and had to be put down. When I demanded their remains so I could have a private autopsy conducted, the authorities told me the bodies had been cremated. A clerical error. The hospital wrote me a check for a hundred grand to compensate me for their mistake. I never cashed the fucking thing."

Many things about O'Bannon suddenly fell into place. All Thompson could think to say was, "Sorry."

"Save it. I have more of a reason to hate the bloodsuckers than anyone here, including you and Compton."

"So why do you cover for Robson when he protects them?"

"Because he's in charge when we're out here. I do as he says, or we die. Besides, Paul has a hard-on for the bloodsuckers, and if I did anything to them, it would mean I'd be banned from camp. I know I wouldn't last a week out here alone."

"Makes sense."

"I'm glad you approve." O'Bannon's voice dripped with sarcasm. "At some point, the opportunity is going to arise for me to get rid of the bloodsuckers without getting myself killed or exiled in the process. When that happens, those fuckers are dead."

Thompson saw his opening. "You may get that opportunity once we reach the facility."

O'Bannon turned back to the colonel, the hint of friendliness having returned. "You know, we may become friends after all."

THE ANGELS SAT around the fire used to warm the coffee, talking animatedly amongst themselves. While none of them

114

would openly admit it, last night's dash through Dover had been an adrenaline rush. It had been a long time since any of them had seen that much excitement, and the thrill of it all felt good.

"So, how many rotters did you get last night?" Emily asked. The word "rotters" sounded like "rottahs" due to her southern drawl. "I only got one."

"Two," said Josephine. "Maybe."

"What do you mean 'maybe'?"

"I couldn't tell because we were going so fast. It's not as easy as it looks in the movies."

"Nothing ever is," said Ari, pushing her glasses up her nose.

"So, how many did you get?" asked Emily.

"None. I shot up a lot of the street, but no rotters."

"The bus was swaying too much to aim properly," added Sandy. "I may have hit one, but I'm not sure."

Leila glanced over at Amy. "I'm afraid to ask how many you bagged."

"You don't want to know." Amy raised the cup of coffee to her lips.

"We're big girls," said Stephanie with a grin. "You can tell us."

Amy shook her head as she drank.

"She won't tell us because she didn't hit anything." Tiara nudged Stephanie. "She's just afraid to admit it."

"Do you really want to know?" asked Amy.

"Yes," most of the Angels answered at once.

Amy sighed in mock exasperation. "Four."

"Bullshit," said Leila.

"You're joking, right?" added Ari.

"Four?" asked Stephanie.

Amy chuckled. "It's not my fault none of you can hit the wall of a barn from the inside."

The Angels responded with good-natured insults and laughter. However, the levity ended abruptly when they all heard the all-too-familiar sound of a rifle bolt being pulled back and locked closed again. They all turned toward the end of the school bus in the direction of the sound.

Two figures stood by the end of the bus. One was a large black man, six feet three inches and at least two hundred and fifty pounds, most of it muscle. Huge biceps bulged under his shirt, as did the veins on his bald palate. He held a shotgun trained on the Angels.

To his right stood a middle-aged white guy with unkempt, graying hair and a beard. Although barely half the size of his partner, he looked just as menacing because of the scowl on his weathered features. He clutched a hunting rifle in his right hand, the barrel pointed toward the ground. A twisted smile pierced his lips, the smile of a bully about to take pleasure in tormenting someone.

"What did I tell ya, Ike? It looks like we've got ourselves some trespassers."

CHAPTER NINETEEN

T HE NEWCOMERS STARED menacingly at the Angels. Ari eyed her Mauser, which sat two feet from her in the grass. Her gaze caught the attention of the bearded man, who quickly lifted his hunting rifle and aimed it at the young woman.

"Don't try it, sweetheart. I'd hate to hafta shoot you."

"Yeah," snorted the giant of a black man. "We got other plans for ya."

Robson felt Natalie start to rise from the fallen tree, but he grabbed her hand and squeezed tight. She followed his gaze across the road where two other men emerged from around the front and back ends of the Ryder. A tall, lanky man carried an AK-47 semiautomatic rifle, the weapon already raised and aimed in his and Natalie's direction. From behind the truck, a barrel-chested man with a mustache trained a double-barrel shotgun on O'Bannon and Thompson, directing them to place their hands on their heads and move toward the center of the clearing. He then turned the gun to Compton and Jennifer, implying they were to do the same.

Off to Robson's left, two more men appeared from around the front bumper of the Mack. One of them, a teenager with long blonde hair tucked behind his ears and held in place with a Yankees baseball cap, pointed an old British Enfield at Rashid and Caylee, motioning with the barrel of his weapon toward the others. The second gunman, a middle-aged man wearing a leather Harley Davidson vest, used an M-16 semiautomatic to threaten the refueling team, who were gathered around the Mack's fuel tank. Daytona and Whitehouse raised their arms and moved to the clearing. Mad Dog sneered. The gunman stepped forward and aimed his M-16 at Mad Dog's head. Slowly and reluctantly, Mad Dog held up his hands and fell back.

Except for the Angels, the gunmen ushered everyone else into the open area between the Mack and the school bus. The two gunmen with semiautomatics stood on either side of the huddled group, their weapons trained on them, ready to fire. The mustachioed gunman circled around and stood behind Robson and Natalie. Ike stepped away from the Angels and boarded the school bus.

The teenager peered into the Mack's bed. His eyes lit up with excitement. He turned and crossed over to the bearded gunman hovering over the Angels. "Hey, Sam. These guys are carrying fifty-five-gallon drums of gas. Four of 'em."

Ike stepped out of the bus. "They have two more drums in here, plus a shitload of supplies, boxes of MREs, and a coupla thousand rounds of ammo."

The teenager stroked Sandy's blonde hair. "Plus, enough pussy to last us months."

Sandy pushed his hand away and screamed, "Fuck you!"

The teenager took the stock of his shotgun and slammed it against the base of Sandy's neck between the shoulder blades. She yelped and slumped forward onto the grass, moaning in pain. The rest of the Angels started to move to her defense but stopped when Ike and Sam stepped forward, their weapons at the ready.

The teenager knelt, clutched Sandy by the hair, and yanked her head up so she faced him. "Oh, you'll fuck me, bitch. Hell, by tonight you'll have fucked all of us."

Ike stepped over to Sarah and used the barrel of his shot-gun to push aside her hair, revealing the scar across her cheek. "Looks like someone already got a crack at this bitch."

Sarah pushed the barrel away. Ike swung a large hand,

slapping Sarah so hard across her face that she spun around and collapsed. He hovered over her, quivering with anger. "Get up, cunt!"

"We don't have time for this," snapped Sam.

"But the cunt needs to be put in her place."

"I'll let you kill her when it's time."

"We're not taking that one with us?" asked the teenager.

"With a face carved up like that?" Sam grimaced. "You want to fuck her?"

"Yeah, why not? I'll just bury her face in a pillow and fuck her up the ass."

Ike smiled menacingly. "I get her ass first."

"Sam," called to the gunman in the Harley Davidson vest. "What should we do with the rest of them?"

Sam thought for a moment. "Get rid of 'em."

"What about using 'em in the zone?"

"Too many mouths to feed."

Robson looked around, calculating their odds of getting out of this. His party had a six-to-one advantage, but the gunmen had surprised them. And the two semiautomatic rifles gave these assholes an edge. The thug in the Harley Davidson vest stood twenty feet in front of Robson, while the lanky one stood about ten feet from Thompson with his back to the colonel. Robson made eye contact with Thompson. He slightly motioned his head toward the lanky gunman with the AK-47. Thompson acknowledged with the barest of nods. It was a damn slim chance, but at least it was a chance. If he and the colonel could take down the two with the semiautomatic rifles, it would give the Angels at least a fighting chance to get to their weapons. But Robson knew he would never cover the distance between himself and the thug in the Harley Davison vest before the guy standing to his rear took him down. He would need Natalie to run interference.

He glanced over, hoping to get Natalie's attention, surprised to see her staring at the Ryder. She would look away for a moment, and then go back to staring at the truck. If she kept that up, she would draw suspicion to herself.

No sooner had Robson thought it when the mustachioed gunman placed the heel of his boot against Natalie's back and shoved. "What the fuck you lookin' at, bitch?"

Natalie meekly lowered her eyes to the grass. "Nothing."

"Bullshit." He shoved her again with the heel of his boot.

"What's going on?" yelled Sam.

The mustachioed gunman pointed toward the Ryder. "Somethin's in that truck."

"What?"

"Don't know. The bitch ain't talking."

Sam turned to the teenager. "Billy, didn't you check it out?"

"No."

"Fuckin' idiot."

Billy cringed, as if expecting to be hit. "Sorry."

Sam turned to Ike and nodded to the Angels. "Keep an eye on them."

"Sure thing, boss."

"You're with me," Sam said to Billy, who fell in behind him. He snapped his fingers toward the mustachioed gunman and motioned for him to follow.

The thug rammed the stock of his shotgun into Robson's back. "Move."

Robson and Natalie did as they were told, joining the others in the center of the clearing. Sam grabbed Natalie by the forearm and dragged her toward the Ryder. As he did, he glanced over his shoulder. "Billy, watch them. The rest of you are with me."

When they reached the rear of the Ryder, Sam shoved Natalie forward. "Open it."

Natalie climbed up on the loading dock, knelt, and swung the latch into the unlocked position. Grabbing the handle, she pulled up. The door slid along its rollers, exposing the blackout curtains.

"What's in there?" Sam asked nervously.

"Trust me," said Natalie. "You don't want to know."

"We'll see." Sam yanked Natalie off the truck, knocking her onto the grass. He stepped back and spoke to the others. "Check it out. If you find anyone inside, kill 'em."

The three gunmen climbed up onto the loading dock. The lanky one pushed aside the curtains with his AK-47 to allow the mustachioed gunman and the one in the Harley Davidson vest to enter and then followed them inside.

A moment later, a scream emanated from the back of the Ryder, followed by gunshots and a growl, an ungodly guttural sound that was neither animal nor human. All three men screamed, the intensity of their panic terrifying. Then, one by one, each cry devolved into a muffled gurgle. The mayhem stopped as quickly as it had started, leaving in its place an eerie silence.

"You guys all right?" Sam stepped closer to the loading dock. "Talk to—"

The thug in the Harley Davidson vest fell from behind the curtains and landed face-first on the landing. The left side of his face had been slashed open, leaving deep claw marks that raked the skin down to the skull. His remaining eye bulged in terror. He clawed at the metal, desperately trying to get away.

"Sam, help me! Don't let them get—"

A roar came from inside the truck. Something grabbed the thug and dragged him back inside as he screamed at the top of his lungs. A second later, they heard the crunching of bones, which ended the anguished wail.

Sam turned around, a blank expression on his face. He stammered, trying to talk, but could not voice any words. Then he saw Natalie lying on the ground, and his initial shock changed to anger. "You cunt! What the fuck's in there?"

"I told you you didn't want to know."

"Fuck you!" Sam raised the hunting rifle and aimed it at

Natalie. She closed her eyes and waited for death. Before he could pull the trigger, another roar sounded from the back of the truck. A pair of taloned hands reached through the curtains and plunged into Sam's shoulders, penetrating deep into his flesh. The claws yanked him onto the landing and into the rear of the truck. Sam shrieked and thrashed around. His screams were still audible when Natalie crawled onto the landing and lowered the door.

From beside the school bus, Ike heard the commotion and rushed to help. He did not get far. As he ran by the Angels, Sarah grabbed the pot of coffee brewing on the fire and threw the boiling remnants into his eyes. He dropped the shotgun to clasp his face, howling in pain. Sarah picked up her Mauser and swung the stock so it collided with the left side of Ike's jaw. Blood and broken teeth spewed from his mouth. He fell to his knees. Sarah lifted the Mauser above her and brought it down against the back of his head, fracturing his skull with a loud crack. Ike toppled forward onto the grass. He tried climbing to his feet but could not. He merely mumbled the single word, "Please."

"Fuck you!" Sarah slammed the Mauser down on his head again, this time with such force that Ike's skull shattered and his skin ruptured, spilling his brains onto the grass. Despite his being dead, Sarah continued assaulting the pulverized skull with her rifle until Stephanie intervened, gently removing the weapon from her hands and holding the young woman. Sarah began sobbing.

After witnessing the carnage at the Ryder and the attack on Ike, Billy dropped his shotgun and ran for the nearby woods, hoping to escape. Robson picked up the shotgun and aimed at the teenager's back, but Thompson stepped forward and pushed the barrel down.

"What are you doing?" asked Robson.

"Give me the gun and your radio, and I'll follow him to see where he goes. If there's others out there, we need to know about them."

Robson handed the shotgun and the radio to the colonel. "Do you want me to come along?"

Thompson shook his head. "No offense, but I can track him better on my own. Get everybody ready to defend themselves in case these assholes have buddies nearby."

"Can do. Good luck."

As Thompson raced off, Natalie joined Robson. "Are you okay?"

"Just a bit shaken, that's all." He stretched his back muscles, feeling a bolt of pain where he had been hit with the shotgun. "How about you?"

"I'm gonna hurt like hell."

"You better go check on your girls."

"I will."

As Natalie started to walk away, Robson reached out and clasped her hand. "That was a gutsy maneuver. How'd you know it would work?"

"I didn't. But it was better than you and the colonel getting into a shootout with those assholes."

As Natalie ran off, Robson turned to the Ryder and stared at it. He had no sympathy for the gunmen and was glad they were dead. Even so, he pushed from his mind any thoughts of what was going on in the back of the truck.

CHAPTER TWENTY

TRACKING BILLY PROVED easier than expected. The teenager was so scared that he barreled through the woods, making enough noise to wake the dead. Or to attract the living dead, if any were around. Thompson followed him at a discreet distance. After running amongst the trees for almost a mile, Billy finally turned toward the road, rested a few minutes to catch his breath, and then set off again. Damn kid was so frightened he never once looked back and had no idea Thompson followed not too far behind.

After another mile or so, Parade Road merged onto a small highway. Billy veered off the asphalt and into a clearing. Thompson cut across to the other side and climbed a hillock before the point where Billy turned off. Carefully broaching the summit, he could easily see the crossroads where Parade Road intersected Route 28 and, directly beneath him, the facility Billy entered.

Thompson radioed his position to the others and waited. Thirty minutes later, Robson, O'Bannon, and Natalie joined him on the hillock. They had brought the armored car if they had to make a speedy getaway, leaving it parked a quarter of a mile away and guarded by three of the Angels. Now the four of them stared down at the compound. As O'Bannon and Natalie kept a lookout for foot patrols, Thompson and Robson used binoculars to survey the area.

Beneath them sat an old self-storage facility that the new occupants had converted into a fortified compound. Twelve

Harley Davidson motorcycles, four with sidecars, and three military-style Humvees sat near the front wall nearest the entry gate. Thompson did a quick calculation. If each vehicle was filled, approximately thirty people were on the compound, minus the five who died back at the campsite. If the disposition of the assailants they had encountered offered any indication, these guys were all thugs and gang members.

From their vantage point, it looked as though the storage cubicles had been converted into living quarters. A few people milled around the compound, primarily men who did not look friendly even at this distance. Each one carried a sidearm or a larger weapon strapped over their shoulders. A few women were visible, but most appeared beaten down and submissive. Thompson assumed they were being used as sex slaves.

No guards were posted anywhere that could be observed. Not that any were necessary. A chain-link fence topped with barbed wire had been erected thirty feet outside the facility, running parallel to the original stone wall and completely enclosing the compound. At forty-foot intervals between the two fences sat men and women chained to stakes hammered into the ground. Each had a worn blanket tightly wrapped around them, their only protection against the elements.

"Can I see?" asked Natalie.

"Sure." Thompson handed over his binoculars. "But you probably don't want to."

Natalie raised them to her face and examined the compound. "Why are those people staked to the ground?"

"An early warning system," said Thompson, unable to conceal the disgust in his voice. "If any rotters break through the outer fence, the screams of the people being eaten would alert those inside to the danger. That's what they referred to as 'the zone.'"

Natalie lowered the binoculars and handed them back to Thompson. "That's inhuman."

Robson agreed. "That would have been us if you hadn't

suckered those assholes into the Ryder."

Natalie's expression became determined. "So, how do we get those people out of there?"

"We don't," said Thompson.

"We can't leave them."

"Our mission's too important to risk it on a humanitarian raid."

Natalie turned to Robson. "Mike?"

"He's right." Robson lowered his binoculars. "There's no way we can rescue them without getting into a firefight, especially now that they know we're here. And they have the defenders' advantage. We'd lose too many people."

"You can't be serious?"

"I am."

Natalie leaned forward to look at O'Bannon. "Help me out here."

"I agree with Mike and the colonel on this one," said O'Bannon. "It's too risky."

"Even if we did get them out, what then?" added Thompson. "There's at least twenty of them in the zone, plus the women inside the compound. They're too weak to take with us, and we can't afford to split our resources to take them back to camp."

Natalie huffed and stared at the ground.

"Shit," broke in Robson. "We've got movement."

As they watched, about twenty heavily armed men exited the main building and spread out across the compound, each heading for makeshift guard towers inside the stone wall.

"Are they going after the convoy?" asked O'Bannon.

"I don't think so," said Thompson as he watched the men climb into the guard towers. "It looks like they're preparing for an attack. They're probably too scared to leave."

"I don't want to take any chances." Robson grabbed his radio and keyed the microphone. "Daytona, do you copy?"

"Loud and clear, boss."

"Load up the convoy and head back to Barnston. Wait for us at the junction with Route 28 and be prepared to move quickly. If anyone other than us approaches, get out of there in a hurry. Understood?"

"Is there trouble?" asked Daytona.

"Just do as I tell you."

"Roger that."

Thompson nodded his approval. "Good call."

"Thanks." Robson keyed the microphone again. "Ari, do you read me?"

"Yeah. I heard your conversation with Daytona. Do you need backup?"

"Negative on that. Get the Angels in the armored car and be ready to haul ass the minute we get back."

"We'll be waiting."

Robson put the radio back in his pocket. "Let's get out of here."

CHAPTER TWENTY-ONE

AVOIDING THE GANG'S compound took over an hour. After meeting up with the others, Robson and the drivers quickly consulted their maps, going over all the nearby roads. They eventually settled on a route that would take them north to the town of Alton and then west toward Gilmanton. Daytona led the way, followed by Mad Dog in the Ryder and Whitehouse in the school bus. Robson followed a minute later in the armored car, hanging back long enough for the quiet to settle back in so he could listen for the tell-tale noise of approaching motorcycles or Humvees.

As the convoy wound its way north along the tree-lined road, Robson noticed that Thompson stood by the back window the entire time, keeping a close watch to the rear.

"Do you see anything?"

"Thank God, no." Thompson moved away from the window and took his seat behind Compton.

Compton shifted in his seat to face the colonel. His voice betrayed his concern. "Are you expecting them to follow us?"

"No. If they were going to come after us, they would have done so by now. After that little asshole related what happened to his buddies, it'll be a while before they leave camp again."

"That suits me fine." Robson took his foot off the accelerator, slowing down enough to let a family of deer bolt across the road in front of them. "But I learned a valuable lesson today. No more letting our guard down. It's too dangerous out here."

"Don't be too tough on yourself," offered Compton. "It's

not easy to imagine what the world has become until you've been out in it for a while. It surprised us when we left Site R. I can't imagine what cities like New York and Tokyo must be like."

"I don't want to try," said Robson. "This is bad enough."

"Trust me," added Thompson. "You haven't seen anything yet."

Robson wanted to ask the colonel what he meant but thought better of it.

The convoy drove along until it arrived in Gilmanton, where it picked up Route 107 and continued west. Here the setting took on a more suburban tone, with strip malls lining either side of the road. Only a few dozen rotters populated the parking lots, with another handful wandering down the road. Most of these barely acknowledged the convoy as it raced past.

"I don't like this," said Robson. "Something ain't right."

"It's the dead rotters," responded Thompson.

"They're all dead." Robson said it in a matter-of-fact tone.

Thompson leaned forward between the doctor and Robson and gestured toward the side of the road. Only when the colonel pointed it out did Robson realize what he was referring to. Scattered along both shoulders were scores of desiccated corpses. From the few that were closest to the convoy as it raced by, it looked as though the back of their heads had been blown off. Piles of charred bones and ashes appeared at regular intervals. The convoy slowed as it passed near the entrance to a Burger King where a stack of rotters had not been torched yet. Strips of decayed flesh and rotted organs dangled from the carcasses, much of the remains already melting into a pile of ooze dripping into a nearby sewer grate.

Daytona's voice blared from the radio, an uncharacteristic tension straining his tone. "Boss, what the fuck is going on here?"

"Yeah," Natalie chimed in from the school bus. "This is freaking us out back here."

"May I?" asked Thompson. Robson passed him the radio. "Nothing to worry about. This is an old site. We're approaching the interchange with Interstate 93. The military cordoned off this area and policed it of rotters to keep it secure to keep the escape route to the highway open."

"Are you sure?" Natalie did not sound convinced.

"Yes, ma'am. We saw this a lot after leaving Site R."

"It's still fucking creepy if you ask me," said Daytona.

★ ★ ★

A MINUTE LATER, the convoy passed a large green sign announcing the interchange with Interstate 93. The other three vehicles slowed as they crossed the overpass, then stopped. Robson watched as everyone climbed out of their vehicles and stepped over to the railing, their attention fixed on something below. Robson pulled in behind the school bus. He, Thompson, and Compton joined the others at the railing.

"What's up?" asked Robson as he approached.

Natalie looked over at him, her eyes wide in horror. She raised a shaking hand and pointed to the interstate. Robson looked down, drawing a deep breath at the nightmare that confronted him.

All four lanes of the highway were jammed with vehicles heading north, stretching as far as he could see. Each exit ramp was blocked by National Guard two-and-half-ton trucks, forcing the vehicles to stay on the highway. The meridian and breakdown lanes were strewn with abandoned vehicles that had broken down. Piles of luggage, much of it opened and ransacked, were scattered across the area. Five hundred yards farther down, a tractor-trailer lay on its side, having overturned as it tried to navigate down the slope of the meridian. Those vehicles still on the road had their doors open or the side windows smashed, with dried blood staining the paint. Corpses littered the area, their bones having been stripped of so much flesh and organs that the bodies never had a chance to reanimate. Scores of rotters wandered amongst the carnage, peering into empty vehicles in search of food.

Robson turned to the south. The same sight stretched in that direction to the horizon.

"Jesus Christ," mumbled Whitehouse. "What happened?"

"Rotters must have overrun them while traffic was stalled." Thompson motioned back toward the strip malls. "They must have wandered down from back there. These people didn't have a chance."

Ari suddenly cried out and ran back to the school bus. She bent over by the front fender and vomited. The others looked down directly beneath them to where Ari had been staring. Jennifer gasped and turned, burying her face against Mad Dog's shoulder.

Below the overpass sat a Lexus SUV with the left rear door ajar. The remains of what once had been a woman lay crumpled on the highway. Inside the vehicle, a baby sat in a car seat, the stump of a half-gnawed right arm reaching up towards them. Lifeless eyes stared at the humans. It tried to crawl out of its seat, but the still-buckled restraining straps kept it in place. It pushed against the straps, snapping at the humans with a tiny mouth that had yet to grow teeth. It wailed in frustration, an ungodly cry more like a wild animal than an infant.

The wail attracted the attention of those rotters closest to the Lexus. They turned in the direction of the sound and, upon seeing food standing on the overpass, began stumbling toward them. Moans of anticipation came from scores of decayed throats, melding into a ghastly chorus. Those rotters on the exit ramps moved toward the overpass.

"We need to get moving, people." Robson stepped back from the railing. Everyone still looked down at the highway. "Now!"

The sharp command snapped them all out of their shock.

One by one, the party fell back to their vehicles. Robson waited until the last person boarded before jogging to the armored car. A rotter reached the top of the exit ramp and stumbled toward him, limping on a right leg hobbled by a compound fracture. As it was no immediate danger, Robson ignored it. Daytona and Whitehouse were already pulling away when he crawled into the driver's seat. Mad Dog passed by on the right, falling in behind the school bus. Shifting into drive, Robson brought up the rear, taking one final look down Interstate 93 as he crossed the overpass.

CHAPTER TWENTY-TWO

R OBSON KNELT BY the rear door of the school bus. O'Bannon and Thompson crouched on either side of him as Compton stood looking over his shoulder, the area map spread out on the grass as they reviewed the route the convoy planned to take that night. Daytona, Whitehouse, and Mad Dog resumed refueling the vehicles after having been interrupted that morning. This time, however, everyone else sat in a circle against the left flank of the school bus, huddled in one group for safety. Half the Angels had spread out around the vehicles, Mausers loaded and ready to deal with any threats, living or living dead. Once the second half finished their MREs, they switched out, giving the others a chance to eat and rest. All except Natalie. She walked the perimeter the entire time, checking in with each of her Angels.

Robson knew better than to let their guard down, despite their not having spotted anyone all afternoon. After leaving the interchange with Interstate 93, the convoy traveled for another hour without incident, following the Daniel Webster Highway before cutting over to Route 11. An hour before sundown, they entered the small town of Andover. The place had seemed deserted, with no traces of life or rotter activity. Robson had ordered the convoy to stop and had each driver rev their engines for a minute. When nothing had appeared out of the side streets, Robson ordered them to shut down and take a break while they waited for nightfall but to remain on guard.

The group finished studying the map, finding it difficult to make out details in the fading light. "Any questions about tonight's run?"

Compton nodded his approval. "I think you have this pretty well covered."

Robson stood, wincing as his knee protested after having knelt in the cold grass for so long. "Thanks. If the route Windows mapped out is accurate, we should have clear sailing until we get to lower New York."

"I hope so." O'Bannon also stood up, rubbing his leg. "I've already had my share of excitement on this trip."

"You and me both."

Thompson got his feet, focused on the combination gas station and convenience store across the street. "Before we move out, I think we should check out the quickie mart."

"Why?" asked O'Bannon with a hint of aggravation. "Most of those places were ransacked long ago."

"I know. But this town seems different. No rotters are roaming around or any signs of mass panic. Maybe the townsfolk were able to keep things under control before they evacuated—"

"Or were killed," interrupted O'Bannon.

"That store doesn't look like it was looted. There may be something there we can use."

Robson stood and looked to the west. The sun had already disappeared below the tree line and would completely set in a few minutes. "We still have plenty of time before we head out. It couldn't hurt. I'll get some volunteers."

"Thanks."

Robson folded the map and handed it to O'Bannon. "Brief Dravko and the others on the change in plans when they wake."

O'Bannon grimaced as if he had swallowed bile. "Why me?"

"Because I want to check on the others and make sure we're ready to roll as soon after sundown as possible."

"It's not like we have to wait for the bloodsuckers to have dinner." The colonel's tone seethed with disgust. "They've already eaten."

"Knock it off," ordered Robson. "Both of you. What happened back there was awkward enough."

"Awkward?" O'Bannon's voice carried to the others gathered by the school bus, causing them to look over. "The bloodsuckers fucking killed humans."

"They killed a band of rapists and murderers," corrected Compton, "who would have killed us first if they got the chance. I don't particularly care what happened to them."

Thompson looked aghast. "You don't condone what happened back there?"

"Not usually. But my only concern is getting the vaccine. If it weren't for the vampires, we'd be dead or—"

The rattling of the Ryder's sliding door being rolled up cut off the conversation. Dravko stood in the doorway, scanning the horizon to make sure the sun had set, and then let the others know it was safe. One by one, the vampires emerged and jumped to the ground, mindful that all human eyes were drawn to them. The vampires looked healthier than they had in months, with a gleam in their eyes and a ruddier complexion to their skin, the result of having fed off humans for the first time in months. Even their manner seemed different, some of the docility they had developed living with humans having given way again to their natural, hunter-like demeanor.

Tatyana exited last, spots of blood staining her blouse. O'Bannon turned away and headed for the school bus.

Robson stepped over to Dravko. "Is everyone all right?"

Dravko nodded. "Who were they?"

"They were members of a gang that took us by surprise. They would have killed us if Natalie hadn't convinced them to check out the Ryder." Robson paused, not sure how to ask the next question. "What happened to the... the...?"

"They're still in the truck." Dravko became uncomfortable,

briefly breaking eye contact with Robson, but quickly regained it. He spoke softly so no one else could hear. "I'd like to take the Ryder behind one of these buildings and dispose of the bodies, if that's okay with you."

"That's probably the best idea."

As Dravko and the other vampires climbed into the Ryder's cab, Robson stepped over to the group gathered by the school bus. "Listen up, people. We'll be moving out soon, so get your things together. I need a couple of volunteers to help the colonel check out that convenience store across the street."

"I'll go," said Jennifer.

"Me, too," said Rashid.

"Count me in," added Josephine.

Mad Dog shrugged. "What the hell."

"Good. This place looks safe, but stay alert and don't let your guard down. We'll meet back here in twenty minutes."

THE GROUP CROSSED the parking lot and headed for the front of the convenience store. Thompson veered off toward the pumps. "Josephine and I will check for gas. The rest of you have a look around inside. And for God's sake, be careful."

Mad Dog led the way to the front door. The glass remained intact, which seemed promising. Standing by the doors, he shined a flashlight inside and scanned the aisles and front counter. The shelves were empty. No debris littered the floor, and nothing seemed out of place.

"What do you think?" asked Rashid.

"Place looks cleaned out," said Mad Dog, "but it doesn't look looted."

Jennifer moved to the window on the far right and shined her flashlight inside. "Maybe the locals took everything they could, hoping to ride out the apocalypse."

"Could be," Mad Dog lowered the flashlight and looked back toward the town, "but if that's the case, where is everyone?"

He placed his hand against the door and pushed. It opened. Stepping into the store, he paused and sniffed. No odor of decayed flesh.

"Hey," he yelled. "Is anyone here?"

Silence.

Mad Dog unsnapped the strap on his holster, removed his Magnum, and stepped inside. Jennifer and Rashid followed. Mad Dog motioned for them to stay there as he walked the length of the store, shining the light down each aisle. When he reached the far wall, he yelled out again. "Is anyone here?"

Again, no response.

Mad Dog walked back to the others. "Looks like the coast is clear. Rashid, check out behind the counter. We'll take the rest of the store."

Rashid gave a mock salute and headed off.

Mad Dog and Jennifer walked up and down each aisle, shining their flashlights on empty shelves. The locals had cleared out everything, from food and drinks to pet food and household supplies. The two met up at the far corner.

"Find anything?" asked Jennifer.

"Nothing." Mad Dog stepped back and yelled down the aisle to Rashid. "Find anything?"

"Just a shitload of lottery tickets. Want to try your luck?"

"Hell, no. This would be the one time I win." Mad Dog flashed his light down a short corridor toward a door that led to the stockroom. "Keep an eye out here while Jennifer and I check out the back."

Mad Dog led the way, pausing in front of the restroom. He knocked on the door, listening for a response from the other side. When he heard nothing, he slowly opened the door and looked in, shining the light around. Closing it, he moved down to the stockroom door, with Jennifer close behind.

Mad Dog knocked, and again he heard nothing. He turned the knob and pushed. Back here was even darker than out front. He sniffed, thankful not to smell rotters.

"Anyone here?"

No response. Mad Dog holstered his Magnum and stepped into the storeroom. As he swung the light around, Jennifer entered, letting the door close behind her. Wooden pallets were piled in the center of the floor. Beside the pallets, two stacks of broken-down cardboard boxes stood five feet high, blocking the loading dock door. The metal door leading to the freezer stood off to their left.

Mad Dog turned the light toward Jennifer, lowering it so the beam did not shine in her eyes. "Shit. They cleaned out back here, too. Not even a cockroach could survive."

"That's fine by me. I hate roaches almost as much as rotters."

"Let's go."

"Wait a minute." Jennifer walked over to the freezer door and grabbed the handle, pulling it toward her. It popped open. "I want to make sure there's nothing in here."

As the door opened, the stench of decayed flesh overwhelmed them. A chorus of moans shattered the silence. Jennifer tried to slam the door shut, but too many rotters shoved against it. She stumbled back, falling into the pallets and nearly toppling over. Mad Dog raced forward, grabbed Jennifer by the arm, and prevented her from falling. As they watched, nearly twenty rotters staggered out of the freezer, filling the far end of the stockroom and blocking the exit.

"W-we're trapped," stammered Jennifer.

"No fuck, lady."

"What are we going to do?"

Mad Dog unholstered his Magnum and cocked back the hammer. "We're gonna kick some rotter ass."

CHAPTER TWENTY-THREE

MAD DOG SLOWLY stepped back from the rotters as they staggered toward him. He used his body to shield Jennifer as he herded her back against the loading dock door, keeping the pallets and stacks of cardboard to his right and the wall to his left. Jennifer crouched, grabbed the handle, and yanked up. The door moved a fraction of an inch and stopped, rattling in its rollers.

"The damn thing's locked."

"No big deal." Mad Dog aimed at the closet rotter, which wore a gore-soiled State Trooper uniform and a motorcycle helmet, and squeezed the trigger. The Magnum roared, sending a .357 round into the rotter's face. The helmet reflected much of the blast, fracturing its face and blowing its eyes out of its socket. It dropped to its knees and tottered for a second before falling over.

Shifting his aim, Mad Dog fired four more rounds, shattering the heads of the next four rotters. Each one crumpled to the floor between the pallets and the wall, blocking the path for the others. A rotter in National Guard cammies tried climbing over the pile of corpses. Mad Dog aimed, but at the last moment the rotter slipped, falling face-first on the floor in front of him.

Behind the National Guard rotter came a former firefighter still in its yellow coat, an axe deeply lodged into its chest above the right breast. Mad Dog placed the flashlight on the stack of cardboard and moved forward. He grabbed the axe handle in his left hand and, lifting his leg, placed his right foot on the rotter's abdomen. It opened its mouth and snarled. Mad Dog shoved the barrel of his Magnum into its mouth.

"Eat this, asshole."

As he shoved with his foot, Mad Dog pulled the trigger. The last .357 round ripped through the rotter's head, splattering skull fragments and brain tissue on those behind it. The force of the round, combined with the concussion, propelled the firefighter rotter backward. It fell into three more rotters, knocking them over.

Rashid burst through the door leading out to the store. "What's going on? Are you—?"

The rotter closest to Rashid, a stubby man in a county deputy's uniform, spun around to face him. Its abdomen was swollen to five times its normal size so that the skin pushed its way through the shirt, which was held together by a single button around the neck. It snarled and lumbered toward the food. Rashid tried to raise his shotgun, but the obese rotter was too close. Before he could back up, the rotter stumbled and, due to its ungainly size, toppled forward onto Rashid. The two crashed to the floor. Rashid felt his elbows crack against the cement floor, the bolts of pain that shot down his arms so intense he nearly dropped the weapon. Fortunately, he did not, for the shotgun clutched in his hands and held across his chest had caught the rotter across the shoulders, keeping it away from him. The obese rotter struggled to get to Rashid, flailing against the shotgun and straining its neck to bite him. With all that weight pressing down on him, Rashid felt the muscles in his arms quickly tiring.

"Hey," he yelled. "How about some help here?"

"In case you haven't noticed, I'm a little busy."

The rotter in the cammies grabbed Mad Dog by the ankle and pulled itself toward him. Mad Dog shook it loose and stepped back. Raising the axe above his head, he brought it down as hard as he could on its head. The blade sliced through the skull and lodged deep in its brain. It shuddered for a moment before going limp. Mad Dog tried to remove the axe, but it remained stuck in its head. Placing his right foot on one side of the ruptured skull, he yanked and twisted. The blade came free with a sickening squish, spilling brain fragments onto the floor.

A rotter in a tattered nurse's uniform closed in on Mad Dog. He slammed the blunt side of the axe blade into its face. It staggered back a few steps. Before the nurse rotter could surge forward, Mad Dog swung the axe horizontally like a baseball bat, slicing the blade through its neck with a single swing. The head flew across the storeroom and smacked into the wall, leaving a gore spot.

From the other side of the sliding metal door, Dravko yelled, "Is everyone okay?"

"No!" screamed Jennifer. "We're being attacked by rotters! Help–"

A rotter leaned across the stack of cardboard boxes and clutched Jennifer's arm. She tried to pull away, but its grip was too tight. Grabbing the flashlight in her free hand, she slammed it against the thing's head.

"Let..."

Jennifer hit it again.

"...go..."

And again.

"...of me..."

And again.

"...motherfucker."

"Lean back," yelled Mad Dog. As Jennifer did, he brought the axe down on the rotter's left arm, severing it above the elbow. He did the same with the right arm. Released from its grip, Jennifer fell back against the wall, panting in fear. Mad Dog swung the axe like a bat, cleaving through the rotter's head directly across its eyes.

Distracted by saving Jennifer, Mad Dog almost did not see the armless rotter coming up on his flank. He jumped to the side at the last second. It stumbled past him toward Jennifer. Spinning around, Mad Dog brought the axe down on the back of the rotter's head, cracking the skull open from its neck to its forehead. It dropped to the ground by Jennifer's feet. She frantically kicked at it as she scooted on her ass into the far corner.

Thompson and Ari rushed into the stockroom in time to see the melee in full swing. Thompson kicked the obese rotter in the face, sending teeth and remnants of lip flying in all directions. It snarled at the intruders. Ari fired her Mauser from the hip. Her aim was off, hitting the rotter in the abdomen. Its gut burst open, spilling a hundred pounds of undigested, decayed meat onto Rashid. She retched at the stench but quickly regained her composure. Raising the Mauser and taking careful aim, he placed a bullet squarely between its eyes. The rotter fell over to one side.

At that moment, the lock on the metal door snapped. The door rolled open, revealing the four vampires standing outside. Each already had morphed into their vampiric forms. The rotters near the rear of the horde turned to greet the new food and lumbered toward them. Dravko and Sultanic raced in first, hacking apart the two closest living dead. Tibor and Tatyana joined them. Tibor grabbed a teenage rotter by the head and squeezed, crushing its skull. Tatyana lunged at a female rotter in a deputy's uniform, tearing off its jaw with an angry swipe of her hand. Undaunted, it continued towards Tatyana until she plunged two taloned fingers through its eyes and gouged, scrambling its brain.

The last few rotters were quickly felled, Thompson taking down two with his Colt .45 and Ari another. Dravko eviscerated a fourth before ripping off its head. They all stood by and watched Mad Dog dispatch the last rotter, knocking it to the ground before he hacked it to pieces in an orgy of axe strokes. When he finally finished, the only sound came from the living panting heavily from fear and exhaustion.

Mad Dog tossed the axe aside and looked at Thompson and Ari, a grin spreading beneath his beard. "What took you so long?"

Robson, Natalie, and O'Bannon rushed into the storeroom. Natalie flinched at the stench and held her hand over her mouth.

"Jesus," mumbled Robson as he swung his flashlight around the carnage. "What the fuck happened?"

Mad Dog pointed to the freezer. "Someone locked a shit-load of rotters inside. When we opened the door, they swarmed us."

"Is everyone okay?"

Rashid jumped up, chunks of gore dropping off him, and ran down the corridor. He made it only a few yards before dropping to his knees and vomiting. Despite his stomach being empty, he continued heaving. Natalie followed to check on him.

Mad Dog looked around for Jennifer. He found her backed into the corner. She clutched the flashlight so tightly to her chest that the beam barely illuminated her. Stepping over to her, he crouched and spoke with uncharacteristic tenderness.

"It's over. They're all dead."

"A-are you sure?"

Mad Dog nodded. "You're safe now."

Jennifer hesitantly extended her hand, clasping Mad Dog's. He helped Jennifer to her feet. Once standing, she rushed into his arms and buried her head into his chest, sobbing. Mad Dog wrapped his arms around her and gently patted her shoulder before leading her to the relative safety of outside.

CHAPTER TWENTY-FOUR

ROBSON FOLLOWED MAD Dog and Jennifer through the convenience store. He was concerned about the woman's mental state, which seemed only natural considering what she had gone through. He said nothing, hoping Mad Dog's tenderness would keep Jennifer anchored in sanity and prevent her from going over the edge.

As they exited the store, Robson noticed everyone outside had gone into lock-and-load mode. The Angels on guard duty had stayed at their posts but were on heightened alert. Those Angels who had been eating dinner a few minutes ago now crouched in a semi-circle in front of the store, their Mausers trained outwards. Everyone else huddled by their respective vehicles, ready to join the fight or bug out at a moment's notice. O'Bannon and Compton waited by the gas pumps.

"What the hell happened in there?" O'Bannon asked Mad Dog. Mad Dog walked by without answering, more concerned with comforting Jennifer and getting her someplace where she would feel safe.

"You can stand down," said Robson. "The situation is under control."

The Angels hesitated for a few seconds before getting up. Swinging their Mausers over their shoulders, they sauntered back to the convoy, hovering around Ari and bombarding her with a dozen questions.

O'Bannon sidled up to Robson. "What situation is under control?"

"The store was empty until Mad Dog and Jennifer opened the freezer. Someone had locked twenty rotters inside. When they opened it, they were swarmed."

"Makes sense," said Compton.

"How so?"

Compton looked up and down the street, although his vision only extended as far as the floodlights on the vehicles. "Look how meticulous this town is. No bodies or abandoned cars in the streets. No barricades. No signs of panic. Whoever ran this town kept a tight ship. If you're going to lock up your rotters, the freezer is ideal. They can't escape unless someone lets them out, and the cold keeps the bodies from decaying. At least while the electricity was still running."

"But why keep them at all?" asked Robson.

Compton shrugged. "Maybe they were waiting until they had enough to make a decent bonfire."

"Maybe," O'Bannon mumbled, not sounding convinced. "But what happened to the people who ran this town?"

As Robson contemplated that unsettling thought, Dravko drove the Ryder around from behind the convenience store and parked near the group of men. Dravko leaned out the driver's window. "Are your people okay?"

Robson nodded. "And you?"

"We checked ourselves out. No bites or scratches."

"That's good to hear. Thanks for coming to the rescue back there."

"You're welcome." Dravko smiled. "We're in this together."

As Dravko drove the truck back to the convoy, Robson turned to see the friendly exchange had not settled well with Compton or O'Bannon. Compton looked frustrated and refused to make eye contact with him. O'Bannon glared at him with a look that bordered between disgust and hatred. Fuck 'em, thought Robson. If Dravko and the others had not shown up when they did, he would undoubtedly have lost people in that stockroom.

Thompson and Rashid exited the convenience store, the colonel walking several paces to the rear. Robson immediately understood why. He could smell the stench hanging off Rashid from here.

"Jesus Christ." O'Bannon gagged. "What the fuck happened to you?"

"Don't ask," Rashid snapped.

Robson and the others stepped back as Rashid passed by. "Get out of those clothes and toss them. Have Natalie give you a gallon of water to wash yourself off."

Rashid looked at him awkwardly. "It's gonna take more than a gallon to wash away this stink."

"I know. But that's all we can spare."

"He's not sitting beside me," joked O'Bannon.

"I love you, too."

A frightening thought suddenly dawned on Robson. "You didn't get any of that shit in your eyes or mouth, did you?"

"Thank God, no. I just bathed in it."

"Make sure you wash your face and hands with antibacterial soap."

Rashid grimaced as he continued back to the convoy. "You guys are all heart."

Fifteen minutes later, the convoy departed Andover. Sultanic took the lead, driving the Mack, while Tibor followed in the school bus. Dravko drove the armored car, with Compton in the front seat and Robson and Thompson spread out in back. Tatyana brought up the rear in the Ryder. Beside her sat Mad Dog and Jennifer, the former wrapping his arm around the girl to comfort her.

They had barely driven five miles before Robson dozed off, lulled by the swaying of the armored car and the exhaustion of the last twenty-four hours.

146

★　★　★

ROBSON WOKE UP slowly, disoriented and only vaguely aware of his surroundings. He did not know how long he had slept, but it must have been a while since he remembered dreaming. Christ, he even remembered the details, though that was not difficult. He always had the same vision, a recurring nightmare of that day rotters had overrun him and Susan outside Newington. Being out here in the middle of rotter hell had dredged up dormant memories.

Usually, he woke from his nightmare in a cold sweat with his heart pounding against his chest. However, what woke Robson this time was not the physical anxiety caused by these hellish visions but the sound of Dravko's voice.

"Sunrise is not for several hours yet."

"Are you sure?" Sultanic's voice came over the radio.

"Yes," Dravko said into the radio.

"Then how do you explain it?"

Robson yawned and stretched his arms and legs. The rear compartment of the armored car had not been designed for comfort. He sat up and leaned against the interior wall. "What's going on?"

Dravko looked over his shoulder. "Didn't mean to wake you."

"That's okay." Robson ran a hand across his hair. "What's Sultanic talking about?"

"Hell if I know. He thinks the sun's coming up."

"Shit." Robson crouched down between the driver and passenger seats. "How long have I been asleep?"

"Two and a half hours."

Robson was still confused. "Then what's he talking about?"

Before Dravko could answer, Sultanic's voice came over the radio again, sounding frustrated. "Is anyone there?"

Dravko keyed the microphone. "I'm here."

"If sunrise isn't for several hours, then can you explain what that glow on the horizon is?"

Robson leaned forward to look out the driver's window. Sultanic was right. A bright yellow glow stretched along a large swath of the southern horizon. He could not see the source because of the surrounding terrain, but something created the light, and it was extensive judging by the reflection projecting off the overlying cloud cover.

Tibor's voice chimed in over the radio. "I see it, too. Any idea what it is?"

Dravko looked to Robson, who shrugged. He keyed the microphone. "No idea yet. Wake up everyone on the bus in case it's trouble."

"I was hoping you wouldn't say that."

Robson pulled out his map and laid it on the floor in front of him, using a flashlight to illuminate it. "Where are we?"

"Route 149. A sign a few miles back said we're about twenty miles from Interstate 87."

By now, all the commotion had roused Compton and Thompson. The doctor sat forward, looking anxiously out the windshield. "Is everything all right?"

"We have lights off to the south," said Robson. He placed his finger on the map. "It looks like it's coming from Glens Falls. Maybe they still have electricity."

"Doubtful," said Compton. "We passed Glens Falls on the way here. The city was pitch black and deserted."

"Well, something's generating a lot of light."

Thompson tapped Robson on the shoulder. "Can I take a look?"

"Be my guest." Robson pulled the map back into the rear of the armored car and made room for Thompson.

The colonel leaned forward and looked out the driver's window. "Shit."

"You know what it is?"

Thompson sat back down. "The light is shimmering off the

clouds."

"So?" asked Dravko.

"I've seen that only once before. In Kuwait back in 1991 after Saddam Hussein set fire to the Kuwaiti oilfields."

"You mean something's on fire?" asked Robson.

"It looks that way."

"If you're right, that's one helluva fire," said Dravko.

Fifteen minutes later, their worst fears were confirmed when the convoy rounded a bend in the road and had an unobstructed view of Glens Falls. A conflagration consumed most of the city. The residential neighborhoods scattered north and west of the river were engulfed as a wall of flames over a hundred feet high marched across the area. Above the city, thousands of sparks flittered across the night sky like giant lightning bugs, many falling back to earth to ignite homes, trees, and parks, merging into the spreading inferno.

The convoy continued along the outskirts of Glens Falls, passing underneath the interchange with Interstate 87 and turning south. It traveled less than a mile when the lead vehicles halted.

Dravko picked up the radio. "Keep moving."

"We can't," replied Sultanic. "Fire's blocking the road."

Dravko pulled the armored car into the parallel lane. A few hundred feet ahead of them, the houses on either side of the road burned furiously. Several flaming trees and utility poles had toppled into the street, blocking their path.

"What now?" asked Sultanic.

Robson took the radio from Dravko. "Head back to the interstate. We'll regroup there. And for Christ's sake, haul ass."

"What's the rush?" asked Dravko.

"If the flames close in on the road behind us, we'll all be burned alive."

Dravko did not need to be told twice. Shifting into reverse, he backed the armored car into a three-point turn and headed the way they had come, pausing long enough to ensure the other vehicles had safely made the turn.

Five minutes later, the convoy gathered near the overpass for Interstate 87. As everyone stepped out of their vehicles, they were greeted by the deafening roar of a city consuming itself. A cool, strong wind rushed past them as the conflagration sucked in the surrounding air, feeding the fire. Robson took out his map and placed it on the hood of the armored car. As the other drivers huddled around him, he studied the map, holding down the ends with each hand so it did not flap in the wind. The fire was so intense that he did not need a flashlight to read it. Unfortunately, the flames did not give him any insight and how to get around this situation.

"Where do we go from here?" asked Sultanic.

Robson shook his head in disgust. "Every other route around Glens Falls either takes us hundreds of miles out of our way or through heavily populated areas."

"What about the back roads?" asked Dravko. "Some side streets eventually have to take us to another major road."

"Yeah, but which ones?" asked O'Bannon. "These maps don't go into that level of detail. What happens if we get stuck in a cul-de-sac filled with rotters?"

"Why don't we go through Glens Falls?" offered Thompson.

Robson shook his head. "You saw the road back there. It's impassable."

"I'm not talking about that road." Thompson pointed above him to the overpass. "It runs right through the neighborhoods and avoids built-up areas. We'd bypass most of the fire. Five minutes at top speed, and we'll be in the clear."

"Too risky. Suppose we run into blocked traffic?"

"We took the interstate from Site R. An accident clogged the southbound lanes, but the northbound ones are wide open. There's nothing in our way for at least twenty or thirty miles."

Robson still needed to be convinced. "We can't take the chance."

"We can't afford not to," added O'Bannon. "Windows didn't have a chance to check out any of the other roads. God knows what we'll run into if we try to go around this. This may not be the best option, but it's the best we've got."

Robson looked over at Dravko. "What do you think?"

The vampire put on a show of bravado. "When do we ever do things the easy way?"

"Then it's settled. We go through Glens Falls." Robson lifted the map off the armored car, almost losing it in the breeze, and folded it. "Keep five hundred feet between vehicles. Sultanic will lead the way in the Mack to clear the path. And for God's sake, don't stop for anything until you've reached the other side. Let's roll."

The small group broke up and headed back to their vehicles. Robson watched them. Sultanic helped Caylee out of the exposed gun mount and made her join him in the cab. He could tell by the vampire's dire expression that he was not happy about leading the convoy into the inferno. As Tibor climbed aboard the school bus, the others bombarded him with questions. Robson could not hear the conversations but could tell by the yells of protest and the way several of the Angels cast him disapproving looks that they disagreed. Even Mad Dog, who was never fazed, shot him an awkward glance. Robson began having second thoughts about his decision, despite the support from the other leaders. After all they had been through, burning to death hundreds of miles from camp would suck.

Dravko slid up behind him. "Are you ready?"

"Not really."

"Do you want to drive?"

Robson shook his head. "I trust you."

Dravko smiled and headed for the armored car. Robson followed and crawled into the back, closing and securing the door behind him.

Sultanic shifted the Mack into drive. The truck lurched

forward, crossed underneath the twin overpasses, and turned toward the exit ramp. Its engine roared as it picked up speed. A few seconds later, the Mack reached the northbound lanes of Interstate 87, traveling at close to fifty miles an hour. By the time Dravko drove the armored car onto the highway, the Mack was merely a dark image against the flame-filled night sky.

The conflagration had not spread this far north, so the first mile remained uneventful. Random embers blew across the sky. Some came to rest in trees, igniting the dry foliage, or settled onto small patches of grass that began to smolder. As the convoy drew closer to the center of Glens Falls, the flames grew denser, consuming everything. At that point, the meridian widened enough to contain a thin line of trees that blocked the southbound lanes from view. Ahead of them, the trees on either side of the highway burned furiously, creating a fiery tunnel the Mack plunged into.

Inside the armored car, Robson and the others felt a spike in the temperature as the flames closed in around them. A mixture of embers and ash coated the windshield. Dravko switched on the wipers. The blades squeaked across the glass, leaving gray streaks. When Dravko sprayed the windshield washer, most of the fluid evaporated into wisps of steam.

Robson felt the sweat forming on his forehead. "This was a bad idea."

Dravko grinned. "Remind me to say 'no shit' if we get out of this al—"

The brake lights on the school bus suddenly flared red and its speed dropped rapidly. Dravko pulled into the outer lane and sped past. As he took second place, he keyed the microphone.

"Why are you slowing down?"

Tibor's voice came over the radio, fear in his tone. "I want to stay far away from Sultanic."

"Why?"

"Because the dump bed is catching too many embers."

"Fuck!" Robson strained through the smeared windshield to see the Mack. Even from this distance, he could see the paint on the fifty-five-gallon drums beginning to smolder. He grabbed the radio from Dravko.

"Sultanic, do you copy?"

Caylee answered, her voice flustered. "We're a little busy here."

"You're about to get even busier. The drums of gasoline are about to explode."

"Fuck!" Caylee yelled into the microphone.

A few seconds later, the convoy emerged from the trees, and the area on either side of the interstate opened. Robson immediately realized they had traded one hell for another. Glens Falls spread out in every direction. Here the fire was less intense because most of the buildings were commercial, composed of steel and concrete that did not ignite as easily as the wooden homes. With little here to burn, the surrounding air was sucked toward the center of the conflagration, creating a convection plain. The winds raced across the highway at forty miles per hour, forcing Dravko to steer into the wind to keep the armored car going straight.

Sultanic veered to the left and drove the Mack toward the shoulder. The others began to follow, but his voice came across the radio.

"Stay on the interstate. I'll catch up."

Robson went to the rear window to keep his eye on the Mack. Rather than veering toward the shoulder, Sultanic headed for an exit ramp. He raced the truck down the ramp and across the interchange, pushing aside a Prius abandoned in the middle of the road. As the Mack entered the incline of the opposite ramp, the dump bed began to slowly elevate. As the angle increased, the drums of gasoline slid along the metal, inching toward the rear. They eventually tumbled onto their side and rolled out the back, crashing to the asphalt. A fireball erupted behind the truck, extending across the ramp and washing over the Mack's dump bed. For a moment, Robson could not see the truck and feared it might have been engulfed. As the fireball dimmed, he could see the truck accelerating up the ramp, tongues of flame licking off the bed. The Mack merged back onto the interstate and fell in behind the Ryder.

From up front, Dravko keyed his microphone. "Sultanic, are you okay?"

"Yeah, but that was a little too close for my liking. Are we almost out of this hellhole?"

"Almost."

The conflagration still roared off to their left but had not yet traveled to the southern, residential outskirts of the city spread out in front of them. With the prevailing winds blowing north, falling embers had not ignited the surrounding homes. Flames from the burning city reflected off windows. Convection winds bent the tops of trees toward the inferno as if nature pointed to where the danger lay. Thankfully, the road ahead was clear, and the convoy sailed through the neighborhood without mishap, covering the next three miles in as many minutes.

Finally, the convoy crossed the bridge spanning the river that marked the southern boundary of Glens Falls. Once on the opposite banks, the homes and commercial buildings gave way to trees and fields, leaving the inferno behind them.

CHAPTER TWENTY-FIVE

APPROXIMATELY A MILE outside of Glens Falls, the convoy exited the interstate onto Route 9 and stopped to assess the damage from their run through the inferno. Daytona and Whitehouse checked each vehicle to ensure they were fit to continue, pleasantly surprised at how well they had fared. All of them had suffered from blistered paint due to the intense heat. The Mack came through the worst because of the explosion from the ignited drums of gasoline; most of the aft half of the dump bed was blackened from where the flames had burned off the paint and seared the metal. Ironically, the two innermost drums in the front right corner of the bed had not broken loose from their mountings. Sultanic and Caylee were fortunate those drums did not explode when the fireball erupted around them, otherwise everyone in the front cab would have been roasted alive. Beyond that, each vehicle looked fine. None of the engines had overheated, none of the hoses or belts had melted, and none of the circuitry had gotten fried.

As the two mechanics went over the vehicles, the others sat near the school bus eating a late dinner. Most of the conversation focused on small talk related to their recent run through Glens Falls. Sultanic told the best story, dramatically describing how he raced through the side streets with his truck bed filled with flaming gasoline sloshing over the rim until he found a safe place to release his volatile cargo. At least, that was how Sultanic told it. Even Caylee seemed animated when telling her part of the saga. It was the first time she had shown any emotion other than depression or anger since Jordan's death.

More importantly, it was the first time humans and vampires bonded in such a manner.

As the Angels changed shifts, Robson pulled out his map and checked their location.

"How far out of the way did our little adventure take us?" asked Compton.

"Not far at all." Robson swigged down a huge mouthful of water from a plastic bottle, still parched from the heat of the inferno. "We originally planned on approaching Saratoga Springs via the Route 9 Bypass. Instead, we took the commercial road."

"Saratoga Springs?" questioned Thompson. "Is that our next waypoint?"

"Yeah. It's a fairly large town about ten miles south of here. There's no going around it, at least not without going through even larger urban centers or traveling a hundred miles out of our way." Robson opened his satchel bag, pulled out a folder, shuffled through it, and withdrew five photographs of commercial imagery. He handed the sheets to Natalie on his left, who passed them along. "According to the last satellite photos downloaded by Windows, the path we're going to take runs through the center of town along the main commercial road. The route looks wide open."

Dravko looked at the photos as they passed by him. Even with his advanced night vision, he could barely make out any details in the dim light. "How can you even read these things?"

"I go with what Windows tells me." Robson grinned. "Of course, if you think she's wrong, you're free to scout ahead for us."

"No, thanks," chuckled Dravko. He passed the photos down to the colonel. "You ain't getting rid of me that easily."

"So, what's the game plan?" asked Natalie.

Robson looked at his watch. "It's a little after midnight. We'll head out in about half an hour. It shouldn't take us long to clear the town. After that, it's open driving until we get to southern Pennsylvania."

"Sounds good to me." Natalie flashed him a flirtatious look.

Robson smiled back, feeling a bit self-conscious. "We'll hit the road once the Angels have had a chance to rest."

THE TRIP TO Saratoga Springs passed without incident. No one saw any signs of life on the run. No abandoned cars, no desiccated bodies, not even rotters. None of them realized they had entered town until the floodlights mounted on the Mack's grill fell upon the sign reading "Entering Saratoga Springs."

Sultanic's voice came across the radio. "Where to now?"

Robson keyed his microphone. "About a mile down the road, we'll come to a large intersection. Turn left onto Broadway."

"Gotcha."

A few minutes later, the Mack slowed as it approached the intersection. The City Center stood off to their left, a giant black structure blocking the night sky. Darkened traffic signals hung above the intersection and, between them, a street sign notifying drivers they were on Broadway. Sultanic veered left and, once certain the street was clear, accelerated. The rest of the convoy followed.

As they rushed down Broadway, Robson glanced around, a bit taken aback at the lack of activity. Not even wildlife roamed the streets. However, considering how well-kept the streets appeared, he figured the town's people had maintained order as long as possible, clearing away stalled traffic and corpses like in Andover. And he remembered how well that had turned out.

The brake lights on the Mack suddenly lit up. From inside the armored car, Robson heard the squeal of stressed rubber. The truck came to a violent stop, the rear end jackknifing slightly as several tons tried to stop short too quickly, then the front end dropped down a few feet and the Mack came to a shuddering halt.

The other vehicles slowed to a more graceful stop. Dravko grabbed the radio.

"Sultanic, what's wrong?"

No response.

"Sultanic, are you there?"

Again, no response.

Dravko put the radio on the dashboard. "Something's up."

"Can't be too bad," said Thompson, pointing to the Mack's forward gun mount. "If they were under attack, Caylee would be shooting."

"What is it then?" asked Dravko.

Robson headed for the rear door. "Let's find out."

Dravko joined him. The two men exited the vehicle and cautiously moved toward the Mack, Robson unholstering his Glock. As they passed the school bus, the side door opened and Natalie stepped out. "Need fire support?"

"Couldn't hurt," said Robson.

Natalie leaned back into the bus. "Ari. Tiara. Josephine. Front and center."

Natalie followed the other two. As they approached the Mack, Dravko moved to the left to look around the truck's front end. Robson wrapped a finger around the Glock's trigger and clasped his free hand under the stock, keeping the weapon aimed low but ready to fire in an instant. When he approached to within ten feet of the truck, he called out softly to Caylee.

"Is everything okay?"

Caylee turned to him and shrugged. "I guess."

"Why'd you stop?"

"I have no idea."

Robson stepped up to the cab, surprised not to see anyone in the driver's seat. "Sultanic?"

The vampire, who had been leaning to one side, popped up suddenly, startling Robson. "I'm here."

"Why didn't you answer the radio?"

Sultanic raised it in his hand. "It fell on the floor when I hit the brakes."

"Why'd you stop?"

"There's a huge sinkhole in the road. I didn't see it until I was on top of it."

Dravko stepped over to the front of the truck and turned to Robson. "He's right. Damn thing's about ten-foot square. The right tire is hanging over the edge, and the left is only partially on firm ground."

"Can you back out of it?"

"Too risky." Sultanic turned off the headlights and flood-lights and shut down the engine. He opened the cab's door. "Too much motion might collapse the sinkhole even further, then we're screwed. We stand a better chance if we pull it out."

Dravko headed back to the school bus. "I'll have Tibor back up to the truck. We should have her free in a few minutes."

"Thanks."

The three Angels came running up to Natalie and Robson, Mausers at the ready.

"What's up?" asked Ari.

"Truck's stuck in a sinkhole," Natalie responded. "You stay here. Tiara and Josephine, take the flanks. Keep your eyes open for rotters."

The three women nodded and took up their positions. Whitehouse climbed into the Mack's cab, shutting the door behind him. He shut off the floodlights and engine, then waited for the order to shift the truck into neutral. Sultanic stepped off the school bus carrying a length of tow chain, one end of which he proceeded to wrap around the Mack's rear trailer link. As he did so, Tibor turned the school bus into a large U-turn, plunging them in darkness as its floodlights lit up the rest of the convoy behind them. A sharp, steady beeping cut through the night as Tibor backed up the school bus behind the Mack.

Robson heard something out of place, like the muffled scuffling of feet, though it was difficult to tell between the idling of the bus engine and the clanking of the chain on concrete. He looked for the source, but his eyes had not yet adjusted to the dark. The sound persisted, but he could not tell from where.

Robson tapped Natalie on the arm. "Tell Tibor to shut off the engine."

Concern crossed her face, but Natalie ran off to do as ordered. Seeing her run off, Dravko wandered over. "Anything wrong?"

"I'm not sure. Do you hear that?"

Dravko listened. "The shuffling noise?"

"Yeah. Where's it coming from?"

"I'm not sure."

The bus engine shut off, plunging the area into silence except for the scuffling. Dravko and Robson listened closely. The noise came from in front.

"Whitehouse," Robson called out softly. "Flip on the floodlights."

Whitehouse complied, bathing the road ahead of them in light and illuminating a horde of more than twenty rotters advancing toward them less than three yards away.

CHAPTER TWENTY-SIX

"ROTTERS!" SCREAMED ROBSON. "Two dozen heading our way and closing fast!"

Robson raised his Glock and aimed at the closest one, a young girl in a cheerleading uniform with no skin on the lower half of her face. Its skeletal jaw snapped at him. He fired off a single round, but at this distance his aim was off. The bullet punched into the dead flesh of the rotter's right shoulder, shattering most of the blade and blowing the bone fragments through the skin. The blast knocked it slightly off balance, but it continued lumbering toward him, the right arm dangling uselessly by its side. The second round passed through its throat, spilling globs of congealed blood through the entry wound. Adjusting his aim upwards, Robson fired a third round. This one caught the rotter directly between the eyes, the hollow point blasting off the back of its head. It fell forward with a wet thud.

Beside him, Ari raised her Mauser and took careful aim on a hulking rotter in a New York State Police uniform. She waited an interminably long time to line up her shot but, when she pulled the trigger, its head exploded. Ari quickly shifted her aim to the next rotter in line, a young female with blonde hair matted by dried blood and wearing the remnants of a county deputy uniform that only partially covered the gaping hole where its internal organs had once sat. A single squeeze of the trigger and the rotter's head jerked backward, showering the horde behind it in a cloud of brains and gore.

From up in the gun mount, Caylee aimed her semiautomatic at the closest rotter in her line of sight, a road worker dragging its partially severed right leg. She released a three-round burst, ripping its skull apart. Once that rotter collapsed, she switched to another and fired again.

Morphing into his vampiric form, Sultanic jumped into the Mack's rear bed and rushed forward to where the remaining fifty-five-gallon drums were stored. Ripping one from its mountings, he jammed his talons through the metal, tore four long gashes down its length, and then tossed the drum over the side and into the horde. He jumped onto the cab's roof and turned to Caylee.

"Fire at the drum."

The drum poured diesel fuel onto the asphalt. Once Caylee had a clear view, she squeezed off a three-round burst. Sparks flew as the bullets slammed into the metal, igniting the expanding pool of gasoline. Flames raced across the street in all directions, climbing up the legs of those rotters standing in its path. The fire surrounded the drum and licked at its surface until the excess gasoline inside ignited, generating a fireball that knocked over a dozen of the living dead.

As the flames lit up the night, Robson saw another swarm of more than a dozen rotters a few yards behind the first. He was only vaguely aware of the Angels rushing out of the bus and taking up position alongside him and Ari. As each woman fell into line, they chose a target. One by one, the rotters fell, but for each one the Angels dropped, more seemed to take their place.

Eight rotters, all in flames, converged on the Mack's cab. Whitehouse opened the door to escape, but they were too close, so he slammed it shut. The rotters reached out to him with burning hands, slapping at the door and clawing at the metal. Tiny licks of flame seared the paint. Beneath them, the spreading pool of gasoline flowed under the Mack, catching the tires on fire. The temperature inside the cab rose dramatically.

Rolling down the window, Whitehouse climbed out and turned, reaching up to find a handhold on the roof. The rotters moaned at the sight of their prey and began frantically clawing to get at him. Thankfully, the spikes welded around the bottom and sides of the window protected him from their grasp.

Unfortunately, they did not protect him from the fire. As the rotters clasped at him, the flames licked off their outstretched hands and lapped at Whitehouse's clothes, setting his jacket on fire. Instinctively, he released his hold on the roof to pat out the flames and fell back into the horde. With his legs still inside the cab, he hung upside down, as helpless as an animal in a slaughterhouse. The rotters pushed against Whitehouse, driving him into the spikes and pinning him against the door. He screamed at the top of his lungs, desperately clawing at the air to escape.

Sultanic leaped to the edge of the cab's roof and reached down, holding on to the mirror mount with his right hand while stretching for Whitehouse with his left. Whitehouse flayed around wildly, too disoriented from terror and pain to notice. Not that it mattered, for the rotters already had torn open his abdomen and pulled out his intestines, feasting on the fresh meat. Whitehouse's legs slipped out of the cab as the last vestiges of life slipped from him. His torso slid off the spikes and dropped to the ground. Sultanic still reached for Whitehouse, leaning even farther into the horde to save him.

Seeing the new source of food wriggling above its head, a fat female rotter in a blood-encrusted housecoat stretched out its hand and grabbed Sultanic's wrist in its charred fingers. He tried yanking his arm away but, because he hung over the side of the Mack, he did not have the leverage. He could only watch helplessly as the fat rotter plunged its teeth into his forearm, slicing through flesh and tissue. Sultanic howled. He yanked his arm away, leaving a chunk of meat in the rotter's mouth, which hungrily chewed and swallowed.

At that moment, Caylee reached the end of the cab. She

aimed the semiautomatic at Whitehouse's head and squeezed off a three-round burst, putting him out of his torment and ensuring he would not reanimate. Switching to full automatic mode, she emptied the magazine into the horde. A few dropped to the ground, quickly becoming engulfed by the flames. Most of the living dead were left unscathed by the assault and closed in around the Mack. Caylee grabbed Sultanic by the back of his collar and pulled him to the safety of the dump bed.

Robson barely noticed what was going down around him, his attention concentrated on the approaching rotters. He had taken down two more when the slide on his Glock locked into the open position. As he popped out the used magazine and removed a new one from his belt, an old male rotter with no arms lurched toward him. Robson slammed the magazine into place with his palm and pulled back the slide, but the rotter had moved in too close, not giving him enough room to aim.

Natalie shoved Robson aside as the old rotter lunged. It sank its teeth into her shoulder.

"No!" Robson yelled. Regaining his balance, he raced over to help.

Natalie barely flinched as the rotter's teeth yanked at her shoulder. She placed the barrel of her Colt .45 against its left temple. Turning her head and closing her eyes, she pulled the trigger. The rotter's head distorted as the back of its skull was blown off. Brains and some bone fragments splattered her jacket. It crumpled in front of her.

"Why'd you do that?" rasped Robson, trying not to sound emotional. "Now you're infected."

Natalie brushed off the gore. Only then did he notice that her leather jacket was untouched except for a few teeth indentations around the shoulder. Natalie smiled at him and winked.

"I barely felt it. Now pay attention so I don't have to save your sorry ass again."

Robson quickly assessed the situation. Most of the raiding party stood on either side of him, plucking away at the horde as if they were in a shooting gallery. The first group had been eliminated except for the five or six still feeding on Whitehouse, so consumed by hunger that they seemed oblivious to the inferno that engulfed them. The remnants of the second group reached the outer limits of the gasoline-fed fire when a volley from the Angels took several down.

Behind him, Natalie gave orders as she walked down the line.

"There're five rotters to our right. Bethany, Sandy, go back up Josephine. Stephanie and Leila, check on Tiara. Ari, make sure nothing's coming at us from the rear."

As the Angels raced off to reinforce the flanks, the remaining girls took down the last few rotters from the second group. With the danger now past, Dravko and Daytona approached the pack feeding off Whitehouse, careful not to get too close to the flames. They each fired three rounds, putting down the remaining rotters.

A few rounds of gunfire sounded from their flanks, and the attack ended as suddenly as it had begun. Silence fell over the area, broken only by the roar of the fire and the corpses' sizzling as the flames charred their remains.

Robson lowered his Glock but kept his finger on the trigger in case any rotters came after them from the dark. "Everyone, sound off."

He felt relief as each member of his raiding party called out, first those around him and then the Angels manning the perimeter. Noticeably absent, however, was Whitehouse.

As well as Caylee and Sultanic.

"Caylee?" he yelled. "Where are you?"

"Here," she cried from the rear of the dump bed. "I need help."

Robson ran over to the Mack, followed closely by the other vampires. Caylee stood at the end of the bed, Sultanic's good arm wrapped around her shoulders for support. He cradled the bitten forearm against his chest, wincing in pain each time he moved. Dravko and Tibor jumped into the bed and lowered Sultanic to the ground where Tatyana supported him. Dravko climbed down to check on his friend. Tibor helped Caylee out of the bed and then dropped himself down.

Dravko pulled Sultanic's arm away from his body and turned it to examine the wound. The look in his eye said what everyone else already knew. The bite was a death sentence. "How did it happen?"

Caylee answered. "The rotters bit him while he was trying to save Whitehouse."

"Is that true?" asked Dravko.

Sultanic nodded. He pulled the arm away and again cradled it against his chest.

Robson stepped forward and patted Sultanic's shoulder.

"Wh-what do we do now?" asked Tatyana.

"There's nothing you *can* do," answered Sultanic.

"Don't say that," said Dravko, the desperation evident in his voice.

"It's true."

Compton rushed up to the group, with Thompson close behind. The doctor focused his attention on Dravko. "I heard one of your vampires was bitten."

Sultanic raised his good hand. "That's me."

"May I see?"

Sultanic held out his arm and turned it to expose the bite. A teacup-sized chunk had been torn from the forearm. Compton shown a flashlight on the wound and then turned the beam away.

"I'm sorry."

Dravko shook his head. "The vaccine you created. Will it cure someone who's already infected but not yet turned?"

Compton hesitated, taken aback by the question. "I'm not sure. We never tested it that way."

"We can at least try, right?"

"Forget it," said Sultanic.

"What do you mean?"

Sultanic looked at Compton. "How long before I turn?"

Compton thought for a moment. "A wound that deep usually turns its victims in eighteen hours. For you, it might be a little longer. I'm not familiar with vampire physiology."

"And we're still at least two days from Site R." Sultanic shook his head. "I'll be one of those things long before we get there."

"We can at least try," said Dravko.

"All you'll do is put everyone else in danger, and then you'll have to put me down like a dog. I don't want that."

Tatyana tenderly placed a hand on his shoulder. "What will you do?"

Sultanic forced a smile. "Something I haven't done in almost two hundred years. Watch the sunrise."

"Are you sure?" asked Dravko.

"We're willing to risk bringing you with us," added Robson.

"I know," Sultanic said to Dravko. Then to Robson, "If I have to die, I want to die with dignity."

"You've earned it." Robson took a few steps back. "Everyone load up. We're moving out in two minutes."

Compton and Thompson returned to the armored car without another word. Caylee followed, but not before she hugged Sultanic, tears flowing down her cheeks.

Tatyana threw her arms around Sultanic, hugging him tight and sobbing. "Goodbye."

He hugged back with his one good arm. "Take care, little one."

Tibor stepped forward, patted his friend on the shoulder, and led Tatyana away.

When the others were out of earshot, Sultanic turned to Dravko and Robson. "Ironic that I died trying to save a human, isn't it?"

Robson stepped forward and offered his hand. "There's a lot of us who would've done the same for you."

"I appreciate it." Sultanic reached out with his left and shook Robson's.

Dravko placed a hand behind Sultanic's head and drew him close. When he spoke, his words were choked with emotion. "See you on the other side."

"Hopefully not for a long time."

Robson and Dravko left Sultanic and headed for the armored car. As he climbed into the back, Robson took the microphone. "We'll take point from here on in. Tibor, you'll follow us. Tatyana, bring up the rear."

"Gotcha," said Tibor.

"Roger that, boss." Mad Dog replied for Tatyana.

The convoy started and pulled back onto the main road, maneuvering over the sidewalk to avoid the fire blocking the street. Sultanic waved to them as they passed. The last image Robson had of Sultanic was of the vampire crossing the street and heading toward the center of the park to wait for dawn.

CHAPTER TWENTY-SEVEN

N O ONE IN the armored car spoke as the convoy left Saratoga Springs. There was nothing to say. Robson stared out the side window into the darkness, only vaguely aware of the shadows that raced past. He tried to block from his mind the image of his fallen comrades. There would be time to grieve for them later. He needed to concentrate on the task at hand so they did not lose anyone else.

That was a lot easier said than done, however. The loss of Whitehouse and Sultanic hit him particularly hard. Except for Jordan, it had been months since the camp had lost anyone to rotters. Robson blamed himself, fearing he had become too complacent about dealing with the living dead. Or too cocky. Maybe he should have deployed the Angels in a defensive perimeter once the Mack got stuck in the pothole. Maybe he should have opted to travel only by day when they could better see their surroundings, or opted for a less populated route, even if it meant adding several days to the trip. Maybe he should have argued with Paul and taken half as many people, making the group a less conspicuous target. The self-criticism got him nowhere, for Robson could come up with a dozen "should haves," but in the end, the result was the same. Too many people had died.

But Robson also knew their deaths were not on his head alone. The loss of three good men in the past few days all had one common factor that went beyond his ability to command. Those deaths had occurred since the arrival of Compton's party. When a rotter infected Jordan during the rescue attempt, Robson initially blamed Compton, although, at the time, he reasoned he was transferring his anger over losing a team member. After what happened back at Saratoga Springs, he began to feel that transferring his anger was more than justified. The doctor had started all this by creating the damn Revenant Virus in the first place. And by his own account, Compton had lost ninety percent of his group escaping from Site R, only to turn around and beg Paul to have his team take him back. Rather than refuse, Paul had seemed taken in by the doctor's promises of a miracle cure and had agreed to send half the camp on a trek hundreds of miles down the east coast on a futile quest. What was the result? Three of his team butchered. The raiding party stuck in the middle of rotter territory, too far along to go back and with the toughest part of the journey still ahead. And with no idea what waited for them at Site R. *If* they ever arrived.

Robson warned himself to be more on guard for the rest of this trip. That caution extended not only to the rotters but also to Compton.

THE CONVOY SPENT the next two hours traveling the back roads of New York. By constantly changing secondary roads, they avoided heavily populated areas. Once on Route 79 South, the convoy traveled only a few miles before Dravko broke the silence.

"We're getting close."

Robson leaned forward to look out the windshield. Up ahead, the floodlights reflected off a large sign along the side of the road welcoming them to Pennsylvania. It twisted down and to the left, the outer support beam bent by a Chevy Tahoe that had crashed into it. The front left door sat open, the mummified remains of its devoured driver hanging out the opening, still strapped into its seatbelt.

To their left, the first sliver of daylight crested the horizon.

Robson moved to the front of the car and crouched beside Dravko. "Let's stop here and switch drivers. This place seems safe enough."

"Nowhere is safe." Dravko was not arguing with Robson, just stating a fact. The vampire picked up the radio and keyed the microphone. "We're going to stop and change over. Tatyana, pull the Ryder up beside the school bus. Tibor, have the Angels form a perimeter once we stop."

"Can do," answered Tatyana.

"Same here," added Tibor.

Dravko slowed the armored car to a stop. The school bus halted directly behind him. Tatyana pulled the Ryder up on the right, its back end sat even with the school bus side door. As Robson watched in the rear-view mirror, the Angels darted off the bus and fanned out in a circle around the convoy, their flashlights on and scanning the area.

Without saying a word, Dravko climbed out of the driver's seat and headed for the Ryder. Robson followed him via the rear door, asking Thompson to take the wheel and be ready to move out quickly if necessary.

Robson caught up with Dravko by the front of the school bus. "Wait up."

Dravko looked over his shoulder. The squint in his eyes warned Robson that Dravko did not want to talk. Even so, he had something that required saying.

"I'm sorry about what happened to Sultanic."

"Thanks," Dravko answered without conviction. He turned and started to walk away.

Robson raced ahead and stood in front of him. "What's wrong?"

"Sorry if I'm not talkative. In case you forgot, I lost one of my people tonight."

"It's not lost on me and most of the others that Sultanic

became infected trying to save Whitehouse."

"I hope you appreciate it," snapped Dravko.

"I do." Robson found it difficult to control his anger. "Sultanic sacrificed himself, and he deserves better than to be ignored. He was a good man."

Dravko's expression softened slightly. "Not a good vampire?"

Only then did Robson realize that, for the first time, he had acknowledged Sultanic as a member of the team rather than distinguishing between human and vampire. "No, I mean a good man."

Robson offered his hand. Dravko hesitated a moment before reaching out to clasp it, giving it a single, firm pump. "For what it's worth, I'm sorry about Whitehouse. He always treated us well."

Robson nodded his appreciation. "We've lost too many good people since Compton's group arrived."

Dravko cast a quick look at the armored car. "Do you trust them?"

"Compton or Thompson?"

"Both."

"Not fully."

"I didn't like those two from the moment they came into camp. At first, I thought it was because they hated vampires. Now I think there's more to it."

Robson ushered Dravko away from the armored car and toward the Ryder. "Compton's holding out on us about something."

"You think he's lying about the vaccine?"

"No. I'm sure one exists. But they're not telling us everything."

Dravko nodded in agreement. "What do we do?"

"Nothing we can do other than keep a close eye on them."

"Easy for you to say." Dravko gestured toward the Ryder. "You're not stuck inside that thing for eight hours a day."

"You guys are safe as long as I'm around."

"I know that." Dravko jumped onto the Ryder's loading dock and spun around to face Robson. "We all do."

"Don't worry. By this time tomorrow night, we should be at Site R. Until then, I've got your back."

"Then I guess I'll see you at sunset." Dravko stood up and closed the rear door, securing it from the inside.

Robson stood for a moment, staring at the Ryder and feeling more at ease now that he knew that Dravko and the others felt the same distrust for Compton. At least now, he did not feel like he would have to go this alone.

"All right, Angels, back on the bus. We're moving out."

Two minutes later, the convoy started to roll again and headed south into Pennsylvania.

THE CONVOY CONTINUED along as the first rays of the morning sun crested the tree line. Route 79 became Route 92 when they crossed into Pennsylvania. Robson followed it to the intersection of Route 6, took that road west for several miles, and then picked up Route 87. He traveled for over half an hour when a road sign appeared ahead of him off to the right.

ENTERING BARBOURS

Robson pulled the map from the visor and flipped it over to the side displaying northern Pennsylvania. After a few seconds, he found what he was looking for.

"We're here."

"What are you talking about?" asked Thompson as he made his way forward. "We're nowhere near Site R."

"I'm not talking about Site R."

A small country road cut across Route 87. Only a few isolated, abandoned buildings could be seen. Robson steered the armored car onto the shoulder and stopped. Behind him, the remaining vehicles pulled off the road and parked.

Compton, slumped down in the passenger's seat, stirred from his nap. Sitting upright, he looked out at the surrounding trees. "Where are we?"

"Barbours."

"Why are we stopping? There's nothing here."

"Exactly." Robson opened the door and stepped out, Compton and Thompson staring at him with a look of confusion. The two men exited the armored car.

By the time Robson reached the school bus, the Angels were deploying in a circle around the convoy. Natalie, O'Bannon, and Daytona came forward to meet him. Mad Dog jogged up from where he had parked the Ryder farther down the road.

"Is everything okay?" asked Natalie, her eyes nervously scanning the area.

"Everything's fine. We're making camp here until sundown."

"I don't think that's a good idea." Thompson stepped up behind him. "We have another seven hours of daylight."

"We need to rest up and regroup."

Thompson disagreed. "If we push on, we could make it to Gettysburg by nightfall."

"It's not as easy as you make it sound."

"Why's that?"

Robson pointed west down Route 87. "Because ten miles down that road, we'll be entering Harrisburg."

CHAPTER TWENTY-EIGHT

THE RAIDING PARTY sat around the campfire, drinking hot coffee and munching on MREs, enjoying their brief respite and the beautiful autumn morning. Then Robson warned them what tonight's run would entail. With the map spread out on the grass before him, Robson traced the route they would follow on the last leg of their trip to Site R. If anyone had thought the worst was behind them, they were sorely mistaken.

As Robson pointed out, Pennsylvania was populated in such a way that no isolated roads could reach Gettysburg. The best route Windows could come up with involved a run of nearly one hundred and fifty miles that avoided Harrisburg. Even that alternate would require them to negotiate the major cities of Kenmar and Faxon, both assumed to be heavily infested with rotters, before turning south for rural country. After that, they would pass through a few large towns before eventually breaking into farm territory for the last few miles to Gettysburg. Three hours of pure hell with numerous chances to be overrun by the living dead.

By the time Robson had finished, the cheerful mood had turned grim and somber.

"Any questions?" Robson asked, knowing he would not be able to provide any satisfactory answers.

"I have one," responded Thompson. He sipped at his coffee. "Why don't we make the run now while the sun's still up? We could cover the entire trip before dusk and travel through the populated areas while it's light enough to see what we're getting into."

"I considered that. The problem is Dravko's people. They'd be stuck inside the Ryder and wouldn't be able to help if we had to fight our way out of a situation."

"Is it worth the risk?" asked O'Bannon.

"Yes, it is. After the Angels, they're the best fighters we have."

"That's not what I meant," said O'Bannon.

"I know what you meant." Robson had a finality to his tone that warned he would not tolerate further discussion.

Thompson either did not catch Robson's tone or did not care. "I think we should leave the Ryder in the middle of a populated area while it's still daylight."

Before Robson could respond, Caylee sprang off the ground where she had been sitting and lunged at the colonel. She swung her hand, slapping him across the face with enough force that the crack echoed. Thompson jumped to his feet, but rather than strike back, he took a defensive posture. After the initial shock, Natalie jumped up and placed herself between Caylee and the colonel.

Still in his defensive posture, Thompson rubbed his cheek. "What was—?"

"Shut the fuck up!" Caylee screamed. "I'm sick of your shit!"

"You got a thing for the bloodsuckers?"

Caylee lunged again, this time being held back by Natalie. "One of those bloodsuckers saved my life last night. Or maybe my life doesn't mean anything to you, either?"

"Your life wouldn't have been in danger if the bloodsuckers hadn't unleashed the Revenant Virus on mankind."

"You mean the Revenant Virus that Doctor Evil here created?" Caylee spat in Compton's direction.

Compton continued to sip his coffee, indifferent to the encounter.

Robson stood and crossed over to Caylee, placing a reassuring hand on her shoulder. "That's enough."

"We should leave *him* wandering the streets for the rotters. That'd be justice."

"That's *enough*, Caylee."

Robson squeezed her shoulder increasingly harder until the pain in her muscles distracted her. Caylee swung her left arm up and back, slapping off his grip. She glared at him for a moment, ready to vent her anger on him, but thought otherwise. Breaking free of Natalie's grip, Caylee stormed away from the group.

Ari stood up and passed close by Natalie. "I'll keep an eye on her and make sure she doesn't wander off."

As the two women walked off, Robson turned to Thompson. "Keep a low profile for the rest of this trip."

"I didn't—"

Robson extended his index finger and shoved it into Thompson's face. "You heard me. Keep your fucking opinions to yourself."

Thompson seethed. His expression toughened, the eyes and lips becoming slits. Robson saw the colonel's right fist clutch into a fist when Compton intervened. Without looking up from his cup of coffee, the doctor uttered a single command.

"Stand down, Colonel."

Thompson shot his boss a glance equal parts anger and disappointment. A tense few seconds passed before the colonel picked up his tin cup, emptied the coffee with a violent flick of the wrist, and stormed off in the opposite direction Caylee had gone.

An awkward silence surrounded the campfire. Jennifer spoke first, trying to help out Robson.

"What now?"

"We rest up as much as possible while we can. We'll head out tonight about seven o'clock. That'll give Dravko's people time to be briefed."

"What about us?" asked Ari.

"You need rest more than anyone. Everyone will take turns guarding the perimeter, one person per quadrant for two-hour shifts. Have Natalie work out the schedule. Everyone else, rest while you can. Dismissed."

O'Bannon got up first, tossing the rest of his coffee into the fire, where it sizzled against the embers before storming off in the same direction as the colonel. The others sauntered away at their own pace to prepare for that night's run. Compton left last, finishing his coffee and MRE before moving off as if nothing had happened.

Robson watched the doctor as he walked away, still unable to get the full measure of the man. He did not know what bothered him most: that the doctor seemed not to care that he had created the Revenant Virus, which all but wiped out mankind, or it did not bother him that most of the others despised him for that reason. Robson assumed Compton would at least be a bit remorseful about his involvement in the apocalypse and hoped he was merely being arrogant or self-righteous and that his nonchalance did not stem from his being a sociopath.

That would be his luck, to be stuck in the middle of no-where with a group of humans and vampires who wanted to tear each other apart and surrounded by hordes of rotters more than happy to help.

Pushing such pleasant thoughts from his mind, Robson went off to find Daytona and prep the vehicles for tonight.

THOMPSON WALKED BACK to the intersection of Route 87 and Dunwoody Road, turning northwest and proceeding down the latter toward an empty home about a quarter of a mile ahead. He had no reason to go there other than as a distraction to keep his mind off the argument with that asshole Robson, and worse, the dressing down he received from Compton. The former did not bother him that much, for he expected nothing better from a vamp hugger. But being humiliated in front of these people by Compton was too much for his pride to take. Shit, he deserved better than that. A hell of a lot better.

Compton would be dead if it had not been for him. He had been with the doctor since the first days of this crisis, serving as his sounding board and supporting his decisions. He even protected the doctor from the criticism and verbal attacks of their colleagues and from rotters. Compton was not the type of man who altered his opinions easily, so what happened back at the campfire could not be written off as the doctor having a change of heart. The only reason he could think of was that he had lost the doctor's confidence, though for the life of him, he could not see how....

The crunching of gravel from a few feet behind interrupted Thompson's musings. Shit, he had been so self-absorbed with his own emotions he had not heard the rotter approaching. In one motion, Thompson reached for his Colt, pulled it from its holster, and spun around to aim.

He was surprised to find himself staring down the barrel at O'Bannon.

O'Bannon stopped short and raised his hands in front of his chest as if to ward off the bullets. "It's cool, man. I'm not the enemy."

"Sorry," Thompson reholstered the sidearm. "My mind was elsewhere."

"You gotta be more careful. Out here, a mistake like that can get you killed."

"I'm sure most of you wouldn't mind."

O'Bannon stepped up to Thompson and looked him in the eyes. "As I said, I'm not the enemy."

"Interesting choice of words." Thompson left the statement hanging.

"I'm not playing word games. I don't like or trust the bloodsuckers any more than I do the rotters. The only difference is that the rotters aren't as cunning. I think you feel the same way."

Thompson nodded in agreement.

O'Bannon's lips twisted into a wry smile. "Neither of us is happy with the vamp lovers around here or with the way Robson's running the show."

"You have that right." Thompson grew cautious about where this conversation might be heading and carefully chose his next question. "What are you planning to do about it?"

"Nothing. And you should do the same thing."

"What do you mean?"

"Lay off with the bloodsucker comments. Like it or not, Robson's in charge out here. Although he's an asshole, he's done a good job keeping us alive so far. Besides, most of the others like and respect him, and none of them would go along with us if we tried anything." O'Bannon cast a disparaging glance back toward the convoy. "Most of them have been buying into this alliance with the bloodsuckers for so long they can't see the reality from the bullshit."

"So that's what you came to tell me?" asked Thompson, the anger returning to his voice. "To lay low and shut up?"

"I'm advising you to lay low and shut up until we reach Site R. Then you and the doctor are in charge, and you'll have the advantage." O'Bannon's voice went softer, not that there was anyone else around who could overhear. "Once you have the vaccine, if you and the doctor decide you've had enough and want to set off on your own, I want to go with you."

"You hate the bloodsuckers that much?"

"It's mostly a question of self-preservation. Sooner or later, it's gonna come down to humans versus vampires, and I don't feel like fighting them by myself."

"I'll mention it to Compton."

"Good." O'Bannon gave Thompson a friendly smile. It was the first time the colonel could recall seeing genuine emotion from the man.

O'Bannon headed back to the convoy, passing by Compton, who approached the two. The two exchanged a few pleasantries. A minute later, the doctor joined Thompson.

"What was that all about?"

Thompson watched O'Bannon as he walked back to the campsite. "He was warning me to lay low until we reached Site R."

"Good advice. You should take it." The colonel started to protest, but Compton cut him off. "Look, I'm sorry I dressed you down back there, but we've discussed this before. Robson's in charge, and we can't go bucking his authority. Besides, like it or not, we need the bloodsuckers to ensure we make it back to the site. Once we get there, we'll take care of this problem once and for all."

"I understand."

"So, we're okay?"

"Yes, sir."

"Good." Compton turned back towards the convoy, motioning for the colonel to join him. Thompson fell in beside his boss. "What else did O'Bannon say?"

"Well, for starters, he hates the bloodsuckers as much as we do."

"That's good. We know we can rely on him when the time comes."

"He did warn me that the rest of the group respects Robson and will probably follow his lead when it comes to the bloodsuckers."

Compton frowned. "That's too bad. I'd hoped we would have more support."

"What happens if they don't go along with your plan?"

Compton thought for a moment. "When the time comes, they'll have to decide which side they want to be on."

Thompson did not like the implications of the doctor's response but decided not to pursue it any further.

CHAPTER TWENTY-NINE

"**W**HAT ARE YOU listening to?" asked Dravko.

"The humans." Tatyana lay on the top bunk, her head pressed against the inner wall of the Ryder. "They're arguing."

"About what?"

"I can't tell."

"Probably about us," chimed in Tibor. "I wouldn't be surprised if they're debating the best way to get rid of us and make it look like we were rotter casualties."

"Enough," barked Dravko. "Tatyana, move away from the wall and get some rest. You'll need it tonight."

Tatyana obeyed reluctantly, mainly because the shouting had ended, and she could no longer hear anything.

Rest was the last thing any of the vampires could hope for. The death of Sultanic weighed heavily on them, not only because he was their friend, but because the scarcity of their numbers was such that the loss of even one member proved devastating. Combined with the uncertainty of what would happen to them in the next few hours, both at the hands of the rotters and their human comrades, they were too agitated to sleep.

After several minutes, Tatyana leaned her head against the wall. "It's quiet out there. I can't hear anyone."

Dravko sighed. "You have to trust the humans."

"Why?" asked Tibor. "They despise us as much as we despise them."

"You hate the humans that much?"

"I despise what we've become living with them. We have to rely on them for our safety, feed off livestock so we don't offend them, and treat them like equals. It's... it's...."

"Demeaning," Tatyana concluded his sentence.

Dravko found himself at a loss for words. He felt the same way at times, although he would never voice those feelings to anyone other than Elena. Nor would he admit that taking down those gang members offered a thrill he had not experienced since before the outbreak. The way each man had screamed and struggled, pumping adrenaline into the bloodstream, sweetening the vital life fluid. It may not have been as exhilarating as a hunt through the streets of New York City, but it provided more of a rush than feeding off cattle.

Strangely, the kill also dredged up an emotion Dravko had not felt for centuries. Guilt. Not for what happened to the gang members, because he could not have cared less about them. They had to die if the rest of the raiding party hoped to survive, the manner of death being irrelevant. The guilt resulted from the awkward position he had placed Robson in. After spending so many months repressing their natural instincts to fit in with the humans, their feeding frenzy only reinforced the vast differences between them. Robson had put his reputation on the line defending them, especially while on this insane mission. For the first time since humans and vampires had reluctantly agreed to join forces, Dravko felt a tenuous bond developing between the two species. At best, yesterday's lapse would make Robson's efforts to defend them that much more difficult. At worst, it could well have undone months of reconciliation.

Still, he empathized with Tibor and Tatyana. "I know it's not our way, but we've had to adapt. Without the humans, we'd be dead by now."

"I could say the same about the humans," said Tibor. "We lost Sultanic because he tried to save Whitehouse, and the humans do not care."

"That's not true. Robson was upset about Sultanic."

"I wish all the humans were as decent as him," said Tatyana.

"Robson's not the threat," admitted Tibor, "but there's only a few like him. Most humans would drag us into the sun without a second thought, especially Compton and the colonel."

"Those two are evil." Tatyana sneered.

"And once we get to their compound, they'll be running the show," Tibor added ominously. "We won't be able to rely on Robson to protect us."

"Then we rely on ourselves," Dravko responded defiantly. "When we get to Site R, we don't stop looking over our shoulders. We stick together or stay with the humans we trust, like Robson or Natalie. No one goes off alone or puts himself in a situation where Compton or Thompson can isolate and take us down."

Tibor raised himself in his hammock and looked over at Dravko. "What happens if Compton or Thompson try something?"

Dravko shrugged. "Then we'll do whatever we have to to survive."

CHAPTER THIRTY

PREPARATIONS FOR THE final run to Site R were completed by noon. Since the convoy would not set out until after dark, Robson advised everyone to get a few hours of rest. Once the others had bunked down for the afternoon, he made his rounds of the perimeter to check on the Angels standing guard duty. Before heading back to the armored car and settling down himself, Robson strolled a quarter of a mile down the road, stopping by a small bridge that crossed over a creek. The road continued straight as far as he could see until it disappeared.

It reminded him of the autumn Sunday drives he used to take with Susan when they would stop for a picnic lunch. A warm sun mixed with the chill of an October day, the two blending into a comfortable afternoon. The foliage had started to turn down here, small patches of red, orange, and yellow blotting the trees. Around him, the sounds of nature echoed through the woods. Birds chirped, insects buzzed, and occasionally some hidden animal scurried through the brush, oblivious to the near extinction of the once most dominant species. This stretch of road lay in stark contrast to the urban nightmare not far removed from them.

Robson did not want to think about what awaited them beyond the horizon.

"A penny for your thoughts?" The voice came from behind him. He turned to see Natalie standing directly there.

"You don't want to know what I'm thinking."

She moved up close beside him. "Worrying about what we'll face tonight?"

"Partly." Robson kept his gaze focused on the far end of the road. "You realize less than ten miles from here sits a horror none of us have ever experienced, at least since the first days of the outbreak?"

"I'm trying not to dwell on it."

A moment of silence passed between them, a few brief seconds where they enjoyed each other's company in a pristine countryside left untouched by the living dead. It reminded Robson of better days. If this raid succeeded, the world might enjoy days like this once again.

"What else is bothering you?"

"Huh?" Robson had only half heard the question.

"You said you were partly worried because of tonight's run. What else is bothering you?

"I'm concerned about what we'll find at Site R. Compton and Thompson aren't telling us everything."

"If it's any consolation, we're all worried about that."

He had not heard any of the others voice concern about their mission. "Really?"

Natalie nodded. "I overheard some of my girls complaining that no one is leveling with us. And Daytona and Ari were bitching about it this morning."

"And here I was thinking I'm being paranoid."

"I prefer to think of it as you being cautious. Whatever you call it, it's kept us alive this long, so don't stop now. No matter what we face in the next few days, my girls are behind you all the way. Especially me."

Natalie reached out and wrapped his hand in hers, gently squeezing it for mutual reassurance.

Robson desperately wanted to take Natalie in his arms and kiss her but refrained from being impulsive. The last thing either needed was a physical distraction that took their minds off the task at hand. There might be time enough for that later.

Instead, the two stood quietly on the road, holding hands and enjoying each other's company.

CHAPTER THIRTY-ONE

T HE SUN HAD set two hours earlier. Everyone had eaten dinner. For the humans, it consisted of MREs and fire-brewed coffee and, for the vampires, stored cattle blood. Afterward, Robson took aside the drivers and those who would navigate and, huddled together in the glare of the armored car's headlights, each reviewed the maps and satellite photos until they practically knew the route to Gettysburg by heart. Even that familiarity did not evoke much confidence, for each member of the raiding party knew that the toughest part of the trip lay just ahead, and the success or failure of this mission could well hinge on what went down in the next hour.

When the drivers and navigators felt confident of what to anticipate, Robson gathered everyone in a circle, bathed in the lights from the armored car and bus. He carefully studied each of their faces, assuming some of those gathered would not make it through the night. A nagging part of him wondered how many more of his people he would lose before they made it to Gettysburg. Pushing aside the negativity and focusing on the task at hand, Robson took a deep breath.

"At the risk of sounding melodramatic, I want to warn you about what we face. A few miles down this road, we'll be entering the suburbs around Harrisburg. The satellite photos don't tell us much. We think it's clear of traffic and debris, but the images are months old. And we have no idea how much rotter activity we'll face. The safest bet is to expect the worst.

"The goal is to make it to Site R. If we don't get Compton

and his team to the facility to get the vaccine, then we've wasted our time and lives for nothing. In other words, every one of us is expendable. So, be careful out there. If any of the vehicles get separated from the convoy, haul ass out of the area and make your own way to Site R. We'll meet you there. If we find ourselves in a clusterfuck of rotters and one of the vehicles gets stuck, we'll try to get you out so long as it doesn't endanger the rest of us. If we can't get to you, you're on your own. We can't risk any heroics that'll get us all killed. Are we all clear on that?"

No one answered.

"Are we clear on that?"

The group responded affirmatively, though with little enthusiasm.

"Good. Compton will ride in the bus with the Angels. Jennifer will go with Tatyana and Mad Dog in the Ryder. Thompson is with Dravko and me in the armored car."

Thompson shook his head. "It's better if I stay with the doctor."

"Sorry, but each vehicle will carry one member of your team. God forbid, if something happens to the bus and the Ryder, I don't want this whole mission to fail."

The colonel started to protest, but Compton cut him off. "He's right. Besides, if these young ladies can't protect me, there's not much you'll be able to do."

Thompson backed down. He turned and stepped away from the group, clearly upset at being dressed down again by his commanding officer.

Robson resumed the briefing, trying to make eye contact with everyone around him. "I don't know if any of you still believe in God after what we've been through the past eight months, but if you do, now's a good time to pray for success. We'll pull out in five minutes. With luck, we'll all meet up at Site R."

The group broke up and went their separate ways. Some

went off into the woods to relieve themselves, while a few found a private spot away from the others and prayed. Only Natalie stayed behind, waiting until the others had cleared out before stepping up to Robson. A look of concern replaced her usual smile.

"Do you think it'll be that bad?"

"We'd be foolish to think otherwise."

Natalie forced a smile. "Expect the worse, hope for the best?"

"Something like that."

"Don't do anything foolish."

"I don't intend to. Me, Dravko, and the colonel can take care of ourselves. I need you to keep an eye on Compton and get him to Site R in one piece."

"You can count on me."

"I know I can."

Natalie stepped forward and wrapped her arms around Robson, hugging him. He could feel the warmth of her body, even underneath the leather pants and jacket. She held the embrace for several seconds.

"Be careful," she whispered.

"You too."

When Natalie finally broke free, she returned to the school bus without looking at Robson. He thought he noticed tears in her eyes. He watched until she boarded the school bus, then made his way to the armored car and climbed into the passenger seat. Dravko sat in the driver's seat, the engine idling. Thompson sat in back. No one spoke.

Daytona's voice coming from the radio broke the silence. "Ready when you are, boss."

"Same here," answered Mad Dog from the Ryder.

Robson grabbed the radio and keyed the microphone button. "Let's roll. And may the wind be at our backs."

Dravko shifted into first gear and eased his foot off the clutch. The armored car lurched forward and slowly picked up speed. Robson glanced into the side mirror. Daytona followed one hundred feet behind them as per his earlier instructions, with Mad Dog bringing up the rear.

This is it, thought Robson, trying not to think about what they faced.

A FEW MILES ahead, Route 87 doglegged to the south and skimmed the outskirts of Montoursville. The town lay off to its left, black and silent. The buildings appeared as dark shadows against the moonlit sky. No more than half a dozen rotters wandered along the road, attracted by the sound of the convoy. Each turned and lumbered toward the approaching vehicles, mindless creatures only aware that food roared nearby. One of the rotters stumbled out into the center of the lane and held up its hands as if to flag down the convoy. In the light from the armored car's floodlights, Robson could see it was once a girl no more than ten years old. It wore blue jeans and a torn red sweater that dangled off its left shoulder, both soiled with dried blood and gore. The skin had been stripped off its right arm, shoulder, and chest, revealing the skeleton underneath the gristle. Dravko swerved around it and continued down the road.

A few miles later, Route 87 again doglegged, this time to the west, and merged with Route 147. Up ahead, the skyline of Kenmar and Faxon cast a dark shadow against the horizon, creating an abyss that the convoy was about to enter. Robson wiped his sweaty palms against his pants leg.

"Get ready," he said to Dravko. "We're about to enter hell."

They spotted the first rotter a few miles outside the city limits, a naked man with only its right arm and torso dressed in a tattered National Guard uniform. It wandered down the center of the road. Dravko veered around it. Three more rotters could be seen a hundred yards ahead and, beyond that, a dozen more moved in the shadows.

"Their numbers are increasing," said Dravko, a barely detectable strain in his voice. "And we're not even in the city yet."

"Probably stragglers that set out looking for food."

"That doesn't bode well."

Robson quickly realized how prophetic Dravko had been. The armored car soon entered the city limits, the dark hulks of gutted and abandoned buildings towering above them like canyon walls. The floodlights illuminated their exteriors, the beams reflecting off the shattered remains of storefront windows and detailing the dried blood and burn marks marring the facades. Abandoned vehicles sat at awkward angles every few yards, having been pulled off to the side to make way for first responders and the military. Some were completely burned and gutted. Most of the others sat with their doors open, more often than not, the insides smeared with human carnage. Debris littered the streets and sidewalks: newspapers, suitcases and travel bags, water bottles, empty food containers, weapons.

Amongst the dross of human society, dozens of living dead spread out across the road, with even more figures lurking in the shadows out of range of the floodlights. From every direction, lifeless eyes fell on the convoy, shimmering in the light's glare. In their stare were none of the remnants of their former humanity. No life, no emotion, no thought. Just a recognition of food. Slowly and unsteadily, they lumbered into the street toward the vehicles, reaching out. One rotter in a Pennsylvania State Police uniform slammed its lifeless hand against Robson's window as they passed, smearing the surface with chunks of decayed flesh.

Dravko swerved around the rotters for the first few hundred feet before the encroaching horde made avoiding them impossible. Two of the living dead stepped right in front of the armored car, one dressed in a business suit and tie, its chest stained with dried blood, the other a nurse with its lower jaw missing. Dravko slammed the armored car into them. The nurse careened to the right, tumbling through the air and knocking three other rotters to the ground. The rotter in the suit took the brunt of the left fender in the chest, being knocked back onto the street where the armored car's left tires rode over it. Inside the armored car, Robson and the others were shaken around as the vehicle bumped over the corpse.

"Christ," said Thompson from the back. "How much more of this do we have to go through?"

"It's about two miles before the turn to the bridge," responded Robson.

"Shit."

"Tell me about it," said Dravko.

He slammed into another rotter in a National Guard uniform. This time a loud pop accompanied the thud of the armored car smacking into flesh. The lights ahead of them dimmed as two of the floodlights shattered.

"Damn it!" cursed Dravko.

"Maybe we should let Daytona take the lead," suggested Robson.

"There's not enough room to risk it. Besides, if we slow down to let him pass and these things swarm us, we might not be able to get going again."

The collective moan of rotters in a feeding frenzy filtered into the armored car despite the thickness of the walls. Robson did not know what unnerved him more, the moans or the sound of dead hands slapping and clawing at the armored car, trying to claw their way to the meat inside. The horde of rotters steadily grew thicker as they converged in the center of the street. Each one Dravko hit sent a spray of gore across the windshield. He switched on the wipers, but the blades only smeared the blood and guts across the glass. The red smears on the windshield and the massive swarm of flies hovering around the floodlights decreased their visibility.

Robson tried to read the names on the cross streets to judge how far they were from their turn. Off to his right, he noticed an electronics store, its front windows smashed in. Boxes flatscreen TVs, computers, and radios littered the ground out front, mixed in with a pile of mummified corpses belonging to looters set on by the living dead and devoured before they could escape with their bounty.

Finally, he saw a sign for Franklin Street. He glanced down at his map and searched until he found it. Shit, they were only a quarter of the way to their turn.

The armored car swerved left, causing Robson to look up. With all the rotters converging in the middle of the road, space opened to the left. Dravko moved into the open lane and floored it, trying to gain as much distance as possible before the living dead surged back around them.

They had traveled about two hundred yards when the hulk of an overturned ambulance loomed in front of them. Dravko veered to the right, whipping around the wreck. The floodlights fell onto the form of a three-hundred-pound rotter that stood naked in the center of the street, its bulging gut drooping across its genitals. It turned to the approaching lights, arms flailing wildly. With the ambulance on the left and the mass of rotters on the right, Dravko had nowhere to go but straight. He slammed his foot down on the accelerator, shifted into a lower gear, and aimed the armored car's right fender at the bloated rotter. Robson braced for the impact.

They smashed into the bloated rotter at over sixty miles per hour. Its stomach exploded, showering the front of the vehicle with chewed, undigested, rotting meat. Several chunks came to rest on the hood and windshield or got tangled up in the floodlight supports. As horrible as the sight was, it could not compare to the stench filtering in through the air conditioning system. Decayed flesh. Shit. Bodily gases. Robson leaned forward and vomited.

"You okay?" asked Dravko.

"Yeah," choked Robson. He gagged, spitting up a chunk of vomitus which he spit onto the floor. His puke smelled better than the living dead.

"Good. I need you to tell me when we reach the turn."

"I'm on it." Wiping his mouth clean, Robson grabbed the map and began comparing it to cross streets.

"What street are you looking for?" asked Thompson, who had leaned forward between Dravko and Robson.

"Market Street. On the—"

The armored car shook, accompanied by another thud of a body striking metal. Both men looked up as a rotter flew over the hood, careening off the windshield before falling away to the left. The concussion shattered the remaining floodlights, dimming the road ahead of them.

"It'll be on the left," resumed Robson.

"Roger that."

Both men kept their eyes glued to the sides of the road, searching for street signs. They found it difficult to see them, racing along a rotter-filled road in limited light, with gore from the crushed bodies splattering the glass every few seconds. Finally, Thompson patted Robson on the shoulder and pointed.

"There. On the corner. It says Sterling Avenue."

Robson ran his fingers along the map until he found the name and scanned farther, looking for Market Street. Shit. It was the next turn. He looked up as the armored car entered the intersection.

"Turn here!"

Dravko spun the steering wheel left. The armored car whipped through the intersection and swung onto Market Street, the tires screeching in protest at the sudden change in direction. Robson placed one hand on the door and pushed, trying to keep himself from being thrown against it. Even as the armored car entered the turn, he knew something was horribly wrong. The vehicle continued tilting to the right, the angle slowly getting steeper until it toppled onto its side. It slid along its right flank, chewing up chunks of concrete before eventually coming to a stop in the middle of the intersection.

CHAPTER THIRTY-TWO

"**N**O!" SCREAMED NATALIE when she saw the armored car fail to make the turn onto Market Street. She held her breath as the vehicle's left wheels left the road, teetered for a second, and then flipped onto its right side. The weight and speed of the vehicle propelled it along, gouging out the tarred surface and plowing through the mass of rotters. It halted after ten yards, the only signs of movement being the tires that still spun on their axles.

One hundred feet behind the armored car, Daytona slowed as he approached the crash site, quickly calculating his options. Natalie jumped out of her seat and ran forward.

"What are we gonna do?" she asked.

"I don't know." Daytona sounded frustrated.

"We can't leave them there."

"We sure as hell can't go outside. Not with all these rotters around."

Tibor stepped up behind Natalie and pointed to the emergency escape hatch in the bus roof. "We could go over them."

"We have ourselves a plan." Daytona's frustration gave way to relief. "Tibor, be ready to move when I tell you. Natalie, get the Angels ready. They're going to have plenty of targets soon."

Tibor stepped back to the emergency escape hatch, unfastened the locks, and pushed it open. Natalie rushed past him, ordering her girls to action. The Angels lowered the windows on the left side of the bus to give them clear shots, then stepped back into the aisle, ready for action.

Daytona grabbed the radio and keyed the microphone button. "Mad Dog, we're gonna try and rescue Robson and the others. Hang tight for a few minutes."

"Good luck, man."

Daytona placed the radio back on the dashboard. "Things are about to get hairy."

MAD DOG STOPPED the Ryder and shifted into reverse. The loud, steady beeping cut through the night as the truck slowly rolled back.

"You're not leaving them?" asked Tatyana.

"Fuck that. But if we sit here and wait, these things will swarm us."

DAYTONA SWUNG THE school bus in a wide arc, driving through the section of street cleared of the living dead by the crash, and pulled the bus parallel to the armored car's overturned undercarriage. He inched closer until the armored car's wheels scraped along the side of the bus. Shifting into park, he looked over his shoulder.

"Go!"

Tibor jumped up and grabbed either side of the escape hatch, pulling himself onto the roof. He quickly looked around. Hundreds of rotters were closing in from all sides. Their collective moaning, mixed with the buzzing of thousands of flies, was deafening. He had a few minutes at most to free Dravko and the others.

Jumping the two-foot gap between the vehicles, he landed on the left side of the armored car and moved to the passenger door. It was locked. He banged on the metal but got no response from inside. This time he pounded. Still no response. Morphing into his vampiric form, he grabbed the door handle and pulled, the muscles in his neck and shoulders straining.

IT TOOK ONLY a few seconds for the first rotters to surround the bus.

"What are you waiting for?" ordered Natalie. "Fire!"

Fourteen rifles went off simultaneously. At this distance, no one could have missed. A dozen heads exploded, showering the windows and the seats in brains and skull fragments. Swarms of flies, dislodged from their feast, flew inside and buzzed around the windows. As the first line of rotters collapsed beside the bus, they were replaced by more of the living dead, each desperate to claw their way inside. Dead hands scraped against the exterior or grabbed the window frames, trying to rip them off. Another volley eliminated these rotters, but more took their place. They were already packed two deep around the bus, with more closing in. The smell of mass decay and spent gunpowder became overpowering, forcing Natalie to place her hand over her mouth.

At the front of the crash site, a single rotter in a tattered jogging suit wedged itself between the two vehicles and pushed its way into the confined space. It stumbled over the front tire of the armored car, falling face-first to the asphalt, leaving scraped skin and broken teeth on the ground. Struggling to its feet, the rotter continued to push its way between the two vehicles.

Behind it, a second rotter with two broken legs noticed the gap and began to pull itself onto the armored car's tires.

TIBOR FELT THE door's hinges start to give way on his third try. He paused, summoned all his strength, and yanked again. This time the grinding and snapping of metal accompanied his groan. A moment later, the door broke free. He stumbled backward, momentarily thrown off balance. Whipping the door to his right, he watched it sail over the edge and crush three rotters under its weight.

Tibor leaned through the opening, afraid of what he might find. He yelled into the void. "Hello?"

"It took you long enough," grunted Dravko.

Tibor breathed a sigh of relief. "Is everyone okay?"

"I've got a broken arm."

"What about the others?"

"I'm fine," Robson called out from the rear of the car. "But Thompson's out cold."

"Pass him to me," ordered Tibor. "And hurry."

Robson lifted the colonel and carried him up front, where he and Dravko hoisted the unconscious body to the open door. Tibor reached down, wrapped his hands underneath the colonel's arms, and pulled him out. He lowered the colonel onto the metal and reached back into the cab. Dravko went first, clasping his good arm around Tibor's and allowing himself to be pulled out. Robson followed close behind, using the driver's seat to climb up. When he reached the open door, Dravko and Tibor each grabbed an arm and lifted him to safety.

Robson looked around and muttered the single phrase, "Holy fuck."

By now, almost two hundred rotters had closed in on the vehicles, most converging on the school bus where they were packed four deep along its left side. Constant gunfire came from inside the bus, dropping the dead in scores. For every one that went down, another surged into its place.

"Come on," said Tibor. "We don't have much time."

Dravko jumped the gap between the two vehicles and headed for the escape hatch, dropping inside. Robson bent over to pick up Thompson, but Tibor stopped him.

"Go ahead. I've got him."

Robson crossed over to the school bus and turned, waiting for Tibor. The vampire lifted Thompson, draped the colonel's right arm over his shoulder, and jumped off the armored car. He landed safely, but gravity pulled the colonel's unconscious body down. His body slid off the rounded roof of the bus and into the gap between the two vehicles. Kneeling, Tibor clutched the colonel's arm, preventing him from falling. However, the dangling legs caught the attention of the jogger rotter. Tibor tried pulling the colonel to safety, but the rotter grabbed his leg and latched on, refusing to let go.

"Shit, one of them has Thompson."

Robson reached for his sidearm but could not find it. It must have fallen out in the crash. He knelt and yelled down the escape hatch.

"I need a weapon. Now!"

DAYTONA HEARD ROBSON'S call for help and checked the side mirror, noticing the jogger rotter grasping at the colonel's legs.

"We've got trouble."

Rashid also saw what was happening and ran to the exit. "I've got this."

Daytona opened the side door. Rashid jumped into the gap and took two steps toward the rotter, removing his .357 Magnum and aiming. Thompson's legs were in the path of his bullet.

"Hey!"

The jogger rotter turned, standing back enough that the bullet would not hit the colonel. Rashid squeezed off a single round that blasted away its head. It fell back against the undercarriage of the armored car and slid to the ground. Tibor lifted the colonel onto the roof and quickly lowered him through the escape hatch.

Rashid spun around and headed back for the door, tripping over the rotter with the broken legs. He fell on top of it and kicked himself off but, in the process, moved closer to the front tires and away from the door. Leaning against the axle, Rashid raised his Magnum, aimed at the back of the rotter's head, and fired. Its head disintegrated.

"Take that, motherf—"

A rotter reached over the tires. Grabbing Rashid by the neck, it dragged him out into the street where four more of the living dead descended on him. The kid did not stand a chance. He had enough time to fire off a single round into the face of the rotter that grabbed him but, before he could move, the other four sunk their teeth into his flesh, tearing off chunks of meat. Rashid raised the Magnum, trying to aim for his head. Before he could do so, a fifth rotter grabbed his wrist and bit into his forearm. Rashid dropped the gun and screamed, his death cry drowned out by the carnage around him.

Inside the school bus, Daytona watched helplessly as the living dead tore Rashid apart. He closed the door and bowed his head.

"Go with God, buddy."

BY NOW, ROBSON and Tibor had lowered Thompson into the bus and joined the others. Natalie and Compton placed the colonel in one of the seats on the right side of the bus.

Robson turned to Daytona, brushing away the flies swarming around his face. "Let's haul ass."

"No need to tell me twice." Daytona shifted into drive and pressed his foot down on the accelerator. The bus did not move. He tried again, applying more gas until the engine roared, but the bus still would not budge.

Robson stepped up behind him. "Why aren't we moving?"

"I don't know." Daytona swatted away some flies that had landed on the gear indicator. "The damn thing's in drive."

A rotter in police riot gear clawed at the door beside Daytona, grabbing hold of the handle and pulling. Daytona glanced over at it, his eyes falling on the side mirror. He saw the rotter corpses piled up alongside the school bus. The converging horde had pushed some of the bodies underneath and around the wheels, not allowing him enough traction to move. Shifting into reverse, Daytona tried to back up, hoping to give himself some room. The bus moved only a few feet before the front wheels became jammed against more bodies.

"Shit."

"What's up?" asked Robson.

"Bodies are blocking the wheels. They've wedged the tires in place."

Daytona shifted into drive and gunned the engine. The school bus shot forward and then jerked to a stop. The rear wheels dug into the corpses, trying to get enough traction to roll over them, but there were far too many. He tried shifting into reverse again but only moved a little farther than before.

"Is it going to work?" asked Robson.

Daytona shook his head. "There's too many for me to get over."

"What now?"

"Someone has to go out there and pull those bodies from around the tires."

Robson looked at him aghast. "Do you know what you're asking?"

"Yes. I'm sending someone out there to get killed." Fear crackled in Daytona's voice. "But if someone doesn't clear the bodies from around those tires, none of us are getting out of here."

Tibor stepped up to Robson. "I'll do it."

"No," said Robson. "I can't spare you."

"You can't spare anyone. I'm stronger than you humans. I stand a better chance than any of you."

"Let him do it," groaned Dravko.

The argument was interrupted when Mad Dog's voice came over the radio. "Daytona, hold on and get ready for the ride of your life."

The four stared at the radio, not understanding. Daytona

went to pick up the microphone when he saw the Ryder racing up behind the school bus in his rearview mirror, the front grill growing larger.

Daytona swung around in his seat, grabbing onto the steering wheel and bracing himself for impact. He yelled over his shoulder, "Everybody, hang on tight."

MAD DOG CONTINUED his slow retreat down the street, his attention switching between what was behind him and the rescue attempt. Even from this distance and in the dark, he could see the battle around the school bus growing increasingly intense. The flash of rifle fire remained continuous, and the spray of gore and dislocated flies hung around the vehicle like a cloud. Mad Dog watched Tibor's rescue, thankful to see Robson and the others being pulled from the wrecked armored car. But the mass of rotters swarming the bus made him uneasy.

Most of the rotters were attracted by the noise generated by the melee around the school bus and lumbered off in that direction, ignoring him. Only a handful of the living dead came after the Ryder, not enough to be of any concern.

Tatyana leaned forward to stare at Mad Dog. "Shouldn't we do something to help?"

"Not much we can do. If we get too close, we'll be in the line of fire."

"We could at least offer a distraction."

"Trust me, honey," Mad Dog winked at the vampire. "They'll be glad I hung back this far."

As the three watched, Tibor and the others climbed back into the bus. However, the school bus still sat there.

"Why don't they get out of there?" asked Jennifer.

"There're too many dead rotters around the wheels. They can't go anywhere."

"What do we do now?"

Mad Dog grinned. "We give them a push."

He stopped the Ryder, shifted into second gear, and headed toward the melee. As he approached the crash site, he veered the truck right and then sharply left, coming in directly behind the bus. When about two hundred feet away, he picked up his radio and keyed the microphone.

"Daytona, hold on and get ready for the ride of your life."

A few seconds later, Mad Dog rear-ended the bus at about ten miles per hour. The windows in the rear door shattered, and those not holding on were tossed about like dolls. Seven rotters trying to claw their way into the back of the bus were crushed between the bumpers, spurting blood and decayed body parts onto the truck's hood. Thankfully, the blow did minor damage to either vehicle, although it did provide enough momentum to force the bus tires over the pile of bodies. Once free, the tires got the traction they needed. The bus lurched forward and pulled away from the Ryder. Mad Dog gave it enough time to put some distance between them before shifting into fourth gear and heading off down Market Street.

INSIDE THE SCHOOL bus, the force of the blow seemed amplified, throwing everyone and everything forward. O'Bannon placed himself against the two fifty-five-gallon drums at the rear of the vehicle and pressed into them; the bump jostled the drums around and knocked O'Bannon to the floor, but neither container moved more than a few inches. Natalie and Compton leaned against Thompson, holding him firmly in his seat. The Angels were not so lucky. Most were too engaged in battle to hear Daytona's warnings and were thrown about the cabin. A couple of shots went wild, one going through the roof just behind Daytona's head. Bethany grabbed onto one of the seats as she toppled backward, snapping her wrist in the fall. Most of the other girls suffered strained muscles or scrapes from bouncing off the seats.

Daytona was oblivious to all that. Before the Ryder bumped into him, he shifted into first gear and slammed his foot on the accelerator, feeling the rear wheels spinning futilely in the blood and gore as if it were mud. Then the truck collided, shoving the bus over the pile of corpses and through the pool of blood. Daytona felt the rear tires spin for another few seconds before finally gaining ground. The bus lurched forward. He let off the gas long enough to shift into second gear and floored it again, thankful to feel it picking up speed. Surging forward, the bus pushed aside the horde of rotters and broke into the open road, rapidly gaining speed.

Daytona took a glance in the side mirror. Gore covered the front of the Ryder, with a rotter arm dangling from the grill. The right headlight and most of the floodlights were busted, but it followed close behind. From the driver's seat, Mad Dog gave him a thumbs-up.

Rotters filled the road ahead of them, though nowhere near as many as on the main road. Daytona maneuvered around the larger groups. The plow blades disposed of the stray ones that got in his way, their bodies rupturing with a sickening thud.

"How much farther?" he asked without taking his eyes off the road.

Robson stepped up beside him, massaging a bruised shoulder. "It's about a mile to the river. After that, we should be home free."

The number of living dead became fewer the farther they traveled along Market Street until Daytona could drive right through them without swerving around or hitting them. After a minute, the headlights shone off the bridge abutments.

"There it is," called out Robson.

Daytona increased speed. A burned-out SUV blocked the right lane, with a naked rotter trudging along in the left. It turned around at the sound of the bus, revealing an empty abdomen. It had taken a step toward them when the bus slammed into it with enough force to throw it to one side. The rotter somersaulted in the air and disappeared over the side of the bridge.

Less than a mile later, Route 15 appeared on their right. Daytona slowed and made the turn, leaving the nightmare behind them.

CHAPTER THIRTY-THREE

ROBSON WAITED UNTIL the convoy entered the farmland along Route 15. Once certain they were safe, at least for the moment, he strolled back through the bus to check on the others. He made his way first to Thompson, who was still slumped back against the seat, unconscious. Natalie stood behind him, her hands on the colonel's shoulders and holding him in place, occasionally brushing the flies off his face. Compton crouched before his friend, running his hands across the colonel's legs.

Robson knelt in the seat in front of Thompson. "How is he?"

"At least he hasn't been bitten." Compton stood and patted down his ruffled hair. "I think he has a concussion. I won't know for sure until I get him back to Site R and can examine him."

"If it is a concussion, will he be all right?"

"With proper medical care and some rest, yes." Compton swiped his hand in front of his face, shooing away flies. "We'll all be better off once we clear away these damn insects."

"And the stench," added Natalie.

"Hopefully, keeping the windows open will take care of that. Let me know if there's anything I can do for him."

Compton nodded.

Robson continued down the aisle, stopping in front of the seat where Dravko sat. "How are you doing?"

Dravko massaged the shoulder above his broken arm.

"Hurts like hell, but it'll heal quickly. By tomorrow I won't feel a thing."

"Good." Robson leaned closer so only Dravko could hear. "I have a feeling I'm going to need you and the others at a hundred percent in the next few days."

"I'll be ready." Dravko nodded in Thompson's direction. "What about him?"

"He's banged up pretty bad, but he ought to be okay in a few days."

"Let's hope we don't regret saving him."

THE NEXT FEW hours passed uneventfully, especially in comparison to the hell they had just left. The next city was Lewisburg, approximately twenty miles to the west. Rotters roamed the streets, but nowhere near the numbers as in Kenmar-Faxon. Daytona and Mad Dog maneuvered around them, avoiding the main concentrations and making it through the city in minutes.

They next encountered Selingrove along the Susquehanna River. The convoy avoided most of the living dead by skirting the city to the east. Just south of the city, an abandoned military roadblock barricaded their path. A line of abandoned cars and SUVs sat on the grass to the left. The scattered weapons and pools of dried blood on the road and grass attested to what happened to those who had manned it and were detained. The roadblock had been designed to stop lone vehicles that violated martial law, so Daytona and Mad Dog drove around the barricade.

After that, it was mostly open roads through farmland for the next hundred miles. The convoy followed country roads far to the west of Harrisburg, taking them through small towns almost completely devoid of the living dead. Liverpool. Duncannon. Marysville. Landsburg. A few rotters blocked the overpass that marked the interchange with Interstate 76, but Daytona pushed them out of the way as the convoy raced by. Near Chambersburg, farmland gave way to woods. The convoy continued until it picked up Route 30 east.

They had traveled only a few miles down this road when Daytona leaned his head back. "Hey, boss. You'll want to see this."

Robson stood up from his seat and stepped to the front of the bus, resting his left arm on the driver's seat. "What's up?"

"That." Daytona pointed to the side of the road ahead of them.

A sign stood off to the side of the road. It read:

ENTERING GETTYSBURG

CHAPTER THIRTY-FOUR

COMPTON STOOD IN the middle of the small access road that led up the hill, half a mile from the intersection with Harbaugh Valley Road. Around him were Robson, O'Bannon, and Dravko. All of them except for Dravko wore night vision goggles. Natalie stood directly behind Robson, her gaze alternating between the access road and the five Angels she had posted in a semi-circle around the group.

"Site R is up there," Compton said, pointing toward the top of the incline.

Robson strained to see the last half mile to the chain link security fence that blocked the road, noticing the mass that shambled around on the opposite side of the access gate. He spoke softly so as not to attract their attention. "It looks like we have a welcoming committee."

"The fucking place is swarming with rotters," O'Bannon noted.

"There has to be a couple of hundred of them," added Dravko.

"Almost four hundred, to be exact." Compton seemed unfazed by his comment.

The others stared at the doctor in stunned silence.

"How do you know that?" asked O'Bannon.

"Two chain link fences form a security perimeter around the facility. About fifty yards on either side of this road, interlocking fences connect the two outer fences, forming a security cage around the entrance." Compton lowered the goggles and looked at O'Bannon. "Before we left, we opened the outer gate, lured all the rotters into the cage, and closed it behind them. Once they were trapped inside, Thompson counted them from one of the security cameras on the roof of the guard house."

"Why would you want to trap them?" asked Robson.

"To clear our escape route, of course."

Natalie moved closer to the group so she could speak quietly and still be heard. "They're so... docile."

"That's because they've been left there for several weeks without food." Compton turned to face the others. "They're mindless creatures that accept their environment. They'll stroll around that cage like guppies in a fishbowl until their bodies rot. Or until something excites them."

Dravko sneered. "In other words, us?"

Compton nodded. Robson felt himself shudder.

"Don't worry," said Compton. "Those fences are heavily reinforced to keep out any crowds that tried to force their way into the compound. Those things aren't getting in unless someone lets them."

"That ain't gonna happen," said O'Bannon.

"One question, doc." Robson removed his night vision goggles, not wanting to look at the seething mass of living dead any longer. "If they're blocking the main entrance, how do we get inside?"

"The same way we got out. Through the back entrance."

CHAPTER THIRTY-FIVE

THE CONVOY EMERGED from the tree-lined street into the small residential cul-de-sac along the compound's perimeter fence. Nine three-bedroom homes stood on either side of the road, each as dark and quiet as the surrounding neighborhood. There were signs that rotters once roamed this area. An abandoned Suburban sat in the driveway of the third house on the right, its doors and hatch wide open. Rust-colored spots began by the driver's door and ran across the driveway to the front door of the house, which sat ajar. A Honda Civic sat at an angle in front of the middle house on the left, its front wheels on the sidewalk, its side windows shattered with streaks of dried blood running down the doors.

Everyone kept an eye out for living dead roaming along the edge of the woods, but no one saw any activity.

Daytona halted in front of a ten-foot-tall chain link fence at the far end of the cul-de-sac. Mad Dog stopped a few yards to his rear. The gate was still closed. The few remaining flood-lights lit up the digital keypad mounted on the reinforced fence support to the right of the gate. A length of chain wound several times between the support and the outer rim of the electronic gate, with a combination padlock holding the two ends together.

"Real hi-tech for a secret government installation," chuckled Daytona when he saw the chain.

Compton, who stood behind him, did not register the sarcasm. "We put that on when we left the compound in case the emergency generators failed and tripped the electronic lock. We didn't want rotters getting inside and wandering around."

"I hope you have the combination?" asked Robson.

"Of course." The doctor turned to Robson. "Shall we?"

"Yeah. Let's make it quick."

Daytona opened the door, allowing Robson and Compton to get out. Four Angels followed behind the men, deploying to the corners of the convoy to keep watch.

As they approached the gate, Robson noticed the digital display on the lock flashed the word ERROR.

"Damn," swore Compton.

"What's wrong?"

"When we left the compound, we converted to emergency solar power. There must have been a temporary outage."

"That means we're trapped out here?" Robson did not relish the idea of gaining access through the main gate.

"No. I have the override code. It means this will take a little longer."

"It's all yours."

Compton raised his head to see the lock through his bifocals and punched in a five-digit code. The ERROR light stopped blinking. A series of red dots ran along the bottom of the display for several seconds before another word lit up: ENGAGED. Lifting the padlock in his left hand, Compton spun the combination lock to the right, left, back to the right, and set it on zero. It popped open in his hand. He dropped the lock into his jacket pocket and removed the chain, draping it over his shoulder. He punched another five-digit code into the keypad. The word on the display switched to OPEN. With a whir, the gate slid aside. Compton stepped through and performed the procedure on the second gate.

As the second gate opened, Compton rejoined Robson. "You bring the vehicles through. I'll wait here and close the gates behind you."

"Gotcha." Robson ran back to the school bus and yelled up

to Daytona. "Let's roll."

"We can't."

"Why?"

"We lost Mad Dog."

WHEN HE SAW Robson and Compton head for the gate, Mad Dog slipped out of the Ryder.

"Where are you going?" asked Jennifer.

"I'll be fine." He reached in and patted her hand. "Take care of yourself."

Without waiting for a reply, he walked away from the truck and headed for the next to the last house on the left. Making his way around to the rear, he opened the gate leading into the backyard and crossed to the kitchen door. It hung ajar, the wood around the jamb busted as if something had broken in. Mad Dog breathed deeply and stepped inside.

Pitch-dark filled the interior of the house. Removing a flashlight from his jacket, he switched it on and headed inside with a familiarity borne of experience. The small wooden breakfast table sat askew, with its accompanying chairs either knocked over or shoved to one side. Across from the kitchen, a swinging door led to a combination living room/dining room. Mad Dog pushed open the door and stepped through.

And felt his heart sink.

The dining room was a shambles. The table sat on its side, its chairs spread helter-skelter across the room. One lay in pieces beside the door underneath a huge gouge taken out of the wall. The glass in the china hutch had been shattered, with shards of broken dishes mixing with the glass on the rug.

He found the living room in a similar state of disarray. Only this time, amidst the broken furniture, were the remains of a female body. The skin that clung to the skeleton had long since mummified, as had the bits of flesh and organs scattered around the body, the remnants of a feeding frenzy. It sat in the center of a pool of dried blood that stained the carpet black. The corpse was barely recognizable, but Mad Dog knew exactly who it belonged to. He knelt beside the remains and gently stroked its leathery cheek. Tears welled up in his eyes. At least she had not become one of them.

Bending over, Mad Dog kissed the corpse on its forehead, oblivious to the death pressed against his lips. He sniffed, clearing his nose of snot.

"Goodbye, Marcia."

Standing up, he stripped out of his jacket and laid it across her face and shoulders. It was the least he could do.

Mad Dog made his way around the blood-stained sofa to the corner of the living room near the front of the house. The tears welled up in his eyes again. The dog crate sat in the corner, unaffected by the carnage. Inside sat the two tiny skeletons of his beloved Cavalier King Charles Spaniels, George and Gracie. Deep down, he had hoped that somehow they had escaped and made their way to safety where they could have fended for themselves in the woods, giving them a fighting chance. Instead, they were trapped in their cage, left to die slowly of starvation while their owner's body decomposed nearby. He did not know who suffered the worst fate.

God knows he had tried to save them. He had left the compound only for a few minutes to rescue his family and bring them back to the safety of the facility, only to find the neighborhood overrun with dozens of rotters feeding on friends who had not gotten out in time. Trying to make it to his house at the opposite end of the cul-de-sac would have been suicide. Marcia had been a tough woman, and he prayed she had taken off with the dogs when the situation deteriorated. When he could not reach his house, he returned to the compound to discover he had been locked out. With nowhere else to go, he had set out on his own, looking for a safe place to ride out the outbreak and hopefully be reunited with his family.

Only she had not run. She had waited for him to come and save them, and she died.

Mad Dog dropped to his knees in front of the crate. The sobs came long and heavy, months of pent-up fear, guilt, and anguish purging all at once. His hand caressed the top of the crate. He could barely make out the bones of George and Gracie through his tears.

"I'm so sorry," he sobbed.

Pulling himself together, Mad Dog stood up and crossed over to the lounge chair that used to be his favorite spot to watch television. Ironically, it was the one piece of furniture that was not broken. He slumped into it, sighing along with the cushions. The flashbacks flooded his mind, providing temporary solace from his pain. God, how many times had he and Marcia sat side by side, each with one of the dogs in their laps, petting their ears as they watched TV and argued about politics, what they were going to watch, and the value of reality shows? Those days were gone now.

Forever.

Reaching for his holster, Mad Dog withdrew the .357 Magnum and placed the barrel into his mouth. The taste of the metal felt so soothing on his tortured soul. Maneuvering the end of the barrel so it sat against the roof of his mouth, Mad Dog's finger gently squeezed the trigger.

"WHERE THE HELL is he?" Robson had not meant to snap at Tatyana and Jennifer. He was pissed at Mad Dog for going off without telling anyone, especially in unknown territory.

Jennifer slid across the front seat and leaned out the window, looking over the spikes surrounding the windshield. She pointed to the row of homes off to the left. "Right after we stopped, he got out and headed for the second house on the end."

"Did he say why?"

"No. He told me to take care of myself."

Dravko shook his head. "I don't like the sound of that."

"We've got to find him. You're with me."

"Okay."

"Jennifer, get on the school bus. Tatyana, take the wheel, and be ready to move if anything happens."

"Gotcha." Tatyana waited for Jennifer to climb out of the cab before she slid into the driver's seat.

Robson led the way to the house, unholstering the Colt .45 he had borrowed from Thompson and switching on his flashlight. The two men had closed to within a few yards of the house when a single gunshot rang out from inside. They broke into a sprint, racing across the lawn and up the front stairs. Dravko rammed his shoulder into the door, knocking it off its hinges, and stepped inside. Robson rushed past him and stopped in the hall, one hand holding the Colt and the other the flashlight, panning the area. Dravko tapped him and pointed into the living room.

The beam from the flashlight fell on Mad Dog's corpse, slumped back in a lounge chair, chunks of his brain and skull dripping from the ceiling.

Dravko placed a hand on Robson's shoulder. "At least he's at peace now."

Robson went to cover up Mad Dog's remains when the blaring of the Ryder's horn caught his attention. A moment later, the two men heard the all too familiar groan of rotters. They rushed out onto the front porch. Tatyana leaned out of the truck window, waving them to hurry up. Ari and Bethany crouched in a firing position by the truck's front fender, ready to defend the convoy.

Around them, a dozen rotters filtered into the neighborhood, drawn by Mad Dog's gunshot. Most came from the surrounding houses, while a few wandered from the woods. Neither their numbers nor their proximity posed a threat.

As Robson and Dravko rushed back to the others, Daytona and Tatyana drove their vehicles onto the compound through the twin security gates. Ari and Bethany waited until the two men passed before they followed. Compton stood by the outer gate, waiting for everyone to pass through before punching his five-digit code into the keypad. The outer gate slid shut. Compton stepped inside, walked up to the second keypad, and punched in his code again. He stepped inside the compound, standing beside Robson and Dravko as the twin gates glided into the closed position.

"That'll keep them out." Compton left the others standing there and strolled back to the school bus.

Robson watched the rotters slowly converge on the gate, clawing at the chain links to get at them. *More like trap us inside,* he thought.

BOOK THREE

BOOK THREE

CHAPTER THIRTY-SIX

THE DIRT ROAD from the rear gate wound its way through the forest surrounding Site R. Both vehicles creaked and groaned as they jostled along the rutted surface, neither having been designed for terrain like this. The discomfort was a small price to pay, though, for everyone got to see an area teeming with life. Isolated by the security fence from the horrors of the rotter world, wildlife flourished within the compound. Every time one of the vehicles banged its way through a pothole, a rabbit or deer would bolt, seeking cover amongst the trees. Turning one corner, the school bus headlights fell upon a beaver standing in the middle of the road. Upon being caught in the glare, it raced ahead of them, its furry behind seeming to shake in defiance before it darted into a small gulley.

Robson could not help but smile. For the first time in months, the world seemed normal.

That delusion quickly evaporated when the road finally broke through the tree line. Ahead of them sat a large clearing at the base of the mountain, stripped of its natural beauty and replaced by the functionality of a military compound. Initially designed in the 1950s to house and protect the Oval Office during a nuclear war, Site R quickly became obsolete as the world's nuclear weapons became increasingly more destructive and was eventually relegated to quartering other, less important government entities. Aesthetics had never factored into the facility's responsibilities. An endless stream of vehicular traffic had crushed down most of the grass, leaving behind an unsightly expanse of churned dirt and gravel. An abandoned two-and-a-half-ton military truck, a stripped-down Humvee, and several rusted metal sheds littered the area. A large swath of trees had been felled along the ascending slope and replaced with a row of metal towers bearing the electrical wires supplying the facility. A tunnel dug into the base of the mountain large enough to drive two trucks through further marred the pristine beauty. The tunnel's entrance glowed red from a string of emergency lights running along its ceiling.

"In there," said Compton excitedly as he pointed to the entrance.

Daytona looked nervously over his shoulder. "Are you sure?"

"We have to be careful not to get too close to the tunnel entrance by the front gate, otherwise we'll excite the revenants."

Daytona nodded. "That's fine with me."

The vehicles carefully entered the tunnel. The emergency lights provided just enough illumination to see by, although there was little inside worth viewing, only smooth rock walls extending into the distance.

"How far is it?" asked Robson.

"About a third of a mile straight ahead, then the tunnel bears right to the access door." Compton kept his eyes focused on the tunnel ahead of him. "There's an entrance similar to this on the opposite end of the mountain."

"Why are the tunnels so long?" asked Daytona.

"Site R was built directly beneath the apex of the mountain. A couple of tons of solid rock lies directly above our heads."

"Wonderful." Daytona did not sound pleased. "We're entering a fucking tomb."

"Far from it." Compton smiled, trying to reassure him. "This facility was designed to withstand a blast of several hundred kilotons. A few hundred revenants pose no threat."

"Unless they trap us inside," muttered Robson.

Daytona turned at the bend in the tunnel. After another minute, Compton pointed to a massive blast door twenty feet square off to the left. "Stop right there. I'll open it, and you can drive in."

Daytona did as told and idled the school bus. Compton jumped out and walked over to the door. He punched a code into the digital display mounted to the right of the door and stepped back. It popped open. Robson whistled in amazement. The door was composed of steel four feet thick. Much to his surprise, the doctor pushed on it with his hand, swinging it aside with the same ease as he might have the front door of his house.

"How the hell did he do that?" asked Daytona. "That thing must weigh a couple of tons."

"It does," answered Jennifer, who had come forward to join them. "It's on special hinges designed to allow one person to close it quickly in case of emergencies."

Robson and Daytona stared at her quizzically.

She grinned. "Each of us had to learn other tasks while we were here to ensure continuity of operations if some of us were killed or incapacitated. I was assigned to the engineering department."

"You must know this place pretty well?" asked Robson.

"Like the back of my hand."

Compton waved them on. Daytona maneuvered the school bus through. Tatyana followed.

Inside the facility, they found a service road two lanes wide. A massive concrete wall blocked their path to the right. Two Humvees with Military Police markings and roof-mounted blue lights sat in front of it. To the left, the road extended deep into the mountain as far as the eye could see. A concrete dome stretched from the outer wall to a height of one hundred feet. In front of them, three buildings, each three stories in height, stretched back for a hundred yards. Daytona pulled the school bus against the wall and shut down the vehicle. Tatyana pulled the Ryder in behind him.

A moment later, Compton stepped back onto the bus. He gestured toward Thompson, who still sat unconscious in one of the seats. "I need to get the colonel to the infirmary so I can start treating him."

"Before you do that, I want to check out the facility and make certain it's secure."

"That's not necessary. We secured it as we left. There's no way a revenant could have gotten in."

"Still, I'd rather be safe than sorry."

"That's no longer your concern, Mr. Robson." Compton spoke in a quiet but firm voice. "I hope I don't have to remind you what Paul said about my being in charge once we arrived?"

Robson did remember and was not happy about how quickly the doctor assumed his authority. Despite his displeasure, he backed down. "No, you don't."

Compton placed a conciliatory hand on his shoulder. "There's an easy way to check this place out. Security cameras cover every part of this facility. Miss Wilson can take you to the control room, and you can conduct your inspection from there. Is that acceptable?"

"Sure." Like he had another choice.

"Good. Now, if I could get someone to help me with the colonel."

"I'll carry him." Tibor came forward from the rear of the bus. Crouching, he slid his hands under Thompson and lifted the colonel off the seat, cradling him like a child. "Lead the way."

Compton hesitated, uncertain about trusting a vampire. When no one else volunteered to assist, he gave in to the inevitable. The doctor shrugged, exited the bus, and led the way to the infirmary on the second floor of the building on the far left. Tibor followed.

Robson mouthed to Natalie for her to send along an escort. She nodded and turned to her Angels. "Ari, take two of the girls and stay with them."

"Roger." Ari choose Emily and Bethany. The three set off after the doctor.

Tatyana had shut down the Ryder and joined the others. "What's the game plan, boss?"

Robson frowned. "To start with, I'm no longer the boss. Compton's in charge as long as we're here."

From where he sat near the back of the bus, Dravko mumbled, "That makes me feel a lot safer."

A few uncomfortable chuckles filled the interior. Robson ignored them. "I want everyone to stay here with the vehicles. Jennifer and I will go to the control room and use the security cameras to scan this place for rotters. Once we're certain the area's secure, we'll come and get you."

"I'm coming along." Natalie stepped forward.

"That won't be necessary," said Robson. "We should be okay."

"It's your own orders. No one travels without an armed escort while in an unsecured environment." Natalie tried to sound forceful, but the look in her eyes indicated she was more concerned with being with him than ensuring his safety.

"Fine. You're with us."

Natalie grinned like a schoolgirl asked to the prom. She took the Mauser from Leila and swung the strap over her shoulder.

Robson let Jennifer lead. The group made their way to the building on the far right. Directly across from them stood another door with a window in the upper quadrant showing the interior. Off to the left sat two rows of lockers while a set of stairs ascended to their right. Jennifer climbed the stairs to the third-floor landing, opened the door, and stepped inside.

Another corridor ran the entire length of the building, ending at a second windowed door at the far end. The interior was designed with typical U.S. Government functionality. Recessed fluorescent lights, light-colored tiled floors, walls painted white, plain wooden doors with plastic plaques mounted on brass frames in the middle of each one. The only illumination came from the red emergency lights, casting an eerie glow along the corridor.

Jennifer led them to the first room on the right. The door plaque bore the word SECURITY. A chest-high counter separated the room. They stood in a waiting area containing only three cheap plastic chairs against the wall. Jennifer went to the far end of the counter, where a break allowed them access to the other side. Here sat several desks with computer terminals. An empty gun cabinet stood in the far corner.

Jennifer led them to a room off the left corner that was only a quarter of the size of the main area, with most of the space taken up by a bank of monitors mounted along one wall, divided into four sets of six screens. Those on the left showed various shots around the facility. Robson immediately noticed the tunnel entrance they had entered through, an entrance he assumed to be the one near the main gate, the blast door, the area with the school bus and Ryder, plus others he was not familiar with. The three sets of monitors on the right showed interior shots of the buildings. One screen among the second set of monitors showed Compton treating Thompson in the infirmary. Beneath each set of monitors, schematics of various sections of the facility and each building had been attached to the metal surface. Each section of the schematic contained one small red and green light.

Jennifer stepped over to a metal box mounted on the wall off to their left and opened it, revealing a circuit breaker. She flipped a large switch at the top labeled GENERATOR into the up position, waited a few seconds, and then flipped into the up position a second large switch beneath it. Each monitor glowed brighter as the facility's fluorescent lights came on.

"That'll give us some more light," she said. "I'll check out the generator and solar panels later to make sure we have a constant supply of electricity."

Jennifer sat down in a leather chair in front of the central console. Robson and Natalie stood behind her.

"Security cameras are located all over the facility," Jennifer explained. She pointed to the schematic on the left. "This shows the location of the cameras in the interior of the cavern. The top screens show the tunnel entrances and the exterior of the blast door. They're permanently locked onto those views. The other screens show the main entrance by the blast door, the motor pool, and the supply depot. I can toggle through them to view the other cameras."

Jennifer pressed one of three lighted buttons beneath the facility schematic. The green light by the blast door entrance changed to the red light, while the red light to the left of the schematic switched to the green one. The scene on the monitor also switched, showing an indoor reservoir. Jennifer pressed the next two buttons, alternating the views on their respective monitors to show a large generator and a rung ladder rising six feet to a small metal platform and door.

"What's that?" asked Robson.

"The ladder? It leads to the room containing the air filtration system. It's located on the far end of the access road." Jennifer pointed to a larger light at the extreme left of the schematic. "It's the only part of the facility that's alarmed."

"Why?" asked Natalie.

"A ladder inside leads up through the ventilation shaft to the intakes on top of the mountain. Once the blast door is closed and secured, that air shaft is the only way into the building."

Jennifer pressed the button again. This time the monitor showed a long cement shaft with a ladder mounted onto one of the walls. The view looked down on top of the air filtration unit from a height of approximately one hundred feet. Another press of the button, and this time the view of the shaft looked up to a series of massive HEPA filters, each almost ten feet long.

"The alarm was installed during the Cold War to warn against commando raids. Now it only goes off when a squirrel or raccoon gets inside the shaft."

Jennifer toggled through the other interior cavern views. The crematorium, which she explained was initially designed to dispose of those who died of disease or radiation after arriving at the facility. The machine shop. The meat locker and food closet.

When Jennifer switched to the last view, Natalie stepped close to Robson, pressing against him for comfort. From the angle of the shot, Robson assumed the camera was located on the roof of the access control building out front. It showed the compound's main gate and the four hundred rotters trapped between the outer and inner security fences. Packed in shoulder to shoulder, they could barely move. They stood listlessly like cattle crammed into the dispatch chute of a slaughterhouse, except these things were already dead.

"Turn that off," asked Robson.

"No problem." Jennifer pressed a button, replacing the view of rotters with the interior of the blast door and their vehicles.

The remaining banks of monitors each had three schematics beneath them representing the floors of each building. Jennifer pressed the SCAN button for each set, and the monitor views changed, showing the corridors, exits, or various rooms, lingering on each for five seconds before switching to another. As the views shifted, Jennifer continued her explanation. She pointed to the bank of monitors on the right.

"This is the building we're in now. It holds the offices, mess hall, security offices... you get the idea. This building in the middle is the dormitory."

"Security kept tabs on everyone?" asked Robson.

"No," answered Jennifer with a don't-be-silly tone to her

voice. "When the facility was in use, security had orders not to monitor the rooms. The cameras were permanently locked onto the three corridors, the two exits, and the common area. At least they were whenever I was on duty."

"You're not into voyeurism," joked Robson.

Jennifer chuckled. "The building on the left also contains offices. But when we came down here from Fort Detrick shortly after the outbreak, the building was reserved for the infirmary and Compton's personal use. Compton converted the larger rooms on the first floor into labs and living quarters. The other two floors are not being used."

Natalie pointed to a set of separate switches on the far right of the console. "What are those for?"

"Those are the master controls for the generator, air filtration system, freezer, and so on." Jennifer pointed to one switch colored red. "That's the alarm system for the facility. And you don't want to touch the one beside it."

"What is it? The self-destruct mechanism?"

"In a sense. That one controls the main gates. Touch that, and you'll let all the rotters onto the compound."

Natalie involuntarily took a step back from the console.

Robson only partially heard the conversation, concentrating instead on watching the monitors for any signs of rotter presence. One image, in particular, caught his attention. "Can you freeze that one?"

"Which one?"

"Second set of monitors. Bottom center."

Jennifer pressed the button, freezing the monitor on a blackened room.

"What's that?" asked Robson.

Jennifer searched the schematic for the green light. "That's Compton's private lab."

"What's in there?"

"I don't know. I was never allowed in. Only the doctor and Colonel Thompson ever went in there."

"Why aren't there any lights on?"

"The doctor must have shut them off."

"But why?"

Jennifer shrugged.

"I want to check it out, to be on the safe side. Where is it located?"

"First floor of Compton's building, third door on the left. You'll need these." Jennifer reached into her pocket and removed a set of keys, which she handed over to Robson.

"I'll go with you," said Natalie.

"You stay here with the radio in case I need to contact you."

"But—"

"I'll be fine. I promise."

Natalie frowned but did not argue.

It took Robson only a few minutes to reach the door leading to the lab. It contained a knob with a lock and a deadbolt, both of which looked new. He tried the knob. As expected, it was locked. He used Jennifer's keys, eventually finding the correct one. A few tries later, he unlocked the deadbolt. Robson removed his Glock and held it in his right hand. With his left, he knocked loudly on the door three times and listened carefully, waiting to see if he heard anything moving around on the other side. Nothing.

"Everything okay?" Natalie's voice came over the hand-held radio.

Robson unclipped it from his belt and held it to his mouth. "Yeah. I'm heading inside now."

"Please be careful."

Robson replaced the radio. He turned the knob and pushed the door halfway open. Not enough light filtered in from the corridor for him to see anything.

"Anyone in here?"

The room was quiet.

Robson raised the Glock into firing position and carefully

stepped inside. He felt around the wall with his free hand until his palm ran over the light switch, and he flipped it on. The fluorescent lights overhead flickered to life.

Robson turned and gasped when he saw a horde of swarmers rushing toward him.

CHAPTER THIRTY-SEVEN

ROBSON FELL BACK until his shoulder slammed against the wall. Screw the pain, he thought. He raised the Glock, knowing he could never fight off so many swarmers but still hoping to take down at least one or two before they tore him apart. He did not fire, however. By now, they should have been ripping into him. Instead, they remained ten feet away, still snarling and clawing. Only then did Robson realize that a Plexiglas partition stood between him and the swarmers. A heavy Plexiglas partition, he hoped.

"Mike, are you okay?" Natalie's voice sounded frantic over the radio. "Mike?"

"I'm fine." Robson took a few steps forward to get into the camera angle. As he drew closer, the swarmers grew increasingly frantic. They clawed at the Plexiglas, some so desperately they ripped off fingernails. One swarmer in an Air Force officer's flight suit gnawed at the Plexiglas, succeeding only in dislodging a few teeth that dropped to the floor. Robson looked up at the camera long enough to assure Natalie he was all right, then turned his attention back to the swarmers.

Natalie sounded only slightly less relieved. "I saw them lunge at you. I thought you were...."

"I would be if it wasn't for the Plexiglas barrier."

"I'm coming down."

"Leave the radio with Jennifer. I want to talk to her." Robson's tone had an icy edge as his initial shock gave way to fury.

A few seconds later, Jennifer's shaky voice came over the

radio. "I'm so sorry. I had no—"

"What the fuck are you people doing keeping swarmers?"

"I had no idea they were there. I never would have let you—"

"Bullshit! How could you not know?"

"S-sir, please believe me. I've never been in that room. That's Compton's private lab. Only the doctor and the colonel ever went in there."

Jennifer had mentioned that to him earlier. So far, she had played straight with him, and his anger with her quickly subsided. However, he was still furious at being lied to by Compton and would have some choice words with the doctor about this later. "Are there any more swarmers or rotters I need to know about?"

"I doubt it, sir. Every other room checked out clean. You saw them for yourself."

"Good enough. I trust you."

"Thank you, sir."

"And stop calling me sir." Robson softened his tone. He looked up at the camera and forced a smile. "I want you to stay there and keep watching the monitors. Let me know if you see anything suspicious. I'll have someone relieve you soon."

"Roger that."

Robson stood against the wall to wait for Natalie, using the time to study the swarmers. He counted seventeen in total. Christ, it had been months since any of them had encountered swarmers, which was fine by him. Rotters were bad enough. Rotters with speed, agility, and increased ferocity were something he would prefer not to deal with. There was something unusual about them, although he could not readily place it.

The Plexiglas containment unit the swarmers were caged in took up half the lab. Two-thirds of the front façade was comprised of double Plexiglas screens, constructed with an inch between them to provide added protection if the swarmers somehow shattered the inner layer. The other third was a steel wall that contained a single metal door with four electronic deadbolts extending from the center at right angles, similar to a bank vault. He noticed another door on the metal wall making up the left interior of the cage. The three inner walls were all made of steel. Thank God whoever built this knew what they were doing.

Robson heard several pairs of feet racing down the corridor. He backed out of the lab with his eyes still on the swarmers. Taking a quick look, he saw Natalie running down the hall as fast as she could manage, a Mauser clutched in front of her. Tiara and Sandy were right behind.

"Everything's okay," he called to them.

"The fuck it is." Natalie panted lightly from the sprint. "There's swarmers in this facility. That puts us all in danger."

"They're sealed up tight. They can't get out."

"They're a threat just by being here."

Robson stepped back into the lab and motioned for the Angels to join him. When the three women entered, the swarmers went wild again, even more frenzied this time at the prospect of food. The three women stayed close to the far wall. Tiara had raised her Mauser, ready to fire from the hip if necessary.

"See. They can't get to us, though not for lack of trying."

Natalie kept her eyes fixed on the swarmers. "That bitch should never let you come in without warning you."

"It's not Jennifer's fault. I reamed her out, but she swore she didn't know about them. I believe her. She said only Compton and Thompson ever came into this lab."

"Figures," spat Natalie. "I don't trust those two."

"Oh, my God." Tiara's face twisted in a look of horror. "They're all military."

Robson took another look at the swarmers, suddenly realizing what he had found unusual about them. Except for a female with long red hair and dressed in a white lab coat, all of them wore battle fatigues from the various services. They were all members of Compton's and Thompson's staff. Being swarmers, they could only have been turned four or five weeks earlier at most. Something else also dawned on Robson. As he scanned each one, he noticed that none bore any noticeable bites or wounds, nor were they covered in blood, which ruled out their being infected during an attack on the facility.

"What the fuck is going on here?" asked Natalie, her fear replaced with anger.

"I have no idea," answered Robson. "But I know who does."

CHAPTER THIRTY-EIGHT

WHEN ROBSON AND the Angels arrived back at the vehicles, Tibor had already returned from the infirmary and was talking to the rest of the group. He noticed them approaching and stepped back to make room for them.

"I was telling the others that Thompson will be all right. He has a mild concussion, but Compton says he'll be back on his feet in a day or—"

"I don't give a shit about the colonel." Robson stopped in front of the group, consciously trying not to direct his anger at Tibor. "Where's Compton?"

"He's in the infirmary with Thompson. The Angels are with him." Tibor suddenly realized something was wrong. "Why?"

"Oh, the good doctor forgot to mention that he has seventeen swarmers locked up in his private lab."

A flurry of responses bombarded Robson. He held up his hands to quiet everyone. "They're in a reinforced cage, so there's no immediate danger. But I'm pissed that neither he nor the colonel thought to tell us about them beforehand."

"Are you sure we're safe?" asked Daytona as his hand felt for his firearm.

Natalie answered. "They tried to get at us, but their cage is solid. They're not getting out unless someone lets them out."

"That doesn't mean we can let our guard down," added Robson. "God knows what other surprises are hidden around here. Until I know exactly what we're facing, everyone is to carry a weapon with them at all times. And no one is to go anywhere without a friend. Is that clear?"

The others nodded or mumbled in the affirmative.

Robson pointed to the center building behind him. "That's the dormitory. I want you to double up with someone so you're not alone and stay together on the first floor. I don't want anyone separated from the rest of the group. Now get some rest. We have a long day ahead of us."

As everyone gathered their gear, Robson waved O'Bannon over. "I need you to do me a favor."

"Sure. What?"

"The guard room in the third building monitors every security camera in this place. Jennifer's on watch right now. After you find a bunk, relieve her. She'll brief you on how the system operates." Robson glanced at his watch. "It's a little after seven now. I'll have one of the Angels spot you around noon."

"Anything in particular I'm looking for?"

"Mostly stray rotters that may be wandering around. And keep close tabs on Compton."

"Roger." O'Bannon followed the others into the dormitory.

Robson waited until Dravko exited the school bus and ushered him to one side so no one could overhear. "I want you, Tibor, and Tatyana to stay in one room and reserve the one across from it for me."

Dravko seemed disturbed by the order. "You're keeping an eye on us?"

"I'm looking out for you. Something about this place doesn't sit right with me."

Dravko nodded slightly.

"Now get some rest and regenerate that arm. We're going to need you at full capacity tomorrow."

Robson waited until everyone had drifted off to find a place to bunk down before turning to Natalie. "It's time we talk to Compton."

★ ★ ★

ROBSON LED THE way to the infirmary. He knew which room to go to because the Angels milled around the door. Ari leaned against the wall. Emily sat on the floor. Bethany crouched between them. The three stood to greet them when they saw Robson and Natalie approaching.

Natalie waved at them to stand down. "Is Compton still in there?"

Ari nodded. "He's with Thompson. Looks like the colonel will be okay."

"Not if I have anything to say about it."

The tone of Robson's voice took the Angels by surprise. Ari looked to the other Angels, then back to Robson. "What's up?"

"I'll explain later," said Natalie. "We'll take it from here. Join the others in the dormitory and find yourselves a place to sleep."

"Yes, ma'am."

Robson waited until the Angels had left before he and Natalie entered the infirmary. Twenty hospital beds filled the ward. Thompson rested comfortably on the one opposite the doorway, an IV drip inserted into his inner elbow. Compton stood by him, jotting notes onto a clipboard. The doctor looked up as they entered and then went back to scribbling.

"I can tell by the look on your face you're not here to check up on the colonel's health."

"Why didn't you warn us about the swarmers locked away in your private lab?" demanded Robson.

"Forgive me," Compton said with sincerity. "I was concerned with getting the colonel medical care and forgot to mention it." He inserted his pen between the clip and the board and hung it on a hook at the end of Thompson's bed. "How did you find out about them?"

"While I was checking out your private lab, they charged

the Plexiglas cage. Scared the shit out of me."

"I'm sorry about that. I planned to warn you about the revenants when we arrived at Site R but, as I said, I was preoccupied with the colonel's health."

"Why didn't you warn us back at camp?"

Compton answered with the shrug of someone who never questioned his original decision but now had second thoughts. "You're right, of course. I never mentioned them earlier because I don't see them as a threat."

Before Robson could argue that point, Natalie jumped. "Who are they? Why are they all dressed in military fatigues?"

"They're some of the bravest men and women I'll ever know." Compton leaned against the hospital bed opposite the colonel. "Each one of them agreed to try out variations of the vaccine. Unfortunately, as you saw, I had several failures before perfecting the serum."

Natalie was aghast. "You mean they were guinea pigs?"

"Volunteers. Every single one was a willing participant. They were fully aware of the risks before I injected them."

"Couldn't you have experimented on animals instead?" asked Robson.

"The results would have been inconclusive. As far as we know, animals are not affected by the Revenant Virus. I required human test subjects."

"What about their families?" Natalie could not let go of the horror of it all.

Compton pulled up the sleeve of his lab coat and began unbuttoning his shirt sleeve as he responded. "Everyone who joined me at Site R was selected because they had no immediate family members. It was necessary if we wanted to concentrate on finding a cure for this virus. And before you think I'm some type of monster, remember that I even volunteered to be a test subject." Compton raised his shirt sleeve, showing them his scarred-over bite wounds.

Though Robson did not necessarily agree with the doctor's

methods, he understood why he had taken that course of action. "Why didn't you dispose of them as they turned?"

"I was hoping to find a serum that prevented humans from catching the Revenant Virus and could reverse the effects for someone newly infected. Unfortunately, there's no such miracle cure. By that time, there were too many to risk exterminating them. The colonel and I felt it better to leave them in the containment cell to deal with later." Compton pushed himself off the bed. "I admit that was an error in judgment."

Robson could not argue that point. God knows he had made quite a few bad calls since the outbreak began. "Is the vaccine ready to go?"

"Not yet. I planned on getting some rest before I begin."

"How long will it take?"

"I must make enough serum for all of us, plus extra for those at camp. I also need to make back-ups of all my notes. Everything should be ready in the next thirty-six hours or so."

"Good. I want to get out of here and back to camp as soon as possible."

"Understandable."

"Everyone is bunking down in the dormitory. I'll have them save a room for you."

"If you don't mind, I'd rather stay here tonight in case the colonel takes a turn for the worse."

Robson thought about it for a moment. "Makes sense. I'll have one of the Angels join you for protection."

"No need to bother any of them. I'm perfectly safe. Besides, I have a radio if I need help."

"Have it your way. I've posted someone in the security room to keep an eye on things. Call them if you need anything."

"I will."

Robson and Natalie left the doctor in the infirmary and headed back to where they had parked the convoy. Once they were far enough away so they could not be heard, Natalie asked, "Do you buy his story?"

"About forgetting to tell us about the swarmers? It sounds legit."

"Maybe." Natalie shrugged. "I still don't trust him."

"He's definitely holding out on us. I'll check out what tomorrow."

"I hate to tell you," said Natalie as she looked at her watch. "It's already tomorrow."

"What time is it?"

"A little after eight."

"Shit. We've been on the go for fourteen hours."

"You need to get some rest."

"I will. First, I want to look around the facility and get my bearings. I don't want any more surprises."

"I'll go with you," offered Natalie.

"No need for that. I'll be fine."

"I can't let you do that." Her smile bordered on flirtatious. "No one's supposed to go off on their own. Remember?"

"I'm too tired to argue." Truth be known, Robson appreciated her company. "Come on. Let's make this quick so we can get some rest."

CHAPTER THIRTY-NINE

COMPTON WATCHED ROBSON and Natalie leave the infirmary, chastising himself for mismanaging the entire situation. Rather than win their trust by getting them safely onto the compound, he had let his concern for Thompson cloud his thinking and forgotten to warn them about the revenants isolated in his lab. He did not blame Robson for being furious. He could only imagine how unsettling it must have been to stumble across them in the manner he did. Robson and Natalie accepted his explanation of why the revenants were present within the facility and why he had failed to mention it to them earlier. Even so, the damage had already been done. None of them understood his reluctance to accept their accommodation of the vampires, which generated a natural distrust between them. This incident only served to widen the rift between the two groups.

Compton shrugged and returned to the hospital bed to check on Thompson. There was nothing he could do about it now. Their distrust did not change his plans. It only made it slightly more difficult to carry them out. He still hoped to persuade them of the righteousness of his intentions. Robson and Natalie were smart, if somewhat misguided, and he still felt they would come around to his way of thinking once he presented his justification to them. If not, so be it. He had a contingency plan to deal with any intransigence.

Thompson checked out fine. His blood pressure was elevated, but that was understandable considering the physical trauma he had gone through. His other vital signs were normal. The intravenous drip would keep him sufficiently hydrated until he woke, which should be in another six or seven hours once the sedatives wore off. The concussion was minor and would heal on its own. He would have a slight headache and severely bruised muscles for the next few weeks, but nothing that a steady dose of mild pain painkillers could not take care of.

The doctor pulled the blanket over Thompson's shoulder and stepped over to his bed. The colonel would be all right. He would need him in the coming days to deal with the others. More importantly, the colonel was a decent man who had been willing to endure many sacrifices to bring the human race back from the brink of extinction. Compton already had lost too many good men and women in the cause.

As he stripped off his lab coat and removed his shoes, his mind wandered to the seventeen revenants isolated in his lab. All of them had put their faith in him and allowed themselves to be test subjects for the vaccine, even after the first tests of the serum failed miserably. Despite each failure, several stepped forward to try out the next variation of the serum, knowing the chances of success were small. He could not bring himself to reward such bravery by exterminating them like used lab rats. Besides, he always harbored the hope that a serum would be found that would reverse the effects of the infection and restore them to normal. Unfortunately, that hope turned out to be fleeting. The vaccine could prevent the Revenant Virus from infecting a host but could not reverse the virus in those already infected. Compton made a mental note that before they left Site R for good, he would have to find a way to release his people from their hellish existence.

He removed the keys and lighter from his pocket and placed them on a metal table. Sliding into the bed opposite Thompson, Compton settled down to rest. In a few days, he would have four hundred doses of the vaccine ready to immunize those here and back at camp and to begin vaccinating those in the government-in-exile. Once they were back in Maine, the President would send a boat to take him to Guantanamo Bay, where a long-range aircraft would fly him to Omaha.

Then the world would hail him as its savior. Not only for saving mankind from the revenants, but also for finally eliminating the vampire threat.

CHAPTER FORTY

THE TOUR OF the facility did not take Robson and Natalie as long as they had originally imagined. Thankfully, they did not find any unpleasant surprises waiting for them. Except for the swarmers in Compton's private lab, no rotters lurked anywhere else, nor would any find their way in. The underground complex was completely sealed off from the outside world except for the air shaft and the entrance to the tunnel, both of which were now under constant surveillance. Since Site R was designed to house hundreds of people in the months following nuclear war and would be more than adequate to keep the raiding party safe and comfortable for the next few days.

One pleasant discovery was that the Humvees parked near the main entrance were still in working order, which meant that when the convoy set out back to camp, they could add a few more vehicles to their number, increasing the safety factor. In addition, each of the Humvees was equipped with four M-16 assault rifles and hundreds of rounds of ammunition, which would be added to the convoy's arsenal. Robson even stumbled across an Atchisson AA-12 assault shotgun, an automatic version of a shotgun that held twenty rounds in a drum magazine. He commandeered this for himself.

Back in the dormitory, they walked the corridor looking for their sleeping quarters. Four rooms down on the right, Robson found a sheet of paper taped to the frame with the words "Robson's room" scribbled in Dravko's handwriting. He opened the door and flicked on the light switch. The ceiling-mounted fluorescent light came on, illuminating the two empty bunk beds. Robson stepped inside and looked around. The place was Spartan, but no more so than his container back at camp.

Natalie followed him inside, closing the door behind her.

"What are you doing?" he asked.

"I'm going to stay here tonight."

"Shouldn't you be bunking with the Angels?"

"You may have kept us alive these past eight months, but sometimes you don't have a clue."

Natalie unzipped her leather jacket and slid it back over her shoulders. Robson could not help but keep his gaze fixed on her breasts. He always thought Natalie was beautiful. But now, with her chest thrust forward, pushing against the white turtleneck and stretching the fabric so it contoured tightly around her, he found her irresistible. She let the jacket drop to the floor and glided over to him. Her left hand slid behind his neck, and her right hand wrapped around his waist, drawing him into her. Before Robson could say anything, Natalie leaned up and kissed him. Her tongue slid into his mouth, the tip gently exploring his own. God, she felt so good. The warmth of her body set his skin on fire. Robson wanted her more than he had ever wanted a woman. But it was not right.

Tenderly placing his hands on Natalie's cheeks, he pushed her head back enough to break the kiss. "I want to make love to you so badly. But this isn't the time or place."

Natalie looked up at him affectionately. "We just spent days driving through hell to get stuck in an underground bunker surrounded by hundreds of rotters. I can't think of a better time."

This time, when Natalie kissed him, Robson did not protest. He placed his hands on her hips and pulled her into him.

As he grew hard against her, Natalie let out a throaty moan. "God, you're hot."

"What'd you expect? It's been eight months."

"Then let's take care of that." Natalie lowered herself onto her knees. Her hands caressed their way over his hips and to his front. She ran her right palm along the bulge in his pants, her fingers massaging him through the fabric. Robson moaned and thrust himself against her palm. Grabbing his belt with her left hand and holding it in place, Natalie unzipped him with her right. His erection pushed through the folds, pointing at her.

Natalie leaned forward. Parting her lips, she slid them over his erection and sucked him in, the warmth of her mouth engulfing him. She moved her silky lips back and forth along his erection, using her tongue to massage the underside of his shaft and, every few seconds, sucking him in as deep as possible until he filled her mouth. He had never been so excited by a woman's touch. Closing his eyes, Robson lost himself in the moment, enjoying the feeling of being throated. After only a few minutes, he felt his balls tighten. He exploded into her mouth. Natalie gulped greedily, swallowing. Only after his erection stopped spasming did she slowly pull him out, her right hand and lips milking out the last drops.

Natalie rose to her feet. She used the tip of her tongue to seductively lick a few drops of semen off her lips. "How was that?"

"Awesome." Robson pulled her close to him, wrapping his arms around her waist as he kissed her. "Let me return the favor."

Now it was his turn to drop to his knees. Robson unzipped Natalie's leather pants and pulled them down over her hips. Her panties were soaked, and her thighs glistened. Leaning forward, he placed his mouth over her mound and exhaled. Natalie moaned and thrust herself against his face.

Lowering Natalie to the bottom bunk, Robson stripped off her leather pants and panties, placed his lips against her mound, and slid his tongue deep inside her. She gasped and fell back onto the bunk. She grabbed the back of his head with her right hand and pulled him tightly into her while she bucked against him. He explored Natalie with his mouth, enjoying the smell and taste of her sex and her warmth. Within minutes, he felt his erection pushing its way through his open zipper. Difficult as it was, he stripped out of his clothes while tonguing her.

Natalie moaned, a long, deep sigh. Robson climbed into the bunk and mounted her. She wrapped her legs around him and pulled him in, bucking against him with every thrust. The two fucked for several minutes with wild abandon, enjoying each other and their passion, and exorcising months of horror and fear. Suddenly, Natalie shoved hard against him, clutching her pelvis tight. Her head fell back, and she cried out as an orgasm shuddered through her body. Seeing the woman he loved in such erotic beauty drove him over the edge. Robson drove his erection as deep into Natalie as possible as he exploded inside her.

Physically spent and emotionally satiated, he collapsed on top of Natalie. The two lovers shifted in the bunk, never breaking their embrace, and silently lay beside each other until they dozed off in each other's arms.

SHIT, THE SHOW'S over. O'Bannon turned his attention away from the monitor showing Robson's room and checked out the other screens. He had always thought Natalie was a hot number to look at, especially in her leather outfit. He never realized what a slut she was until now. Maybe now the bitch would not be so uptight. Of course, he could say the same about Robson.

O'Bannon massaged his hard cock through his pants. He wished Tatyana was here so he could get his rocks off. It had been over a week since he had last fucked her ass, and after watching Robson and Natalie, he could use some relief. Unfortunately, she had decided to bunk down with the other bloodsuckers, so that was out of the question for now. No big deal. She was more than willing to take it whenever he wanted, so he'd tap her later. First, he would have to find a place to fuck her without anyone spying on them, which would be hard considering how inundated this place was with security cameras.

He locked into place the security camera for the vampire's room and the camera for Robson's room if he and Natalie woke up horny, and then sat back to wait out the rest of his shift.

CHAPTER FORTY-ONE

STRETCHING IN HIS bunk, Robson felt his muscles groan and snap, a result of last night's strenuous activity. Not that he minded. A few aches and pains were a small price to pay for the contentment he felt. His eyes still closed, he rolled over and felt around the bunk for Natalie but, after several seconds, realized she was not there. He opened his eyes and scanned the room, hoping to find her sleeping in another bunk. Although it was difficult to see anything in the dim illumination emanating from the fluorescent ceiling lights glowing in the corner, he saw she had left. Glancing at his watch, he noticed it was almost five o'clock. He had slept the entire day away. No wonder Natalie had ducked out.

Robson slid out of bed. The floor felt unusually cold against his bare feet. But then, this whole facility was cold and damp despite the central heating. Thank God they would not be spending too much time in this place. Bending over, he picked up his clothes scattered across the floor, putting them on piecemeal. Only when he grabbed his shirt tossed under the bunk did he notice the message Natalie had left him. Robson smiled when he saw the 7.62 mm shells from her Mauser arranged on the mattress in the shape of a heart.

After getting dressed and using the bathroom, Robson headed out, figuring he would drop by the security office to see where the others were. However, upon entering the admin building, he was attracted by an aroma drifting from the mess hall he had nearly forgotten about since the outbreak. Bacon, eggs, bread. And coffee. Real, freshly brewed coffee. Robson did not care if a hundred rotters were lying in wait. He had to get some of that.

As he entered the mess hall, Robson noticed most everyone else had the same idea. Most of the raiding party was seated around the room, eating and chatting amongst themselves. Natalie sat with some of the Angels along a table by the wall. She raised her mug of coffee and blew him a kiss. A second group of Angels and Caylee congregated around another table, intent on a sheet of paper spread out in front of them, the schedule for sitting watch. O'Bannon and Daytona huddled at a third table, laughing at a shared joke. Dravko's crew was nowhere to be seen, which was not surprising considering they ate in private. Nor did he see Compton or his people, which made him feel uneasy.

Robson made his way through the tables, exchanging friendly greetings with everyone as he headed for the counter. Ari came out of the kitchen. She wore a white cloth apron, its front spotted with food stains. She had pulled her hair up in a bun. Robson grabbed an empty plate and stepped up to the grill.

"Morning, boss."

"Morning." Robson held out his plate. "Man, it smells good."

"Thanks. I used to be a short order cook at a run-down greasy spoon near where I went to college."

"Were you any good at it?"

Ari shrugged as she spooned a mound of scrambled eggs into his plate, followed by two slices of toast and six strips of bacon. "It beats an MRE."

"No argument here." Robson took back the plate. He picked up a strip of bacon and popped it into his mouth. He had forgotten how good it tasted. "Where'd you find all this stuff?"

"In the freezer. The military has enough supplies in here to feed us for months."

"Sounds as if you like it here."

"Screw that. It's like living in a mausoleum. At least we'll eat well." Ari nodded to the end of the counter. "Coffee's down there."

"Thanks." Robson grabbed a mug and headed for the dining area. He noticed Thompson entering the mess hall, walking slowly and unsteadily. Jennifer strolled beside him. She kept pace with the colonel but did not help him, although Robson assumed she hovered close to assist if he needed it. The colonel shuffled down the mess hall, finally grabbing a seat at a table near the halfway point. He sat down hard on the bench, wincing in the process. Jennifer bent over to help him swing his legs over the bench and under the table, but he politely waved her off. One at a time, and with considerable effort, Thompson positioned his legs until he faced the table. Jennifer gently patted him on the shoulder, spoke quietly to him, and then headed for the counter to get his breakfast. As she passed by Robson, she greeted him with a cheery hello.

Robson took his plate over to where Thompson sat and slid into the bench opposite him. "Good morning."

"That's a matter of opinion." The colonel tried to say it good-naturedly. He took a deep breath and blanched.

"What's wrong?"

"The smell of the bacon is turning my stomach."

"You don't like bacon?"

"I love it. But, right now, my stomach doesn't."

Robson shifted along the bench a foot, hoping to distance the aroma from Thompson. "Compton says you'll be fine. Just a minor concussion and some banged-up muscles."

"He told me the same thing. Doesn't change the fact that right now my head's throbbing and my stomach's doing flops."

"You'll be fine in a day or two." Robson scooped a forkful of scrambled eggs into his mouth.

"I know. I hate being on sick call when there's so much to

do." Thompson leaned across the table. "What happened back in town?"

"Compton didn't tell you?" asked Robson through a mouthful of food.

Thompson shook his head and winced.

"We were racing through Kenmar-Faxon. The place was overrun with rotters."

"I remember that."

"Our turn came up quickly. Dravko tried making it without slowing and flipped the armored car. You and Dravko got banged up bad. You got a concussion. Dravko broke his arm, but at least it'll regenerate quickly."

"How did we get out?"

"Daytona pulled the school bus alongside, and Tibor pulled us out."

"Tibor?"

"Yeah." Robson pushed another strip of bacon into his mouth.

"How many…? Did we lose anyone?"

"We lost Rashid. A rotter got between the bus and the armored car. Rashid took it out, but the others got to him before we could save him." Robson hesitated.

"Who else?"

"Mad Dog before we entered Site R. While Compton was opening the rear gate near the housing area, he wandered off into one of the houses and shot himself."

"Shit." Thompson bowed his head and closed his eyes for a few seconds. "It was his house. He had left the compound to try and rescue his wife when we went into full lockdown. Poor bastard was stuck out there with all those rotters. It's a miracle he made it to Maine."

"He was a tough son of a bitch."

"Tell me about it."

"What was Mad Dog's real name?"

"It doesn't matter now."

An uneasy silence passed between the two men, interrupted only when Jennifer arrived with a tray containing two plates of food and two cups of coffee. She placed the tray in front of Thompson but did not notice him grimace.

"My God. Did you see the spread Ari cooked up?"

Robson raised a fork piled with scrambled eggs and slid it into his mouth. Thompson moaned and reached for one of the mugs.

"Just coffee for me."

"You need to eat," said Jennifer as she slid onto the bench beside him.

Thompson sighed and pulled the plate toward him. Picking up his fork, he swirled it around the plate, pushing the eggs from one side to the other before finally taking a bite.

They ate and chatted idly. At least Robson and Jennifer did. Thompson spent most of his time rearranging his food, occasionally chewing on a small morsel of eggs or sipping at the coffee. Everyone else finished their meals and sauntered out of the dining hall in small groups, except for Natalie who joined them. After several minutes, Dravko and Tibor entered. The two vampires looked around and, spotting Robson, came over to the table.

As they approached, Thompson swung his legs over the bench and stood to face them. Dravko slowed down and approached cautiously, with Tibor taking up a position to the left and just behind him, neither certain what to expect. Even Robson was prepared to intercede if necessary. The colonel made his way toward Tibor, his eyes locking on the vampire. As Thompson drew closer, he stopped in front of Tibor and extended his hand.

"I heard you saved my life back there in town. Thank you."

Tibor hesitated for a moment, taken aback by the gesture. He finally grasped the colonel's hand and gave it a single pump. "You're welcome."

"I mean it. I owe you." Thompson released Tibor's hand.

"Excuse me. I have to go. It's not the company. I need to get some rest."

"I'll go with you." Jennifer placed her utensils on the plate.

"I'm all right. You stay here." Thompson gave them all a half-hearted wave and sauntered off.

Tibor watched Thompson leave and then turned to the others. "That was weird."

"Damn unusual," added Dravko.

"At least he no longer considers you a threat." Robson drank a large sip of coffee. "How's the arm?"

"Great." Dravko held it up and flexed it several times. "Good as new."

"Glad to hear it. I'm surprised to see you here. You usually don't eat with us."

"I know." Dravko sat on the bench opposite Robson as Tibor stood behind him. "I wanted to touch base on what the game plan is."

Robson grinned. "In a hurry to leave?"

"Hell yeah. I'll take my chances up top in the sunlight rather than stay stuck in this glorified coffin surrounded by rotters."

"Amen to that," chimed in Jennifer.

"We should only be here for two or three days at most. Long enough for Compton to prepare some doses of the vaccine and create backup files for his research." Robson finished off his coffee. "Once that's done, we'll head back to camp."

Tibor huffed. "That's not very comforting considering what we went through to get here."

"We can bypass the populated areas. One of the routes Windows offered skirted most of the major population centers by running farther to the north and west. Problem was, it added several hundred miles and another day to our travel. Considering what we went through to get here, I think the detour is worth it."

"No argument here," said Dravko.

"Do we have enough gas left?" asked Tibor.

"We do now. Natalie and I walked through the facility after we arrived and took inventory. The military has this place well stocked, including hundreds of gallons of gasoline. We can refill the fifty-five-gallon drums and load up with some spare jerry cans we found in the motor pool. That should give us more than enough to get home. Dravko, I'd like you and your people to take care of that."

"Can do."

Robson nodded. "We also found a lot of other supplies. Non-perishables, medicines, clothes. And enough ammo to equip a small army. I want to take that with us rather than abandon it. The Angels will start loading them onto the bus and truck."

"What if Compton disapproves?" asked Dravko.

"Fuck him." Robson suddenly remembered that Jennifer was seated with them and turned to her. "Sorry. Nothing personal against your boss."

"No need to apologize," said Jennifer. "I've thrown my lot in with you."

"That's good to know." Robson turned back to the others. "We also found two Hummers parked by the main entrance. We're taking them with us so we'll have a backup if the bus or truck breaks down."

"What about sitting watch with the security cameras?" asked Dravko.

Natalie leaned forward. "My girls and Daytona have volunteered to sit most of the shifts, so we're covered on that front."

"Are you sure?"

Natalie nodded. "Thanks, though."

"Besides," added Robson. "I need you and Tibor to load the vehicles with supplies. With your strength, you two can get it done in half the time we could."

"You really want to get out of here, don't you?" asked

Dravko.

"You have no idea how badly I want out. Once Compton has everything ready, we'll hit the road." Robson looked around at the others. "Okay, gang. Let's rock."

CHAPTER FORTY-TWO

THOMPSON MADE HIS way from the mess hall to Compton's office at a plodding pace. His hesitation derived not so much from his concussion and aching muscles but because he needed time to contemplate. Even more so than the bumps and bruises to his body, his entire psyche had been dealt a resounding blow, one strong enough to change his way of thinking.

For his entire military career, which spanned almost thirty years, he had sworn to defend the United States against all enemies, foreign and domestic. He had done so without hesitation, whether those enemies sat across from him on the Fulda Gap or the DMZ on the Korean Peninsula, roamed the streets of Mogadishu or Sarajevo, or hid out in the mountains of Afghanistan or the Iraqi desert. Even after the outbreak of the virus, his enemies were clearly defined—the revenants and the vampires who had unleashed this horror on mankind. In those instances when he had to kill the enemy, he had been able to dehumanize them, mentally distancing them from their humanity by derisively viewing them as commies, gooks, or ragheads. Because they were not among the living, it was easy to dehumanize the revenants or bloodsuckers. Until now.

Upon first arriving at Fort McClary, he had been as taken aback as the doctor by the presence of vampires on the compound. He did not trust the bloodsuckers. Nor did he have much confidence in the humans for blindly putting their faith in them, feeling Paul and the others had allowed the rotter apocalypse to cloud their better judgment and bring the enemy into their fold. It was why he went along with Compton when the doctor said if Paul could not be entrusted to ensure the safety of what was left of the nation, it was up to the two of them to do so. Yet the more time he spent with Robson's team, the more he realized that somehow this bizarre alliance worked. Despite there being only a handful of vampires left in the world, Elena had willingly banished one of her own to certain death to maintain the détente between the living and the undead. And rather than retaliate, which would have been the natural instinct, the vampires constantly put their lives on the line to protect the humans. Sultanic had become infected trying to save Whitehouse. Tibor had risked being turned by revenants to rescue him from the armored car, despite his open hostility toward the vampires. Deep down, Thompson knew if the roles had been reversed, he would not have done the same.

The world had changed immeasurably in the past eight months. More importantly, so had his way of thinking.

Though the realization had been slow in coming, Thompson now knew Compton was wrong to try and eliminate the vampires. The two of them had devised a plan to dispose of them shortly after arriving at camp. Until today, he had every intention of carrying it out. Now his conscience could no longer allow it. He had to convince Compton to abandon the scheme, which would be more challenging than it sounded. Whenever the doctor got something stuck in his head, he pursued it with a single-minded determination. He still viewed the situation in black and white, refusing to see the shades of gray that had developed. Thompson had finally seen the truth, although to do so he nearly had to forfeit his life. If he talked to Compton and explained that the situation was not as clear cut as he himself had seen it only a few days ago, maybe he could convince the doctor to stand down. No one would argue that mankind had experienced almost total genocide thanks to the vampires. Yet that did not alter the fact that what Compton intended was no different. Whether it was four vampires or four billion humans, genocide was still genocide, and he would have no part in it.

Hopefully, he could convince Compton to see things the same way.

Thompson carefully planned out what he wanted to say, walking around the lab building several times until he felt confident he had chosen the correct words. Once he had rehearsed his speech a dozen times, the colonel entered and headed for the main laboratory. As expected, he found Compton hard at work on the computer, burning his notes onto CD-ROMs. Summoning his courage, Thompson opened the door and stepped inside.

Compton was so engrossed in his work he did not hear him enter. The colonel knocked on the open door. "May I come in?"

Compton glanced over his shoulder briefly before turning back to the computer. "Please."

Thompson closed the door behind him and crossed the lab until he stood behind the doctor. "How much more do you have to do?"

"Not much. The last batch of vaccines is incubating now. In the meantime, I've been transferring my files to four CD-ROMs and two thumb drives. You and I can each carry a thumb drive, and I'll give the CD-ROMs to Robson and his people. That should give us enough backup copies to ensure at least one of them gets to Omaha." Compton looked up at Thompson. A look of concern shone on his face. He spun his chair around to face the colonel. "How are you feeling?"

"Better than yesterday."

"Are you still in pain?"

"A little, but nothing the drugs can't manage. Why? Don't I look well?"

"You look well enough. You seem distracted."

"I am. But not by the pain." Thompson took a deep breath to steady his nerves. He pulled out a chair from the adjacent workstation, turned it to face Compton, and sat down. "I wanted to talk about your plans for the vampires."

Compton looked out of the corner of his eye at the security camera. The tiny red light glowed, signifying it was not transmitting. He leaned closer to the colonel and lowered his voice. "Everything's set. Once we inoculate Robson and the others, t we'll take care of the vampires."

"That's what I want to talk to you about. I think we should reconsider."

"You have a better plan?"

Thompson shook his head. "I don't think Dravko's people deserve to die."

"Dravko's people." Compton spoke the words slowly, emphasizing each one. He leaned back in his chair and studied Thompson, his brow crinkling with disapproval. "You're beginning to sound like Paul and the others."

"Maybe they're right."

"Do you honestly believe that?"

Thompson paused for a moment as he considered his response. "Yes, I do."

Compton broke eye contact and pushed his chair back to his workstation. "I'm beginning to think the concussion is affecting your judgment."

"My judgment's fine."

"Really? You're starting to exhibit the same affectation for those creatures as Robson and the others."

Thompson stood and crossed over to the doctor. "I realize this sounds strange, especially coming from me, but I've watched how the vampires interact with the rest of the group. They seemed to have integrated themselves until they think and act like humans."

"But they're not human," Compton shot back in a low but stern voice. "Wild animals can be trained to live with humans, but they're still wild animals and usually turn on their masters. You'd do well to remember that the vampires released this hell onto mankind in the first place."

"I know. And they suffered for it as much as we did."

Compton turned to face Thompson. "And because of that, I'm supposed to forgive them? Let's hug and make up, and hope they don't bite us in the neck while we're embracing?"

"Yes."

Snorting in disgust, Compton returned to his work. "You should go back to bed and rest. I need to finish up."

"You need to listen to me," Thompson said forcefully, growing impatient. "Like it or not, the vampires are integral to Robson's group. And we need Robson if we hope to get the vaccine back to Omaha, mass produce it, and start taking the world back from the revenants. If you go ahead with your plan behind Robson's back, we're screwed. We'll be lucky if he doesn't take the vaccine and abandon us here."

Compton sat back in his chair, focusing his eyes on the wall as he contemplated what the colonel had said. Thompson did not say anything, desperately hoping he had made a connection with his friend.

After several seconds, Compton spun his chair to the colonel, his normal pleasantness returning. "You're right. Not only about needing Robson, but also about being honest with him. We owe him that much."

Thompson felt every nerve in his body relax. He had psyched himself up to anticipate the worst, although he was unsure how he would have dealt with that situation. Fortunately, Compton saw reason.

"Thank you, sir."

"You're the one who deserves my gratitude. I never would have made it this far without you." Compton looked at his watch. "It's getting late. You should get your rest. You're going to need it for the ride back."

Thompson stood up and pushed his chair back to its workstation. "What about you?"

"I want to finish the backup files of my notes before I go to bed."

"As long as you take your own advice about getting some rest. Good night."

"Good night." Compton waited until Thompson reached the door before calling out. "And colonel, thanks again for looking out for me."

"That's what you pay me for, sir."

Exiting the lab, Thompson returned to his room, suddenly feeling emotionally and physically drained.

CHAPTER FORTY-THREE

DRAVKO AND TATYANA had spent the past few hours loading up the school bus, the Ryder, and the two Humvees with all the supplies they had discovered in the facility. They would be more than adequately stocked for the run back to camp. They had tapped into the facility's fuel storage tanks, topped off the remaining fifty-five-gallon drums, and filled more than a dozen jerry cans found at the motor pool. In addition to the eight M-16s left in the Humvees, Daytona had discovered an arms locker off the main security room that contained another twenty M-16s, five shotguns, ten Glock 23 semiautomatics, a .357 Magnum, thousands of rounds of ammunition, plus two dozen each of smoke and concussion grenades, all for crowd control. All the weapons were divided up amongst the convoy, except for the Magnum which Robson had commandeered for his own use. The remainder of the stash included surgical equipment and medical supplies, two biohazard suits, three portable generators, crates of engine oil, containers of bottled water, and as many boxes of MREs as they could fit onto the vehicles. Jennifer had even found in the infirmary twenty pints of whole blood Robson confiscated and surreptitiously passed to Dravko.

Packing the vehicles had been time consuming. They had to make sure not only that everything was divided in such a way the loss of one or two vehicles would not mean the loss of any one group of items, but they also had to make certain there was enough room for the group to travel comfortably. The

Ryder housed the three generators and the bulk of the supplies, while the two Humvees fit what few things could be stored in the cargo area. When it came to the school bus, every other row of seats was packed as tightly as possible and the contents tied down.

"That ought to do it." Dravko finished securing the last of the supplies on the school bus. He stood up, stretching the muscles in his arms. "Where did Tibor run off to?"

"I sent him off to the fire and rescue station to see what he could find," answered Tatyana.

"That was over an hour ago."

"You want me to go check on him?"

"No. I'm sure he's okay. But we could have used his help."

As if on cue, Tibor emerged from between the lab and dorm buildings pushing a cart filled with gear. He wore a huge smile, which wrinkled the scar across his face in an awkward manner. Since Tibor rarely smiled, Dravko reasoned he must have stumbled upon something good. He and Tatyana stepped off the bus to greet him.

"What did you find?"

"There wasn't much there that we could take with us. Mostly axes and some heavy duty crowbars we could use as weapons. But look at this."

Tibor beamed as he removed what looked like a silver blanket and unfolded it. When he spread it out in front of him, Dravko saw that it measured eight feet square.

"What is it?"

"An asbestos blanket. I found ten of them amongst the rescue supplies."

Tatyana looked puzzled. "What are they used for?"

"You throw them on somebody who's on fire to douse the flames."

Now it was Dravko's turn to be puzzled. "You plan on spontaneously combusting on the ride home?"

Tibor's smile morphed into a frown. "They're heavy and

267

impervious to fire, which means they're also impervious to sunlight. I figure we put three on the bus, three on the truck, and two with each Humvee. That way, if we get trapped on any of the vehicles at sunrise, we can protect ourselves."

As a demonstration, Tibor bent over and whipped the blanket over his shoulders. It covered him completely.

Dravko nodded his approval. "Good idea."

Tibor stood up straight and refolded the blanket. "I'll put them into the vehicles. How much more do we have to load up?"

"We're done."

"Oh. Sorry." The tone in Tibor's voice, though, indicated he did not regret missing most of the hard work.

At that moment, the blast door opened. The three vampires braced themselves, not sure what was on the other side. They were very relieved when Robson and Thompson entered. The colonel closed the door behind them.

"I didn't know you went outside," said Dravko.

"We wanted to check on the radio antennae to see if we could get a message to Omaha."

"Any luck?"

"No," said Thompson. "Looks like a bolt of lightning struck it. Everything's fried."

"Can you fix it?"

Thompson shook his head. "Not without an engineering squad. No big deal, though. The radio's still intact. I'll remove it from the communications room and take it with us. We should be able to reach Omaha with it once we're back in Maine."

"Do it in the morning," said Robson looking at his watch. "It's getting late, and we need to get some rest."

"No arguments here." Thompson offered a friendly salute and strolled off.

Robson turned to Dravko. "You almost done?"

"Pretty much. We have a few more things to pack up and

then we're good."

"Looks like I'm not needed here. Call me if anything happens." Robson headed off to the dorm building.

Once both humans were out of earshot, Tibor leaned closer to Dravko. "It looks like the colonel is taking a liking to us."

"Maybe. I still don't trust him or the doctor."

CHAPTER FORTY-FOUR

ROBSON ENTERED HIS room and flicked on the light switch. A soft voice startled him.

"It's about time you showed up."

Robson spun around. Natalie lay in the bottom bunk, the blanket pulled up around her. He immediately noticed her shoulders were bare and smiled in anticipation. "Have you been waiting long?"

"Long enough. And I'm chilly."

Robson slid out of his leather jacket. "Is it too cold in here?"

"That's not the reason I'm chilly." Natalie pulled the blanket down to her waist. She wore nothing underneath. Her dark hair flowed over her shoulders and rested on her breasts. He admired how beautiful she looked. For so many months he had thought of Natalie as a soldier, the leader of the group's rotter hunters. Only in the past few days had he seen the other side of Natalie—the passionate, vibrant, exciting woman she truly was.

"Hurry up and join me."

"Patience," said Robson as he began stripping out of his shirt. "God things come to those who wait."

Natalie ran the tip of her tongue across her lips. "I can't wait."

"What would the Angels say?"

"They're happy for me. They think if I'm getting laid, I won't be as much of a hard ass on them."

"Come on. I love your hard ass."

Natalie frowned. "You're such a romantic."

Robson sat on the side of the bunk to take off his boots. Natalie scooted closer, running her hand along his back. "Why didn't we do this sooner?"

Robson did not immediately respond. He knew the reason why. It was because of Susan. The guilt flooded his conscience. He had not acted earlier on his feelings for Natalie because he did not deserve to love again.

Natalie sensed his mood and drew closer. Her tone was tender. "It's Susan, isn't it?"

He sighed deeply.

"You can't go on blaming yourself for what happened. You couldn't have saved her."

"I didn't even try." It was the first time Robson had admitted that to anyone. He shifted on the bunk so he could face Natalie, but kept his head lowered so he would not have to look her in the eyes. "When we were trying to escape, she couldn't keep up. I got ahead of her, and when I looked back, she was being chased by swarmers. Half a dozen closed in on her. She screamed for me to help, begged me to save her. Instead of going back, I ran on ahead. I... left her to die."

Robson looked up, expecting to see Natalie glaring at him in horror and revulsion. Instead, he saw only sympathy and understanding. Tears formed in her eyes and rolled down her cheeks.

"You've been living with that the whole time?"

All he could was nod and avert his gaze again.

Natalie placed her hands on Robson's face and raised it, forcing him to look at her. "Stop beating yourself up. You have nothing to feel guilty about."

"How can you say that? I killed Susan."

"No," Natalie said forcefully. "The swarmers killed Susan. You couldn't help her without getting yourself killed. All you did was watch her die. Everyone here has watched a loved one die because they couldn't help them."

Robson clasped Natalie's hands and gently pulled them away from his face, then lowered his head in shame. "The guilt is killing me."

"Don't let it. You may not have been able to help Susan but look how many lives you've saved since then. None of us would have survived this long if it wasn't for you. Everyone at camp owes their lives to you. So don't fall apart on us now. They need you." Natalie cupped his face and turned it towards her. "I need you."

Robson felt nothing but adoration and respect for Natalie. Instead of condemning him, she had offered him acceptance and understanding. It was more than he could have hoped for, and so much more than he deserved. If Natalie could forgive him his sin and still love him, then maybe he could afford to do so. At that moment, all the pent-up emotions that had eaten away at his soul dried up. Anger. Guilt. Self-loathing. Solace filled the void, a solace he had not known for months. He burst into tears, relieved that his pain could finally be reconciled.

Natalie reached out, wrapped her arms around him, and pulled him close. She comforted him until his crying devolved into a series of heavy sobs. Maneuvering Robson so he laid beside her on the bed, she wrapped the blanket over them and held him close until they both fell asleep in each other's arms.

CHAPTER FORTY-FIVE

*W*HAT A FUCKIN' *waste of a day.* O'Bannon yanked open the door to the dorm building with enough force that it slammed against the outer wall, the bang echoing throughout the facility. Cracks spider webbed through the glass pane. O'Bannon could give a shit about the door or whether he woke the others. He did not even bother closing it behind him. Instead, he stormed down the corridor heading for his room.

After his shift monitoring the surveillance cameras in the security office, he found himself with nothing to do because the Angels would man the remaining shifts. He went to check in with Robson, hoping to help him plan the route back to camp, only to find out not only had Robson and Natalie plotted the return trip without him, but he and the colonel had then gone topside to check on the radio antenna. *So much for being third in command.*

Jennifer had suggested the fuckin' bloodsuckers were packing the convoy for the ride back and could use his assistance, but he'd be damned before he helped them. He grabbed some rest, or at least tried to. The shift work had screwed up his schedule. He laid there for two hours but still could not fall asleep. Saying the hell with it, he decided to take a tour of the facility. Rather than occupy him for a few hours, it merely provided him time to stew in his own anger.

He had a right to be angry. He had spent months tolerating Paul's turn-the-other-cheek bullshit when it came to the bloodsuckers. When Compton first arrived at camp, he could sense the doctor and the colonel knew the score when it came to dealing with them and hoped they could get Paul to see the light and finally purge the world of this evil. Instead, this mission had only imbedded the tolerance of the bloodsuckers into the others. No one seemed upset about how Dravko and the others had savaged those bandits back in Pennsylvania when given the chance. That could just as easily have been their group, and more than likely *would* be before too long if someone did not stop them. Rather than see the bloodsuckers for the monsters they were, Robson and the others thanked them. Like a pack of sheep thanking the wolves for inviting them to dinner. Even Thompson seemed to have a change of heart after Tibor had saved him. Big fucking deal. The bloodsuckers had saved a few of them during this mission, but that could not balance out the billions of humans turned into rotters due to them.

However, the free time did give O'Bannon a chance to think things over. He knew he could not stay any longer with Robson and the others, waiting patiently for Dravko to turn on them. As difficult a decision as it was to make, especially after seeing how dangerous the world had become, he had made up his mind that if an opportunity presented itself on the way back to camp, he would set out on his own. If not, then he would ask Compton to take him back to Omaha where at least he would get the chance to do something good for the country.

Entering his room, he found Tatyana waiting for him. She lay across the bed, the covers pulled up around her waist. Her clothes sat in a pile on the floor. As he closed the door, Tatyana rolled over and propped herself on one arm.

O'Bannon looked away and slid off his jacket. "What are you doing here?"

"Waiting for you." Tatyana pulled down the covers to reveal her naked body.

As attractive as he found Tatyana, she was not human, and right now he wanted nothing to do with her. "Not tonight."

"Come on," she cooed. "It's been a week since we've made love."

"We don't make love. We fuck."

"So, let's fuck."

Tatyana partially morphed into a vampire, allowing her teeth to grow into fangs. She bared them at O'Bannon and snarled, the gesture meant to be one of seduction. It had the opposite effect, however. In that moment, Tatyana represented everything he hated. Not just the vampires, who destroyed his world and reduced him to a daily struggle to survive in rotter hell. She personified his sense of isolation in a twisted world where the only thing that cared for him was a bloodsucker, and his own self-loathing for feeling attracted to something he despised so fiercely. Instead of inspiring lust and passion, her gesture filled him with fury and hatred.

Grabbing Tatyana by the shoulder, O'Bannon flung her off the bed onto the hard floor. She responded by arching her pelvis and plunging a finger into her sex, masturbating until her lips glistened. He yanked his pants down around his ankles and dropped to the floor behind Tatyana. She fingered herself furiously, her breathing becoming a shallow moan. Leaning over, O'Bannon rammed his cock into her. Tatyana bucked into him. Her head arched back as she practically howled in ecstasy. It did nothing to excite O'Bannon. He did not want to fuck. He wanted to hurt.

He began slamming his cock into her as violently as he could. After the first few strokes, her moans changed to grunts. She tried to squirm free. O'Bannon clutched Tatyana by the hair on either side of her head and yanked her into him, holding her in place as he violated her.

"Stop it. You're hu—"

O'Bannon raised her head and slammed it against the floor, momentarily stunning her. Her squeal of pain drove him over the edge. He slammed his cock as deep into her as possible just as he exploded. Tatyana moaned. Not in passion, but in anger and humiliation.

When he was spent, O'Bannon climbed off Tatyana and stood. She quickly scurried away on hands and knees, backing herself against the opposite wall where she curled up in a fetal position. "What was that about?"

"You said you wanted to fuck, so I fucked you." O'Bannon picked up Tatyana's blouse from off the floor and used it to wipe off his dick.

"That wasn't fucking," she yelled. "That was rape."

"You wanted honest emotion, bitch. You got it." O'Bannon flung the stained blouse at her before pulling up his pants. "Now get out."

"But I love you."

"Love me?" O'Bannon spun around. His fists clenched in anger as he fought back the urge to cut off Tatyana's head. "You're not even human. You have about as much emotion as the rotters."

"Why are you trying to hurt me like this?"

"Because your kind destroyed my world."

"I had no part in that," Tatyana cried. "You're still alive."

"No, I *exist*. My life is now a daily struggle to survive in the hell your kind created. And the worst part is that the only thing that cares for me in this miserable world is a fucking inhuman bloodsucker."

Tatyana rose to her feet slowly and deliberately. O'Bannon noticed the pain and anguish she had felt a moment before was now replaced by a sneer of revulsion. *Good*, he thought. That emotion he could deal with. She fully morphed into her vampiric form. Her fingers elongated into talons, the palms out to her side and ready to attack, as her lips curled back to expose the mouth full of fangs. Her eyes turned crimson, intensified by her hatred. She growled as she moved toward him.

Without taking his eyes off Tatyana, O'Bannon reached up to the top bunk, stuck his hand under the mattress, and removed a pair of stakes. Holding one in each hand, he assumed a knife fighting stance.

"Bring it on, bitch."

Tatyana stopped and eyed him. He could not place the emotion he saw in them, uncertain whether it was fear or disillusionment, not that it mattered. When she took a tentative step backwards, he knew he had won.

"You'd really kill me?" she asked.

"In a heartbeat."

Tatyana reverted to her human form, a shattered expression on her face. "Didn't I ever mean anything to you?"

"You're a mattress, hon. Something to sleep on." Still holding the stakes in each hand, he used his right foot to kick her clothes across the floor. "Now get out before I stick this in you."

Bending over, Tatyana scooped up her clothes and raced out of the room, forgetting to close the door behind her. Once the sound of her running feet faded down the hall, O'Bannon stepped over to the door to shut and lock it. He strolled back to the bunk and crawled into bed, still holding a stake in each hand in case Tatyana or one of the other bloodsuckers tried to even the score later that night. He did not have much time to contemplate that option, though, since he fell into a deep sleep shortly after his head hit the pillow.

CHAPTER FORTY-SIX

THE ROTTERS WEDGED between the two perimeter fences shuffled along in one mass, each following the other in a glacially-slow clockwise movement that after several hours would bring them back to where they started. According to the logbooks, they had been trapped between the twin gates two weeks ago so the convoy could slip out of the facility unscathed, and since then had been endlessly circling the closure. It reminded Ari of the cattle she used to watch on her grandfather's farm as they were herded into a confined area before being shipped off to slaughter. Except these things did not evoke the same empathy in her the cows did.

Even so, Ari could not take her eyes off the monitor that belonged to the security camera focused on the front gate. She had been transfixed by the horde for most of her shift in the control room, unable to avert her attention. This was the first time she was able to truly study the rotters up close, or at least as close as the camera could get her. By zooming the lens in and adjusting the angle to track them, she watched select rotters for fifteen or twenty minutes at a time. It left her feeling empty and depressed.

At one time each of these things had been an individual like her. They had loved ones, they had jobs or classes or something that occupied their lives, they had felt love and anger, happiness and despair. They had harbored dreams and aspirations that did not include joining the ranks of the living dead. The key word here was "had." As she watched them hour after hour, she saw nothing that indicated feelings. No signs of physical pain. No signs of emotion. No signs of individual thought. They huddled around each other, a mindless mass stripped of every shred of humanity. The only tenuous link they had to the living was their instinct to feed.

At one point, a deer wandered out of the darkness and approached the fence, coming to within a few feet before the rotters saw it. Those closest to the deer began moaning and clutching at the chain links, sloughing the decayed flesh off their fingers. The others around them joined in, oblivious as to what caused the commotion, generating a mass frenzy. As expected, the deer bolted back to the safety of the forest and, once it was gone, the rotters quieted down and resumed their shambling.

Then something caught her attention. She noticed it at the far end of the monitor. Shifting the camera to the right, she focused on a female rotter pressed up against the fence and wearing a soiled and torn hospital gown. It moved more awkwardly than the others because it protected something cradled in its left arm. When the rotter shifted slightly so it faced the camera, Ari saw that it clutched a baby. The umbilical cord was still attached, draping down from the infant's belly before disappearing under the gown. Its tiny arms and legs twitched, while its tiny mouth suckled on the mother's emaciated breast.

Ari wanted to weep from despair. She reached up with her right and fingered her mermaid pendant, a gift from her own mother on her sixteenth birthday, and now her only link to humanity.

Daytona entered the room, holding a thermos of hot coffee. "The cavalry has arrived."

"Thank God." For the first time in hours, Ari looked away from the monitor.

"Watcha doin'?"

"Studying the end of mankind."

He glanced over at the monitor. "Jesus, kid. Why are you torturing yourself like that?"

"They're hard to ignore." Ari glanced back at the monitor. "Don't you ever imagine who they were when things were normal?"

"No."

"But look." Ari pointed to the monitor. "There's one rotter in there wearing a cheerleader's outfit. One is dressed in a tuxedo. Another one's in a business suit. I can't help but wonder what they were doing when they were turned."

"I don't think about it because I don't want to think of them as human. They're not anymore. If I think of them as people, I wouldn't be able to kill them." Daytona placed his hand gently on her shoulder and squeezed. "And you shouldn't be thinking of them that way either."

"It's hard not to."

"They're dead, kid. Their souls are in a better place. What you're seeing there are walking corpses."

Ari wanted to believe him, wanted to reassure herself that there was nothing human left in their shells of a body. Then her eyes fell on the rotter mother clutching her dead infant and she started to doubt.

"Come on, kid. Shift's over. Get some rest. You need it."

Ari turned away from the monitor and stood. She wished Daytona a good night and headed back to her room, trying to force the image of rotter maternal instincts from her mind. Though she doubted she ever would.

CHAPTER FORTY-SEVEN

ROBSON WOKE UP to find Natalie cuddled against him. He lay there for several minutes, admiring everything about her. How her chin rested on his chest and one arm draped over him, protecting him. How she breathed deeply yet sedately, a sign she felt safe around him. How even though they were buried hundreds of feet underground and surrounded by rotters, she could still sleep with a smile on her face, content with what life had thrown her way. The other night when they made love was the first time he had been with a woman since the outbreak began, and he had almost forgotten how alive the touch of another person made you feel. His contentment went beyond the physical, which had been fantastic. Emotionally, he felt more alive than he had in months. Despite having admitted he left Susan to die, Natalie still wanted to be with him, and trusted him enough to open her heart. Even more importantly, her faith had allowed him to forgive himself. With that heavy burden lifted from his shoulders, Robson could now begin to live again.

Natalie awoke a few minutes later. She greeted him with a warm grin and a good morning kiss, which led to a passionate embrace. They made love, this time slowly and sensually, savoring the moment, exploring each other physically and emotionally, and strengthening the bond between them.

After showering and getting dressed, they headed for the cafeteria. As they walked, Natalie clasped his hand, sliding her fingers between his and gently squeezing. Robson found the dichotomy striking. Over the past few months, he had watched Natalie shoot rotters with military precision, standing her ground against packs of the living dead without flinching. Now she acted like a teenager going to the prom. It made him adore her even more.

If he could find such happiness in a world as fucked up as this, there may be hope for what little remained of mankind.

As they entered the cafeteria, Robson noticed that the others were already eating breakfast except for Compton, Thompson, Jennifer, and Tatyana. Everyone watched him and Natalie intently. A small band of Angels and Caylee were seated by the counter leaned closer and began chatting in hushed whispers. Dravko, who sat against the wall with Tibor, raised his coffee mug to Robson as if giving him the thumbs up. Robson was not sure why, but he felt extremely self-conscious.

That feeling was intensified when they stepped up to the counter and grabbed some plates. Ari stuck the ladle into the scrambled eggs and asked, "I suppose you two will want an extra serving to keep your energy up?"

"Jesus," said Robson as he felt his cheeks flush. "How many people know?"

"Everyone." Ari began serving.

"How?"

Ari grinned broadly. "Thin walls and gossip."

Robson stared at her, speechless.

"Relax," said Ari as she dropped several strips of bacon on each plate. "We're all happy for you."

"Thanks." Natalie beamed.

"It's about time. What took you two so long to hook up?"

Natalie leaned to her right and gently nudged Robson in the arm. "He's shy."

Robson figured by now his complexion must be the same color as the tomato juice.

Grabbing some coffee and utensils, the two crossed the cafeteria and took a seat with Dravko.

"Morning, boss." Dravko took a sip of coffee. "Rough night?"

"Don't you start." Robson quickly scooped up a slice of bacon because, truth be known, he was famished after the morning round of lovemaking. "Where do we stand with the preparations?"

"We're all set to roll once Compton's ready. We finished packing the vehicles. There's barely enough room in there for us, but we're bringing so much stuff back with us we won't need to make a supply run for months."

"Good. Once we get back to camp, I want to stay put for a while."

"I'm sure you do," Tibor said with a grin.

Before Robson could respond to the quip, Dravko continued. "Daytona checked out the vehicles before he went on shift. He says they're fine. So once the vaccines are prepared, we're set to go."

"Good. The sooner we leave this place, the better I'll feel."

"I don't blame you. This place makes me nervous."

"Which route are we taking home?" asked Tibor.

Robson took a drink of coffee to wash down his bacon. "Natalie and I charted a way home that takes us north to upstate New York. Then we'll swing east, cut across central Vermont and New Hampshire where rotter activity should be minimal, and return home via Portland. It'll add a couple of hundred miles and a few days to the trip, but we'll avoid major population centers."

Everyone nodded uncomfortably, not wanting to remember what they had gone through outside of Harrisburg.

"Once we figure out who the drivers will be, we'll sit down and go over the route. I have copies of all the maps in my room."

The conversation devolved into small talk for the next ten minutes. The Angels finished their breakfast and filed out in small groups, most of them casting an approving glance at

Robson and Natalie. She smiled back while he tried to hide his embarrassment. Soon the only ones who remained were those seated at their table and O'Bannon, who sat sullenly on the opposite end of the cafeteria, drinking coffee and staring at the wall.

Jennifer entered the cafeteria. She looked around and, upon seeing Robson, made her way to him.

"Good morning," said Robson as she approached.

Jennifer looked at her watch. "Shit. It is morning. I've been working with Compton all night to copy his notes and formulas."

"When will the vaccines be ready?" asked Natalie.

"They're done. We finished the last batch about an hour ago. That's why I'm here. The doctor wants you to join him and Thompson in the lab."

"Now?"

Jennifer nodded. "If you can. They're waiting for you."

"Should I come along?" asked Dravko.

"I wouldn't. Compton doesn't want to be around you any more than you want to be around him. No offense."

"None taken," Dravko replied.

Robson stood to leave. Natalie wolfed down the last of her coffee. "Hang on. I'll join you."

As the two crossed the mess hall, O'Bannon rose from his chair and approached. "Mind if I come along? I'd like to hear what he has to say."

"Be my guest."

The three left the mess hall and headed for the lab.

CHAPTER FORTY-EIGHT

A S ROBSON, NATALIE, and O'Bannon walked down the
hall of the laboratory building, the anticipation seemed
palpable. With the last batch of vaccines completed, they could
head back to camp, which suited Robson perfectly since he
hated this facility. Once in Maine, he could concentrate on
ensuring Compton and the vaccines reached Omaha so the
remnants of the government could begin inoculating troops so
they could take back the country from the rotters. And who
knew? Maybe he and Natalie could one day live a normal live.

He knocked on the door to the medical lab. A few seconds
later, Thompson opened the door and ushered them inside.
Compton stood by a sink in the corner of the room, meticu-
lously washing his hands. On a table in front of them sat four
steel briefcases, each the length and width of a laptop computer
and eight inches thick. Three were closed. The lid to the fourth
lay open. Each half of the briefcase was filled with dark gray
foam bedding. One hundred glass vials four inches in length sat
in four rows of twenty-five, each inserted into holes equidistant
from one another. Robson assumed these were to transport the
vaccine. To the left of the briefcases stood a wooden stand
holding another eighteen vials. Beside that sat a cloth pouch
folded over and a Taser.

Compton finished washing his hands. He flipped off the
excess water and wiped his hands on a towel. "Thank you for
coming."

"Jennifer said you've finished preparing the vaccines."

"Finally, yes." The doctor dropped the towel onto the counter by the sink and crossed over to the table. "Each of these cases contains one hundred doses. I've also made six copies of the formula and my notes. I'll keep one each with me and Thompson. The others will accompany each case. We'll put one in each vehicle in the convoy. I figure that way if we lose any vehicle on the way back, we don't lose all our work."

"Good thinking."

Compton moved over to the wooden stand. "These vials are for us. I'll inoculate each of you before we set out."

"How much time do we need before the vaccine takes affect?" asked Natalie.

"An hour at most. Once the vaccine makes its way into the bloodstream, you'll be immune to infection if a revenant bites you."

"Thank God," said Natalie.

Robson counted the vials. "You're three doses short. Have you already started the inoculations?"

"No. All the doses are prepared."

"Who's not getting inoculated?" asked Natalie.

"The vampires."

Robson felt his chest tighten at the doctor's cavalier answer. Instead of yelling at Compton, which was his initial reaction, he demanded in a sharp tone, "Why are they being left out?"

"Because the vaccine is not effective on vampires. Their physiology and blood type are too different to be compatible with any vaccine prepared for humans."

"You knew this when you arrived at our camp?"

"Of course."

"And you still allowed Dravko and his people to risk their lives on this mission without telling them the vaccine wouldn't help them?"

Thompson stepped up beside the doctor, trying to diffuse the deteriorating situation. "Mike, before you get angry with us, remember it wasn't our decision to have Dravko's people join us. We wanted to leave them behind. When we first mentioned to Paul the idea of retrieving the vaccine, he insisted it be a joint effort between humans and vampires. He wouldn't entertain the idea of a humans-only run down here."

"Did you warn him the vaccine was ineffective on vampires?"

Thompson shook his head. "We thought about it but, in the end, we decided not to. We were afraid that if Paul found out, he wouldn't sanction the mission."

Robson was still furious. "Why didn't you tell *us*?"

"Would you have gone on this mission if I had?" Compton asked the question honestly without trying to be condescending. He spread his hands out on either side of the cases, like a messiah calling forth his flock. "You must understand that getting this vaccine safely to Omaha may be the only chance mankind has of surviving the Revenant Virus. I'll do whatever it takes to accomplish that, especially if all it takes is keeping the truth from you and ruffling a few feathers."

As angry as he was, Compton could not argue with the doctor's reasoning.

Natalie stepped over and looked at the open case of vials. "Can you create a vaccine for the vampires?"

"It took months to create the vaccine for humans, and that was only after seventeen failed attempts at inoculation. They probably wouldn't survive the trial stage."

"I'm willing to take the risk," snorted O'Bannon.

Robson glared at him furiously.

"This is what I have for them." Compton moved over to the cloth pouch and pulled it toward him. He unfolded the flaps, revealing three medical hypodermic needles safely nestled in cloth slits. A dark red fluid filled each hypodermic needle. "Each hypodermic needle contains a highly concentrated dose of the Revenant Virus, enough to change them over in a matter of minutes. The transformation will be quick and relatively painless. We'll administer the injection as if we were giving them a vaccine and, when they turn, we'll stun them with the Taser and dispose of them."

Everyone stared at Compton in disbelief. It took Robson several seconds for the words to register. Before he could protest, Compton continued.

"I originally intended to use morphine or another sedative, but being uncertain about their physiology, I thought this was the best way to ensure success."

Robson stepped up to the table across from Compton and stared directly into his eyes. "You... you're talking about infecting Dravko and the others and executing them."

"Of course," replied Compton, as if he was responding to a student who could not grasp a simple theory. "We must infect them first, otherwise they'll fight back. This is the most humane way I could think of to euthanize them."

"Euthanize?" Robson backed away from the table to rejoin Natalie and O'Bannon, all the while keeping his gaze fixed on Compton and the colonel. He suddenly wished he had brought his sidearm with him. "You're talking genocide."

Compton's expression hardened, the pleasant features showing disapproval. "I take exception with that word. I'm not talking about killing anything human. The vampires are *things*. Ridding the world of them is no different than putting down a family pet."

O'Bannon sneered. "Except we'd feel bad about putting down a pet."

Robson stepped a little closer to Natalie, suddenly feeling outnumbered. He glared at the doctor. "And you thought I'd go along with this?"

"I thought you were a reasonable man," Compton shrugged. "Clearly I was mistaken."

"How can you think this is reasonable?" asked Natalie.

"Because it is." Compton spoke not as someone pleading his cause, but as someone attempting to get others to see the light. "The vampires have always been the enemy of mankind.

They stole and released the Revenant Virus to keep us preoccupied with saving our own lives so we wouldn't hunt them. They're responsible for the murder of seven billion people. The only reason they allied with you was to save themselves. Without you, the vampires would have become extinct months ago. I don't see Paul as some visionary who is ushering a new era of peace with the vampires. Paul is the one who aided and abetted mass genocide, not me."

"We've had no problems with the vampires since they joined us," argued Natalie. "They've changed."

"Have they?" Compton placed his hands on the table and leaned closer. "Once man has turned the tide on the revenants and defeated them, then what? Do you think Elena will still be willing to abide by your peace when the one thing that posed a threat to them is gone? Do you think the vampires will be content living off the blood of farm animals? Like us, they'll want to rebuild their numbers. They'll start with you and the others in your little camp. Maybe Paul and the rest of you are naïve and trusting, but not me. I have an opportunity to rid the world of two evils plaguing mankind, and I'm going to take advantage of it."

"I'm with you, doc." O'Bannon spoke with a conviction and enthusiasm Robson had never seen before.

He looked at Thompson. "Did you know about this?"

The colonel averted his eyes. "Yes."

Since persuasion did not work, Robson tried the only tool he had left. His authority. "Sorry, doctor. I can't allow this."

Compton chuckled. "It's not your decision."

"I'm in charge—"

"No," Compton cut him off. "You're in charge when we're on the road. In this facility, *I'm* in command."

"But—"

"This discussion is closed."

Robson noticed O'Bannon had moved away from his group and now stood at the end of the table closer to Compton.

Thompson remained behind the doctor, avoiding eye contact. Robson figured he had better get out of here now before one of them got the idea to detain him. He turned around and headed out, pushing Natalie along in front of him. As he opened the door leading into the hall, he glanced at the others, almost expecting to see them coming after him. Thankfully, they stayed on their side of the table and watched him leave. Once in the hall, he grabbed Natalie by the hand and rushed for the building's exit.

"I can't believe I was stupid enough not to see this coming."

"Do you think he'll really go through with it?" asked Natalie.

"Yes. Which means we have to work quickly if we hope to stop him."

"How?"

"I'm not sure yet." As they exited the building, Robson looked over his shoulder toward the lab. No one was following them. "Call everyone together for an emergency meeting in the mess hall. And tell everyone to bring their weapons with them."

CHAPTER FORTY-NINE

COMPTON WATCHED ROBSON and Natalie exit the lab, realizing he had severely miscalculated their reaction. Although he figured it would take some convincing, he had hoped to persuade them to his way of thinking and garner their support. What he had not counted on was their irrational loyalty to the vampires. Whether their thinking resulted from Paul's influence or from some twisted form of the Stockholm Syndrome, whereby the humans began to identify with the vampires with whom they were held captive, the result was the same. Not only could he not rely on Robson's cooperation but, judging by his and Natalie's speedy exit from the lab and the way he had kept a suspicious eye on him, Robson would most likely work to stop him.

"That didn't go as well as I hoped," said Compton.

"I didn't expect anything different from him." O'Bannon stepped over to the doctor. "Robson's always been an apologist for the bloodsuckers. And as for Natalie, wherever Robson's cock goes, she'll follow."

Compton turned to Thompson. "And what happened to you? Why the sudden lack of conviction?"

"It's not a lack of conviction." The colonel raised his head. "I was surprised by the change in plans."

"What change in plans?"

"I thought we agreed not to kill the vampires."

Compton felt himself growing frustrated with the colonel. "We agreed not to keep it secret from Robson."

"A lot of good that did," snorted O'Bannon.

"It'll make things more difficult, that's all."

Thompson stepped closer to the doctor. "You're not seriously going ahead with this?"

"Of course," Compton said, closing the open case of vaccines. "Only now we'll have to deal with Robson and the others as well."

"*Deal with*?" Thompson looked dumbfounded. "You intend to murder them, too?"

"Call it whatever you want. I have an opportunity to get rid of the revenants and the undead, and I'm not going to throw it away because of some misguided affectations on the part of Paul, Robson, and the rest."

"But they fought alongside us. Hell, they sacrificed one of their own to make sure we got here safely. Doesn't that count for something?"

"The vampires teamed up with Paul's group only because they faced extinction from a common enemy. Once that common enemy no longer exists, this alliance of convenience will fall apart."

Thompson became uncharacteristically belligerent. "Are you sure you're not going to such extremes out of guilt for what you've done?"

"I have nothing to feel guilty about," responded Compton in a calm voice. Though he had every right to be furious with Thompson for challenging his authority as well as his integrity, he felt sorry for the colonel, knowing the man was struggling to rationalize his sense of duty and loyalty with his sentimental attachment to the bloodsuckers for saving his life outside of Harrisburg. He paused long enough to make eye contact with Thompson, hoping he could reason the colonel out of his emotional turmoil. "I didn't create the Revenant Virus as a weapon, and I wasn't the one who released it. I now have a chance to rid the world of the two greatest evils facing it. If I don't take advantage of this opportunity, and the vampires begin preying on humans again, *then* I have a lot to feel guilty about."

"I wish it hadn't come to this, sir." Thompson's eyes hardened, filled with grim determination. He took three steps back from the doctor, unholstering his Colt in the process. Withdrawing the firearm, the colonel aimed it at his boss. "Dr. Compton, I'm taking command and placing you under—"

An electronic zap cut off the colonel. That was when Compton noticed O'Bannon standing behind Thompson. He had taken the Taser from the table and shoved it into the colonel's lower back against the spine. Thompson's body stiffened and convulsed. O'Bannon reached around front, grabbed the Colt by its barrel, and yanked it out of the colonel's hand. Once the colonel was disarmed, he turned off the Taser. Thompson dropped to the ground, crumpling into a moaning heap. O'Bannon stuck the Taser into his pants pocket and slid the Colt between his pants and the small of his back.

"You okay, Doc?"

"Yes, thank you. You took a chance. What if the security cameras saw you?"

"No chance." O'Bannon crossed to the corner of the room where the camera was mounted onto the wall. "The red light is on, which means nobody's watching."

"Good thinking."

O'Bannon pulled a chair over underneath the camera, grabbed a fire extinguisher from its wall mount, and stood on the chair. Holding the extinguisher in both hands, he slammed the base against the camera several times until it eventually tore from its mountings and shattered onto the floor. "That ought to keep them out of our business for a while."

"We only need a little while."

O'Bannon climbed down from the chair and returned to Compton. "You realize that once Robson gathers the others together, he'll be coming after you, right?"

"I'm aware of that. But we'll be gone before then."

"We?" O'Bannon grinned. "Does that mean I'm part of the team now?"

"You and I *are* the team." Compton motioned toward Thompson lying on the floor. "Bring him along. And hurry. We don't have much time."

Hoisting the colonel over his shoulder, O'Bannon followed Compton out into the hall and down to his private lab, waiting as the doctor unlocked the door. Signaling for O'Bannon to wait, the doctor stepped inside and looked up at the security camera in the corner. Seeing that the power light was red, he reached up and yanked the wires, ripping them from the wall. The red light faded out. Compton stepped inside and held open the door, directing O'Bannon to the center of the room.

When O'Bannon stepped inside, the seventeen swarmers inside the Plexiglas cage lunged Plexiglas, slamming into the surface with a dull thud. O'Bannon jumped back and looked to the doctor for reassurance.

"Don't worry. That cage is steel and reinforced Plexiglas. They can't get to you."

"You sure?"

"Would I be here if they could?" Compton moved to a floor-mounted examination table in the center of the lab. "Bring him here."

O'Bannon did as he was told. As he dropped Thompson onto the table, Compton rummaged through one of the drawers on a nearby counter and pulled out a pair of hand-cuffs. Returning to the examination table, he latched one end of the cuffs to its leg. Before he could lock the other end, Thompson swung his arm weakly and brushed away the doctor's hand.

"Wh-what the hell are y-you doing?" Thompson tried to roll off the table, but O'Bannon grabbed pulled the Taser from his pocket and shoved it against the colonel's lower spine, zapping him. Thompson screamed and spasmed before falling unconscious.

"Help me with him before he wakes up again," said Compton.

O'Bannon placed the Taser on the table and pushed Thompson onto his back. He held the colonel's left arm down as Compton locked the free end of the handcuffs around his wrist. The two men stepped back and stared at the colonel.

"What now?" asked O'Bannon.

"Now we arrange our escape." Compton headed for the door. "Follow me."

CHAPTER FIFTY

A S HE DID every hour, Daytona toggled the security cameras inside the facility into cascade mode so they would give him a display of every room. He did so as much to alleviate the boredom as for security reasons. As the monitors slowly toggled through the various views, he opened the thermos and refilled his coffee mug.

Turning his attention back to the monitors, he saw nothing unusual. Tatyana strolled through the facility, looking upset. He made a mental note to avoid her until she cooled off. Almost everyone else was gathered in the mess hall for some type of meeting. He would have to check with Robson later to find out what they were discussing. Hopefully, they were going over the plans for their return home. Other than that, things seemed quiet. Though he did notice the cameras were out in the research lab and Compton's private lab. It was probably a malfunction. He would mention it to Robson after shift change. Daytona locked the hall camera outside the private lab onto permanent display mode, which would allow him to warn the others in the unlikely event the swarmers broke out.

He was taking a long drink of lukewarm coffee when O'Bannon entered the security room. Daytona swiveled his chair to face him. "What's up? Come to see if any of the Angels are in the shower?"

"I'm here to relieve you."

Daytona looked at his watch. "Shift change ain't for another two hours."

"I know. But I can't sleep, so I figured I'd come by early and give you a chance to get some rest."

"I thought Bethany was spotting me."

"She was, but Natalie changed the schedule. She wants Bethany somewhere else."

Something did not settle right with Daytona, and the one thing he had learned since the outbreak began was to trust his instincts. He looked quickly over at the screen and back to O'Bannon. "How come you're not at the meeting?"

"What meeting?"

"The one being held in the mess hall."

"I guess I wasn't invited." A weird expression briefly flashed in O'Bannon's eyes, but then disappeared. Daytona thought it might have been worry. "So, am I relieving you or what?"

"Let me check with Natalie."

Daytona turned to get his radio, which was on the desk by the monitors. As he reached for it, the blank screen to Compton's lab reflected O'Bannon pulling a bayonet from the sheath strapped to his ankle and lunging. Daytona grabbed the thermos and spun around, flinging it at O'Bannon's head. O'Bannon brought both arms up in front of his face, deflecting the thermos. Daytona used the chance to bolt out of the chair and slam his left shoulder into O'Bannon's exposed abdomen, knocking him back against the wall.

Clasping the chair in both hands, Daytona lifted it over his head and ran at O'Bannon, intending to slam it down in him. O'Bannon slid across the floor and kicked out with his leg, catching Daytona in the l ankle. Daytona tumbled forward. He dropped the chair to the floor and fell on top of it, knocking the wind out of him. O'Bannon scrambled to his feet and circled behind him. Daytona tried to push himself up and regain his breath but made it only a few inches when he felt O'Bannon clutch his shirt by the collar and yank him to his feet. A second later, a bolt of pain shot through his body as the bayonet blade sliced into his back and up into his chest, puncturing his right lung. Daytona gasped from the shock but found it impossible to inhale. He wanted to fall forward but could not because O'Bannon held him upright by his collar.

The pain erupted into an excruciating agony when O'Bannon twisted the bayonet, shredding his lung. It felt as though someone had set fire to Daytona's chest, overwhelming his senses. His vision blurred and narrowed, and then his world went black.

O'BANNON SLOWLY LOWERED Daytona to the floor and pulled the bayonet out of his back. He kicked Daytona in the gut to see if he was still alive. No response. "All clear."

Compton entered the room. He barely gave the body a passing glance. "Are you alright?"

"Yeah." O'Bannon wiped the bayonet blade on Daytona's shirt. He stood and grimaced, stretching his back and rotating his shoulders from side to side. "Just a bit winded from the asshole throwing me into the wall."

"You'll live." Compton lifted the chair back onto its legs, pushed it over to the console, and slid into the seat. He checked the various monitors, pleased to find everyone gathered in the mess hall. "Good. They haven't formed a lynching party yet."

"Give them time."

"Time is something they have precious little of." Compton stood, input a few commands into the fuse box's control panel, and returned to the main console.

"What are you doing?"

"Creating a distraction. I've set the main power to go out in fifteen minutes. Everything will shut down except the emergency lights and primary security features."

"So how does that help us?"

"While they're trying to figure out what happened they won't be looking for us." Compton looked over his shoulder. "It'll give us a chance to escape."

"Sorry to bust your bubble, Doc, but there's no way we can steal a Hummer, open the blast door, and get off the site before they catch us."

"True. But we won't be going out the front door."

O'Bannon was totally confused. "I thought there was no other way out."

Compton raised his hand toward the schematic of the underground facility and pointed to the end farthest away from the buildings. "There's a door here to the air filtration system. An access ladder leads to the intakes near the top of the mountain. It's heavily alarmed. Once the power goes out, we'll be able to make it to the surface without anyone knowing."

"And how do we get back to camp?"

"Thompson stationed three Humvees near the intakes. That way, if revenants overran the facility, anyone who made it through the emergency escape would have a way to get to safety."

"You had this planned out all along." O'Bannon clapped Compton on the shoulder. "You son of a bitch."

"I'll take that as a compliment." Compton pressed ENTER and set the shutdown commands into the system. He swung his chair around to face O'Bannon. "I'm going to grab the vaccines. You get the maps from Robson's quarters. Once you have them, follow the main access road to the far end of the facility. That's where the access door to the air filtration system is. We'll meet there in ten minutes and make our escape when the power shuts down."

"Sounds good to me."

"One more thing before we go."

Compton typed a command into the system. O'Bannon concentrated on the monitor focused on the blast door leading into the facility. As he watched, the bolts holding the door disengaged. Once unlocked, it popped open, leaving a two-foot gap. Compton punched another command into the console. A red light began flashing on one of the monitors. O'Bannon looked up, horrified to see it was coming from the monitor focused on the main gate. The gate shuddered and slowly began sliding to one side.

"What are you doing?" asked O'Bannon.

"Making certain there are no witnesses." Compton stood up and headed for the door. "Come on. Time is of the essence."

OUTSIDE THE FACILITY, a red light atop the chain link fence comprising the main gate switched on. The rotating beam flashed across the horde of more than four hundred rotters trapped between the twin fences. Only a handful even seemed to notice, staring up at the light with curious disinterest. None of them had any idea what it meant. There was no reason to.

When the fence's motor came to life, those rotters closest to the gate moaned in anticipation, long ago having equated noise with food. As the inner gate slid to the side, it dragged along those rotters adjacent to it that got caught up in the links. The others made their way through the opening. Most staggered and stumbled, having been cooped up so long their limbs remained stiff and atrophied. Not that it mattered, however, for they were no longer trapped. In one mass, the rotters surged forward and began to slowly disperse across the compound.

CHAPTER FIFTY-ONE

"SO THAT'S WHERE we stand." Robson finished relaying to the rest of the raiding party the confrontation he and Natalie had with Compton. Everyone who had thrown their lot in with he and Natalie sat around the mess hall, except for Daytona, who stood watch in the security room, and Tatyana, who was wandering around the facility. Those two could fend for themselves for the next few minutes. As for the others, they listened with a growing sense of confusion and betrayal, still unable to believe the type of people they had allowed amongst them. Robson noticed several of the Angels subconsciously cradled their weapons as they listened. Tibor clenched and unclenched his right fist, while Dravko visually struggled not to morph into his vampiric form. Dravko was the first to speak.

"Let me get this straight. Compton wants to inject us with the Revenant Virus, stun us when we turn into swarmers, and then kill us?"

Robson nodded.

Dravko turned to Natalie. "This is not an exaggeration?"

"No."

"Doesn't he realize that by infecting us, he'll be creating swarmers with incredible strength that'll be that much harder to destroy?"

"I don't think he's thought that through," said Natalie. "To him, this is the most humane way of disposing of you."

"Humane?" snarled Tibor. "I say you let me and Dravko take care of them. We'll at least give them a fighting chance."

"No." Robson said forcefully, cutting off further discussion. "We're not going to sink to their level. First, we'll arrest the three of them and destroy the hypodermic needles with the virus. Jennifer, are there any prison cells here where they can be detained?"

"There's a small holding cell across from the security offices in the admin building. It's large enough to hold them." Jennifer's eyes searched the room. "I hope no one here thinks I had any part in this. This is the first I've heard of Compton's plan."

"Don't worry," said Robson, trying to sound reassuring. "No one here lumps you in with them. Shit, we were all taken in by the doctor."

Ari raised her hand. "After we arrest them, then what?"

"Then we figure a way to transport them back to base and let Paul and Elena decide their fate."

COMPTON AND O'BANNON entered the medical lab. The doctor made his way to the table with the vaccines. He grabbed the pouch with the three hypodermic needles filled with the virus and handed it to O'Bannon.

"Take this and keep it safe in case we need it."

"What about the vaccine?"

Compton took two of the steel briefcases from off the table, holding one in each hand. "I'll take these. It'll be enough to start inoculating Omaha when we get there."

"Shouldn't we destroy the rest?"

"We don't have time." Compton motioned to the clock mounted on the wall. "The power will go out in less than ten minutes. Get the maps and meet me by the air filtration room. And hurry."

The two men raced out of the lab and headed for the main thoroughfare.

★ ★ ★

TATYANA SAT IN the driver's seat of the school bus, struggling with her emotions. She had long since gotten over the pain of what O'Bannon had said to her and how he had used her all these months. Right now, she had enough to do trying to handle her own shame. Shame at falling in love with someone who obviously never cared for her. Shame at allowing herself to be treated so horribly. Shame of being taken advantage of by a human. She realized now she had allowed herself to become his mattress out of her own sense of self-loathing at being a vampire. That ended as of today. Maybe she did not want to be the undead, and did not ask to be turned, but there was nothing she could do about it now. The reality was that she was a vampire, one of the few left in the world. As painful as the time she spent with O'Bannon was in retrospect, it had taught her one valuable lesson.

Tatyana was proud to be a vampire and would never be pushed around again.

As the shame changed to anger, Tatyana wiped away the last of her tears. She would go to Dravko, explain what had happened, and ask him to forgive her for being so naïve. After that....

Tatyana saw Compton and O'Bannon exit the lab building. She slid down behind the steering wheel so they would not see her. The doctor held two briefcases in his hands, though she had no idea what was in them. Knowing the doctor, it could not be anything good. She watched as he turned and headed for the opposite end of the facility. O'Bannon went in the other direction, ran a few yards, and disappeared inside the dormitory.

Something was wrong. They were acting too suspiciously. She thought of calling Robson on the radio and letting him know but then thought better of it, not certain whether he would believe her. No, she had to confront O'Bannon directly and find out what was going on.

Exiting the school bus, Tatyana crossed over to the dormitory and followed O'Bannon inside.

CONSCIOUSNESS SLOWLY RETURNED to Thompson, fighting its way through a fog of pain and disorientation. His head throbbed, drowning out his senses. He had no idea where he was and had only a faint awareness of muffled movements and moaning close by. He tried to roll over, but his left side was paralyzed. No, he slowly realized. He had movement in his arm, but it was limited. Something restrained him. Despite the agony, he rolled onto his left side and sat up. His back spasmed, the pain so powerful he nearly passed out. Summoning all his willpower, he steadied himself on the edge of whatever he sat on. The movement and moaning pounded on his eardrums, though still muffled. Taking a deep breath, he slowly opened his eyes.

The light scattered across his irises like a kaleidoscope, forcing him to squint. His stomach heaved, spewing its contents across himself and the floor. He tried to raise his left hand to wipe off his mouth, but it moved only a few inches and stopped.

Thompson opened his eyes again. This time the pain, though intense, was not as severe as before. Through his blurred vision, he focused on his left hand, but could not make out anything. Only after several seconds did his sight clear enough that he saw the handcuff attached around his wrist, anchoring him to a metal examination table. Resting on the corner of the table sat a Taser.

Suddenly the memory came to him of pain radiating through his back until it shocked him into unconsciousness. O'Bannon. The son of a bitch must have used the Taser on him while he was arguing with Compton and then they handcuffed him here.

But where was here?

Looking around the lab, his eyes fell on the steel container off to his left. The swarmers inside pressed against the Plexiglas, scratching and gnawing at the surface to get to him.

Shit.

Taking several deep breaths, Thompson tried to focus his thinking. He had to find a way to get out of here and warn Robson about what Compton planned.

DAYTONA COUGHED. THE agony of that single action woke him up. He spit blood onto the floor. Not a good sign. Gasping a lungful of air, he cried out as his right chest erupted into a fireball. *I don't have much time left,* he thought.

He rolled onto his hands and knees, nearly passing out from the pain that wracked his entire right side. He concentrated on standing, tightly clutching his right arm against him to ease the torment and using his left hand to grasp the console and pull himself to his feet. When he stood, the entire room started to spin. Daytona felt his legs become wobbly. He supported himself on the rim of the console, barely preventing himself from collapsing.

Glancing up at the monitors, he saw someone had opened the front gate and released the rotters onto the compound. He reached for the radio to warn Robson and the others and, as he did, his vision rapidly narrowed and his senses collapsed. In that instant, Daytona knew he was about to die.

Before the life drained from his body, Daytona summoned all his strength and slammed his hand against the red button. He collapsed onto the console and slid to the floor. The last sound he heard before death took him was the claxon of the emergency alarm reverberating through the facility.

IN THE COMPOUND, the blaring of the claxon cut through the silence of the night. Nearly four hundred rotters searched the sky for the source, knowing sound meant food. A teenage rotter in a torn Goth girl outfit listened for a moment before looking up at the speaker mounted on top of the tunnel entrance. Slowly pivoting on a shattered ankle that caused its right foot to drag sideways along the ground, it lumbered toward the noise until it reached the tunnel entrance. An even louder noise echoed from deep within the tunnel. To its decayed mind, the louder noise meant more food. With a groan of anticipation, the Goth rotter set off into the tunnel.

Other rotters noticed and followed, which in turn attracted even more of the living dead. Within minutes, the entire horde was making its way into the access tunnels.

CHAPTER FIFTY-TWO

B ETHANY STARTLED WHEN the claxon went off inside the mess hall. "What the fuck is that?"

"The emergency alarm," replied Jennifer.

"What does it mean?" asked Robson.

"Could mean anything. It's set off only from the security office."

Robson removed his radio from his belt and keyed the microphone. "Daytona, what's going on?"

No response.

"Daytona, are you there?"

Still no response.

"What is it?" For the first time since he had known her, Natalie looked truly scared.

"I don't know. But there's only one way to find out." Robson withdrew the Magnum from its holster. He flipped open the chamber, checking to make certain it was loaded, and slid it back. "Jennifer, you know how to shut down the alarm?"

"Yes."

"Good. Come on. Natalie, Dravko, Tibor. You're with us. We're going to the security room to find out what's going on. The rest of you stay here until you hear from me. Let's move."

The small group exited the mess hall. Robson stopped them and pointed to the staircases leading to the third floor. "Dravko, you and Natalie take the middle stairs. Tibor and Jennifer will take the one at the far end. We'll meet outside the security office."

The others nodded and rushed off, climbing their respective stairs. Robson walked the length of the building to the front stairwell and began ascending, his weapon drawn and at the ready. By the time he reached the third-floor hallway, the others were already waiting.

"Any signs of Compton?" asked Robson.

Dravko shook his head.

Robson pushed open the door and stepped back.

"Daytona, are you there?"

When he got no reply, he quickly stepped inside and placed his back against the wall to the left of the jamb. He kept the weapon aimed as he scanned the room. Natalie followed behind him, her firearm drawn and held down in front of her. She fanned out to the right, moving to the end of the room and vaulting over the counter. Landing on the other side, she raised the weapon into firing position and walked the length of the room, looking for anyone waiting to ambush them. No one was there.

"Clear," she said as she lowered the firearm, though she still clutched it in her right hand.

Dravko and Jennifer slid by Robson and entered the monitor room. Jennifer's gasp confirmed Robson's worst fears. Rushing in, he saw Daytona lying crumpled on the floor in front of the console in a pool of blood. Clearly visible on his right side was a gouged-out wound. It looked thick and deep, as if it had been made by a bayonet, and only one person in the group carried one of those. Though Robson knew it was useless, he crouched and placed two fingers on Daytona's carotid artery. As expected, no pulse.

"Fucking O'Bannon. He must have done this a few minutes ago. The body is still w—"

"Jesus. Fucking. Christ." Natalie drew out each word as if each were its own sentence. The quiver in her voice turned Robson's blood cold.

He looked up at Natalie, about to ask what was wrong,

when he noticed her staring at the console. His gaze followed hers to the monitor displaying the scene outside the tunnel. It showed four hundred rotters spread out across the compound, most of them shambling toward the tunnel entrance, attracted by the sound of the siren.

"We're fucked," said Dravko.

"No, we're not." Natalie unhooked her radio from her belt. "Ari, do you read?"

"Loud and clear."

"Gather the Angels and meet at the main door to the facility."

"What's wrong?"

"I'll tell you later. Now haul ass." Natalie slipped the radio back onto her belt.

Robson reached out and clasped her hand. "You can't do this. There's no way the Angels can take on so many rotters."

"What choice do we have? If those rotters swarm the entrance, we'll never make it out alive. Our only chance is to stop them before they get here." Natalie sounded confident enough, but her eyes betrayed her desperation.

The worst part was Robson knew she was right. "Go kick ass. And be careful."

"I always am." She gave him a quick kiss before running out of the security room.

Dravko leaned forward, examining the monitors. "What I don't understand is how Compton plans to escape. If the rotters trap us in here, won't they also trap him?"

"Not necessarily." Jennifer maneuvered her way to the console and pressed a button that shut off the alarm. She then toggled through the views until one of the monitors showed a long shot of the thoroughfare with Compton heading for the far end. "I thought so."

"What?" Robson also leaned closer.

"He's heading for the air filtration system. There's a ladder there that leads topside."

"But aren't the vents sealed?"

"Yeah, but he has the access codes. There's also a couple of Hummers stored near the vents in case of an emergency evac. If he reaches them, he'll be home free."

"Then we have to make sure he doesn't make it topside." Robson started for the door, but Dravko stopped him.

"I'll go."

"It's my job."

"He has too much of a head start. You'll never catch up with him in time. I can." Dravko bared his fangs. "Besides, I owe the fucker for what he planned to do to us."

Robson nodded and watched as his friend departed.

Jennifer continued to flip through the various security cameras. "O'Bannon and Tatyana are in the dormitory. It looks like she's following him, but I have no idea where they're going. I can't find the colonel anywhere, but I don't have connectivity to either the research lab or Compton's private lab. He could be in one of them, but I can't be—"

The security room plunged into total darkness as all electricity to the facility was cut. The pitch black lasted only a second before a red emergency light came to life in the corner behind them, bathing the room in a crimson glow. A second later, the monitors came back on, displaying snowy screens for a few seconds before powering up. They showed the entire facility as being without power, save for the occasional red emergency light.

"What the fuck happened?" Robson slammed his fist against the top of the console.

Jennifer ran over to the fuse box and opened it. "Shit. Compton programmed the computer to shut off the electricity. All we have is emergency lighting, the security cameras, and the locks to the blast door."

"Can you fix it?" demanded Robson.

"Yeah," Jennifer began punching codes into the control panel, "but it'll take me several minutes to reboot the system and get power back online."

Robson spun around to Tibor. "Go get O'Bannon and bring him here. I'll tell you exactly where he is."

"What if he resists?"

"Then break his legs and drag him here."

A sardonic sneer twisted Tibor's lips. "With pleasure."

Robson turned back to the console, his eyes darting from one monitor to the other. By now the first fifty rotters already had entered the tunnel and were slowly making their way to the blast door. *Christ*, he started second-guessing himself. *I hope I'm making the right decisions.*

THE ANGELS AND Caylee were waiting for Natalie when she arrived at the blast door. They all seemed nervous, which was natural under the circumstances. When they saw Natalie's expression, though, their apprehension turned to outright fear.

"What's going on?" blurted Ari.

"Compton opened the main gate and let the rotters onto the compound. And thanks to that damn alarm, they're entering the tunnel and heading this way."

"H-how many?" stammered Stephanie.

"All of them."

"Dear God." Tiara swallowed hard and, for a moment, she looked like she might vomit.

"We've never faced odds like this before. If any of you don't follow me out that door, I promise you no one here, least of all me, will think any less if you. But we have to try. If those rotters swarm around this door, we're trapped." Natalie looked at each of her Angels as she spoke, searching their eyes for any signs that they might not be able to handle this battle. "Who's with me?"

All sixteen Angels responded in the affirmative.

Caylee stepped forward and partially raised her hand. "I want to help."

"You stay here."

"By myself? No fuckin' way. Besides, you need all the help you can get."

Natalie raced over to the twin Hummers parked near the blast door, removed one of the M-16s and several boxes of ammunition, and rejoined the Angels. She handed the weapon and the boxes to Caylee. Caylee pulled back the bolt on the M-16 to make sure it was loaded.

"Are you ready?" asked Natalie.

Caylee slid the bolt back into its firing position. "Let's rock."

Natalie smiled and nodded. Under the circumstances, it was the only response she could think of. Taking her radio, she called the security office. "We're heading out."

"Roger," responded Robson.

Natalie moved over to the blast door, which was already partially ajar, and pushed it open all the way. The Angels tensed, half expecting to see rotters stream through the opening. Thank God they were not that close yet. Natalie quickly ushered her girls into the tunnel and followed the last one out. She paused in the opening to key her radio.

"Mike, can you read me?"

"What's up?"

"Once I'm in the tunnel and have closed the door, bolt it shut behind me."

A pause before Robson responded. "You realize if I do that, you may not be able to get back in?"

"I know. But we can't risk any of the rotters getting by us."

No response.

"I'm in charge of security around here," Natalie barked at Robson in a stern tone she did not mean. "Do as I tell you and secure the door behind me. Understand?"

Another pause, but this time he responded with a half-hearted, "Yes."

Natalie slid the radio back onto her belt as she stepped out into the tunnel, then pushed the blast door shut and waited. With a metallic whir, the bolts slid back into place. The click they made as they locked sounded like a death knell. She placed a hand on the cold metal, wondering if she would ever again see anyone on the other side. Looking up at the security camera, she mouthed the words, "I love you." She hoped to God Robson saw them, because deep down she feared this would be the last time she said them.

Turning to face her Angels, Natalie saw them standing around her. She could see in their faces fear and uncertainty. Yet none of them had opted to stay behind. They would face the rotters together, even if it meant they all died together.

"All right, Angels." Natalie stood straight, trying to project a confidence she did not feel. "You always said you'd follow me to Hell and back. Now's your chance."

Natalie marched off for the tunnel entrance, with her Angels falling in behind her.

CHAPTER FIFTY-THREE

ROBSON TURNED AWAY from the monitors, knowing if he watched the nightmare about to play out in the tunnel, he would be of no use here in the security room. He looked over at Jennifer, who frantically worked inside the fuse box.

"I could use power any time now."

"It's not gonna happen." Jennifer glanced over her shoulder at him, her expression a mixture of anger and defeat. "Compton hosed this system pretty good. To fix it, I'm going to have to take everything offline, including the emergency lights, security cameras, and blast door."

"Fuck." Robson slammed his hand against the console.

"Sorry."

"It's not your fault." He turned back to the monitors. Almost everyone was accounted for. The Angels were running down the tunnel to meet the horde. Compton was down at the other end of the facility, waiting by the door to the air filtration room, with Dravko having just left the admin building and racing to him. O'Bannon entered his and Natalie's room, with Tatyana not too far behind. Tibor was still heading down the stairs of the admin building, heading for the exit. The only person he could not find was Thompson, which made Robson nervous. The colonel knew enough about this facility to fuck up the situation even worse than it already was. The only locations Robson did not have visual access to were the two labs. He needed to know the colonel's whereabouts.

"Don't waste any more time trying to get that thing back

online. I need you to help me find Thompson."

Jennifer stepped over to join him. "He's not on any of the cameras?"

"No. But the two in the labs aren't working. Can you check them out for me?"

"Sure."

Jennifer headed for the door and ran out of the security room.

THOMPSON STRAINED AGAINST the handcuffs, pulling on them as hard as he could to get that extra few inches without dislocating his shoulder, hoping to reach one of the drawers on the surrounding lab stations where he hopefully would find something to help him get free. Despite the ache in his muscles and the pain in his ball joint, he could not get the tips of his fingers closer than three inches to any of the handles.

He was weighing other options when the lights suddenly flicked out, leaving only the eerie red glow of the single emergency light above him. The sudden loss of electricity chilled his blood, though not because of the darkness. Two loud, metallic clicks accompanied the darkness. The colonel felt his heart rate spike as he watched the electronic locks on the inner and outer doors of the swarmer container disengage. The bolts slid back into their cylinders, allowing each door to pop open a few inches. It was enough.

One of the swarmers turned its head to the sound. Seeing the door ajar, it rushed over and shoved it open. With a moan of anticipation Thompson heard even through the Plexiglas, the swarmer stumbled into the containment corridor and headed for the metal door leading into the lab. The others followed.

Grabbing the Taser off the exam table, Thompson set the voltage gauge to its highest setting, and clutched the weapon in his right hand. He stood chained to the exam table, ready to meet the onslaught.

THE ANGELS ROUNDED the corner where the U-shaped tunnel turned right toward the exit. They came to an abrupt halt. Fifty yards ahead was a mass of the living dead shambling toward them. They filled the tunnel, ten rotters wide and deeper than any of them could see. The reek from of hundreds of decayed bodies crammed into so confined a space overwhelmed Natalie's senses, making her eyes water. Even worse was the overpowering stench that clogged her sinuses and mouth. She fought back the urge to gag by concentrating on the pervasive buzz from thousands of flies and wasps feeding off the living dead and each other.

On seeing the fresh meat in front of them, the horde moaned in unison, an ungodly wail that echoed off the walls, making it sound as if the Angels were surrounded. The rotters surged forward. Natalie noticed several of her Angels backed away. She could almost smell the panic threatening to shatter their cohesion.

Stepping through her Angels, Natalie spun around and faced them, forcing the girls to focus on her rather than the rotters. "There's no time for pep talks. We need to kill them if any of us want to make it out of here alive. We fight until only one side is left standing. Are you ready?"

The sliding back of rifle bolts answered her question.

The first group of seven Angels and Caylee stepped forward and formed a line abreast across the tunnel. Each of them raised their weapons and lined up their sights on a rotter head.

"Don't wait for my order," said Natalie. "Fire whenever you're ready."

A volley of rifle fire shot down the tunnel. Eight rotter heads exploded, showering the tunnel walls and those behind them with skull fragments and chunks of gore. The bodies collapsed to the ground, finally at rest. Other rotters surged forward, filling the gap.

The horde slowly drew closer.

OUTSIDE OF ROBSON'S room, O'Bannon withdrew his sidearm from its holster. He did not think Robson would be there but wanted to be ready. O'Bannon pushed open the door and stepped inside, swinging the gun from one side of the room to the other. Once certain he was alone, he re-holstered the weapon. Crossing over to the small wooden desk, he rummaged through the folder of papers, looking for the one with the revised route back to camp. Several maps lay on top of the pile, but those were from the disastrous run down here. He tossed them onto the floor, searching for the correct ones.

"What are you doing in here?"

O'Bannon glanced over his shoulder to see Tatyana blocking the door.

"I asked you a question."

"Can't you hear the alarm?" O'Bannon went back to sorting through the papers. "Robson asked me to make sure the maps were safe."

"I doubt that." She entered the room, still hovering by the door. "What were you doing with Compton a few minutes ago?"

Tatyana's voice made him nervous. It was cold and harsh, and slightly inhuman. He had heard that tone before from vampires trying to control their anger, when they struggled against the urge to let their emotions take control and to morph into their vampiric form. Because her intentions were uncertain, at this moment she posed a menace. With his back still to Tatyana so she could not see what he was doing, O'Bannon slid the cloth pouch from inside his jacket and placed it onto the desk.

"Are you spying on me?"

"Do you blame me?" Tatyana moved closer, her manner

stalking.

O'Bannon opened the flaps of the pouch, exposing the three hypodermic needles.

"You lied to me." Her steps as she approached were slow and steady.

He removed two of the hypodermic needles from their slits and placed them on the table.

"You treated me worse than a common whore." She stalked up directly behind him.

He removed the plastic covers to the needles and plungers, then clutched one hypodermic needle in each fist, the needles extending beyond the bottom of his hands, his thumbs on the plungers.

"You took advantage of me," Tatyana hissed. O'Bannon felt her cold dead breath against the hairs on the back of his neck.

"I didn't hear you complaining as I fucked you."

"You used me." The snarl was purely animalistic, intermingled with the grinding of fangs. Tatyana grabbed O'Bannon by the shoulders and spun him around. As he expected, she had morphed into her vampiric form, leaving behind little semblance of her human beauty. The soft skin had hardened, becoming dark and leathery. The silky hair that once flowed over her shoulders now hung in clumpy strands. Deep furrows along the brow and the pulled back cheeks distorted her face. A pair of blood red eyes sunk deep into their sockets glowered at him, the adoration they once held now replaced by hatred and a feral lust for his blood. She clutched the collar of his shirt with hands deformed into talons and lifted him into the air. Her lower jaw dropped open, exposing a gaping maw filled with jagged fangs. Tatyana twisted her head, aiming for his neck.

"Now it's my turn to use you."

O'Bannon sneered. "Not yet, bitch."

He brought his hands up between Tatyana's outstretched

arms, jamming the hypodermic needles into her neck as she bent over to feed on him. He shoved his thumbs on the plungers, injecting Tatyana with two lethal doses of the Revenant Virus. She released her grip and stumbled backwards, slamming into the corner of one of the bunk beds, the hypodermic needles still stuck into her neck. Clutching at her throat, she began ripping away the flesh with her talons, trying to tear out the infection.

"It burns!" she bellowed.

"Of course, it burns." O'Bannon turned back to the table and quickly rummaged through the remaining maps. "I injected you with enough of the Revenant Virus to turn every one of us into one of those things in minutes."

Tatyana reached up with a shaky hand, clasped one of the hypodermics in an uncertain grip, and yanked it free. The needle broke off in her neck, while the plastic vial tumbled out of her grip and clattered to the floor. She tried to talk but, her voice came in rasps.

"I'm g-going to make you p-pay for that."

"I doubt it." O'Bannon found the maps and pulled them out of the folder. Folding them in half lengthwise, he slid them into the inner pocket of his jacket. When he spun around to face Tatyana, he was shocked to see how rapidly the virus had worked. Her complexion had turned sallow and lifeless, with black blotches and exposed spots of decay erupting through the skin. The crimson eyes had glossed over, becoming gray and smoky. Blood drained from her mouth, blackened and partially congealed, forming clumps that plopped to the floor.

"You'll be dead any second now."

Mustering what little strength she had left, Tatyana snarled and attempted to lunge at O'Bannon. He did not even bother moving aside. She took two shaky steps and dropped to her knees, tottering unsteadily for a moment before falling forward. Her face slammed into the floor with a loud crack. Tatyana twitched violently once before her body went slack. A hushed sigh slipped from her throat as the remnants of her life passed from her.

O'Bannon reached behind and grabbed the pouch, folding the flaps closed to protect the last hypodermic needle. As he headed for the door, he did not even cast a glance at Tatyana, his only thought being to clear the area quickly before she reanimated as one of the living dead.

THE SWARMERS POURED out of the Plexiglas cage and into the small corridor separating the two steel biohazard doors. Though ajar, the outer door slammed shut under their weight, providing Thompson with a temporary reprieve. He looked up at the camera, hoping to get help from whoever was on duty in the guard room. His heart sank when he saw the coaxial cables and power cord dangling from its rear panel. Grabbing the restraints of the handcuffs with his right hand, he pushed the metal as hard as he could, trying to slide it over his hand. It went as far as the joint of his thumb and stopped, straining against the bone. Damn. That left him with only one option.

Pulling the handcuffs farther up his wrist, Thompson tightly gripped the metal restraint and took a deep breath. He jerked the cuff down toward his hand, slamming the metal into the thumb joint. Despite bracing himself, he screamed as the metal shattered the bone. His thumb went limp and bent inward at an awkward angle, but the cuffs slid over his hand and along his fingers. At least he was free.

The sound of swarmer moaning increased, causing Thompson to look over his shoulder. One of the swarmers had discovered the edge of the steel door and had pried it open enough to push its head through. It stretched its neck toward Thompson, decayed, gore-encrusted teeth snapping the air. Shoving its left arm through the opening, it clawed at the metal, desperately trying to get free.

Most of the swarmer's torso was through the door when

Thompson scooped the Taser from off the exam table and rushed over. It opened its jaw wide in anticipation of food, presenting a prime target. The colonel placed the weapon against the swarmer's forehead and squeezed the trigger. Hundreds of volts were discharged, arching through the creature's skull. One of its eyes exploded. Froth formed around its partially-chewed-off lips. It convulsed violently as the electrical current cooked its brain, burning out what little motor function remained.

Rather than buy him a few extra seconds to escape, his stunt shortened it. The electric crack and death howl startled the other swarmers enough that they pulled back from the door. As the pressure against it eased, the door sprung open. The fried swarmer's corpse collapsed across the jamb, lodging it in place. With their path now clear, the swarmers jumped over the body and rushed into the lab.

Thompson already had dashed for the exit and might have made it were it not for his injury. He grabbed the knob, but because of his broken thumb he could not get a good grip, his hand slipping off the metal. Placing the Taser between his left arm and torso, he used the right to open the door. Before he could get out, the swarmers attacked.

The colonel grabbed the Taser from under his arm and jammed it into the neck of the first one to reach him, the female in the white lab coat. Its arms and head flailed as the current passed through its body, but the effort was not enough to save him. The remaining fifteen swarmers lunged at the colonel from both sides. Decayed hands yanked at his clothes and dug into his skin. Thompson raised his arms in front of him and swung them from side to side as he backed up, trying to break their grip, but there were too many. He tumbled over backward, with the three closest swarmers collapsing on top of him. Once on the ground, the colonel did not stand a chance.

One swarmer each clawed at a limb, using their bony fingers to strip off clothes and flesh. Thompson was frantic from panic and pain. Every nerve in his body screamed with agony, overriding all his other senses. His bowels and bladder emptied. His vision narrowed. He was only vaguely aware of his own screams and the munching of the swarmers as they chewed his flesh. He thrashed around, mostly out of instinct, trying to break free. The three swarmers held him down, bending over to feast on the meat of his thighs and right arm, ripping off chunks of skin and muscle between their teeth. A fourth swarmer twisted at the colonel's left arm, ripping it out of its socket like a chicken wing. Once the skin and muscles tore free, it jumped up and dashed to the corner to feed in peace.

Two others dropped to their knees on either side of Thompson and tore open his abdomen. His agony spiked as they plunged their hands into his open cavity, clutching at anything that looked edible. A swarmer in Air Force fatigues wrenched out the colonel's stomach and bit into it. The organ exploded, covering its face in undigested food and stomach acid. It barely noticed the burning on its skin as it devoured the delicacy. The larger of the two clutched its fingers around a length of intestine and pulled it out, unwinding the slippery coils as it shoved as much as possible into its mouth. Attracted by the dangling coils of moist food, the two swarmers near the colonel's legs lunged for the intestine, clutching it in decayed hands. The three creatures fought over the intestines, ripping it apart until each had its own length, shoving it into greedy mouths.

By now Thompson had slipped into shock. He did not even feel the last swarmer as it knelt beside his head and placed its hands into the colonel's mouth. It yanked his jaw open, dislodging the lower half with an ungodly crack, then bent over and began feasting on Thompson's tongue.

The remaining eight swarmers tried to find a place to feed but were driven back by the others at each attempt. They soon gave up and moved toward the door, attracted by a human voice coming from down the hall.

"COLONEL," CALLED OUT Jennifer as she approached the lab. The open door to Compton's private lab was fifty feet away. "Are you there?"

On hearing the chorus of moans coming from the lab, Jennifer started to back down the hall, her eyes fixed on the open door. She gasped when three swarmers stepped into the corridor. They looked around, trying to find the source of the noise. Finally, the lifeless eyes of the closest swarmer, a large man in Marine Corps battle fatigues, fixed on Jennifer. It snarled, desiccated lips rearing up over a skeleton-like mouth. The other two spun around, catching sight of Jennifer, their snarls joining in the chorus of death. The three bolted down the corridor toward her, with another five racing out of the lab to join in the sprint.

Jennifer knew she could never beat them to the exit. Her only chance, slim as it seemed, was to seek refuge. Sprinting the ten feet to the main research lab, she opened the door and rushed inside, slamming it shut and flipping the lock as the swarmers reached the door. They pounded and scratched on the thick glass, moaning in unison for the food on the other side. Jennifer ed her weight into the wood, trying to hold it in shut as she slid the deadbolt into place. She reached for the keypad, hoping to engage the electronic bolt lock, but cursed when she remembered that with the power off it would not be online.

Each time the swarmers slammed into the door, it strained on its hinges. It would not hold out much longer. Her eyes scanned the lab, looking for an escape. Unfortunately, the only way out was right into the jaws of the swarmers.

Removing the radio from her belt, she keyed the microphone, looking for help.

ROBSON WATCHED THE nightmare unfold on his monitors as a cold emptiness gripped his stomach. The situation was spiraling out of control, and he remained helpless to do anything about it. A minute ago, he had watched O'Bannon murder Tatyana by injecting her with a concentrated dose of the virus. Now he stared at the monitor as swarmers dashed out of Compton's private lab and hunted down Jennifer. He assumed the power outage must have released the locks to the special containment chamber the doctor had rigged which, if correct, meant over to a dozen swarmers were now loose inside the facility. He watched as Jennifer ducked inside one of the labs and closed the door behind her. She was safe, but only for a few minutes. Robson could tell by the way the swarmers pounded at the wood it would not hold up against their weight for long. He checked the monitor for the lab, realizing it was one of those in which the security cameras had gone blank. Damn, he had no way of know—

"Please, help me." Jennifer's frightened voice crackled over the radio. "I'm trapped in the medical lab with a bunch of swarmers trying to get at me. Is anyone there?"

Robson grabbed his radio. "It's Robson. Are you hurt?"

"I'm fine," she huffed. "But not for long. There's eight swarmers outside the lab trying to break their way in."

"I see them." Robson already was on the move, grabbing his AA-12 as he ran out of the security room. "I'm on my way."

"Hurry. This door won't hold them out for long."

"I'm halfway there." Robson bolted down the stairwell, taking the steps two at a time.

By rushing out of the security room when he did, he failed to notice the small group of twenty rotters entering the access tunnel from the far end, shambling toward the Angels from their rear.

TATYANA'S EYES POPPED open. She stared blankly at the ceiling, the image colorless and murky. It did not register with her, though. Nothing did. All cognizant thought had died along with her body, leaving only basic motor functions and the need to quench the hunger consuming her. Tatyana rolled onto her side and unsteadily climbed to her feet, shaky arms using the bottom bunk to support herself. She had no conscious thought of her movement, going through the actions out of instinct. When she stood, she teetered precariously, her sub-primitive mind trying to adapt. Slowly she grew used to the strange numbness in her legs and took a few tentative steps. Cloudy eyes searched her surroundings, catching sight of the open door leading into the hall. Noise came from that direction. Though devoid of all rational thought, her mind registered the sound and equated it with food.

With shuffling and faltering steps, Tatyana headed for the door.

THE BATTLE INSIDE the tunnel had been raging for only a few minutes, but it already had taken on a perverse rhythm: the crack of a rifle shot, followed by the dull thud of a bullet striking meat, and the thump of a corpse collapsing to the ground. A mist of congealed blood and brain matter splattered the walls and those rotters to the rear. Amy emptied her magazine first, taking down eight in rapid succession. She stepped back behind the second line to reload. Tiara took her place. As each of the Angels in the first line expended their ammunition, they also fell back, allowing one of the girls from the second line to pick up the fight.

The stench of hundreds of living dead mixed with the acrid odor of spent gunpowder. A cloud of whitish-blue smoke formed around the Angels, unable to dissipate within the confines of the tunnel, burning their eyes and making it difficult to see. Even worse were the insects. Every shot that tore through one of the rotters kicked up flies and wasps, many of which now swarmed around the Angels. Each of the girls had to pause every few seconds to cough, clear their eyes, or swipe away the insects. Many of the girls were stung in the face by the crazed wasps, distracting them as they slapped at the bugs. The drop in the rate of fire gave the rotters a slight advantage, allowing them to close the distance between them and the Angels.

Like the rising waters of a flooded river, the horde of living dead continued to surge forward, undaunted by the onslaught of bullets. For every one dropped, another took its place, oblivious to everything but the food in front of it. The gap between humans and rotters steadily narrowed.

TIBOR WHIPPED OPEN the door to the dorm building, nearly colliding with O'Bannon who was on the way out. The human skidded to an abrupt stop, then backed down the hall, his eyes warily fixed on the vampire. Tibor stepped inside and let the door close behind him. He stood in the center of the corridor, blocking the way out.

"Where are you going in such a hurry?"

"Stay the fuck away from me." O'Bannon continued backing down the hall.

Tibor followed, keeping pace with the human. O'Bannon dropped the papers he was carrying. Holding a cloth pouch in his left hand, he used his right to open the flaps. He removed a hypodermic needle from inside the pouch, pulled off the plastic coverings protecting the plunger and needle, and clutched it in his left hand. His thumb hovered warily over the plunger.

When Tibor reached the papers, he bent down and picked them up. He recognized them as the maps Robson and Natalie had prepared outlining the northern route back to camp.

"Going somewhere?" asked Tibor as he stood. Rolling them into a tube, he shoved them between his pants and the small of his back. "And without inviting the rest of us?"

O'Bannon withdrew his revolver with his right hand and aimed it at Tibor. "Give me back the maps before I have to hurt you."

"*You* hurt *me?*" Tibor laughed, but not from any sense of amusement. He was tired of playing games with this human. His teeth morphed into fangs, which he extended for O'Bannon's benefit. "I'll show you what pain is."

O'Bannon stopped backing up, leaving a good ten yards between him and Tibor. He held the revolver in one hand and clutched the hypodermic needle in the other like a knife. "Don't come near me or I'll do to you what I did to Tatyana?"

"Where is she?" snarled Tibor.

At that moment, Tatyana stumbled out of the dorm room twenty feet behind O'Bannon. Both men stared, taken aback by the image. Since Tatyana had died in her vampiric form, she had reanimated the same way. A monstrosity hovered in the doorway, half undead and half living dead. She was unsteady on her feet, bracing herself against the wall. Her head lolled for a second before lifting, catching sight of O'Bannon. Something flashed in her cloudy, murky gray eyes. Tibor was not sure if it was merely one of the living dead recognizing food or the last synapses of Tatyana's cognizant thought remembering her murderer. In either case, she growled and lunged at O'Bannon, her taloned claws poised to tear him apart.

O'Bannon spun around to face her. Raising the revolver, he took careful aim and fired a single round. The bullet struck Tatyana in the forehead directly above the left eye, punching through her head and ripping out of the back a chunk of brain and skull that plastered the white wall. It hit with such force it knocked Tatyana back onto the floor. He quickly spun around again to face Tibor, threatening him with both the revolver and the needle.

"Okay, asshole. You're next."

Tibor responded with a deep, sinister chuckle. "I don't think so."

From behind O'Bannon, Tatyana climbed to her feet, her head bowed. He turned around, his eyes widening in horror.

The gaping hole in her head was healing itself. Her brain regenerated, chunks of organic matter forming in the space torn away by the bullet, while the fractured plates of her skull extended over the wound. Within seconds, it looked as though she had never been shot.

"You forgot the rotters take over the characteristics of their host," sneered Tibor. "For us, that includes rapid regeneration."

Tatyana's head shot up, her eyes fixing on O'Bannon. He raised the revolver to fire again, but this time Tatyana was ready. Her left arm shot out, slapping O'Bannon's gun hand with such force that the bones in the wrist shattered. He cried out and dropped the gun, his hand hanging limp. Tatyana plunged both hands into his chest, stopping only when they slammed against his sternum. O'Bannon gasped. He reached out, weakly clutching at her arms in a futile attempt to stop her.

"Please," he rasped.

Tatyana leered at him. Grabbing O'Bannon's ribcage, she yanked to the sides with her considerable strength. A loud crack echoed through the corridor as the sternum broke in half. The ruptured ribcage tore open his chest, shredding the skin and spraying Tatyana in blood. O'Bannon's body went limp, remaining upright only because Tatyana still clutched him by the ribs. She lowered her head and began to feed from his exposed chest.

COMPTON LOOKED AT his watch, shifting his wrist until the face caught the red glow from the emergency light. Unconsciously he reached into his pocket and withdrew his lighter, fumbling it in his hand and occasionally slipping open the top. Something was wrong. It had been almost fifteen minutes since the alarm had sounded and ten minutes since the power had gone out. O'Bannon should have been here with the maps long ago. Maybe he had changed his mind about betraying the others. Or maybe the alarm was because someone had found him trying to steal the maps. If so, the others would be coming for him next. No matter the reason, siding with O'Bannon suddenly seemed like a liability.

Not that it mattered. The primary objective was to get the vaccines and the accompanying data back to Omaha, even if that meant sacrificing everyone in the facility to achieve that end. Leaving O'Bannon behind was a no-brainer. He would like to have had the maps prepared by Robson since they would have provided him with a pre-planned route that avoided blocked roads and revenant activity, but he could no longer afford that luxury. Each of the Humvees parked topside contained maps of every state east of the Mississippi, so he would have to make do with those.

Compton flipped the lighter closed and shoved it into his jacket pocket. He climbed the short flight of stairs leading to the air filtration room and stepped inside. The access ladder extended close to three hundred feet straight up. A difficult climb, especially with the two steel briefcases, but it had to be done. Clutching one briefcase in his left hand and lodging the second under his left arm, the doctor began the slow climb topside.

DRAVKO RUSHED DOWN the access road that ran the length of the facility. He was still several hundred feet from the end and, despite the dark, could make out Compton's heat signature by the door to the air filtration room. The doctor glanced at his watch and then headed inside. Dravko's lips curled into a sardonic smile. He had Compton trapped.

ROBSON REACHED THE outer door of the admin building and peered through the window. A group of swarmers in military fatigues crowded around the door to the research lab fifty feet down the hall, banging and clawing to get in. He counted at least half a dozen, maybe more, though he could not be certain considering how close they were bunched together. There were more swarmers than he wanted to face by himself, but he did not have much of a choice. Even from this distance, he could see the door jamb giving way. Unless he acted in the next few seconds, Jennifer would wind up as an MRE for these things.

Robson flipped off the safety on his AA-12. Taking a deep breath to steady his nerves, he pushed open the door and stepped into the corridor. The swarmers ignored him. He raised the shotgun and aimed it down the hall at head level, then yelled out.

"Hey, assholes."

As one, the swarmers turned in the direction of the voice. Upon seeing him they charged, a snarling pack filling the hall. Robson waited until they were within twenty-five feet before squeezing the trigger.

The weapon discharged its entire magazine of twenty rounds in seconds. The effect on the swarmers at so close a range was devastating. Bodies twisted in unnatural positions. Limbs were amputated. Heads exploded. Chests erupted. A cloud of blood and gore formed around the swarmers as the shotgun shells tore them to shreds. The attack ended in less than five seconds, churning the creatures into a pile of shattered corpses. A pool of dark-brown blood filled the corridor from wall to wall.

Robson waded through the bodies, his shoes squishing through the blood and gore. When he reached the door to the research lab, he knocked.

"Jennifer, it's all clear. Open up so we can get out of here."

He heard the deadbolt being slid to one side. A moment later, the door swung open and Jennifer rushed out, throwing her arms around his neck.

"Thank God. That door wouldn't have held out much longer."

"You're safe now." Robson stepped back, gently breaking the hug. "Let's get out of here while——"

Moaning from farther down the corridor caught their attention. More swarmers ran out of Compton's private lab, attracted by the noise. Fresh meat and bright red blood covered their mouths and chests. They did not pause as they entered the hall, instead breaking into a sprint toward him and Jennifer, outstretched hands grasping for the food. Robson did not have time to reload. Instead, he shoved Jennifer back into the research lab, slamming the door shut behind them.

"FUCK." AMY DROPPED her Mauser and bent over, clutching her eye.

Natalie pushed her way through the first line of Angels. "What's wrong?"

"A fucking wasp stung me."

Natalie picked up the Mauser and led Amy out of the front line. Sandy moved up in her place. Once the two women were clear of the firing line, Natalie placed the Mauser against the wall and lifted Amy's head.

"Move your hand."

Amy did. Natalie looked at the eye, trying not to grimace. The iris was veined and bloodshot, and the eyeball itself had started to swell, pushing against the lids. Amy had to get medical attention, which she would not get until they finished out here.

"How does it look?" asked Amy.

"It's gonna hurt, but you should be okay in the long run." Natalie grabbed the Mauser. "I'll take it from here."

"No." Amy took back the Mauser. "I can do this."

"Are you sure?"

Amy nodded, wincing from the pain. She rejoined the line, taking the opportunity to reload and moving into Bethany's place when the latter expended her magazine.

Bethany's firing was off. Because of her bandaged broken wrist, she could not hold the Mauser, instead resting the barrel on her outstretched arm to fire. With every shot, the recoil jerked the rifle to one side, spoiling her aim. Cocking the bolt to reload proved nearly impossible. Caylee stepped over and switched weapons.

"What's that for?" asked Bethany.

"It's easier for you to shoot with this one. I set it to three-round bursts."

Bethany laid the barrel of the M-16 on her arm, lined up on a rotter in a runner's outfit, and pulled the trigger. Two rounds slammed into its chest and the third struck it in the neck, decapitating it. Caylee patted Bethany on the shoulder, then took down a rotter in a soiled three-piece suit.

Natalie felt proud of her girls. She hoped they would live to see tomorrow morning. They had been keeping up a steady stream of fire against the rotters, and had been downing them by the dozens, yet if seemed to do no good. Despite the body count, the living dead never seemed to thin out. Every time the Angels changed lines, the ones reloading fell back a little farther than before, seeking safer ground against the advancing horde. Natalie had not been keeping track, but by now they must have fallen back at least to the blast door.

Looking over her shoulder to check her location, Natalie's heart skipped a beat. Twenty rotters were approaching from behind. The closest, wearing a postman's uniform blackened with dried blood and dragging along a tattered mail bag, had closed to within fifty feet. Christ, if she had not turned around when she did....

"Rotters coming up on our rear," she yelled.

Most of the Angels in the second line stopped reloading and looked up, fear filling their eyes when they realized they were about to sandwiched. Natalie refused to let panic overcome them.

"Second line, about face and fire when ready."

Stephanie finished reloading. She raised the Mauser, aimed, and fired off a round that blew out the postman rotter's eye. It moaned and toppled over backward. Stephanie did not notice, already taking aim on a fat, naked rotter without a left arm. Within seconds, the Angels in the second line joined in the decimation of this new front of rotters.

WHEN THOMPSON'S EYES finally reopened, his mind had no comprehension of where he was or what had happened. Or even who he was. He only knew he hungered. He found it difficult to stand up without an arm and with chunks of his thigh muscles missing but, after several failed attempts, he grabbed hold of an old table and used it to raise himself on wobbly legs. When he tried to walk, he nearly toppled over, tripping over a large section of intestine that dangled out of his ripped open abdomen and wound around his feet. Thompson clutched the coil in his one good hand and ripped it out, flinging it aside. With uncertain steps, he stumbled out into the hall.

Several swarmers hovered around a door to his right, snarling and scratching at something on the other side, probably food. There were too many of them, so getting his fair share would be impossible. Some deep part of his brain he was barely conscious of told him that more food could be found outside the building.

Thompson set off down the hall, supporting himself on the wall as he grew accustomed to walking on ravaged legs. Passing by the swarmers gathered around the lab, he made his way to the end of the hall, out the open door, and stumbled down the stairs. He tripped on the last step, crashing face-first onto the cement and knocking out several teeth. He struggled back to his feet, standing quicker this time as he became more familiar with his body. Looking around, he did not see any food. Thompson moaned, the hunger almost unbearable.

Instinct told him to turn right. Thompson set off down the access road, ignoring the buildings where food might be hidden. Instead, he wandered in the direction of the air filtration room.

ROBSON AND JENNIFER backed up across the room until they bumped into the counter running along the opposite wall, all the while keeping their eyes fixed on the door. The eight swarmers outside pounded and scratched at the glass and slammed their weight into the wood, crazed by their previous feeding and frantic for more. After one particularly heavy blow, the window shattered. A large crack appeared down the center of the wood. Decayed arms jutted through the empty pane, frenetically grasping and clutching at the humans. The combined weight of the swarmers and the intense pounding rapidly weakened the door. Robson saw the crack growing larger and noticed the hinges pulling away from the jamb. They had a few seconds at most.

Robson removed the empty magazine from the AA-12 and pulled a new one from his jacket pocket. It was a smaller magazine that contained only ten rounds. This was going to be close.

"Do you still have the Magnum?" asked Jennifer.

"Yeah." Pulling the revolver from his holster, he handed it to Jennifer. Jennifer flipped open the chamber to make sure it was loaded, closed it, switched the safety to off, and cocked back the hammer. She aimed at the door and spread her feet shoulder-length apart. She flashed Robson an encouraging smile and nodded toward the shotgun.

"You ready?"

Robson raised his AA-12 and took aim as the door burst apart and the swarmers poured in.

DRAVKO DARTED UP the stairwell to the air filtration room, taking the steps two at a time. He pushed open the door and rushed inside, knocking over three of the jerry cans filled with gasoline. The lid on two of them fell off, allowing gasoline to slosh onto the floor. Dravko jumped across the room onto the access ladder so as not to get his shoes soaked.

One hundred feet up the ladder, Compton stood on one the rungs, staring down in disbelief. The doctor glanced up at the exit more than two hundred feet above. Rays of sunlight streamed through the grating and lit up the opposite wall. Compton began climbing as quickly as possible, although with his left arm and hand clutching two of the briefcases, his progress was slow. The doctor must have known he could not make it topside before Dravko caught him.

Which made the game of cat and mouse all the sweeter.

"What's the hurry, doctor?" asked Dravko tauntingly.

Compton continued climbing.

"You haven't given Robson's team their vaccines yet."

The doctor's panting became more audible.

"And I hear you have something special for us." Dravko's voice took on an ominous tone.

Compton climbed frantically, moving so fast his right hand nearly slipped off the rung he reached for. With a frightened gasp, he leaned into the ladder and wrapped his arm tightly around the rung. The sudden action caused the briefcase under Compton's arm to slip. It dangled precariously close to falling until the doctor closed his left arm tight around the sides and maneuvered his right hand to pull it back into place.

Seeing his chance, Dravko glided up the ladder, crawling hand over hand two rungs at a time. He covered the distance to Compton in seconds, stopping beside the doctor. With his right foot and hand anchored on the ladder, Dravko stood with the left side of his body hanging into the shaft. He grabbed Compton by the shoulder, preventing him from climbing any further.

"Going somewhere, doctor?"

"Yes," Compton replied cockily, his arrogance having returned. "To take back my world from the rotters you released on us."

"And you plan on doing that by setting the rotters against us?"

"Use evil to purge evil." Compton turned his head to look back at Dravko. "Very Biblical, don't you think?"

Dravko sneered. "Don't be so smug. As much as you hate my kind, at least we don't kill each other."

"How noble," said Compton contemptuously. "Let's see if you practice what you preach."

Compton lifted his left arm. The briefcase slipped free, dropping down the shaft. It careened off a rung and ricocheted off the opposite wall. The blow popped open the lid, spilling the twenty-five vials of vaccine down the shaft. Everything crashed to the floor below. Each of the vials shattered, mixing the vaccine with the gasoline. Compton used his thumb to flip the latch on the briefcase in his hand. The lid opened, tilting the briefcase at an angle. Several vials of vaccine slid out of their foam rubber compartment, smashing on the ground. Compton waited for the last vial to hit before letting go of the handle The briefcase tumbled down with the other.

The doctor leaned closer to the ladder, switched hands holding the rung, and leaned back out into the shaft so he faced Dravko. "That was the last of the vaccine. You kill me, your human friends won't make it out of here alive. Unless, of course, you see this as the perfect chance to get rid of the last of the humans."

"You bastard."

"I am." Compton laughed. "So, what'll it be? You let me live, and Robson and the others live. Or you kill me and condemn them to become revenants."

Dravko sneered.

"You have only two options."

"Wrong again." Dravko morphed into a vampire.

Compton tried to climb away, but Dravko clutched his shirt collar and pulled him closer. The doctor struggled, slamming his hand into the vampire's wrist to break the grip, but it did no good. Dravko banged Compton's head against a rung, and then leaned over and plunged his teeth into the doctor's neck.

"No!" Compton screamed. He thrashed around to break free, but Dravko only sank his teeth deeper into the doctor's neck, drawing out his life blood. After several seconds, Dravko pulled away. He ran his tongue across his blood-covered teeth and lips, savoring the meal.

Compton cowered against the ladder, his right hand cradled against his bloody neck. He pulled away his hand and stared at the bright red blood dripping between his fingers.

"What did you do?"

"You forgot the third option." Dravko morphed back into his human form, staring at Compton during the transformation. "I turn you into one of us and make you reproduce the vaccine."

Compton placed his hand back over the wound. Blood gushed between his fingers. "Y-you can't be serious?"

"I am. You'll bleed out within an hour, and by tomorrow night you'll revive as a vampire. And since I'm the master, you'll have to obey me. You'll make as much of the vaccine as I tell you to."

"No," Compton squeaked. He looked at the vampire with eyes draining of life.

Dravko nodded, a perverse smile on his lips. "You're about to become my vampire bitch."

"No!" This time Compton screamed the word. He released his hand from the ladder and slipped into the shaft. His body plummeted through the air, crashing to the ground in a mangled heap among the briefcases and jerry cans, the blood from his ruptured body forming a pool that mixed with the spilled gasoline and vaccine.

SHAMBLING ALONG THE access road leading to the far end of the facility, Thompson's attention was attracted by a pair of loud noises. Though he could not comprehend the sound of two steel briefcases striking cement, his dead mind instinctively knew noise meant food. Trying to get his bearings, Thompson headed in the general direction of the sounds.

A moment later, he heard a human scream followed by a dull thud. By now he was close enough to the sounds to know they came from the room at the top of the small flight of stairs. His mind did not connect the thud with a body crashing into the ground. All it knew was the scream came from a human, and humans were food.

With an anticipatory growl of satiating his hunger, Thompson bolted down the access road and scrambled up the stairs.

NATALIE STOOD BETWEEN the two lines of Angels, brushing away the wasps and flies hovering around her head. She kept a close watch on both groups of rotters, carefully gauging their rate of advance. The twenty rotters approaching from behind posed the lesser threat numbers-wise. However, until the Angels cleared them out, no one could fall back from the main horde. And the rotters to their front, now down to under a hundred, were drawing dangerously close. What concerned Natalie was how slowly the Angels were clearing out the living dead. Her girls were missing their targets at an increasing pace, registering more misses or torso hits than head shots. She did not know if it was stress, physical exhaustion, or the distraction caused by the gun smoke and bugs. For whatever reason, the Angels were losing their mark. At this rate, they would be overrun before they could kill them all.

Only five rotters remained from the group to the rear. Ari and Leila took down one each with a single head shot. Tiara aimed on a rotter in football uniform still wearing its helmet. Her first shot deflected off the helmet, ricocheting harmlessly against the tunnel wall. Her second shot went straight through its left eye. It stiffened for a split second before crumpling to the ground. Sandy took down a rotter in a waitress uniform with two shots. Leila went after a rotter in blue overalls stained black with dried blood and grease but kept missing. Her first two shots went wide to the left, and her third thudded uselessly into its shoulder, before the bolt to her Mauser stuck open. Amy stepped in and fired a near perfect shot in the center of its forehead that blew its brains and skull out the back.

Natalie looked forward. The closest rotter was less than twenty feet away.

"Fall back on me."

Natalie moved off toward the opposite end of the tunnel, carefully avoiding the corpses and pools of gore that blocked her path. Most of the Angels followed, except for Emily and Bethany. Emily fired off three rounds in quick succession, dropping a rotter each time. After the third shot, the bolt of her Mauser stayed open. Before Emily could fall back, a rotter in a policeman's uniform charged her, its arms reaching out. Emily brought up the butt of her Mauser hard, connecting with its face. The blow tore off its jaw, which flew across the tunnel and smashed against the wall, and spun the rotter around. Emily backed up a few steps and turned to join the others a hundred feet down the tunnel.

"I thought I told you to fall back?" snapped Natalie.

Emily smiled. "I couldn't waste those good shots, now could I, honey?"

Bethany fired off three rounds from her M-16, each shot barely missing a fat female rotter in a house coat closing in. Bethany stepped back, bumping into the rotter Emily had maimed. It spun around and grabbed at her, clutching her leather jacket by the collar. She tried pushing it away with her left hand but could not get enough force because of the broken wrist.

Caylee rushed forward and slammed the butt of her Mauser into the rotter's face. Its skull fractured from the blow. Releasing Bethany, it turned to lunge at Caylee. Caylee again slammed the rifle butt into its face, knocking it down. Standing over the rotter, she repeatedly crashed the rifle butt into its head, smashing its skull open on the second blow, but continuing to pummel the thing even after it had been killed.

Bethany took several steps back and yelled, "Watch out!"

Caylee never looked up. She did not see the rotter in the house coat come up behind her, and only realized it was there after it sunk its teeth into her shoulder. Caylee never cried out. With her right hand, she shoved the rotter back, its teeth tearing out a chunk of flesh. She spun around and started pummeling its head with her Mauser, seemingly oblivious to the other two moving in. They grabbed Caylee and dragged her to the ground, ripping open her abdomen and yanking out her intestines.

Bethany stood dumbstruck, but only for a second. As three rotters made their way toward her, she fell back to join the others. There would be time to mourn later.

Maybe.

The remaining horde continued their advance on the Angels. There were only forty or so left. But at least her girls had a minute to catch their breath.

"What's the ammo situation look like?" asked Natalie.

"Bad," answered Ari. "I'm on my last clip."

All the other girls responded likewise.

"Then make every shot count."

"TATYANA." TIBOR SPOKE her name softly.

She looked up from O'Bannon's ribcage, a piece of his flesh dangling from her mouth.

Tibor morphed into his vampiric form and bent over slightly, ready to attack. Tatyana dropped O'Bannon's corpse and stared at Tibor, her head cocked to one side. He could not tell whether she recognized him or merely sizing up her next meal. It did not matter. She had to die.

Tatyana growled and lunged.

Tibor sprang toward her. The two collided with such force he had the wind knocked out of him. Tatyana used the momentary advantage to clutch him by the throat with her right hand, squeezing shut his windpipe. Thankfully, he did not need air to live. As she plunged her head toward his neck, Tibor grabbed her by the throat, holding her in place. The combination of her vampire strength and rotter ferocity was greater than he thought, and he felt his arm giving out. Quickly, he wrapped the talons of his left hand around the arm clutching his neck and yanked to one side. The talons sliced through her skin and bone, severing her arm at the elbow and breaking him free.

Tibor released his own grip on Tatyana and jumped to the left. She fell forward, slamming face first into the wall. Before she could react, Tibor moved around behind her, pinning her torso against the wall by shoving his knee into her back. She thrashed violently. He clutched her hair in his left hand, struggling to hold her head still. With his right, he reached around front, careful to avoid her mouth, and dug his talons into the left side of her neck. Mustering all his strength, he pulled his hands apart. The talons tore out her throat and his left hand shattered her spine, ripping Tatyana's head from her body. Her torso collapsed to the floor.

Still holding her head, Tibor saw it still lived, its mouth biting the air to get to him. Holding Tatyana's head between his hands so it faced away from him, he squeezed until he heard the bones fracture. Her skull collapsed under his grip, the fragments shredding her brain. He knelt and placed the lifeless head by her body.

"May you finally at peace, little one."

COMPTON GRIMACED. BOTH his legs and left arm were broken, and he suffered trauma to most of his internal organs. He tried to sit up but could not, an indication he also had a spinal injury. The fall should have killed him. The fact that it did not meant the vampire blood coursing through his veins must already be working. He had wanted to commit suicide to prevent himself from becoming one of them, but it looked like his attempt was in vain. He would bleed out, writhing in agony in his last minutes, and then come back as a vampire.

He smelled gasoline fumes, suddenly realizing he sat in a pool created when the jerry cans overturned. He still had one chance to spare himself from the inhuman fate awaiting him.

Despite the searing pain, with his right hand, Compton reached into the pocket of his lab coat, rummaging around for his lighter. His fingers brushed against the metal surface. Thank God it was still intact. He grabbed it and began to pull it out.

A noise from the doorway caught his attention. Compton strained his eyes to look in that direction. Thompson stood there, his thighs ravaged to the bone and a gaping, bloody hole where his abdomen used to be. The colonel glared at him with lifeless gray eyes. His lips curled into a snarl as he dived through the doorway, landing beside Compton. He grabbed the doctor's head and lifted it off the floor. Excruciating pain shot through Compton's brain, almost blacking him out. That agony paled in comparison to the torment he experienced when Thompson leaned over and plunged his teeth around the doctor's left eye. Compton howled as he felt the teeth slice through his skin and scrape along bone. The colonel closed his jaw and yanked, ripping out Compton's eye and tearing off huge chunks of his cheek and face. Thompson leaned his head back and chewed, popping the orb between his teeth. The last image Compton saw was the man he had murdered cannibalizing him, his flesh and the nerve endings to his eye dangling from its mouth.

Somehow, through the pain, Compton managed to with-draw the lighter from his pocket and flick it on. The tiny flame ignited the gasoline, turning the floor into an inferno engulfing the two men. Thankfully for Compton, by now shock had overcome him and he did not feel himself being incinerated. Thompson, oblivious to pain, still knelt by the doctor's body, continuing to feast on the charred flesh.

DRAVKO CLIMBED THE ladder when he saw Compton pull out the lighter, racing to escape the flames. He ignored the groaning of the living dead, the screams of torment from Compton, and the whoosh as the gasoline ignited. The heat pelted him but posed no danger. He only stopped climbing when the temperature leveled out and a cool wind filtered in from the shaft above him, the air being drawn in to feed the flames below.

Dravko stared down. Despite all the horrors he had wit-nessed in his hundreds of years as a vampire, none compared to what took place below. Despite the inferno that burned away at him, Thompson continued to feed off the doctor. Eventually the stench of cooked flesh wafted its way up the shaft, accom-panied by the sizzling of roasting meat. Popping noises soon joined the ghastly chorus as organs fried and erupted. After several minutes, Thompson wavered and collapsed onto Compton, everything that gave his body the semblance of life having been seared out of him.

Wrapping his arms around the rungs of the ladder, Dravko tried to make himself comfortable. He felt neither regret nor satisfaction his enemies had died such horrible deaths. All he felt was frustration over having to wait up here until the fire died down enough for him to escape.

ROBSON AIMED AT head level and fired a short burst from the

AA-12 as the swarmers burst into the lab. Beside him, Jennifer fired two Magnum rounds. The hail of gunfire shredded the first four swarmers through the door, shattering skulls and blasting heads. Shielded from the onslaught by those in front, the last four pushed past the others, spreading out to the right and left as they rushed into the room and sought out their prey.

Jennifer withheld fire until the two coming after her lessened the range, not wanting to waste ammunition. She carefully lined up her shot on the first swarmer, a young sergeant who used to flirt with her when they were confined to the facility. The .357 round blew its head clean off its body, the concussion knocking it over backwards. Before the body even hit the ground, she switched her aim to the second swarmer. Since it was too close to line up the shot, she fired off two rounds in rapid succession. The first missed, but the second punched a neat hole in its forehead. A spray of blood and gore blossomed from the back of its head. Although permanently dead, momentum continued to drive it toward Jennifer. She dodged to the left at the last second, letting the body slam against the wall beside her within a meaty thud.

Robson concentrated on the two swarmers that lunged for him. He raised the AA-12 and fired off a three-round burst. The bullets slammed into the closest swarmer, tearing off its right shoulder and head, and propelling the mangled corpse to the rear. It fell against the second swarmer, knocking it off balance as Robson fired a second three-round burst. All the rounds slammed harmlessly into the opposite wall. The swarmer snarled and charged. Robson pivoted, reacquired aim, and pulled the trigger. Nothing happened except the sound of the hammer striking an empty chamber.

He raised the AA-12 horizontally in front of him as the swarmer darted the last few feet between them. The move saved him, but only for a moment. The swarmer crashed into Robson, shoving them both against the wall. Only the length of the shotgun pressed against the swarmer's chest prevented it from getting to him. It pushed against the weapon, its teeth frenziedly snapping precariously close to Robson's face. He could smell the rotting contents of its stomach through its gaping mouth. Robson felt the strength in his arms giving out.

Jennifer stepped over and placed the barrel of the Magnum against the swarmer's temple. It turned to face her and growled as she pulled the trigger, exploding its head across the lab. The torso remained erect, still pressing against Robson. He jerked the AA-12 forward, toppling the headless body to the floor.

Robson fell back into the wall and slid to the floor. For the first time since he had encountered the living dead, he began shaking, his nerves frayed to the breaking point.

Jennifer knelt beside him, gently rubbing a hand across his scalp, pushing away the sweat.

"Relax. It's all over now."

"What if there's more out there?"

"Then we're screwed." Jennifer flipped open the chamber to the Magnum and emptied the six spent shell casings into her hand.

"I'M OUT," YELLED Ari as she fired off her last round.

"Me, too," chimed in Amy.

Fuck, thought Natalie. There were still twenty-one rotters left. At least that number was manageable for what would happen next.

"All right, Angels." Natalie withdrew the crowbar from the pouch that dangled off her belt. "This is the part where we get close and personal."

The other girls withdrew their melee weapons. Natalie studied each of them. A few like Emily and Sandy had already placed themselves in that psych-out zone for hand-to-hand combat. The rest looked tired and resigned to their fate.

"A couple of more minutes and it'll all be over." It sounded lame even to Natalie, but it was the best pep talk she could come up with. She brandished her crowbar like a baseball bat. "Let's rock."

The Angels waded into the rotters.

Natalie stepped up to the closest, a woman in a business suit, its white shirt ripped open to expose a chest denuded of skin or breasts. She swung the crowbar, the curved end catching the rotter where the jaw connected with the skull, shattering the bone and knocking its head to the side. When it turned back, its mouth draped open at an inhuman angle, the jaw attached only by the still intact tendons on the right. It chewed at her with its upper jaw, the bottom dangling uselessly. Natalie spun the crowbar around in her hand and jammed the straight end up into the rotter's mouth and through its palette. The rotter jerked for a moment. Congealed blood and brain matter dripping down the crowbar's shaft, and then it went limp. Natalie shifted the angle of the crowbar so it pointed down, allowing the rotter to slide off the metal and drop to the ground. She paid no attention to it, concentrating instead on the two closing in on her.

Sarah came to her defense, holding her machete above her head. She brought it down as hard as possible on the first rotter's head, cleaving down to the nose. The other one, a fat topless man with no arms, ignored Natalie and lumbered toward Sarah. She tried to remove the machete, but the blade was lodged in the first rotter's skull. As the armless rotter approached, she kicked out with her right leg, shattering its kneecap and dropping it to the ground. Sarah placed her foot on the first rotter's chest and pushed back, wiggling the machete in the process. The blade came free with a slurp, spilling chunks of brain across the rotter's scalp. By now the armless rotter had crawled up to its good knee. Sarah spun around, swinging the machete in a long arc that sliced off its head.

Natalie passed Sarah and patted her shoulder in thanks. It was all she had time for. Around her, the rest of the Angels were hacking their way into the remaining horde. Emily gutted a rotter in a nurse's uniform with her hunting knife. Tiara hammered repeatedly on another's skull with her crowbar, continuing the assault even after it dropped to the ground. Doreen had plunged her crowbar through the left eye of a rotter, twisting it around to scramble its brains.

Amy raised her crowbar and swung at a rotter wearing the orange vest and yellow helmet of a road worker. She misjudged, missing it by an inch. As her right arm passed in front of it, the rotter grabbed it. Before she could respond, it leaned forward and sunk its teeth into her leather jacket. Amy screamed and yanked her arm away, expecting to see chunks of torn flesh. Instead, she ripped a dozen teeth out of the rotter's mouth.

Josephine ran up to Amy, shoving her crowbar deep into the rotter's mouth. "Were you bit?"

Amy frantically felt around her arm, fearful of feeling blood. All she found were a few teeth stuck into the leather. "Thank God, no."

"Good." Josephine jerked the crowbar to the right, tearing off the rotter's jaw.

Amy joined in, clutching her crowbar in both hands and driving it through the rotter's skull, venting her fear and anger. She lodged the metal in it so deeply she could not dislodge it.

Ari made her way into the swarm, her machete drawn back to swing. She suddenly froze. In front of her shambled the rotter mother with its baby clutched to its chest, feeding off the flesh of its dead mother's breast. The mother rotter reached out its free hand and grabbed for Ari. Ari could not bring herself to kill it. She stood motionless, knowing she was about to die.

"Leave her alone, bitch." Leila rushed to Ari's defense, coming at the rotter mother from the side and driving the end of her crowbar into the side of its skull. Leila continued shoving, plunging the metal deeper into its head and pushing it sideways until they both crashed against the tunnel wall. She twisted the crowbar from side to side, scrambling the brain. The rotter mother finally went limp. Leila let it slip down the wall and waited until it had collapsed, then placed a hand on its chest while she used the other to remove the crowbar.

Suddenly, Leila screamed. She dropped the crowbar and stood up, holding her hand. The rotter baby was attached to it, biting down on her small finger. Blood flowed from around its tiny mouth. Leila flicked her hand, tossing the thing to one side where it landed in a heap on top of its mother. Leila fell to her knees, staring at the wound in shock. Natalie rushed over to check on her, holding Leila's hand by the wrist and examining the bite. The wound was not deep or large, and in fact, it had only broken the skin in one place. But it was more than enough to infect her. Leila looked up at Natalie, her eyes pleading that it would be all right. The look on Natalie's face told her the truth.

Ari stepped over to where the rotter mother lay. The baby crawled toward her, making it only a few feet before being held back by the decayed umbilical cord. It stared up at her and wailed. Ari raised her foot and crashed the boot down on its head, crushing it with one blow. She turned and joined Leila, sitting beside her friend and hugging her.

"I'm so sorry," Ari finally sobbed, hugging Leila tightly.

"It's not your fault." Leila clutched Ari's arm. The two women rocked back and forth.

As the rest of the Angels took down the last of the rotters, each one came over to check on Leila. They knew without asking that their worst fears were coming true. No one spoke. They just stood around to be there for their friend, enjoying the last moments with her.

CHAPTER FIFTY-FOUR

T HE SURVIVORS STOOD in a semi-circle by the tree line opposite the tunnels' entrance. Behind them sat the Ryder, the school bus, and the two Humvees, their engines idling and their headlights illuminating the area.

After the battle with the rotters, everyone had moved quickly to hit the road. Amy's eye was badly swollen and enflamed by the wasp sting, forcing her to wear a patch. They had treated it in time so, with luck, she would not lose the eye.

Even more fortunate, in his haste to escape the compound, Compton had not destroyed the other two briefcases containing vials of the vaccine. Jennifer administered one dose to all the humans in the group. The two briefcases were loaded one each aboard the bus and the Ryder to help ensure at least some of the vaccine would make it back to camp.

No one even attempted to clean up the facility. The two research labs were left alone, with the bodies of the swarmers scattered around. The tunnel could not have been picked up if they had tried. Four hundred corpses littered the main half of the tunnel, rotting in a pool of congealed blood that seemed to ripple because it teemed with so many maggots. The only bodies they picked up were those of their fallen comrades—Daytona, Tatyana, Caylee, and Leila. Compton and Thompson were nothing but a pile of charred bones. No one bothered to cover O'Bannon's mangled corpse, although Robson did put a bullet through its head to make certain it did not reanimate.

Now the group stood around the makeshift graves of their

four friends. Mounds of dirt marked their final resting place by the trees, each bearing a makeshift cross made of wooden slabs lashed together at their crossing. Even Tatyana's grave bore one. Despite her being one of the undead, somehow it did not seem right to not give her the same respect as the others.

No final words were spoken aloud. There was nothing to be vocalized. Everyone said their own private goodbyes.

Robson assumed most also tried to exorcise their own personal demons. He saw it in the faces of those standing around the graves. They appeared tired, sullen, defeated. The confidence the group had displayed when leaving Camp had been shattered between the betrayal by their own and the onslaught of the rotters. The survivors, especially the Angels, had stared into the face of living death closer than they had before and walked away with deep wounds to their psyche. None of them would ever be able to deal with this rotter world the same way again.

After several minutes, Robson broke the silence. "Okay, people. Mount up. It's time to head back."

One by one, the members of the group stepped away and headed to the vehicles. Dravko stepped forward, kneeling and touching Tatyana's grave, and then he and Tibor walked over to the Ryder. Ari removed her mermaid pendant from around her neck and draped it over Leila's cross. She whispered, "I'll never forget you." Wiping a tear from her eye, she joined the others.

Robson and Natalie were the last to leave.

Before boarding the school bus, Natalie motioned toward the tunnel entrance. "We left the blast door open. Shouldn't we lock it before we go?"

"No," Robson said firmly. "Leave it for the rotters. They deserve it. There's nothing but death in there."

Natalie boarded the school bus and climbed into the driver's seat. Robson made his way to the Humvee that would serve as the point vehicle.

The convoy crossed the facility's grounds and passed through the main gate. At the end of the access road, Robson turned left onto the main street. Each of the other vehicles followed. No one bothered to look back.

Once on the main street, the convoy gained speed, leaving Site R behind them as it began the long journey home.

Acknowledgments

Though it sounds strange when talking about a zombie novel, I did try to keep the book as true to reality as possible. I'm grateful that while researching *Rotter World* I picked up Jonathon Mayberry's *Zombie CSU: The Forensics of the Living Dead*, his analysis of how a zombie outbreak might unfold. It provided unique insights when creating my living dead world.

A debt of gratitude goes to Permuted Press, especially Jacob Kier for offering me this great opportunity. Felicia A. Tiller, my editor, worked closely with me to tone down some of the more sexually graphic scenes and tighten up the manuscript. I appreciate her professionalism and friendship; however, any errors in the final product are mine to own. I would be remiss if I didn't give a shout out to Zach McCain for his excellent cover art. [NOTE: For the original printed edition.]

As always, a special thanks to my family and friends who tolerated the long hours I spent in front of the computer, especially my house rabbits. [NOTE: When I wrote this novel, I had six rabbits as pets. I would not adopt the dogs and cats until later.] I realize every attempt to chew through the power chord was a cry for attention. To all of you, thanks for sharing me with the living dead.

About the Author

Scott M. Baker was born and raised in Everett, Massachusetts, and spent twenty-three years in northern Virginia working for the Central Intelligence Agency. He has traveled extensively throughout Europe, Asia, and the Middle East, incorporating many of the locations and cultures he has visited in his stories. Scott is now retired and lives outside of Concord, New Hampshire, with his wife, his stepdaughter, two cats who treat him as their human servant, his Boxer Roxie, and Fred, a Bassett Hound puppy who is a lovable bundle of energy.

Scott is currently writing the *Nurse Alissa vs. the Zombies* and *The Chronicles of Paul* sagas, his latest zombie apocalypse series, as well as his paranormal series. Previous works include *Operation Majestic*, his first science fiction novel described as *Raiders of the Lost Ark* meets *Back to the Future* – with aliens; *Frozen World*, his first non-zombie post-apocalypse novel; the *Shattered World* series, his five-book young adult post-apocalypse thriller; *The Vampire Hunters* trilogy, about humans fighting the undead in Washington D.C.; *Yeitso*, his homage to the giant monster movies of the 1950s that he loved watching as a kid; as well as several zombie-themed novellas and anthologies.

Blog: scottmbakerauthor.blogspot.com
Facebook: facebook.com/groups/397749347486177
MeWe: mewe.com/i/scottmbaker
Twitter: twitter.com/vampire_hunters
Instagram: instagram.com/scottmbakerwriter

YouTube:
youtube.com/channel/UC5AyCVrEAncr2E0N5XoyUdg/playlists
Wyrd Realities Homepage: www.wyrdrealities.net
TikTok: tiktok.com/@scottmbakerwriter

You can also sign up for Scott's newsletter, which will be released on the 1st and 15th of every month. He promises not to share your email with anyone or spam the recipients. The newsletter contains advance notices of upcoming releases/events and short stories from the Alissa, Paul, and Tatyana universes that will not be available to the public. You can sign up by going to the link below.

Newsletter: mailchi.mp/0b1401f1ddb2/scott-m-baker-writer

Made in the USA
Middletown, DE
14 May 2023